BEASTS OF LONDON

METHOD OF THE KILL
BOOK ONE

JONATHAN MALONEY

SKYNATION PUBLISHING

Beasts of London
(Method of the Kill #1)

Edited by Renee April and Lydia Fuller
Cover design by Dayna Watson

ISBN 978-0-6455708-8-5 (paperback)
ISBN 978-0-6455708-7-8 (hardcover)
ISBN 978-0-6455708-9-2 (digital online)

www.skynation.info

For my grandmother, Margaret, who taught me to dream, even if they couldn't come true.
And for my father, Gregory, who taught me what it was to grieve.

CHAPTER 1

A TERRIBLE IMAGINING

I*magination is a most terrible thing.*

This was the thought that occurred to Mr Bartholomew Bartleby. There had been other thoughts before this, in the series of events that had led up to this moment, but none of them had been with any measure of clarity as to be called cohesive.

In many circumstances, an imagination might prove a most wonderful boon, a gift upon one's creative expression. But in an improper time and place, the very strength of the imaginative mind can become its curse; it can be, simply put, a most terrible thing.

In this instance, when one had the singular misfortune of fate to find themselves bound, blindfolded, and gagged upon the floor of a fast moving carriage, imagination instead filled all the gaps of the denied senses with possibilities most dreadful and final.

It was noted idly by Bartleby that this was an unusual experience in his line of work. Unusual, but perhaps not wholly unexpected—which was part of the reason he felt a sense of inevitable acceptance. As though an event long anticipated and feared had come to pass, and now the sufferer could be resigned to it.

But he had to admit, this was not exactly a comfort.

In fact, if he was able to properly verbalise, or at least express himself, he would surely have done so to illustrate the depth of his affront in the matter. Instead, all he could do was lay where he was, bound and gagged, left to wonder.

All he had done was ask questions. Curious ones that pertained to the most burning mystery of the time. True, they were questions with blood upon them. Older blood than the other perpetual stains, old enough that such inquiry should not have eschewed such a response.

He had asked those questions, and asked some more, and written the answers in his little book. And slowly, a picture began to form around them. A picture with a singular, gaping hole in its heart, a void which bore a face, a name... and a fear. Surrounded by all the questions, all the inquiries, there was a white page mystery, a blank space where the story should have been, and Bartleby was determined to fill it.

His mission had driven him onward and eastward, into the belly of the wretched beast. The bloated streets of blood, arteries that were choked with filth and refuse, the unwanted and unforgivable. That empty picture yet ever beckoned, and so he had scurried from one cloying alleyway to the next, from one dank drinking house to another, where the smell of slow dying pickled upon the air, and found himself on the grimy, Godless streets of deepest, darkest London.

The answers had come harder, but they were there and all the more profitable. A few tuppence here, even a shilling there, as long as his hand was kept fast to his purse when the urchins with hard eyes and fast fingers came brushing against him. This patient purveyor of truth and revelation came ever closer to finding the brush strokes, and thus he pressed on, a slight man in a threadbare suit with a notebook clutched in his hand like a protective badge—a sight so incongruous that the roaming beasts in tattered cloaks with tattered faces made of old violence had not touched him. But they had watched, and they had waited.

He had been getting closer to the prize. He could feel it with the worry that was in the air, the space between the words that were filled with a treacle thick silence, the hard looks, the raised prices. The twinge of anticipation began to be replaced by its sister sensation of dread. The wolves had ceased their circling, and he had not had the chance to realise when the balance had tipped, before a bag was thrown over his head and a club had struck the back of his skull. Dimly, he had been dragged by wordless, heavy men with heavier scents of sweat, tobacco, bad food, and dreadful efficiency of violence, and thrown thus into the very carriage that had then become his entire world.

The first question he could have asked had been answered by the gag, the hood lifted enough for it to be stuffed forcefully between his teeth, filling his mouth with the flavour of mothballs and other unspeakable humours. The second question was answered with a foot that had set his ribs to creaking. That ache about his chest now set itself in symphony with his skull, as Bartleby lay still, waiting and imagining, and hating what imagination was now rendering unto him.

The carriage never slowed. He was aware of it beneath him, his body lifting and bouncing with its rough movements. This immediately lent him to realise that this was an expensive carriage. A cheaper carriage was a noisy affair—especially at this speed—and there *was* speed, a sensation of fierce motion that made his poor addled head swirl disagreeably. But the insulated interior kept the majority of the sound out; for the most part the discomfort instead came from the vibration that rose up from the hard wheel over ground—*ground*, but not cobblestone.

They were outside of London surely by this point. Just how long had he lain in a stupor? It was admittedly a less pressing thought than the ever growing dread of where he was going, but there was no answering that question either.

His hands ached. The cord that held them together bit through his coat along with the autumn chill, bringing with it the shudder that promised the coming winter. With his hands bound, his options of movement were rather limited—not least because the shifting of a boot alerted him to the fact he was once more under observation—but he nevertheless opened and closed his hands to get blood moving again. A most uncomfortable journey, but to what end? Were the questions he had dared to ask so dreadful in their answering that this was the conclusion? He shifted his head then, trying to rub his face against the floor to pry the gag loose.

A faint sound, a whickering of metal against leather. Then a soft tang, right in front of his face. Even through the hood, he could sense a cold hardness of steel, and the faint hint of oil from the scabbard to keep the draw loose and swift.

A voice spoke somewhere above him, the tone thick with phlegm.

"You be quiet and easy as a mouse there, mister. Wriggle too much and I'll nail you down."

It was a rusty voice, rumbling from the pit of the stomach, wrought wicked by rot and liquor. There was a grin in those words, but there was no humour in it, and even less in the long blade that rested but scant inches from Bartleby's quivering nose.

His spirit quailed. The unspoken questions that had risen so stridently in his heart withered into darkened silence. He shifted no more, huddled and shivering from more than just the cold, as he was raced towards the unknown on the unwilling wings of fear.

The horses were near played out when the carriage wheels changed in tone. A grinding sound, the rasp of fine gravel underneath that muted the clop of the hooves and the rattle of the carriage as it slowed to a stop. That change in sound and tempo had been anticipated for some long minutes by Bartleby, denoting an approaching end to his journey. He startled as the door was opened and his legs were seized. Unceremoniously, he was dragged clear, landing with a sharp retort upon the ground, where he lay groaning.

Words were said above him, words he focused on despite the roaring of his own panicked breathing. Words such as 'payment', and 'stables', and 'resting', that 'the matter would be handled'.

The matter would be handled. He being the matter, he being the thing to be handled. There was no comfort in that statement, and so he hunched inwards, hoping against hope to be forgotten as a whimper escaped him.

Strong hands took his arms and shoulders and pulled him to his feet, but they would not work beneath him. The hands were much stronger than he was, and they were well practiced in the handling of menfolk who were in no condition to move under their own power. They dragged him onwards, over gravel, up stairs. A door creaked open, and a voice spoke in wintry tones.

"This way," and that indeed was the way that Bartleby was dragged along.

They were inside the building. A large, cold building, scarcely warmed by fire. There was little light either. Dim candles here and there, provided brief radiance that was only barely visible through the hood that Bartleby wore. Another door was opened, and then warmth flowed out upon him—blessed warmth—and more light. A fire was burning, not fiercely, but comforting nonetheless and, for the first time, Bartleby was fully aware of how cold he was. His teeth would have chattered together were it not for the gag that denied him.

He was shifted about, moved with ease; a joint preparing to be dressed by a butcher. A chair with a hard back and a soft bottom was set under him. A knife shone in the dark with razor-edged intent, and the cords were cut at the wrist. There were sensations of movement, though the gag and hood were left alone, and then the large thudding footsteps retreated, and the door closed. Bartholomew Bartleby was left alone.

No. Not alone.

The realisation came quick and sudden, but there was no indication to reveal it. There was no sound of a presence, though there was not silence. The room was awash with other sounds, of crackling fire logs, of creaking floorboards, of panicked heartbeat and rushed breath. But amongst that there was a stillness, a sensation to the air that was patient and watching.

His fingers shook as Bartleby reached up to the awful gag, pulling it from his mouth with a gasp of relief. He swallowed with a dry tongue and tried to rasp a question to the air, feeling both certain and a fool at the same time.

"Is there someone there?" A squeaking voice, dried by lack of saliva and abject terror, forcing the words out.

An oppressive silence that grew by the moment. And then—

"You have come a long way today, Mr Bartleby."

The voice that spoke was cold. Cold as winter seas and just as bleak. The voice of God for all Bartleby could guess, and though it was blasphemy to think of it, it nevertheless held a power to it—the power of life or death as Bartleby knew.

A deliberate step, and then another, and through the veil of the hood covering his face still, Bartleby could make out a tall, dark shape looming over him, moving out of the shadow into the firelight. He moved, flowing through his limited vision with a slow, deliberate pace, to sit down in a chair opposite him.

"You can remove the hood, if you wish."

The accent was difficult to place; a gentleman's delivery, a Romani roll, a Frenchman's burr, and an Englishman's lacquer laid upon every word. Again, that cold bleakness, a hardness to the words of cracking ice and steel. The voice was not pleased with him. It was not pleased *at all* and there was, in that voice, a promise of a baleful stare and a stony expression.

Bartleby removed the hated hood slowly, blinking in the bright light of the fire until his eyes stopped watering and, though he might have looked around the room, his vision was arrested instead by the seated presence in front of him.

The promise of the voice had been kept. Grey eyes watched him with the ferocity of flint, sharp and waiting. The man before him was handsome, in that his features were clean, but somewhat unkempt. There were scars, faint but noticeable, and hard lines at his brow and jaw that could tighten easily into either stern disapproval or cold, hard rage. A close cut, but still scruffy, beard and moustache, neither overgrown, the black hair speckled with grey and swept back. The cheeks were hollow, the bones sharp. It was an unremarkable face, and it gave nothing away, save for an inexplicable—and intense—degree of anger. It was not a look that inspired much hope.

Bartleby could not pull his gaze clear to look properly at his surroundings. So, the edge of his vision took in details instead. The figure before him was lounging in his high backed, velvet lined chair. One hand laid across his midsection. He wore a long coat of darkened grey gabardine, the collar wide, high, and somewhat severe. His waistcoat was plain and functional black. High boots, not simple shoes, rested upon the richly carpeted floor. There were marks upon the boots, marks of wear and work, of scrubbed off mud. Despite how well-dressed he was, there was a seeming shabbiness to the man in how he held himself—hardly the decorum of a gentleman. But that expression was one of razor-edged command, and he watched Bartleby now with waning patience.

Bartleby could take it no longer, and cleared his throat.

"I am glad we can finally meet, circumstances aside, sir. You *are* the one I have been looking for, are you not?" His voice was raspy still, his throat dry. Reaching up, Bartleby adjusted his cravat and collar as best he could, but it did little to soothe. Without moving otherwise, the figure opposite him shifted his grasp and pointed a single finger to Bartleby's right, away from the fire. Following that directing digit, the suffering man's gaze alighted upon—blessed be!—a steaming teapot, a plain teacup, a saucer of sugar cubes, and other wondrous indicators of the presence of a finely-brewed pot of tea, the scent of which now struck Bartleby and brought with it a sense of relief. He nodded his thanks to the figure, who did not answer or change his rigid, unwelcome expression.

An awkward moment followed. The stare remained, the silence with it, and were the situation not so dire, it might have been viewed as almost comical with the way Bartleby poured his tea, added milk and sugar, and then held it in his hand, his fingerless gloves grasping it firmly. A saucer was considered and dismissed—his nerves would have set it to rattling. So he clasped it and huddled on his seat, raising his eyes to the figure opposite him again.

"If you do not think it too forward of me, sir." He took a sip of the tea, feeling it soothe his parched throat and return his senses. "But you *are* him." The figure did not stir, but something thickened in the air.

Who was he, to make this accusation at all? A little man, shorter than average, skinny and starved and seemingly half grown. Younger than he looked—not yet twenty winters—soft-skinned with a thin, pale face topped by a shock of mousey brown hair. Green eyes that were afraid and yet determined, and shifted around the room rapidly, ever returning to the seated figure as though dragged there, who appeared to have reached an internal conclusion.

"This is the point of the conversation where I illuminate you, Mister Bartleby, though it may have come swifter than you prefer." The seated figure watched the fire as he spoke. "You are here because I wished to ask you questions, not indulge you the chance to ask your own. Therefore, I will forgive your impertinence in your first statements, but will not allow further until I deem that you may do so." There was a clipped finality to the words, and Bartleby blinked as he stared, somewhat struck by the sheer audacity. Here he was, kidnapped from the streets by a man who looked more akin to a highwayman than his surroundings accounted.

But his mind suddenly halted and reversed back over the previous conversation, such as it was. Unable to stop himself,

Bartleby realised just how he had been addressed, by his name and not by one of his many, many easily given pseudonyms. A name he had *never* given to any whom he had questioned, in the hope to avoid this very situation.

The man opposite him tilted his head. "Let us begin this matter with yourself. You are Mister Bartholomew Bartleby, employed, by charter, to the Historical Society of London, occasional writer and informer for the The Times, and of 15b Lancashire Lane, London." He leaned back. "Tell me, did your parents begrudge you entering into the world before they cast you aside?"

"I beg your pardon?" The response burst forth from his lips before Bartleby could stop himself, as if a finger was suddenly and unexpectedly pressed upon a raw nerve.

"You can beg for such if you like, but I am in no mood to grant you anything beyond that cup of tea." The response was quick and hard. "You are a ward of the state, and you have a name given to you of such incongruity that it feels almost vindictive to grant it. Based on what little evidence I have, I am inclined to believe you were unwanted from the start." The lounging man steepled his hands. "You are certainly unwanted *here*. It was not my wish but necessity that brought you to me, and not my choosing. Now, answer me clearly. How came you by such an unfortunate naming?"

Bartleby set his jaw. "My name is a fine one, sir, for it is *mine*. As for my parents, I could not attest to them, but I am sure they had their reasons. And begging your pardon once again, granted or no, it was not my idea to come to your home." He was amazed that he kept his voice level; his head was pounding with rushing blood and the dull, agonising ache of the blow he had taken earlier, but he was steadfast in that moment, clutching his teacup so tightly that the liquid trembled.

"This is not my home. This is simply a building in which I dwell." A quiet correction, but Bartleby was betrayed by a moment of confusion. Was that not the very definition of a home, after all? The figure shrouded in shadows and half-lit by firelight continued.

"As for you not deciding to be here, your choices are what led you to this place. The fact you could not see the result of such choices is the fault of nothing but the lack of your own foresight in the matter." The eyes glowered a moment. "You really felt you could ask about such events as you did, and get neither response nor consequence, when all around you were silent? I had hoped you were intelligent." He sank into the high backed chair, a spectre falling into shadow and out of the firelight.

As fragile as his ego was in such matters, Bartleby felt a scorching sense of embarrassment in that moment, but it was met by a wall of anger. What little veneer of manners faded; he set his teacup down firmly on the saucer with a clinking sound.

"*Sir.*" He intoned it firmly, his voice steadying in his rising wrath. "Be damned to your pardon. I asked those questions to find a man. The one man who could answer the question that has haunted the city of London for six years, and each time blood runs down a dark alleyway, people ask again if *he* is back."

The shadow in the chair was still. Though they seemed to merely be listening, the air became colder, the fire somehow becoming muted and wan. But Bartleby would not be daunted, not now, not after so long.

Not when he was so sure, at last.

"I have searched and hunted in the deepest corners of London, and found answers to questions I did not even know to ask. But I found you. I found the answer to the riddle of *him.*" Bartleby's voice grew in confidence. "Because you are the man who killed him, are you not? You are the one who killed Jack the Ripper."

The stillness and unspoken words returned, but Bartleby could see the hands of the seated man. They tightened upon each other, with a gathering anger and fearsome purpose.

There was a knock upon the door. Bartleby leapt in his chair as the boom of knuckles upon wood went off like a cannon shot. But the seated figure did not move, he merely responded to the knock. "Come in." Flatly stated, caught in a moment which did not desire interruption.

Bartleby turned his head as a door behind him opened with a creak, and a man stepped inside, halting after a few steps at rigid attention. The newcomer was elderly, thin, and severe, with a grey bun at the back of their head, pulled so tightly it seemed to wrench all the skin of their face back. The thin flesh that remained gave them the uncomfortable appearance of a living skull. Nevertheless, despite such a villainous visage, they stood straight backed and tall. Their clothing—black and white with a long tailed coat—was perfectly tailored and bereft of creases, but entirely humble. This man was a *butler* in every conceivable way, yet he defied his description of being a *servant,* and was instead something else. Above all, he was intimidating to Bartleby, in a way the other man in the room was not, but he could not put his finger on why.

"Sir." If the voice of the seated man was cold, this was the voice of frozen, empty expanses of glacier ice, a winter given words. The butler did not look upon Bartleby, but he disapproved. He radiated a never-ceasing sense of disapproval, and that sensation focused upon Bartleby as though through a lens.

"Master… *Cutter* wished to inform you that he forgot to bring in our guest's luggage, as it was quite bulky. He wishes to let you know it can be brought inside forthwith once *payment* is made." Acid dripped from select syllables. The figure in the chair did not move. Finally, there was a shadow of a shrug from the depths of the chair, and what might have been a nod.

Bartleby found himself sweating again and, without thinking, he pushed himself to his feet as the butler turned, closing the door firmly behind him, even as Bartleby stepped towards it.

"So it was important to you, what you brought." The words came from behind him, and he turned once more, straightening up.

"It is, sir. I spent all I have on it." He stood still but radiating anxiousness, watching the door through which the butler had departed until a shadow appeared at his shoulder just as the door opened once again, and Bartleby tried to look in two directions so abruptly that he near whipped his head clean off of his shoulders.

The seated man had approached without making a sound. He was simply *there*, at his shoulder and standing still. Closer, those hard grey eyes looked past him, and Bartleby backtracked away from the doorway.

The butler had returned, and handed over, with great difficulty, a rather large and curious carry bag, done in an arrangement of straps to be borne upon the back. He handed it over to the man, who took it—and Bartleby, who had carried the heavy device for many months, was surprised that he made no indication of the obvious weight whatsoever.

Wordlessly, the figure carried it over to a table and set it down. Once more, the butler faded into non-observance behind the clicking of a door. Bartleby moved towards the man, who was intently unveiling the lacquered wooden box within the carry bag, set in a square around eighteen inches along each side, and half again as high. Bartleby reached him just as he opened the lid.

The device within was carefully set; the wax cylinders adjacent it on each side, a curious collapsed brass metal flower stowed atop it. It was a box, with a small crank upon one side, much like a music box. There were signs of careful work and painstaking metal crafting on the device, which appeared to have been folded down into its current state, but could well be taken out of it and made to function. It was the pride and joy of its owner, and the way that Bartleby leaned towards it longingly, was plain to see.

"A phonograph. I have not seen one like it before, however." The cold voice had a note of fascination in it. A hand rested on the wood, moving carefully along it.

Bartleby could bear it no longer. He stepped in close and interposed himself, protecting the box from the inspecting figure. Getting the point, the older man stepped clear and away, putting both his hands behind his back to watch in silence.

"There is no other like it," Bartleby stated. "I designed it myself."

The box was a bit battered. One of the waxen cylinders was damaged, but the remainder were intact. The mechanism on top of the device itself was slightly misaligned, but a few movements, and the tightening of a pair of bolts soon put it right. He breathed a sigh of relief, running his fingers over the damaged cylinder regretfully.

"I found a damaged, discarded one, and purchased it with what little I owned. I then figured out how it worked, how to use it, and then I set about improving it. There is no other like it in all the world." Reverently, he set the cylinder down and opened the lid of the device, revealing the etching needles, the turning clockwork windmill, currently set and still, but waiting. "I have been carrying it around, recording what I find when I find the people I am looking for. People who do not want to be found, but have stories that need to be heard. People like yourself, sir."

The standing figure was eyeing the mechanism of the device with a calculating air, speculative and thoughtful. Hoping to bridge the distance somewhat, Bartleby spoke hopefully. "Do you like it, sir? I note you have a touch of fascination to your eye, as you look upon it."

The grey eye just spoken of flickered in his direction with a faint hum from the one it belonged to. "No. In fact, I despise it entirely. If you attempt to turn it on in my presence, I shall cast it into the fire, and yourself along with it, should you protest." He turned away and moved to stand before said fire, which to Bartleby's eye now appeared worryingly short on fuel to burn.

Bartleby's heart raced. He had been threatened before; many a time, actually, in his life and in his line of work. But there was something entirely coldblooded and factual about how he had been threatened now. It was disquieting, and he paused in his half-hearted attempt to wind up the clockwork mechanism that would allow the device to record the conversation. He lowered his hand and stepped back from it.

"Can I ask why it upsets you so?" He worded it carefully, while remaining protectively in front of the phonograph to ward off any sudden attacks.

The man standing at the fire shrugged without turning, broad shoulders rising and falling slowly. "I have my reasons. And they are mine alone."

Bartleby took a deep breath, steadying himself. "I seek answers, sir. I shall not be leaving this place until I secure them, either."

A hand reached out and collected a cast iron poker by the

fireplace, setting about to disturbing and breaking apart the burning coals. "You are not wanted here, Mister Bartleby," he said in a level tone, without looking at him. "You are the very picture of the unwanted, in all aspects of your unhappy life. You were brought here because I willed it, but not because I wished it. I would have been happier if I had never known of your existence at all, and that is no one's doing but your own."

"You do not strike me as an all together cheerful sort of person, sir." Bartleby tried to force some humour into his voice, but it fell flat. He coughed instead, to cover for the lack of laughter, and closed the lid on his portable phonograph.

He turned to face the man who now stood by the fire, his expression dour and grim as he watched Bartleby. "You asked before if I was unwanted. I may be unwanted here, sir, but I would like to think that, for the world at large, I am needed. People need to hear this story, sir. They need to hear that the man they still fear is dead."

He held out his hand, his eyes intent as he met the older man's eyes with an energised confidence born out of nervousness. "Mister Bartholomew Bartleby, sir. Might I know your name? For the purpose of the record?"

The older man watched him with the look that a lion might wear when the prey managed to thwart it. The hand remained hovering in the air, unshaken and inviting thus. It was stared at briefly with baleful eyes, and then the man approached Bartleby, towards the outstretched hand, and then right past it, towards a counter and decanter of amber liquid upon it.

"The Whitechapel Killer was no man." He spoke succinctly, firmly, and ignored the request to give his name—not even allowing that slight concession as he busied himself, just at the edge of the firelight. Liquid poured out of the crystal into another, a delicate glass that was lifted. "He was not a man at all."

There was a moment of purest confusion. Bartleby sat perplexed and aghast, before speaking in shock and confusion. "Are you saying Jack the Ripper was a *woman*, sir? I refuse to believe such a thing."

A snort of disgust was his answer, and nothing more, the man shaking his head as he returned back to his sunken chair, sitting back down into it. Bartleby shifted in place and then sat down opposite, looking warily to his phonograph, unsure if he should ignore the demand and start the recording, or if this was some sort of game. A pointed nose and part of a face peered out of the shadows at him, and those glittering, gleaming eyes watched Bartleby, gauging his reaction. He opened his mouth to speak, but the shadow was ahead of him, rather than following, and cut him off.

"Before I tell you anything, you tell me this. How did you find me, and what drove you to do so? What drives Mr Bartholomew Bartleby to dig so deeply to find that which I worked *very* hard to ensure would never be found?" There was menace in those words, but curiosity as well. A frustration tempered with professionalism.

Bartleby took a deep breath, rubbing his hands together and suddenly missing the warmth and comfort of his tea.

"My work for the historical society involves making a record of stories of the times, of recording snippets of history, and grasping what might be missed as part of it, lost along the wayside. A scholar records history, but that recording is based upon the information that people like me uncover." He turned, and grasped his teacup, holding it in both hands again. "I ask questions. I am quite skilled at it—I ask questions people do not see the harm in answering, because they do not realise the story that they are in fact truly privy to. I ask about days, and dates, and things that they saw, who did what." He turned the cup around in his hands, and took a sip of the cooling tea, his gaze drifting downwards, a frown on his face. "The Ripper mystery has been one that has been on the mind of London—indeed, on the entire civilised world—ever since the headlines first struck. Five dead women, torn to pieces, each worse than the last. And no killer caught." He shook his head. "A mystery. Even now, six years later, people have not forgotten him, and people still think he is out there. The Ripper mystery was my case, my piece of history to record, so I went out into Whitechapel and started to ask questions, to see what part of the story could be gleaned, to see if there was more to it for the books.

"I started to hear things. Between each memory, there were these… strange silences, or words and phrases. Talk of a man who asked strange questions, not like the ones the police asked, on strange subjects they did not understand. Who had a strange smell about him, like spices or herbs. Who never gave his name, but some nevertheless seemed to know who he was. When I found one of the ones who knew him,, they would not say. I wanted to know why the man asked such *strange* questions. About what drove *him* to do things, and why no one spoke of him." He looked up from his teacup. "A man whom people feared but would not name. And I found that strange, sir. I found it strange that people who would talk about 'Old Merry Jack' would not speak of the man with strange questions. They would tell me as little as possible."

A finger lifted from the glass, hovering out of the darkness, and pointed at him. "But you did get a name. You would not be here without having a name first. I shall not ask who said it you—I already know who told you. I suppose I should have expected it. But you learned a name. All the police and all the journalists and investigators of London, all asking for names and this and that, crawling through the muck and you, little Mr Bartleby, you found out things other people could not or would not." The levelled finger lowered. "It was either luck and providence, or skill and effort. I would know which."

Bartleby was muted a touch, saying nothing as he held his tea, but his grip tightened as a flicker of smugness lit a fire in his soul then, a surety of knowledge. It smouldered there, with the confidence that he had found who it was he had been looking for.

For a moment, the silence dragged, and he wondered if it would simply roll on, two men in shadow by firelight, unwilling to speak, dragging on until dawn and the ending of the world, unless one or the other dispelled the quiet.

Another of those contemptuous snorts was his sarcastic salvation. "All the effort in the world could be expended in fruitless endeavours, and most lives are wasted in such ways." The glass vanished into the shadow again. "Perhaps hard work came into it as well, experience guiding you on the road. However, luck is something else. Luck is something you cannot account for, but sometimes have to rely on." The glass reappeared, and the man opposite leaned forward. "But I would wager on your luck now, Mister Bartholomew Bartleby. I would wager heavily upon it. Can you guess upon which way I would place the gamble to fall?"

There was something in the way he said it. Something about those words had a dagger in it, giving Bartleby reason to pause and hesitate. He did not answer the question, seeing a trap of presumption when presented with it, but instead spoke hesitantly. "The man who told me your name... a Mister Caldwell... may I ask what became of him? For I assure you, he did not mean to tell me what he knew. I caught him unawares. There was no malice in his admission."

The hard set eyes did not waver. "I shall let you guess

upon what happened to Mister Caldwell. He knew full well that the betrayal of confidence would cost him dearly, and it is a price I have ensured he has paid already." Bartleby's mind swarmed with images of bodies wrapped in sackcloth, set with stones and cast into the Thames, the great graveyard of the underbelly of London.

"Do you intend to kill me, sir?" He spoke it quietly, surprised at how clearly he said it. For he was shaking within, his heart pounding in his throat as his fear rose up, but his voice was somehow steady. He looked the man opposite him full in the face.

A flicker of the lips into a smile, but it was bereft of humour. "Say my name."

Bartleby took a deep, ragged breath, holding it for a heartbeat before letting it out. The man before him had not answered his question, and that, perhaps, was confirmation in of itself, as his dreadful imagination then promised him. Then, falsifying a confidence he did not feel, he spoke.

"You are the man who killed Jack the Ripper. You are Jean Reynard."

CHAPTER 2

THE DOOR OF DESPAIR

The smile flickered and turned grimmer still. There was no more confirmation than that. "And do you wish to meet your end, Mister Bartholomew Bartleby?"

He hesitated, before softly shaking his head. "No, sir. I wish to learn."

A barking sound was the reply. It took Bartleby a moment to understand that Reynard had, in fact, laughed, a single sound closer to a reflexive snap rather than actual amusement. "Ah, but it is a thing to witness ignorance when it is so terribly blithe in its countenance."

Bartleby flinched at that, and grasped his hands together on his lap, the fingers interlacing and his knuckles whitening. "I have a responsibility, Mister Reynard. I have a need to know the truth of what happened, and a noble imperative to make that truth known."

There was a soft chuckle, as sour as an unripe lemon. Reynard sat back, sinking once more into the darkness, sipping from his glass. "So simple. A truth is known, and spoken. But you clearly did not listen to me before. That should already tell you how things shall inevitably go, should you speak on this matter to the public."

The glass appeared again, shaking in the air in an idly mocking manner. "When I fetched this for myself, do you remember what I said? I told you the nature of the Ripper. You ignored part of what I spoke, and stumbled instead to the simple idea of gender, but you misplaced your aim of questioning. You do not even know what the right question is to even *ask*, so how can you possibly understand the depth and nature of the truth?" The voice was loaded with contempt.

Bartleby lowered his eyes, staring down at the fingerless gloves of his hands. Something stirred in his heart then, an all or nothing, a desperation based on despair. He would never get another chance—he may never get another morning. The cold starkness of that thought struck home with leaden weight to his stomach, but it was met with a stirring of his pride. The wrong questions? He had gotten *this* far when no one else had, and the dismissiveness of this fact rankled within him. He swallowed that flash of anger and gambled on his luck once more, with his words.

"Then show it to me. Tell it to me. If I learn it and believe you, then I will know. If I do not, Mister Reynard, and I cannot accept it, then I will think you a madman. But either way, you could snuff my life out and no one would ever be the wiser—so what does telling me matter, if that is what you intend to do?"

A long silence greeted him. Reynard sat, reclined back in his chair, and crossed one leg over the other. The glass, near empty, rested easily in one hand, the other upon the leather clad arm of the chair. His free hand rapped his fingers thoughtfully on the leather, in another one of those drawn out contemplations.

Bartleby could not bear it, as the threat of ending hung overhead, as the fire burned lower, the dreadful waiting that bore ever onwards—getting this man to speak was like pulling teeth! And this time he could not wait, but spoke agitatedly. "What are you thinking, sir? I have a right to know."

"A right, is it?" There was a disgusted tilt to the tone. "In truth, I was studying you. I was curious. What is reality to you, Mister Bartholomew Bartleby?"

The young man's vision clouded with exasperated confusion. This man made so little sense to him! And he seemed to flit from topic to topic, from one line of thought to another. "I do not understand. Reality is what is true, is it not?" This brought out another of those not-so-genteel snorts once more from the shadows.

"Reality is a thing that each soul crafts for themselves, from perceptions given to them, through what they see, what they hear, what others hear, what others see, passed along the line. Everyone creates their own reality, Mister Bartleby. From the King on his throne, to the madwoman speaking to souls long dead at old gravestones, reality is a thing they've each created for themselves. All mad in their own ways, great or small."

The seated man slouched further, if such a thing were possible. "If I am going to tell you the truth of the Whitechapel murders, Mister Bartleby, I would have you use that excellence in finding what is truth, by remembering what the *truth* I have already given you actually is."

Bartleby paused at that, looking confused. The fingers started to rap on the arm of the chair once again in annoyance.

"I told you before, what the Ripper was. Not the whole of it, but enough of it. Did you listen, or did you let your reality craft what you heard into something else instead? Something easier? If you are as skilled as you pretend to be, as you had to be to find me, then you were listening and you should remember. Think back. What did I say?"

Bartleby thought hard. What had he said? He had said that the Ripper had not been a man, and thus he sprung to the startled outburst of the murderer being of the feminine variety, but that, too, had been met with quick contempt. But he had said more than that, had he not?

Bartleby blinked, slowly. "You said that he was not a man at all. And not a woman. So… what was it?"

The rapping fingers slapped down together on the arm of the chair, almost like a single strike of applause, and then a single finger raised threateningly. "If you ask if it was an animal, we are done here. Think harder."

Bartleby was at a loss, and it showed in his countenance, his mouth opening and closing several times, before he shook his head in abject silence and utter confusion, his baffled expression lit by firelight as he desperately wracked his brain, overwhelming him to the point of overwrought frustration.

And all the while, Reynard, the man he had searched for, the man he had come looking for answers from, watched him with the relaxed, speculative—and yet nevertheless intent in its predations—expression of a cat observing the mouse that it had gravely wounded, but not yet struck down. But as the silence drew on, his upper lip lifted in annoyance and his brow furrowed down. For a moment there had been engagement, even excitement, but at this sign of failure, the disdain returned once more.

"Look at you." He said it softly, watching Bartleby as he near gasped like a fish withering out of water. "You come asking for the truth, you get so close to it. You even ask for it after I have warned you of it. And here you are, unable to shift out of your perceptions just enough to contemplate the impossible or the unspeakable, because you just cannot bring yourself to that point."

He sighed, rousing himself and moving back to the table with the crystal decanter, shaking his head. But a whisper followed him.

"Tell me. I must know." The voice shook raggedly somewhat, then spoke louder. "I must."

Reynard stood at the window, with one hand upon the decanter, turning the glass stopper slowly, steadily, lifting it before setting it down. "How set upon reality are you, Mr Bartleby?" He did not turn his head. "If I told you the truth would change your perceptions, the very foundation upon which you stand, would you still demand it? Would you then walk the tightrope of madness to seek its terrible semblance?" He turned back to Bartleby, a shadow within shadows, framed by the open window behind him, and the night sky that shone down upon him in a darkened halo. "I hold the door of despair open before you, boy. Choose carefully, for if you accept what I tell you, there can be no return from it."

Bartholomew Bartleby stared at this odd, strangely terrifying man who spoke in mad riddles. And mad he seemed, and not for the first or last time that night, Bartleby wondered if all his research, and how it had led him here to this mysterious figure, was flawed—that he was in the grip of some scheme or even a strange joke or ploy.

But there was something about him, this Jean Reynard. Something about the way he stood, and the look in those grey eyes—eyes that had seen the world through a lens unspeakable. A queer feeling rose in Bartleby's gorge, a twisting in his stomach as though a serpent roiled about in its dying throes within him, its venom pouring forth. A choice lay before him, an absolute that he did not want to take. He wanted to shake his head, to stand, to leave, to cast off all those months of searching and ask to be returned to London, to go home, and to throw himself into his bed and forget any of this had ever happened.

And so it was with no greater surprise than his own that he heard himself speak aloud. "I am sure, Mister Reynard. I came this far."

If the man could see his consternation at his tongue seemingly betraying him, Reynard did not show it. He simply snorted softly, and turned back to the decanter. There was a final pause before he poured himself a larger portion than before, and then he spoke clinically.

"*Morticorpus voratrix*. The official, and scientific name, for what is otherwise known as a 'ghoul'. In old literature of great Araby, it was *ghul*." He set the stopper back with a soft *clink* and raised the glass, taking a sip. He turned around to Bartleby, watching him steadily to gauge his reaction.

Bartleby stared at Reynard as though the man had slapped him. From the way Reynard sedately sipped at his drink once again, he had entirely expected such a reaction.

"I *beg* your pardon, Mister Reynard. A what?" He spoke with an incredulous tone, as though he was entirely sure he had misheard what had been said.

The older man sighed with the faintest irritation, and started to stroll about the room, seemingly at random. "A *ghoul*, boy. A type of the walking dead, a cursed reanimated with cannibalistic tendencies. Originated in ancient Araby, but the affliction either spread over time or was here under a different name. Exact records were lost during the terror of the Crusades, and the Dark Ages. A century ago they made their way into our literature, so I would wager that they were here well before that, as the transition to the point such things become apparent is usually terribly late." He took another sip, and looked back at Bartleby. There was little to be read from the expression, but there was nevertheless a glint in the eye that spoke of dark, almost sadistic, amusement at seeing the young man before him so baffled. Amidst his confusion, Bartleby could not help but think that the man was playing with him for some sort of twisted satisfaction.

Reynard turned away and continued on. "Varied in shape and form, they all have in common their strengths and vulnerabilities. The Whitechapel Killer was of a sort I've not seen before or since. It was unusual perhaps in its habits, but not in its motives, nor in its actions." He took another slow sip of the drink. "Its primary motive, as it is with all of its ilk, was to satisfy itself on human flesh. Unlike its fellows, the Whitechapel Killer did not wish to wait until its victims were dead."

Bartleby was flabbergasted. This was the rambling of a madman, the drivel of a performer; there was no truth in this. There could not be. He could not have come all this way and suffered through such a night of fear and doubt to be then inflicted with this. But then Reynard looked at him, with no humour, no bravado. There was no gauging to see if the con was working, there was no nervous energy in that gaze. Just a cold, unyielding openness that said, with such a ferocity in the eyes that it was near a physical force, that what had been said was the truth he had so pursued.

"I hunted the Whitechapel Killer. I learned its habits." Reynard spoke without blinking. "I tracked it by scent and by pattern. I looked in places that the police did not. I look for monsters, Mister Bartholomew Bartleby. I look for monsters, and I kill them."

Bartleby felt his mouth open, but no words came out, his mouth opening and closing. The man staring at him sighed.

"Look at you. Unable to decide whether to call me a madman or a charlatan. So entirely confident such a short moment ago, even when I warned you of what the truth was, even when I told you to be prepared for it, and here you are. Any moment now you would laugh, but you think that if you do, you will not leave this room alive." He did not elaborate if that last thought was correct or not, but the nonplussed expression spoke volumes of its own. "You are here, Mister Bartleby, so that I might tell you the truth and decide then what to do with you. If you are to prove an inconvenience, I will be rid of you. If you are an asset, I will make use of you, in whatever fashion I see fit."

Bartleby stirred his courage at last, his expression screwing up into anger with his bafflement. "I would like to think that I have some measure of say in this matter, Mister Reynard."

"You might think that, but you do not." The reply was flat, before it was followed up with a dismissive snort. "Sat in your chair as though you are stuck to it, unsure whether to laugh or cry, to stay or run. Unable to even *contemplate* if what I said was true. Tell me, Mister Bartleby, what is it like in your world?"

"My world? It is the same as yours, sir." The affront remained in the tone.

"No, it is not." Again, that flat dismissal. "You are so far from me in this moment, as I am from you, that we may as well be at opposite ends of the Earth. So I ask you, what is your world like? A world that you, with all your years and wisdom"—a phrase spoken with laden contempt—"can fully claim to be the truth of what is?"

At this, Bartleby could take no more. He rose to his feet, strident, and at the end of the little patience he had left. "For God's sake, man, do you really think you can convince me of all this nonsense, with words no less?"

The man opposite him did not move. But the coldness

around him seemed to somehow congeal, the air getting thicker.

"I have no need nor desire to convince you of anything. I do not *care* about you, Mister Bartleby. But I am asking you if you wish to *see*."

There was something about the way he said it that brought Bartleby up short; a threat, a promise, and a black amusement. He opened his mouth, and closed it.

Reynard saw the hesitation. And for the first time he truly smiled, but there was a malice in it. "You want to see it, but you will not admit it. You are a beast of curiosity, and even if you will not say it outright, you are already a slave to it—to the notion of knowing, to see what drove the mysterious *Jean Reynard* so very clearly mad. So, Mr Bartleby, I ask you—are you ready to stop talking, and to *see?*"

Caught between bemusement and fear, Bartleby could find no answer, nothing that was satisfactory. What did this man *mean?* What was he going to show him that would convince him of the words, of the insane notion that the creature that had haunted London all this time was some sort of… fairy tale creature? He wanted to laugh, to shake his head, but the man was so terribly *intent* in his stance, his words, and those pitiless eyes that watched him. If it was a madness, it was so forthright and fierce that it was unlike any he had seen before. So very clear and honest and, while a madness, it was nevertheless one that burned of truth.

Bartleby had to know.

"See what?" he asked quietly, ever wanting answers. Ever wanting insight. But the man before him would not offer it.

"The unbelievable, Mr Bartleby. Cosgrove!" The name was spoken in a bark and the doors to the room once more opened to reveal that dreadful visage, even as somewhere near, a grandfather clock began to toll, counting down to the eleventh hour, as Reynard continued.

"Take Mr Bartleby to the carriage—you know the one. Sit him down, and have Mr Cutter watch him for the time being."

The curt nod of the butler—the humble name of Cosgrove sat upon him with all the accuracy of calling a cut-throat razor a letter opener—was all the answer given or needed. But Bartleby found the voice of protest rising in his throat.

"But it is the depth of the evening! Where could we possibly go at this hour?"

But the grim Reynard cut him off. "No questions until we are underway, we do not have the time for it. I shall be along shortly. And Mr Bartleby?" He reached over, picking up the hood that had covered Bartleby's face, and tossed it at him, the young man catching it by reflex. "Wear that."

The world went dark as Cosgrove plucked it from unresisting fingers and shoved it overhead after a moment of hesitation. A hand as cold as a gravestone gripped one arm and pulled him along. The door closed. The cold night came rushing back as the utterly bewildered Bartleby, too worn out and lost to protest, was dragged off into the unknown.

REYNARD RAN his hand over the abandoned phonograph. Careful, speculative, noting the workmanship as Cosgrove appeared behind him, looming out of the dark. A slight smile played on the master's face, but there was no humour on it, seeming somehow harder upon his face than without it.

"Fetch me Delilah, and my coat," he said absently, tapping one finger on the phonograph. "One of a kind, and he was right." He sighed, shaking his head, and turned to the dresser where the whiskey decanter stood. However, this time, he did not reach for the glass, but rather opened it, and pulled something out. A wide leather belt, upon which were set two scabbards, clad in finely-tooled leather, and two blades—an old, long-handled hand and a half sword, and a shorter, thinner blade. He hoisted it over a shoulder, and shrugged. "Truly, an age we live in."

Cosgrove gave him a nonplussed look. "I do recall overhearing, if you will forgive the keenness of my ears sir, that you despised his adapted creation." His tone of voice was disdainful as his expression, but Reynard gave the smallest of shrugs, gazing down on the mechanism.

"It represents a future that will forget the past through its own relentless advances—as all things are forgotten. What it records will be less important than the device itself, no matter how precious those words might be, and the machines to come after it, whatever they might be, will be the same." He started towards the door. "So I will loathe it for the inevitability it represents. But I will also be fascinated by it." He paused, pulling the larger blade clear of its scabbard by some inches and inspecting the steel a moment, speaking absently. "For where and what manner of fool would I be, if I did not study that which I despise?" His gaze flicked upwards to the other man. "Now fetch me Delilah."

CHAPTER 3

THE ROTTED CHAPEL

Bartleby stood on the threshold of the manor, trembling and holding his hands together, futile in his efforts to ward off both chill and terror.

There was movement around him, the hood rendering him blind and dulling his hearing along with it, but he could detect motion. The shifting of a carriage, the sound of horses being lead, the crunch of foot, of hoof, and of wheel on gravel in mixed measure. He put up with it for a few moments more, before his fear manifested itself into defiance once again, and he reached up to wrench off the hood, blinking in even the dim light of torch and candle.

To his displeasure, his attention was immediately arrested by an individual standing only a little way from him, leaning against a wall directly in his field of vision, and watching Bartleby intently. Cutter—it felt ignominious to place 'Mister' before his nomenclature—was picking at his fingernails with a paring knife, watching Bartleby with an altogether unpleasant expression, upon an already unpleasant face.

The bulky, battered thug straightened, making a sucking

sound between his teeth. "Think you were told to put that on, lad. Not take it off."

Bartleby stirred in the seething pit of that fear-born defiance. He straightened his skinny shoulders as best he could, while trying to meet that knowing look. "I was told to put it on, but the length of time it was to remain on was not specified." His tone was cordial, but he could not keep the sardonic tilt to his words to cover up the fear.

Cutter gave a laugh then. A silken, soft sound, high in malice and portent. He made the knife vanish with a flick of his wrist and eased himself off the wall to draw closer, hands going to the pockets of his coat. He had knives far more worrisome in those pockets, Bartleby knew, but truth be told he probably didn't need them; the man could likely rip him apart with his bare hands, and he knew it.

You watched me without saying anything. Watched me all the way here and just now. Bartleby realised, his blood running even colder. *You* like *watching people quivering in terror. What sort of creature are you?* But he already knew. Bartleby had known such beasts all his life.

"Clever boy, aren't we? Clever enough to find your way here, clever enough to come back from meeting the boss, and clever enough to have a smart word fly from your tongue at a moment's notice." He filled all of Bartleby's vision at this point, an exquisitely unpleasant experience, to the point of being nauseating as fine, foul details were made ever more apparent. Scars across the nose and cheek, ingrown hairs amongst the stubble, bloodshot eyes, and the remnants of foul meals lodged between twisted teeth. If Bartleby had doubted that the existence of a ghoul was a real thing before, it suddenly became easier when Cutter was so close to him.

He was ripped from his contemplation as blackened metal was flashed before his face, just in front of one of his eyes. A short, nasty blade of black iron and a raw edge, flicked from a wrist.

"Think I might cut that tongue loose, see if it sings for me when I poke it," Cutter mused with a leer, his breath foul as it washed over Bartleby, and he wondered why he had not yet wet himself in panic. The knife drew ever closer as a hand came up, ready to grab at a throat and let the cutting begin—

"Easy there, Mister Cutter. You will break our guest if you keep such things up."

The new voice was musical and light, with a Welsh accent that added that ages old beauty to every syllable. Cutter froze, locked in place momentarily as his eyes swivelled behind him. His head turned slowly, and Bartleby took the moment to peer past the brute.

The newcomer was an odd figure. Clad in simple enough clothing—a worn coat and breeches, with slip on shoes rather than boots—he stood with a stance best described as crooked. His hands were in his pockets with his elbows out wide, his shoulders stooped and his back bent, he had his head on an angle to look up at Cutter, while being taller than him if he stood straight. His features were oddly ageless, smooth but his hair was grey and swept back from his brow. He was also oddly bulky, too—the shoulders were broad even though they slung downwards, the hands, though long and slender-fingered, had a strength to them. He was a juxtaposition in the flesh, and for whatever reason, even though his posture and the pleasant smile on his face spoke of far kinder nature than the man before him, Bartleby was unable to ignore the fact that Cutter had frozen at the sight of him.

The tilted head and the almost too-bright eyes that glimmered silver in the lamplight, watched Cutter for a long moment with that same friendly smile, and Bartleby had a thought—Cutter was not the only one who enjoyed seeing someone in fear.

"Let him into my care, goodfellow—there's a lad." The words were kind, with no hint of malice to them. They remained, lurking in the air, bouncing off stones and whispering along the grass. "Run on with you now. You look like all your teeth are about to fall out, if you linger much longer."

It was a truly bizarre threat, and one that Bartleby did not understand in the slightest, but Cutter, who had not yet managed a single word, gave a most undignified yelp and scurried clear, turning and moving away with whatever dignity remained to him. Bartleby exhaled, sagging, suddenly exhausted as the danger passed.

A hand clapped onto his shoulder, rooting him in place as though he had become one with a mountain. The strangely crooked man was there now, holding Bartleby up by one hand, his head still at that strange tilt, his lips split in a wide grin that showed far too many teeth.

"And what do we have here, a lost lamb in a bright-dark world, bidding the shadows follow him not?" He trilled a musical little laugh that sounded sweet while putting Bartleby's hackles up. He opened his mouth, stammering, but the crooked man shook his head to still him. "Now then, now then, sweet child of spring… may I have your name?"

Bartleby, in a more normal frame of mind, would not have answered the question. There was something quite wrong about the nameless creature before him, a hint of unquiet that never went away. Something about him seemed *twisted*, as wretched as his posture. He beheld Bartleby with those shining eyes and waited patiently for an answer without blinking.

"Bartholomew," Bartleby stuttered. "Bartholomew Bartleby."

The crooked man gave a nod, closing his eyes as he sucked in a slow, slow breath, as though tasting the name on his tongue, which he stuck to the side of his cheek for a moment as he contemplated, looking skyward as he did so. "A name overlong, I fear. Let us carve away at it, and give you a simpler name until we deem to return the other to you." He winked, the grin returning, all too bright, all too many teeth. "How about 'Barty'?"

Barty blinked. "But my name is—"

"Barty, I know," the crooked man said cheerfully. He was steering Barty along now. "As for my name, that is not for the telling, leastways from this tongue. Made that mistake a time too many, a time too many indeed." He shook his head and made a faint whistling note that had a sorrowful echo to it as it fell, his expression flickering into the plunge along with it before abruptly shifting back to the amicable cheer instead, so quickly that Barty had trouble keeping up. "No time for such things, no time in all the skies for such songs and singing, no," he went on cheerfully, and with that hand, guided Barty towards the carriage that waited, a blackened beast breathing in darkness, a hound ready to leap away. A pat on the shoulder, as Barty carried on, like a puppet on a string and with just as little will of his own.

But on the threshold, that grip froze in place and locked Barty where he was. The stranger was at his ear then, his words a murmur that swum through Barty's ear itself and latched onto his brain with ice cold claws. "A word of advice, lostborn son of secrets, child of doubting dreams—whatever it may be that you encounter this night, remember this warning —do not scream. Do you understand, yes... yes? Do not scream. Screams will take morning from you, tomorrow, and all the ones after."

Barty wobbled in place at this. This dread warning

somehow all the more terrible than the crude ones given by Cutter; something about this madfolk murmuring felt more real and unreal at the same time.

He was not given the opportunity to respond. The crooked man patted his shoulder, and his tone turned louder and kind once more. "There's a lad, on you hop." Releasing that iron grip, he turned and sprang up into the carriage seat above so quickly that a squirrel rushing up a tree trunk would have been agog at the sight—Barty was too dazed to properly take it in, as instead, with wobbling legs and a shaking hand, he clambered into the carriage itself to sit down.

"Finally." Reynard was sat in the opposite corner, once again cloaked in shadow. Barty could only recognise him by his boots, of which the foot of one was tapping upon the floor that Barty had arrived upon, curled up and face down. A lifetime ago, despite all the aches that he still felt from it. There was something curious between them however—a black box, long and thin, one end resting on the floor, the other near reaching the ceiling. It was wedged between the two opposite facing benches of the carriage, almost as tall as Barty himself but only around eight inches wide. It was an odd sight, and the featureless box granted him no answers as to what was within it.

Reaching to the chair beside him, Reynard picked up a scabbarded sword—an archaic longsword, Barty was surprised to note—and banged the pommel of it upon the roof of the carriage three times. A light-hearted chuckle slithered through the window, and there was a click of a tongue before the carriage lurched forward suddenly, jolting Barty about before he righted himself. Jean did not move at all.

"I see you made acquaintance with my footman, Mister Barty." Dryly, as the carriage picked up speed rapidly, the horses moving as though the crooked man was chasing them.

Barty found himself bouncing this way and that. He nevertheless felt obliged to respond. "My name is not Barty, it is…" He trailed off, as something escaped him. "I mean, it is…"

"'Barty' will do well enough for now… Mister Barty. You have more important things to be concerned with."

Barty shook his head at this sardonic interruption, glaring at the man who had arranged his kidnapping. The spark of defiance amidst the dread flared once more in his soul. "I doubt you are taking me somewhere to kill me, at least like this," he snapped in response. "What do I have then to worry about?"

His imagination flared as he asked the question, much as it had on the carriage ride to the manor. *Any number of things, you fool*, his own voice admonished him soundly in his mind.

But Reynard gave a bleak chuckle, amused and unworried. "Such a prosaic fear you have. But when your life is all that is left to you, I suppose one must cling to it." He shook his head, still drenched in shadow as moon and starlight replaced that of dirty torches and lamps. "What concerns you now is just how badly you wish to learn the truth."

Barty opened his mouth, but Reynard cut him off with an upheld palm. "I do not doubt that you wish to, that much has been made clear already. What I *do* wonder is just how prepared you are for it, and how willing you are to embrace it." Those broad shoulders shrugged, his features barely visible in the gloom. "The hint given to you was one you were not ready for, so, if you want to learn more as you truly say, about me, about the hunt, and about Jack, I will need you to convince me."

Grinding his teeth together, Barty considered the words spoken. "I have no idea how to do that, beyond what I have already done to find you."

Reynard shook his head, disappointment ringing in the snort of his reply. "Try. What would you be prepared to surrender yourself to, to know the answers?"

Barty struggled with that, his gaze lowering as he shoved down his irritation, his exhaustion and fear, and tried to answer the question honestly. Absently, he noticed that the ride of the carriage had smoothed out. *Strange*, he wondered absently. He would have thought that the rural roads would have been far, far worse than those in the city itself. This was smoother than a train, and it was growing gentler still.

He could hear singing; beautiful words he did not recognise, in a voice he did not know, but could only have been the crooked man. It lulled him a moment, before the single tap of Reynard's growing impatience ripped his attention back. He took a deep breath and spoke, trying to shut that compelling song from his mind. This night was proving too much for him, *had* proven too much for him, but he gathered of himself what he could.

"I want to know," he said, speaking slowly at first, but as he went on his words came faster and easier. "I cannot really explain it more than that. I want to learn the truth of it, I want to know what really happened. I do not believe you, not yet—but I *want* to. If you say he was this thing, a ghoul—then I want to see it proven. I want to find out what I do not know."

He was amazed that he said it clearly, and fully. He was even more amazed that he meant it, and was not simply trying to find the words that Reynard wanted to hear. The man opposite him nodded once, and fell silent, sinking back into shadow once more. Though he had said nothing in reply, Barty got the distinct impression the conversation was over. All that was left was the singing of the song, louder now, and soothing, as the starlight grew brighter and the moon shone its beams into the carriage's corners.

The carriage stopped abruptly with a jerk. Barty was startled along with it, bouncing so firmly off the seat backing that he nearly fell onto the carriage floor. The song was gone. It was still nighttime. Everything was very dark, as the clouds had returned to devour the lights above, the glimmer of moonlight alone now dim and tremulous.

Jean Reynard was climbing out of the carriage. Barty absently noted how gracefully he did so—clambering out of a carriage was something that easily could become awkward. Nobility relied upon footmen who could provide steps while wriggling their forms through doors that were just a touch too small for them, burdened by expensive clothes and tall hats that made the process more complicated than it needed to be. Jean had no such problem. He leapt clear without need for steps, boots crunching, securing his sword belt even as he strode forward. There was nothing about the man that was not confident, intimidatingly so.

Barty, for his part, clambered out with the clumsy movement of someone who seldom, if ever, rode in carriages, and who had no clue where he was or was even fully confident of where the ground was in the darkness. Why had the footman not lit a torch or lamp?

They were amongst trees, from the looming shapes, but on the edge of a forest. There was an abrupt opening in the tree line, and in that opening stood Reynard's silhouette, both hands at his back and staring outwards. Barty, bewildered, followed after him, moving to stand alongside him before Reynard shot out a hand and caught him by the shoulder, fingers cold and hard, biting down painfully to make him wince. Whereas the crooked man's hold had been immovable,

Reynard's was akin to the bars of a cage closing in to crush the occupant.

"Mind your step, Mister Barty. That is a fall you are not quite ready for." Baffled, Barty blinked and peered, then reeled, his mouth turning dry as a break in the clouds gave the moon enough power to render the world visible, though in shades of black and grey alone.

Though the cliff they were on was not especially high, it was enough of one to give pause and worry. Barty could hear the sound of water below, flowing smooth and free. And past that, a low wall surrounding a lumpen field—a field covered in standing stones, small crypts, and headstones—in the distance a great black shadow that could only have been an ancient chapel loomed.

"A graveyard?" Barty said, unable to restrain his bafflement. "Where *are* we?"

Ignoring him, Reynard pointed a finger and spoke in a low tone. "If you want answers, you will find them. In that chapel, you will have the answers to everything you seek. Are you prepared to make such a journey?"

Barty stared at the pitch black structure, a deeper blot amongst other blots. There was no sign of life about it whatsoever.

"Is this some sort of test? A joke of some sort?" Barty tried to sound indignant, but the place was so *quiet*. There was the creak of tree branches and the soft groan of wind, and nothing more. Not even a single hoot of an owl. It did not feel that the world was perhaps sleeping—no, it felt like it was *waiting*.

"Do I look amused, Mister Barty?" Reynard's gravelled voice was flat.

"I could not say, sir. It is far too dark here," Barty quipped back, but his heart was not in even that poor jest. Something about the night-obscured features watching him hardened even further, if that was possible.

"I ask again, Mister Barty." The name still wrangled, but he could not make his lips move to argue it, as that grip on him tightened. "Are you prepared to make such a journey?"

He had come this far. Through fear and outright terror, he had made it this far. He had been searching for these answers for months and months, all to satisfy the unending call in his thoughts. To find this man and learn about him, the one who ended the most infamous murderer in the history of England.

He was powerless against that urge. He answered it, and Reynard both.

"I am," he said thickly, forcing it from his lips. He straightened up, preparing to get back on the carriage. "I am ready to go."

"Excellent," Reynard said in a deadpan tone, releasing his grip on Barty. "You have until morning to get there."

Barty nodded to this without realising immediately the strangeness of the statement, but before he could even form the question, Jean went on in that same, flat tone.

"Allow me to help you on your way."

Barty barely grasped what he meant by that before he was abruptly shoved, the world tilting around and in on itself. He reached out for the ground but did not find it, turning in mid-air to see the shadow of the man who had pushed him off the cliff, before the bone-freezing chill of the stream closed over him in a roar, cutting off the scream in his lungs and filling them with water instead.

Barty rolled and tumbled, bouncing off stones as he tried to fling himself to the surface, screaming for the air that his fall had smashed out of him. He could not swim, but the stream was shallow. Utterly drenched, he dragged himself clear, clawing his wretched form out of the water, in a manner akin to a corpse pulling itself from a welcoming grave. He lay there on his back, gasping, his whole body aching and numb, spitting out water, as white and red spots swam in the darkness of his vision.

Dimly, he realised the carriage above was moving on. Carrying on down the road—towards the chapel? The madman had pushed him off a cliff and tried to drown him! Was he leaving him there to die? Had it all just been a trick to get him out of his home and kill him? Barty did not know. He could not know anything right now, except that Jean Reynard was a mad bastard and that he hated him very much. Very much indeed.

There was a faint note of grey in the sky. The light of the false dawn approached, as the sky brightened with the promise of the sun to come. It took a long time of him simply laying there before he came to understand what it meant, and, with a groan of agony, rolled onto his stomach.

Whether Reynard was going to be there at the chapel or not was irrelevant at this point; Barty had spent enough nights cold and shivering in the depths of a miserable winter in not-so-merry London to know this sort of cold was bad, and that the only shelter in sight was the chapel. He needed shelter. He needed dry clothes, a fire, and a hot meal.

Perhaps half a brick to hurl at the head of a cruel man, if fate decreed such a thing was within his mercy.

But he had to get moving, even if his body screamed at him as he gingerly pushed himself to his feet. Nothing felt broken at least—just as though his whole body had become a great, damnable bruise instead.

His teeth were chattering violently. Ice was forming on his clothes, which cracked as he stumbled along. He weighed twice as much as he normally did, but he pushed onwards. He had to at this point, though the temptation to lay down and forget was an overwhelmingly powerful one. To stop would put another body in the graveyard, except this one would be above ground.

It was at this point Barty remembered where he was, and could not help but pause. The graveyard stretched out before and around him. Quiet headstones stared with the eyes of those who mouldered beneath them, turning back to the dirt from whence they had come. He could not read any of them, for the stones were weathered and old. These people had been dead and buried from a time before he had even been born, and yet their memory lingered on.

He felt guilty for his struggles in that moment, for the contemplation he had of giving up and lying down amongst the dead. What jealousy those bones would feel, for one that still could walk while they became nothing. What would they give to wear his unworthy skin, so that they could live again? Kingdom of Heaven or no. Barty forced himself onwards, grinding his teeth together to stop them chattering, hugging his arms across his frozen chest.

He tripped on a stone, falling flat on his face. Searing agony flew through his numbed toes and already bruised features, sharp needles of misery flaring out bright, and the urge to scream came loud and fierce. But even as it crawled from soggy lungs to claw its way up his throat, he bit down on his tongue to keep it at bay. He did not even think about why he did it at first, but as he felt heat form in his mouth, and blood trickled down his throat to drown the screech, he recalled the advice that the crooked man had given him.

Do not scream, he had said.

No matter what, he must not scream.

It saved his life. Because, in that moment, he heard it, as he sat in the shadow of an ancient, rotting gravestone, being worn down grain by grain by wind and rain, hidden in its shadow even from moonlight.

A menacing menagerie of mixed sounds. Muttering and clicking, scraping and snarling. A spitting voice, a voice of thorns and brambles, thick with blood and madness both. They were muttering something, a figure out there in the gloom, but the voice was a dark and dreadful thing, even for the worst streets of London. Barty did not think his blood could get any colder, but that muttering set frost from the deepest depths of a black ice night through his veins, stopping him solid in place as his heart pounded a new, terrified beat.

"Heard it, we did. Heard the nasty little thing crawling, yes? Smell it, we do. Stinks like fear. Smells like flesh. How long, how long? Too long, too long. Where are you, my tasty little sweet?"

He could make out the words, and the sound of movement, somewhere to his left. Distant, but growing closer. There was a liquid edge to each syllable, and a gurgling laugh, high with malice and horror. Vaguely, sat upon the ground and in the shadow of the gravestone, Barty could see it. A lump of darkness in the void, crouched and curved. It was larger than a man, quite substantially so. It appeared bulky until he could make out its limbs—long, slender, reaching out for gravestones and pulling themselves along, the bulk instead seeming to be a great mass of rags cloaking it. Hands as large as dinner plates with long, curling fingers, the tips glinting in faint moonlight. It —whatever it was—moved like a spider prowling; each time its hands touched stone, there was a scrape and click of its fingers.

Much of it was buried in shadow. But he did not need to see more than he did, because sight did not nearly convey the depth of its presence. It *projected* foulness, spewed it forth from its being to the entire world around it. Whatever *it* was. For under not even the most casual of inspections could Barty have even contemplated that it was a man.

The thing made a snuffling sound, a lump in its midst around where the shoulders would be stretching out, as it sniffed the air, and that high, wheezing laugh came again, a sound so vile that Barty twitched with the need to run, now sitting silent with one hand clamped over his mouth, forcing it painfully shut to keep in the chattering of his teeth and the scream he had buried in his lungs wanting to escape.

Do not scream. Do not. Do not make a sound at all.

"Come now, little mouse, little whisper, who comes to Clickerclack's web, hmm?" The hideous voice had a wheedling tone to it. Pleading, almost kind, but there was a growling undercurrent to it. "We can dance together, you and I, yes, yes—dance and sing and scream together, you and I." The snuffling came back, and exhaled then with a sigh of some obscene pleasure. "I have missed the flesh of the fearful. You smell so sweet, little lost mouse, yes."

The head on the end of the obscenely long neck swung this way and that, searching, prying. It was close. Too close for any measure of comfort, but the terrified Barty would have been afraid if this hellspawn was on the other side of the world. There was no state of reality where this creature, whatever it was, would not haunt his darkest dreams, dreams that were familiar. Memories of a small child, growing up amidst strangers, spending his nights hiding from voices calling his name with malice in their false promises, wheedling and sibilant. He had learned to hide then. It was keeping him alive now.

Was this what Reynard had meant, when he had spoken about knowing the truth? Was this thing, this… *Clickerclack*, it called itself, the thing that a disbelieving Barty had been so wary to take on as a true entity? If nothing else, it was a damnable means of education.

Instinct took over. The stone he had tripped on was still there, just at the edge of the gravestone's shadow. For the first time since he had found himself observing the prowling night-mare, he dared himself to move before the thing got closer.

It was singing now, a low and horrible tune, scratching and splintering on the air. There were no words, but there was no need—it sounded like an animal in pain, like a slaughterhouse at work. It was enough to set the ears to bleeding, even as it sniffed and snuffled away. The head was turned, the thing itself perched on a pair of gravestones at this point—its hands clutching to one and what were possibly its feet clinging to another. Barty closed his hand on the rock, lifted it, and then —as quick as he dared—threw it as hard as he could.

The aim, of course, was to create a distraction. A sound off somewhere for the thing to investigate while he himself crept away quietly and carefully. But there were a number of things playing against Barty as he made the attempt. The first was obvi-ous, in that his body was desperately cold and was not quite responding to his own commands for the time being. In staying still for the few minutes that he had, chill had set into his muscles, making movement awkward. The second issue was that he had severe trouble taking his eyes off the crouching horror, fixated on it from the illusionary safety of his gravestone nook. Lastly, the stone in his hand was a good bit of field granite—hardly a pebble by any means, near as large as his fist, which gave it good heft and weight, but made directing it less easy than one might hope.

So, instead of performing the far more helpful action of lobbing the rock past the thing called Clickerclack, the lump of stone sailed through the air directly at it.

Barty realised his mistake as the projectile was about to

impact, and his heart nearly leapt out of his throat in his sudden horror. A horror which was fully realised a second later when there was a loud *crack*, as the rock smacked into the wretched being's skull.

It was knocked off its perch by the impact, making a high shrieking sound that was part a yelp. There was confusion and shock in its tone, as it tumbled to the ground in a spindly-limbed heap, flailing about in a clot of darkness and rotted cloth. Barty felt his heart drop down from his mouth, down through his stomach and bring it along for the journey, through his legs and into his shoes. For a few desperately hammering heartbeats, he sat there in frozen shock, as the creature thrashed about and twisted itself back upright from its fall. That wretched inhuman voice rose into an ear-piercing shriek of rage as the being screamed its fury, breaking the stillness of the night to pieces.

"YOU WRETCH! YOU HURT CLICKERCLACK!" Barty was locked in place as the rags shifted to reveal a gaping maw in the midst of it, much too large for a human mouth—it was long and thin, merging down the throat and to the chest itself, as though the whole jaw had been ripped clear, and yet it still functioned, full of gleaming teeth.

In the awful revealing, Barty was trapped in that moment, before his body decided to simply take over from his brain, ruling that the mind which guided it had chosen to just… stop working for the time being and, that said, the body was going to have to do the work itself.

Terror proved a potent anaesthetic, adrenaline and panic combining into a powerful panacea that dismissed exhaustion, freezing cold, and locked limbs, to set Barty scrambling. Whatever price he would pay for it later was one he would worry about when it came due, but as the rising, hateful shriek from behind him poured fear down his spine, his body found ways to keep him moving that he had never known he had until this moment. The chapel was ahead, maybe a hundred yards, maybe twice that, he could not tell properly. It did not matter. It was the only promise of safety in the nightmare surrounding him, so he bolted for it as fast as he could.

Behind him, screeching its rage in its loathsome voice, bereft now of any semblance of even the most vile of pleasantries, came the thing called Clickerclack. It pulled itself over the gravestones, howling its hunger and hatred in a long note. Barty did not dare to look back, to see it scuttling like a vile spider over the graves after him, trying to catch him up on its long, stiff limbs. It was gaining, but Barty was running swift as the wind, with not a sign of slowing down at all. Despite that, Clickerclack drew closer.

He could feel the wretched thing nearing, the scratching dig of claws on stone and soil, the wheezing air of a chasing predator. As a hare might attempt to outmanoeuvre a fox, he flung himself sideways along a row of gravestones as Clickerclack leapt, sending it sprawling and tumbling—its body well-built for pursuit, but not so much for sudden changes in direction. Barty had felt a clawed hand, massive and foul, pass over his head as he stumbled in the abrupt shift. Clickerclack was snarling words in either a language Barty did not know, or it was simply incoherent in its fury, and he was in no position to find out which. The chapel was just ahead.

There was a touch of light now. The world lit in shadows of grey as the sun threatened the horizon, but did not yet crest it. Barty dared a glance behind him and regretted it, as the howling monstrosity scrambled towards him, leaping from gravestone to gravestone. The thing wanted blood, and the only blood in sight was his own.

Clearing the low steps of the chapel, he did not slow. An old structure of blackened granite, glistening in the dew of the nighttime air, it looked abandoned, forgotten, whoever had tended it long gone. It sat there, rotting, and even now showed no sign of life or care to the lone struggler seeking sanctuary in its walls, praying that the light of God still yet lingered to banish this pursuing beast away.

He scrambled to one side, as Clickerclack crashed violently into the wall where he had just stood. Sparks flew from the granite as claws scored the stone, flaring bright in the darkness as Barty darted away. His heart was hammering, his body screaming, his lungs on fire, as his blood turned to lead. But the fuel of desperation and terror pushed past all of that, and through the madness and nightmare, the desire to live was still strongest of all.

Reach the chapel by morning, that was what he had been told. Reach the chapel to get all his answers. It was the only choice he had and, nearly sobbing, he scrambled towards the front doors, climbing up the rows of steps two at a time before slamming into great double doors of rotting wood—and they did not open. He pushed and shoved, but nothing shifted. He was trapped.

He turned as the shrieking roar came from behind him. Turning, his terrified gaze took in an awful sight. The creature, Clickerclack, was mid-air in a leap towards him, its four limbs spread apart as it did so. It was a cluster of rotten rags, the limbs stretching out of it pale and befouled, its open maw gaping. It crashed into him, into the doors, smashing them with the weight of the impact and bearing Barty along with them, blasting the air out of him as the overpowering, unholy *stink* of the thing bore him down as surely as its fetid mass, and they burst into the chapel itself. Barty's vision turned blurry as he hit the stone floor, hard, before the world swam back into dreadful focus.

The creature was atop him, all four limbs holding it up

above him as it looked down, and for the first time, Barty was able to make out the details fully. The eyes were surprisingly, shockingly humanlike—bloodshot perhaps, brown as a sewer drain, but human. That was where all the familiarity ended and the horror began properly.

The thing was hairless, entirely so, with the flesh a mixture of dead grey and bruised, yellowing purple, that which could be seen under the matted layer of filth covering both it and the stinking rags it wore. The face was mostly human, but the jaw was completely distorted—it could open enormously wide, and was doing so now, exhaling the single most vile smell that Barty had ever scented, strong enough to choke him and make his eyes burn. Almost too much to see the rotten, twisted fangs that made up the impossibly large mouth, like a muzzle where the lower jawline appeared to take up the entire throat, down towards the chest. The eyes gleamed with triumph, drool spilling out as a long tongue, that looked like a gleaming red serpent, slid out from the void that was the open mouth. Barty was dead, and all he could do in that moment, winded and pinned, was give a squeak of terror, his last testament to a world that had turned entirely mad in the course of but a single day.

And then, a ray of light, bright and fierce, joined by a sardonic, almost disgustedly bored voice. "You were quite nearly late."

Trapped man and leering monster both snapped their vision deeper into the chapel. It was a ruin within, the roof collapsed inwards, and amidst that rubble stood a figure. There was a flare of light and a beam of it extended outwards beside him, sat upon a pile of wreckage—a thieves lantern, with a window open to reveal the trapped glow hidden inside, shone directly into the face of Clickerclack.

The monster squinted, baffled, then it spasmed and shrieked in its hideous voice a single word.

"YOU!" It reared up in that moment, uncoiling like a twisted puppet pulled upwards, but it was too late. The chapel burst bright into light and horrible, booming noise, the scent of gunpowder raw and full, cutting sharp through the stink, and suddenly Clickerclack was flung through the air as though slapped by the hand of a giant.

"Yes. Me," Jean Reynard said, moving forward. From his prone position, Barty watched him, agape, as the man strode past him without even looking down at him. The huntsman's gaze instead was fixated on the thing he had just gunned down with a double barrelled rifle, the barrels still smoking. He opened the breech as he went, the spent shells lifting away, pulling two more from his belt. Barty crawled after him. He did not know what else to do, but he had to see.

"It has been some time, Clicker." Jean's tone was even, and that only added to the menace. He strode through the shattered doorway, unhurried even as the thing crawled away from him, leaving a blackened trail of fuming slime as it went. It was whimpering, a horrible sound that was as disgusting as it was pitiful, a smashed spider dragging itself away before the job of its death was done. Jean loaded the rifle and rested it on his shoulder, pointing skyward, before reaching into his coat with one hand. "But with all that you have done, you know what happens now." There was a terrible sort of smugness to his tone, as he set a cigarette to his lips, lighting it, and then tossing the flaring star of the match clear.

"No! No!" Clickerclack whined, still dragging itself away, as the sky brightened with the promise of the rising sun, its glow forming on the horizon. In so doing, the ruin of its form in the aftermath of the gunshot was revealed as it went.

The solid, brutal slugs had ripped through the rags and

body, tearing chunks of flesh and bone with it from the face and torso. One eye was gone, black liquid oozing from the burst socket, and the flesh was scored with oozing wounds more akin to tearing. It was clearly agonising, but the creature continued, its voice bubbling with a different kind of liquid as fluid flowed into its mouth.

"Nothing wrong, nothing wrong we did! Sweet as lambs, sweet as lambs we have been! Nothing to call the Hunter, nothing to call them at all!"

"And yet, here we are, and what did I see? You chased that poor young man, Clicker. You clicked and you clacked and what were you going to do at the end when you had him? Sing him one of your songs? Call him the lullaby of the dead? No, you and I both know what you were going to do." Jean's hand was back on his belt as he talked around the cigarette, clenching it between his teeth as he spoke. Barty moved to his feet, wobbling and shaking as his mind tried to catch up with the words being spoken. Jean sighed, shaking his head. "But I suppose a ghoul cannot help what it is, can it?" His tone turned harsh, cold and accusing. "Flesh eater. Bone chewer. Know you prefer babes but you'll get any meat that you can, as long as it is human." He looked around briefly, gazing across the empty graveyard before looking back to the wretched, bleeding huddle before him. "Guess you ran out of bones, found yourself wanting something fresher?"

"No! No one comes here! No one supposed to be here!" Clickerclack wailed, covering its head with two spindly hands. Now, as Barty drew closer, it looked ever more pathetic. Its voice was reedy and thin, and desperately, terribly afraid. Pleading for mercy in a man that gave no indication of having even the faintest amount in him. "Clickerclack just wanted to be left alone! Alone!"

Jean snorted, but Barty felt a tremor run down his spine in

that moment, a new sliver of ice running through his bones, his horror giving way first partly to pity despite himself, then to sickened realisation. "You used me." He could not help but say it in a mere whisper, but Jean's grey gaze shot towards him out of the corner of one eye, even as the end of the cigarette flared bright.

"You *used* me," Barty said again, his voice growing stronger, his sickened shock turned to a rising fury, stoked by exhaustion and shock. "You used me as bait for this, this…" He gestured with desperate futility towards Clickerclack, who remained crouched and whimpering throughout. "You brought me here to lure him out!"

"I brought you here to show you the *truth*, boy," Reynard snarled back, his tone laden with contempt. "You did not believe me, and credit to you—but I did not have time for your doubts. This is the kin of the one you were 'investigating'. Take a good look at your first ghoul."

"So few of us! We are so few!" Clickerclack gibbered, as it rocked back and forth, still bleeding on the ground. "The unwanted! The unheeded! We just want to be left alone!" It shuddered and grovelled, pushing its broken face into the ground. "It hurts Clickerclack!"

"I am sure it does. Let us settle things then, shall we?" Jean snorted contemptuously. He brought the rifle around to his shoulder, settling it in place easily as he levelled it at the whining monstrosity. But Barty rounded on him, pale with fury, drunk with the adrenaline still burning into his brain. Standing between the monster and Reynard, fearless even of the loaded gun, he vented his sudden, mad rage.

"You put me in the path of this *thing!*"

Reynard lowered his gun a fraction, his brow beetling down. "I heard you the first time, boy, now get out of the way." He moved to step forward, but Barty, livid and wild, stepped to meet him and shoved both hands at Jean's chest with a curse of frustration.

The night had been too much. Without sleep, without a chance to rest, freezing cold and still soaked, exhausted and put through terror after terror, Barty finally snapped, unable to think of anything save for unleashing his frustration on the one he blamed squarely for all of it.

Jean's face froze. It was not simply shock, or surprise, but something more profound; like a wolf that had been bitten by a mouse, who then decided to square up and carry on the fight. Bewilderment, before it turned in an instant to merciless fury, cold and inexorable. Barty felt his strength suddenly quail in that shift, that glowering expression, a storm that swept his own fury away. But then behind Barty came a snarl, and the world tilted.

In the moment that Barty had blocked Jean, the ghoul Clickerclack had reacted. Whatever play at pain it was making was cast aside as it snarled, and that awful maw gaped wide. More than a foot long, the lower jaw unpeeled like a foul flower to allow the seemingly endless coil of its tongue to lance out.

It was thick, circular, more akin to a glistening red rope or intestine than a simple tongue, and the point of it was a horror of its own—tipped with a gleaming spear of what appeared to be bone, sharp and barbed. It shot out for Barty, quick as an arrow, slithering obscenely fast through the air but Jean was faster. Without wasting breath on a warning, he shoved the quaking man aside, letting the shotgun fall to the gravel at his feet, as he snatched the tongue out of the air with both gloved hands, quivering with the strain as the bladed point of bone waved and thrashed like a trapped snake, slashing at the air inches from his face.

Jean bit down on the cigarette as Clickerclack snarled. All

countenance of cowardice and whining was gone; it clutched at a gravestone to hold itself in place, it's single eye blazing as it tried to use its tongue to stab at the one who had shot it. Barty had fallen from Jean's shove, rolling on the ground to stare up at the nightmarish display.

Monster and man strained against each other, a low growl with different echoes coming from each, but wearing the same colour of rage. Jean shifted his grip, but his arms trembled as that bladed tongue tip continued to slash and wave at him, whipping so fast through the air that it whistled with its passage. Twisting his hands suddenly, he got his shoulder in and turned, releasing the tongue with one hand, and reaching into the depths of his long coat with the other. There was a flash of silver steel, slashing upwards, and Clickerclack suddenly reeled backwards. A howl from hell's darkest depths roared out to the heavens as the ghoul tumbled away, thrashing wildly and clutching at its mouth, as the serpentine tongue retracted rapidly—but not all of it. Three feet of tongue, with the bladed end still twitching grotesquely, was flung down on the ground in front of Barty, as Jean turned the dagger he now held in his grip, the blade black where it had sliced through that spasming muscle, and hurled it in the same motion.

The blade spun through the air, sinking into Clickerclack's spindly shoulder. But he wrenched it clear with long, clawed fingers immediately, heedless of the injury, and leapt, reaching outwards. Jean charged to meet him. All in the space of a few racing heartbeats, while Barty was still experiencing the hurt of fresh bruises on top of those that had already formed.

A sword was pulled from the depths of Jean's coat, the longsword flashing at the striking claws. Despite the slenderness of his frame, Clickerclack showed an awful amount of strength, far beyond what muscle and bone should have allowed. With this inhuman power, the creature bore down on Jean and forced him back, claws and blade sending up sparks in the growing dawn before the sword struck true, sinking into the depths of the rags and into the torso where it lodged home. But Clickerclack ignored the sword now sticking out of it—like all the injuries it had taken so far—and pressed Jean backwards, lifting him off the ground, as the Jean released his sword and caught Clickerclack's ghastly hands by the wrists to stop them from plunging into his body. With that unnatural strength however, it was able to pick him up with ease, and slammed him bodily against an ancient standing gravestone, pinning him there.

Moments passed, as the pair strained at each other; the strength of Reynard extraordinary yet not enough to hold the thing back. The ragged edges of claws drew ever closer, before the mouth opened wide in that hideous maw once again, stretching wider and wider, opening enough to bite a man's head clean off his shoulders—which was clearly what Clicker-clack intended to do.

There was a *click*.

Barty had never picked up a gun before, let alone fired one. He had witnessed it, of course, and heard of it, and even watched pheasant hunting before on a rare and wonderful occasion, but never touched one. He had picked up the shotgun without even thinking about it, and the moment he had, it had felt strangely easy. There was a familiarity to it he could not explain, almost like it was meant to sit where it did, that the stock was supposed to meld with his shoulder. It was a comfortable feeling, but there was a dreadful, compressed power to it that made his skin tingle.

When he had seen Reynard brawling with the creature, he

had been spurned into action. The discarded shotgun was right there, and if the man he had sought out for so long was killed, as much as he was angry at him, it would not save him from when the monster came after him next. He had no choice; he had to end it. So he ran up, placed the barrel next to the creature's head and pulled the trigger.

Unfortunately, all that came was the click. While the rounds were loaded, the breech closed and the gun safe to fire, there was a simple measure that Barty did not understand yet; he had failed to pull back either of the hammers that fired the barrels, and thus, when he pulled the trigger, there was nothing but a *click* of metal on metal as that trigger pulled back, and did precisely nothing. Barty froze. Clickerclack turned his dreadful visage towards the cowering young man, and wrenching from Jean's grip it raised one hand to swipe.

But as fast as the monster was, Reynard was faster still.

Jean's hand, now freed, gripped the hilt of the sword sticking out of Clickerclack and rammed it home. The wretch howled and released him, but Jean was not done. Getting a two-handed grip on the hilt, planting his feet and tilting his body, he ripped the sword around and out. Metal sheered through flesh and bone, and whatever unnatural strength holding that creature together proved useless against the edge of the blade as Clickerclack was carved in twain.

The upper half fell, the legs spasming and twitching, foulness steaming from each. The upper body flopped, gasping and grunting, the clawed hands scratching pointlessly at the dirt as the thing refused to die, and tried to crawl away.

Jean stood over it, breathing hard, before he spat his doused cigarette at the stunned Barty, and snapped. "You are supposed to *cock* it first, you dolt."

Barty did not say anything, as Jean turned back to the stricken Clickerclack. This time it was truly beaten, truly defeated—there was nothing left of it that could fight back. It was a gruesome sight, pulling its upper half away in futility, whimpering and blubbering as it went. A trail of black slime poured from it, bubbling and steaming. Jean stood over it, head cocked to one side, watching the destroyed monstrosity that somehow still lived.

"Resilient, aren't you?" Jean's tone was cold. He reached once more into the depths of his coat. "Do you know why, Barty, he is not yet dead? Because he already is." He pulled a flask from his coat, opening it as he trailed after the crawling, whining Clickerclack, even as it slowed, its attempt to flee nothing but instinct and utterly futile. "Dead for centuries, some. Just forgot how to die, and were so afraid of it, they did everything they could to not. All he had to do was make the choice; to have someone else die for him." He sniffed the open flask, still following. "I wonder, did you struggle with it? Did you hesitate at all?" he asked Clickerclack, his nose wrinkling at whatever it was he smelled. Nodding in satisfaction, he upended it and poured the liquid over Clickerclack, who gave a gasping wail and lifted its hands to cover its face, desperate to protect itself, as the raw, sharp scent of alcoholic spirits filled the air with an acid tang. "I would wager you convinced yourself it was a small evil. Just the once, after all. Just one life, and you could keep living. That was what really mattered, did it not? Just a small evil."

Clickerclack had stopped. One eye looked up at Jean, who crouched down now, resting his elbows on his knees as he leaned forward, his coat pooling around him. He reached into his pocket and pulled out a match. Turning it between his fingers, he watched Clickerclack, who turned its one remaining eye to Barty, and in a bubbling, slurred voice, croaked out a single word. *"Please."*

"I would apologise, but we both know you do not deserve

one," Jean said, as Barty stood there, his tongue cloven to the roof of his mouth, shaking in the non-existent breeze, unable to look away. Jean struck the match, which flared bright. "But you do deserve this. All of it and more." He tossed the match.

The flame caught instantly, and surged into terrible life. It lit the courtyard of the chapel in a coruscating blaze as a high-pitched shriek of despair blossomed from the depths of the inferno, a desperate, weakened thrashing in its midst. As the ghoul burned, Jean did not move. He squatted there, splattered with black blood, unblinking and lit in those hellish flames, as the creature burned to the death it had for so long fled from.

The high collar of his coat buried Jean's face somewhat, but what could be seen lit by the flames was detached. He observed the spasming creature that could no longer make a sound, but instead screamed in a tiny, high pitched scream that hurt the ears, even though it was barely audible. When Reynard spoke, his voice was as empty as his expression.

"Three children went missing over the course of a month. All of them within ten miles of this place. They never found them, and they never will. There are only bones left now." He nodded to the decayed chapel. "I found them in there. " He made a sound that might have been of disgust or of despair. "I arrived too late, once I got word. Clickerclack had already taken another. I remember watching her mother screaming out her name into the night until her voice tore, trying to call her home. Jane, her name was." He shook his head. "She was nine." He fell silent.

There was a *click* behind him. Different to before, and one Jean apparently recognised. "You learned how to cock it then." He slowly stood, turning from the burning monstrosity as the fire raged, but the movement amidst the flames had now ceased.

Barty, at this point, looked precisely like what he fully was —a man entirely at the end of his tether. He was teetering where he stood, shivering and holding the shotgun at his shoulder, but pointed low. The end of the barrel weaved about as he stood, torn between taking aim and lowering it entirely.

"You… promised me the truth." His words were slurred with exhaustion, the cost of his night of madness coming home to roost. All the adrenaline, terror, and pain had left him shattered, and now the only thing that kept him to his feet was that one promise, that single offer, that had set him towards this very time and place. "I want the truth."

Jean cocked his head, setting both hands behind his back. With this movement, his coat opened, showing the blades, the holstered pistols and more besides that had been hidden within. But he made no move towards any of them, gauging the wobbling Barty for a long moment before coming to a conclusion.

"When I was early in my career, I learned about ghouls. They are rarer these days. Harder for them to hunt." He nodded idly over his shoulder. "Clickerclack here was one of the older ones—he may have existed for centuries." He glowered over his shoulder a moment, his upper lip twitching and setting his moustache along with it before looked back to Barty. "To become one, they have to eat one of their own blood—a child of their own—to stave off death." He grimaced, shaking his head. "But once they have done so, everything leaves them. No pain, no cold, no heat. Not even sanity remains, but it's not hard to see that they were mad to begin with."

"And Jack? The Ripper?" Barty still wavered, but he returned to that point with a demand. Jean exhaled and went on, looking irritable—but not worried, despite the gun pointed at his feet; In fact, he seemed worryingly used to the situation.

Jean sighed, exasperated despite his level tone. "A newly made ghoul. The only one I have seen in the city before. Early in its transformation, and with different tastes to most." He made a sour face. "Clever, despite all that. Not so smart as to hunt as successfully as some, but clever enough to get away with it." He shrugged, looking skyward. "I tracked it down, ran him to ground in a shack in Whitechapel, and burned him to ashes. Nothing more than that."

"How did you know what he was? What to even look for? Who *are* you?" Barty set the shotgun to his shoulder properly and raised it. The look he got from Jean was now not exasperated, but coldly angry, as he glared down the barrel at Barty.

"I am a Hunter, boy. I knew what he was, because that is what I was trained to know. I knew how to track him, because that is what I learned to do. I had that which the police, and everyone else who tried to catch him, did not—I had the strength of knowing." He brought a hand up, slowly, and held it palm outwards. "Now give me back Delilah, and we can get out of here."

Barty was bewildered, and it showed as he blinked stupidly. Jean's patience snapped. "The *gun*, boy. Look at the engraving, on the stock." His tone was far from detached at this point. Barty did not even think; he dropped his gaze and tilted the gun and indeed, a name was etched in black, burned into the walnut stock, in fine cursive script—*Delilah*. A strange name for a gun. A strange thing to have a gun with a name, for that matter.

The whole thing took but a moment, but it was a moment too slow. Reynard closed the gap so swiftly that for the poor, broken Barty he was simply *there*, once again demonstrating a speed and surety of action that seemed inhuman. One hand grasped the barrel and turned it away, and the other slid in fast and clamped over the hammers that would have struck each chamber. When Barty's fingers instinctively jerked on the triggers, the hammers clamped down on Jean's hand and stuck there, but the gun did not go off. He barely winced, but now he was right in Barty's face, glowering down at him. This close, the scent of smoke was on him, but it was those grey, glowering eyes that froze Barty in place now, a mouse in the gaze of a wolf.

"What are you going to do to me?" It was a stupid question. There was no bravado in it, nothing but quavering fear. Jean raised a brow, then gently tugged the shotgun from Barty's nerveless fingers without resistance and, with a bit of shifting about, lowered each hammer and uncocked the gun, pointing it safely away before he responded.

"I am going to *do* nothing to you. You should know full well already if you went home and tried to tell this story, not a soul alive would believe you. People are good at pretending things that they do not understand do not exist." That baleful glare down the length of his nose did not relent, but a slow, cold smile formed. "However, I will give you an offer, one I know you will not refuse. Come with me."

He might as well have slapped him. Barty was startled, confused, then angry, then looped back to confused again, his exhaustion propelling him through the kaleidoscope of emotions so swiftly it left him dizzier still. "Come with you? Why would I…why would I *ever* do that?"

The cold smile flashed into a grin, but there was no joy in it. It was the bare-fanged smile of a wolf, bloodied and triumphant after the kill. "For the exact same reason you came here at all, Mister Barty," he said, his voice low and dangerous. "You wanted to know. You *still* want to know." He stepped back, and gestured out to the rising sun over the graveyard. "I can show you everything you fear, and everything you *don't*, but should. You looked for me to know what no one else wanted to. You came to this place because you had to, but it was what you wanted, too." He pointed at the young man. "You could have run. But you ran at the devil with a loaded gun. You know as well as I, Mister Barty, you cannot go back again. Not after this night."

Barty was shivering. There was something about Jean Reynard in this moment. Before he had been cold, he had been reserved. But here and now, he was animated and alive. There was a sort of dark, gleeful energy about him, despite the horror of the place. Despite the black blood that stained his coat, the still smouldering corpse of the unliving monstrosity he had killed, and the bones of the murdered children that Barty could feel the weight of, bearing down on him from the chapel. Jean looked horribly, inexplicably excited. Barty could not understand it. Not yet. But he *wanted to*.

And more than that, the madman, the Hunter, was right. He could not go back. He could not go back to his single room in a little house that was not his own. He knew the dark secret, had had it shoved in his face, and smelt its rotting breath. He had watched it die. He had to know more. He had to know everything. Something scratched at the underside of his brain, cold claws tickling at the tingling meat, and beckoned him onwards.

Jean Reynard stood before him, and Barty could see he already knew the answer, could read it in his face. One hand was held outwards. The other held the shotgun, Delilah, over his shoulder. A wild sight of a wild man, wearing the trappings of civilisation, yet in no way a part of it. "Well then, Mister Barty… do we then have an accord?"

A few moments passed before, with a shivering, shaking hand, Barty reached out to take the one offered to him. A grip that could crush rocks squeezed his, as Barty shook his bargain with the devil—though a different kind than he could have expected—before he found his voice.

"We do."

CHAPTER 4

AN URGENT MISSIVE

During his early years, Barty had the notion impressed upon him that rising early with the dawn was a necessary, and even divinely mandated, act. Only thugs, criminals, and others of a misbegotten nature slept through the day and wandered the night. As he opened his eyes, this was the first thought that registered in his groggy mind, as he witnessed a setting sun, slowly drifting down towards the horizon. An idle realisation that lingered before it was drowned in the recollection of the previous evening, a process that was helped along by the screaming of his bruised, battered body, as he dared to move any of his limbs at all.

It felt like he had been hit all over as he slept, by someone who disliked him very much and had been using a very large stick to vent his displeasure. He groaned, squeezing his eyes shut, not yet sure of what hideous misdeed he could have done to deserve such a punishment.

He heard a voice he recognised, distant and yet harsh, and he shuddered involuntarily. With one hand over his face, he opened an eye, peering out into the fading light.

He was sitting in the coach once again, wrapped in a blanket, the chill warded away and his clothes dry. The blanket was rough, crude, and probably used to usually cover a horse instead, but Barty was grateful for it. It felt a bit like armour in this moment, protecting him from the outside world; the world, and the man in it whose life he had been flung into.

Even at this distance he could make out Jean Reynard as he walked along the gravel path outside the manor. There was a set to the shoulders and head as he walked that had nothing of the stoic stillness he had exhibited when they first met; no, as he walked, he seemed to prowl with the step of a man looking for a fight, his head moving sharply as something caught his attention. There was nothing relaxed about it. Even here, in what should have been a place of safety, there was no difference between his movements as they had been in the graveyard.

The graveyard. The chapel. The ghoul, Clickerclack, the child eating monster that had almost made a meal of them both. Barty shuddered again as that nightmare fluttered up again on evil wings, sinking into his memories and lodging there like a cancer.

After the accord had been struck, the crooked man had brought out the coach from where he had been hiding it, further down the road. He had made a fire, and helped Barty to it wordlessly to get him warm and dry, as Reynard had worked tirelessly to raid a small wood bordering the graveyard to gather a supply of dry lumber, cutting down more when the amount proved insufficient. Barty wondered why he had let no one help him, why he had not brought some of his men along, as he watched Reynard remove his coat and carry log after log into the depths of the chapel. It soon dawned on him what was happening but he did not quite believe it until, after hurling the remnants of the monster Clickerclack through the shattered doorway, Reynard had finally set the chapel on fire.

It had taken a good couple of hours. There was plenty of old wood inside but Reynard had wanted to make sure of the building's destruction. And from his little campfire, in that little graveyard buried in the nook of hills, Barty had watched Reynard stand before the chapel as the interior turned into an inferno, black smoke billowing from it as the rotted remains burned away in the light of the rising sun.

He had not remembered falling asleep. He had not remembered getting into the coach either, or the journey back. He remembered the nightmares however; the clawing fingers, the gaping maw, the high pitched shrieking—

"You are awake, lost child?" The musical voice was close, but it took Barty a moment to locate it.

The head of the crooked man peered out from the roof side edge of the coach window, upside down. Silver hair fell around it in a fountain as that handsome, ageless face gave a wide grin, innocent as a child and as wicked as one with a secret. Barty blinked, realising that the crooked man was lying lengthways on the roof of the coach above his head. He glanced to the opposite window, and saw a pair of bare feet kicking up and down that proved his guess.

"We thought you would sleep forever, you slept so soundly. Not the first time we have seen it, not at all, but hardly the most comfortable way of doing so." His musical voice was light, cheerful. "Glad and sad are we, that it is not the case. Sleep is such a blessed thing." The head lifted up again, out of sight, but Barty knew he was still there.

Something about the crooked man made Barty very deeply uncomfortable. Not least the way he spoke and behaved, which had an air of wrongness to it that danced on the very edge of madness. The things he spoke about were strange, and the way he addressed things stranger still. *Like a cat*, he thought, an impression that had been dancing around in his thoughts since he first met the crooked man.

"I still do not know your name," Barty croaked. His mouth was dry, he realised too late, and he coughed. There was a light thump above him, and the feet shifted as the crooked man rolled sideways onto his back, before the legs lifted up and—like a jester or circus performer—he rolled in a somersault off the roof, all sinew and seemingly so light he may as well have had no bones in him at all, moving to lean on the coach window from the opposite end to which he had just been observing Barty. The fluidity of it all left him dizzy.

"Call us what you will, child of the spring, Mister Barty." He grinned as he said it, eyes sparkling akin to cold gemstones under frost-touched light. Laughing at a joke only he knew, and one that was thick with playful cruelty. "If it is one we like at the time, we shall answer to it."

More and more like a cat, Barty thought, considering his own lacklustre efforts in the past to attract the attention of such a beast. He dismissed it as the crooked man opened the door of the coach, with grandiose gesture and a bow as though to greet an honoured guest. The message was clear, and Barty felt compelled to answer it. He pushed himself to his feet carefully to descend out of the carriage, wincing at every movement.

He wobbled, and nearly fell. The crooked man reached out and caught him, faster than a snake and much stronger, and Barty was steadied again. Despite the strangeness of the man, this was the first bit of kindness he could remember truly being shown since he had arrived into this mad series of events, and it had a restorative effect, as well as tugging tears to his eyes.

He took a deep breath, and nodded, feeling genuine gratitude. "Thank you, sir," he said, his voice a bit thick. "If I fell over at this moment, I do not think I could get back up again." A pause then, as something else caught up with him. "That is the second time you have offered me a kindness."

The crooked man's head tilted at this, looking surprised as well. Barty, sensing the confusion, decided to elaborate. "When you warned me not to scream, I remembered. In the graveyard, I did not scream. It kept me alive—and I thank you for it. You saved my life, sir." Saying it made it startlingly clear in his thoughts. The crooked man *had* saved him, with that simple but strange bit of advice.

The reaction of the crooked man was a mixture of surprise and a queer sense of pride at the revelation. It was a peculiar thing, but in that moment Barty felt that he, too, was not used to genuine gratitude. Rather unexpectedly, he bowed low, in a gesture of exquisite courtliness that bore no mockery.

"You are, in fact, most welcome." The crooked man's words were kind, and he straightened to offer Barty his arm. "Come. Let us get you something to restore you. You look a fright."

Barty did not have the strength to refuse him, and gratefully took the offered arm. Despite its slenderness, it easily held Barty aloft as they moved towards the manor. As they drew closer in silence, two things roused in Barty's thoughts.

The first was immediate. The manor was in fact a hive of activity, but rather strangely so. The various shapeless, nameless figures of the previous evening were making their way this way and that, carrying various objects, boxes, and luggage —*out* of the manor. Clearly a trip was being made of some kind, but Barty found it odd that so much was being taken. Even candlesticks were being hauled out of the place, brought along by a rather untoward looking man who appeared nothing at all like a servant. It was almost like the place was being cleaned out by a pack of thieves.

The second was something that nagged at his thoughts, another memory from the night before. Last night, the coach steered by the crooked man had departed the manor and reached the graveyard within an hour at the very most. But the return journey, under daylight, must have taken hours longer. They had departed at very early morning, only a couple of hours past sunrise, and now the sun had set, slipping below the horizon as torches and lanterns started to illuminate the scene.

"How did we—" Barty began. It made no sense. The crooked man stopped beside him, a thin, delicate eyebrow lifting in a question, the twitch of a smile already having the answer hidden within it. "How did we get to the graveyard so quickly, last night? It had to have been miles away. We rode all day to get back?" He was baffled, turning to look at the crooked man fully, who was doing his utmost best not to break into a delighted grin, before he finally surrendered and laughed, giving Barty a hearty, happy slap on the shoulder that rocked him down to his boots.

"Excellent! I do love it when people notice. Men of the stone are normally too polite to mention it when they realise." He held up a long, pale finger. "But grant me a name, Mister Barty, and I *might* tell you the reason why."

Barty was lost a moment; the crooked man's strange way of speaking was something he was still yet struggling to adjust to. The closeness of traditional manner of speech interlaced with terms that, while poetic, seemed to hold a significance that Barty himself did not understand. It was for this reason he answered truthfully, unable to disseminate into something else.

"Until now, I"ve been thinking of you as... the Crooked

Man," he said, unable to stop it tumbling from his lips. This made the subject of the nomenclature twist slightly, his shoulders shifting and his head tilting further, akin more to an owl inspecting something than a normal, human movement. And still he was grinning, but the change in angle made it seem wider, brighter, and altogether less human. Coupled with a long, languid blink, and absolute silence from the crooked man, Barty felt his reassured spirit quail once more into fear, before a soft, pleased chuckle issued from behind that wide grin.

"Crooked Man. Almost insulting, but honestly given and earnestly gathered, a name that has weight. I think I like it…. I think. I will need to ruminate on it a while." The crooked man nodded then, straightening, and held up his long finger once more. "But as is my want, I shall splinter and weave it into something simpler, and sturdier. From here on, you may call me 'Crook'." He nodded, satisfied. A decision had been made. A name was given in kind to one given previously, and the world was mostly in balance. Crook, as he was now on in Barty's thinking, was pleased. This was clearly entirely to his satisfaction.

"But yes. I shall think on it a while before I go revealing my secrets. There needs to be a few after all, does there not?" The grin remained, but the eyes glittered as Crook reached to a pocket and pulled out what appeared to be a brown lump of paper, which he unwrapped with his thumb to reveal some sort of waxy-looking material of a darker brown hue than the paper it was held in. "Toffee, in the meanwhile?"

Barty was hungry. He did not think of a reason to refuse and so, still disorientated, he reached for it to take it with a nod.

Jean's hand came out of the growing gloom and smacked Barty's away from the offering, the menacing features looming up out of firelight with a baleful look on his face. "Don't be doing that, trickster. He does not know the rules yet."

Crook laughed, high and clear, and held up both hands as he released Barty from his support and skipped backwards, dancing with glee and not at all offended, even as the confused Barty rubbed at his bruised wrist. "A game without rules is all the more fun, Hunter! You know how I lack for playmates these days. And look at him! So innocent! So pure! He does not yet know the half of the songs to be sung. I would have my fun with him before he turns boring." He grinned at Barty, that same innocence paired with malice, and winked, the glittering of one eye going dark for a brief instant. "I'll leave him in your care then. And forgive me my little games, Mister Barty. I fear they are in my nature, but for what it is worth, I do quite like what you have given me. Crook by name, Crook by nature! Ha!" He twirled on one foot, grinding gravel under his bare heel, and sauntered off.

Jean watched him go, his jaw working. He cast a glare out of the corner of his eye towards the baffled Barty. Finally, he seemed to shrug. "You will figure it out, or you will not," he said cryptically. "Come."

He turned and strode away towards the manor without another word. Back into that prowling walk, shoulders tight, his coat rippling as he stalked along. Barty opened his mouth to protest, but was shocked to find that he was following Reynard. Trotting after him, acutely aware of the rumbling in his stomach after the debacle of the denied toffee, he was absolutely mystified—not to mention offended—that he had been so firmly rebuked in accepting what was just a gift.

Yes, his thoughts intruded sharply. *But it was a gift from Crook.*

This brought him up short, but he was not sure why. There was something nagging at his thoughts now, not something he could remember, but something he couldn't at the edges of his realisation. Something had changed in him, something he could not figure out, but it had to do with Crook. Something about names, something about giving them, about changing them, about—

A large, dark man nearly walked through him. The bulky figure gave Barty a glare under beetling brows, in response to which he scuttled to one side and fell back into Jean's wake. He was walking into the manor proper now, into the large entrance hall, where a couple of men were bustling about with a large trunk which jangled as it passed. Everyone gave way to Reynard, who paid them no heed; he was looking for someone.

Dimly, Barty came to understand. This was not packing. These men were not simply transporting goods from one location to the next; they were *taking* them. As he watched people pass, carrying paintings and other effects, even carved wooden chairs, he became uncomfortably aware he was witnessing theft on a grand scale. He was about to say something, but he knew Jean was hardly a fool; that much was clear. In his realisation, Barty remembered something.

"You said that this was not your home."

Jean, frowning as he gazed up a staircase, shifted his gaze towards Barty without turning his head, gazing at him sidelong and narrowing his eye.

"When we first met," Barty went on, his voice growing more sure, "you said this was not your home. Merely a place that you were dwelling." He swallowed. "Who does this place belong to?"

Jean grunted and turned his gaze away. "A rich lord, currently dwelling in another of their homes, perhaps enjoying the pleasant weather of southern France," he said dismissively. "I do not remember their name and I do not care to. But they were not here, and I needed a place to stay."

"You were just *squatting*?" Barty could not keep the shock out of his voice. Suddenly, he was not witnessing a crime—he was absolutely a part of it. A trip to the colonies, at least, was on the cards, but more likely he'd be hung if the authorities came calling.

Jean was unphased. "It was a house. I needed it. Right now, however, I need something else." He reached out, grabbing a man by the collar as he passed—with what appeared to be half a suit of archaic armour under one arm—and halting him midstep in so doing. Dragging them around easily to face him, Jean plucked the armour from the man's grasp and let it fall to the floor with a loud clatter. "You. Find me Cosgrove, my butler. Tell him I am waiting for him here." The man opened his mouth, a rough-looking thug that was stitched out of scars, but he closed it again at the look Jean shot him, then nodded and slunk away like a whipped dog. Jean paid him no heed the moment he had let him go.

Barty was struck by the sight. It was a sort of terrible charisma about the man. Barty had witnessed confident people in his life. Many of them wandered headlong and blindly into hubristic arrogance, ignorant and wilful—people who gave orders perpetually expecting them to be obeyed, because of their station, money, or power. Seldom were their orders disobeyed, but when they were, they were left gobsmacked, and oftentimes hysterical in their ludicrous outrage. He had seen it before many times—in the rich, the powerful, in wives and husbands, and in parents and children. It manifested in many ways. There were also others who commanded, not because of what they were, but *who*. It was ingrained into them. Theirs was the ability to command with confidence and assurance, but that was earned. It was respected. And it was rare.

Jean Reynard did not command like either of those; he commanded with something altogether more savage, something more dangerous. He was not a man who was used to being disobeyed. But seeing him manhandle a man who looked like he murdered for enjoyment only, he had not been simply confident… no. He had been daring the man to object.

He *wanted* them to object.

"You are wondering why the theft," Jean said sourly, shaking his head. Barty said nothing, but pulled his rough blanket closer about himself, hiding behind its meagre protection. "Securing your retrieval was not cheap, Mister Barty." Jean went on coldly. "I had to pay for that service somehow. This will do." He looked around. "Not how I would prefer to normally do things. But the bloated fool who owns this place will not miss it. He doesn't need it. These men do—they have families to feed. Think of it like that. A redistribution if you will."

"You were so eager to find me? That you… that you were willing to pay like this?" Barty's ongoing bewilderment was not lessened by this knowledge. Jean snorted, straightening back up, stilling himself with an effort, before he answered in a cold, sharp tone, speaking very carefully and concisely.

"You were absolutely determined to track me down, Mister Barty. Determined, when I had made it very clear that I did not *want* to be tracked down." His brows beetled down, as he shifted one foot and kicked the dropped piece of armour to the side with a loud clang as he carried on. "When someone is that determined to find me, I normally put aside time to find them first. I could not afford to do that, with Clickerclack soon to be hungering for another child. So I sent someone else instead, and that someone required payment."

He gestured idly. "This was at hand. Whoever you were, at the time you were not so important as to spend my own coin on the matter. And Cutter took a risk in getting his hands on you."

Barty swallowed, looking around. "I am surprised you…" he trailed off, until once again Jean was looking at him out of the corner of one eye, his brow furrowing down further. Taking a breath, Barty continued. "I am surprised you went to such effort, instead of simply… doing what you did to the barkeep who gave me your name."

Jean scowled in response. "And what do you think I did to him, then? Based on our conversations so far." He presented an odd picture for the moment. He looked like a man who wanted to be pacing on the spot, but with the full realisation it was a waste of effort to do so. Nevertheless, that buttoned down fury kept Barty on edge; Reynard radiated a sort of instinctual anxiety in everyone around him. Men stayed out of his way, and away from his gaze as they moved through the manor.

He must be terribly lonely, Barty thought suddenly. It leapt up, unbidden. But the hunter was waiting for an answer to his question.

"I can only hope you did not kill him," he answered honestly. The barkeep, Caldwell, had been honest, a little slow, and a kinder man than many in the more desperate streets of London's fouler districts. Barty had managed to coax the name 'Reynard' from him after asking enough clever questions. He had been quite proud of it, but now, in the face of his unknown fate, he felt sick.

"Earlier I advised you not to find out," Reynard said coldly. "That remains true even now." He exhaled, grimacing at something, grey eyes distant as his jaw twitched. Then, it clamped down harder and he refused to speak, going darkly quiet. Something, however, was weighing on him heavily, so much so that even those broad shoulders were dragged down by it. Barty wanted to ask but he could not find the words—he did not know where to start with this man. He was a mystery, and a desperately dangerous one at that.

Nevertheless, just as he opened his mouth to try, Cosgrove appeared at Barty's elbow. Whereas Jean exuded a sort of repressed violence in his being, the butler Cosgrove was the embodiment of the cold finality of a tombstone. Barty could have sworn the room temperature dropped by several degrees at his sudden appearance, a feeling only magnified when he cast a baleful look upon the still blanket-wrapped Barty. As the place was torn apart by the looters, he looked at Barty as though it were somehow his fault. A look from his master might kill, but Cosgrove's would erase one's entire bloodline from existence entirely.

"You sent for me, sir," came his gravestone intonation. In that greeting, Barty imagined the unspoken question; *shall I have him buried somewhere shallow, sir? Preferably immediately?*

Reynard pointed one gloved finger at Barty. "Find him some food and clothes. Something that fits him which looks vaguely respectable," said the man who's coat still bore black bloodstains from the monster he had killed. "And let us be out of this place in an hour. We have outstayed our welcome."

Cosgrove's expression did not change, but there was frost growing upon it. He did not look at Barty, but he did not have to to make it plain that this was not something he wanted to do. He brought one hand to his mouth and gave a sharp cough into it, then held out a piece of paper in his other hand, gaze lowered. "Before I do so, sir, I have received this telegram on your behalf. From Master Adam. From *London*, sir."

Adam, Barty thought. A familiar sort of name, in how it was addressed, but not one he had heard before now. The way he had said the name of the nearby city had been significant in of itself—not least of all because of the reaction it had in Jean, who went still a moment, then strode over and snatched the telegram from Cosgrove's offered hand. Jean opened it, muttering. "London? What are they doing there? It is not like they can—" he cut himself off suddenly, his fingers tightening on the piece of paper so abruptly it tore in his grip. He went very still.

Barty wanted to ask something, but Jean's expression forbade it utterly. He had gone rigid, shock giving way to something colder, something harder. Somewhere behind that grey gaze, a door had shut, and it was bound in iron and chain. Barty suspected it would not open again.

"Cosgrove, see to what I said." Jean's voice was flat, and cold. "Get the carriage loaded. We are going to London."

Cosgrove bowed with that executioner's precision and turned away with a single sharp, slicing beckon to Barty. While he did not have the most eager desire to follow the butler, there was no arguing the matter at this point. Jean had turned and begun to stride away with the swift aggression of a man who wanted to put a fist through the whole world.

The butler was silent. He did not bother to look at Barty, who was nevertheless surprised at how efficiently and obediently he obliged Jean's request. They strode with purpose down a long hall and into the stone confines of a grand kitchen. Well stocked and well cared for, with signs of meticulous maintenance and preparation of solid food. Evidence of the latter was the smell, a rich heated scent that set Barty's mouth to watering. A weathered hand shifted a chair at the table and Barty was sat down before being supplied with fresh bread, not long from the oven, with a generous helping of butter and sharp, tangy jam. While he was satisfying the ravenous hunger he'd been ignoring for far too long, Cosgrove left the comfortable kitchen to raid whatever wardrobes he could find and, by eye, measured his charge up. Various garments were brought along and, wordlessly, Barty was wrangled into each of them. Soon, Barty found himself wearing a long coat, similar to Jean's own but not as worn or, he had to note, concealing so many weapons. New pants, a plain but sturdy doublet and shirt, and a brand new cravat. But best of all were the boots. Cosgrove was, despite the terror he presented in his coming, clearly a genius at gauging a foot, and the boots that Barty now wore were better than any he had ever owned in his life. They were already broken in, and slipped onto his feet with ease. The soles—real leather!—shifted easily and comfortably under his feet, which was a strange sensation in so many ways—before this, the cheap boots that Barty had previously were such that one could clearly and most uncomfortably feel the texture, coldness, and wetness of whatever ground he had walked upon.

But these? These made him unsteady with how removed they made him feel from the ground. Unsteady, but yet so very comfortable. His stomach full, his clothes warm, his old garments gone, Barty steadied himself on his feet under Cosgrove's baleful eye, and checked his reflection in a mirror. Properly dressed, he felt confident. Let the old butler glower at him. Barty was starting to get used to his presence already—the boldness of the one who had ignored all danger in tracking Jean down was starting to come back.

"Do not take advantage of Master Reynard." They were the first words that Cosgrove had said, the very first he had given to Barty directly, and it took Barty completely and utterly by surprise. He turned on the man, wobbling on his feet a bit thanks to the unfamiliar boots.

"I beg your pardon?"

Cosgrove was looking at him flatly, steadily, and his expression was no longer merely cold. It was the sort of cold that burned, that withered a man down to the bone. The newfound confidence wilted in an instant. Cosgrove nevertheless repeated himself. "Do not take advantage of Master Reynard, young man. I assure you that you will soon regret it."

Barty was shaken. Not least because of the incongruity of the statement—Jean had kidnapped *him* after all, not the other way round, and it was Jean that had brought him to the hunting grounds of Clickerclack. What was this man getting at? He found his cloven tongue where it was hiding, and responded, "I would have that explained, sir. How can I possibly take advantage of him?"

Cosgrove bristled. "He is not your path to recognition, young man. He is not here for you to make a story of his life, and to win fame for yourself. You *do not*, under *any* circumstances, get to take his story and make a penny from it, are we clear? Not one. The day you do is the day your race is run, do you understand my meaning?" This was different. This was not like before. Before, Cosgrove was simply cold. Aloof. He still was now, every syllable cracking with the ice covering it, but his eyes were filled with a sort of pre-emptive rage. A loyal hound with its fangs bared, standing before a stranger to protect their master from threats real or imagined.

Barty was still unsure. After a moment, he steadied himself, frowning. "That was not why I am still here, sir. It..." he trailed off, then shook his head. "Yes, sir," he agreed. There was a time and a place for such things. But Cosgrove was not going to tolerate them. Not at this moment.

The butler glowered for a few seconds longer, then gave the smallest, barest nod of acceptance, reluctance overshadowing all.

Of course, Barty thought. *He thinks I just want to make a story out of this. Find my fortune. But no one would ever believe it. I would be laughed out of The Times and down the street.*

However, those thoughts continued, as Cosgrove turned away and led him out of the kitchen, *why the fierceness? He looked ready to strike me down on the spot for him. To* protect *him. Why? What inspires such a feeling?*

Barty was not the slightest bit sure, but he was becoming increasingly aware that things were far more complicated than they appeared. Reynard was a harsh, callous man with little respect on the surface for anyone or anything. He lived in houses that were not his and took things that did not belong to him to give to others. Most of all, he very clearly did not care much whether Barty himself lived or died—at least, he had not last night. It was not much of a stretch of imagination to think he felt similarly about anyone he met. And yet, a man who considered lives expendable and seemed to dare the world around him to start a fight, somehow inspired loyalty strong enough that a man who, for all intents and observations, had a heart entirely of stone, had just made it very clear to Barty, that if he somehow hurt *Reynard* that they, Cosgrove, would bury him for it. This did not add up to Barty. It did not even come close.

But the burrowing worm of curiosity wanted to find out.

They returned to the hall, which was somewhat more empty now. Cosgrove paused, and a hand reached out to pluck a sturdy, narrow brimmed bowler hat from a nearby coat rack. Dusting it off carefully, he turned to Barty and shoved it at him wordlessly. Used to this sort of thing by now, Barty perched it atop his messy hair, straightened it, and spread out his hands.

"How do I look?" He did not expect an answer, but he could not help but feel quite proud of himself. He had never been dressed in such good clothing in his life.

"Acceptably ridiculous," Jean said as he strode into the room without slowing. He did not even look at Barty, who was a bit crushed. Jean uplifted his chin to his butler, who nodded in return.

"I did the best I could with what I had available, sir. But one can only do so much with wet clay when a kiln is lacking." His tone was not so much dry as it was caustic. It seared away any pretense towards pride that Barty might have felt, and cut the legs out from under him.

Jean did not even notice the destruction his charge was undergoing. Instead, he was speaking to Cosgrove in the firm tone of one expecting an argument. "I will need you to go to the Loch house while I am in London. Take one of the coaches there along with anything I am not taking with me."

The butler startled, then his voice returned in a clipped tone. "Sir, I—" he began, glancing to Barty, but Jean cut him off.

"I need someone there to have their hands on the armoury, Cosgrove, and the files, in case I need them. With Adam already in London, and everyone else gone, you are the only one I can trust to do it." The butler went paler still, but lifted that axe of a nose in a stiffening of his upper lip. "Very well, Master Reynard," he said in an iron tone. "And your… ward here?" His murderous gaze flickered to Barty. *Remember what I told you. Remember what I promised.* Barty did not need to hear him say it.

"He will be coming to London. He will be working the case alongside me," Jean said dismissively.

"I am?" Barty could not keep the startled response from his lips.

"You are," Jean snapped back without turning around. "I want you somewhere I can keep an eye on you."

"I am quite sure if he accompanied me I would be able to

sufficiently take care of him, Master Reynard," Cosgrove said carefully. Barty fretted. There were shallow graves in that near future Cosgrove offered.

"No, I do not think so," Jean replied, with a measure of regret… perhaps? Barty had the uncomfortable feeling that Jean had understood the implication as well. He did not like it. "He might prove useful at this point. And besides, it is not like there's anyone left to assist me, is there? I made sure of that." He said it in a tone of dry amusement, but there was no smile on his face. Cosgrove's expression, for the first time since Barty had seen him, wavered into something else; the merest flicker of hidden emotional turmoil, before it once again hardened into a mask of implacability.

He inclined his head sharply in that headsman's blow of a nod. "Very good, sir. I shall see to it immediately." He marched away, spinning on one foot with head held high. He was angry. Not even that frosty exterior could hide it.

And then Jean and Barty were alone together once again. The hunter was inspecting Barty with a more critical eye now, looking him up and down. In the end, he simply nodded, and walked back towards the front doors. He did not say anything, and he once again did not need to. Barty was not far behind him.

CHAPTER 5

A DAMNABLE INCONVENIENCE

The carriage ride back to London was a quiet affair as they travelled along the night time roads. Crook was not singing this time, and the sky above was completely dark, the moon buried in thick clouds. The carriage was dark within but well-lit outside, as the muted landscape of England rolled past, murky and somewhat miserable at this hour.

Cutter had been well paid in whiskey by the time Jean found him as they left the manor. They had shaken hands on the deal they had made and put paid to their contract for the time being; Cutter was never there, and Jean likewise. The manor keeper, whomever it was that had been watching over the place before it had been invaded by the gang and the hunter, was not mentioned. Barty wondered if they were even still alive. How long had they been using the place? He had no idea, but Cutter had been utterly thorough. Anything that looked like it was worth something had been taken. All of it would fetch a penny or two in the black markets of London.

Before long, they would all pop up somewhere in another rich house, until the cycle began all over again.

Barty wasn't sure how he felt about it. He was nervous about his stolen clothes too, wondering if someone was sure to recognise them. As the journey rolled onwards, he started to imagine scenarios in his head of what would happen if—or when—someone realised he had been part of the crime in that manor, wearing evidence of it on his person. He felt like someone would, and not long after that he would be hanged. What would he do, if he ever heard one of the police shout at him to stop? Wait for them to arrest him? Run? Confess everything?

His overactive imagination was working the same terrible curse upon him in a different framing on the way back to London as it had been upon leaving it. This time however, his position was altogether more comfortable—and there was a subject to distract him, which finally dragged him from such useless ruminations to consider *it* instead. Or more accurately, *him*.

Jean sat in the depths of the carriage, keeping into the shadows of its heart rather than sitting close to windows. He was a still blot of darkness, with but the glitter of his eye visible on occasion. He stared out one window, from what Barty could make out, but in this journey he was reminded of their first meeting. Back then, Jean had felt infinitely dangerous, harder, colder. He felt like that now. Waiting, silent, calculating. Now that he knew what he *was*, the understanding came easier.

But what else did he *know* about the man? Not much. Hardly anything, to think about it, save for what he had gleaned by listening. The conversation with Cosgrove that he had overheard had revealed much. He had people who listened to him, who obeyed him, and allies too—but for some reason, precious few of them. No mention of family, or friends. Not even colleagues. Did they simply not exist? Were they a thing that simply did not warrant mentioning? What was the story there?

Despite the warning from Cosgrove, and his adherence to it in that he would not write anything down, would not try to peddle the story at all, he could not turn off the fascination that had prescribed him to the career he had found himself in. Barty wanted to know things. The same mind that had taken the phonograph—which now sat strapped to the roof of this very carriage—and figured out how to make it work more efficiently, also looked at people and tried to figure out what made *them* work, to better understand them. And in his short years, nothing had been more interesting to him as this mysterious, terrible man.

It was Jean that shattered the stillness, with customary bluntness that somehow still managed to sound refined. "When one is attempting to ascertain the character of another, Mister Barty, they generally do so by asking questions. Not making a foolish face as they imagine such statements in their head."

Barty winced, even as he wondered how the man had been able to make out anything in the non-existent light in the carriage. Had he been that obvious? But he took courage from it nevertheless—after all, what was there to lose at this point?

"It yet occurs to me, that I know nothing about you, sir," Barty replied finally, summoning up what dregs of earnestness remained in him. "Still, after you promised me the truth, and after showing me that, that *thing*..." He shook his head, shaking away the shuddering. Jean said nothing, but Barty could see him staring out into the void of darkness beyond the carriage. With no demand to stop, he mustered his courage and pressed on. "I have so many questions, so many I feel full to bursting. Where did you come from? How did you learn to become this… What did you call it, a hunter?" He shrugged helplessly, but was feeling animated once more. "The way you said it, sounded like it held a special sort of significance. But more than that, why? Why do all this, how did it start? All I know about you is you hunt beasts—"

"Monsters." Jean cut him off suddenly, coldly. Barty fell silent, as that glittering grey gaze shifted in the shadows to stare at him once more. He was silent for a time, letting the word hang as the carriage rattled along, before he continued in that same cold, clinical tone. "Monsters have the ability to reason. To think. To plot, plan, and deceive." He fell quiet again, glowering at Barty before looking back out the window again. "As for the rest of your questions, I do not feel inclined to answer them. I find the idea of hearing my own voice talking about myself would put me into an even earlier grave than the one destined for me. The whole procession is beyond my ability to stomach."

"But I thought, after everything—" Barty stammered, but Jean once more leapt down his throat to catch his tongue, sharp and harsh.

"You thought what? Because you ran back into the fight, thought you had saved my life, that somehow I would open up to you?" He snorted sourly before muttering, "You would have had more luck with that if you had actually managed to *fire* the bloody thing."

"Then why bring me with you?" Barty replied, a trace of irritation creeping in with the confusion, despite his best efforts to conceal it.

"Because a man is dead in London," Jean replied flatly, "in circumstances that call for my attention. He is… was… a man of some importance, and one that I knew for some years."

"Then you would call him a friend, I presume," Barty managed.

Jean shook his head, once, amidst the shadows. "An acquaintance. I do not have friends, Mister Barty. Friends are a liability I can no longer afford, and have not the patience to entertain."

Barty fidgeted. "Then what exactly am I?" He dreaded the answer, but the compulsion to ask was too strong. If he had no means to know more about this man, then he could at least know where he stood.

"You *were* a damnable inconvenience," Jean shot back. "Someone who was dogged enough to trace my steps through every obstacle set before you, to find me. Someone I could not ignore while dealing with a child-murdering monster. You *were* an absolute irritation. Then a liability." He scowled. "I am not sure what I expected when you were dragged into my presence. I expected someone so determined to be more impressive, not a wrung-out rag, a gutter rat scurrying along in the shadows masquerading as a hound." He could not conceal even a shred of the contempt in his tone. Barty was wounded to the quick. Jean exhaled then, expelling some of his remembered exasperation.

"But… as hard won as it might be, I *do* extend credit where credit is due. You did manage to find my name. You would have found your way to me eventually. No one unexpected has done that in a very long time." He shifted his gaze back to the huddled, miserably chastened Barty. "And you *did* pick up the gun to assist in the graveyard. Despite that, it was not your most impressive feat." A flicker of a chuckle, cold and somehow despairing. "You managed to survive as well, Mister Barty. You managed to live. That is something that only luck can explain, and lucky people are useful. I have a use for you, Mister Barty, and I intend to see that through."

Barty did not feel comfortable at this. "You make it sound like I am some sort of an asset, something to be used," he accused.

To his ever increasing discomfort, Jean nodded. "And you would be entirely correct," he said, without a trace of emotion in one direction or another. "You are useful to me in that you can find answers to questions people do not want to answer, and you are useful in that you are lucky enough to survive. This is something in of itself, but you have already played your hand in this matter, and revealed what it is *you* want. Fortunately, it is something only I can give." He sounded smug about it.

Barty was irritable, and that boundless irritation beat back his dread. "And what is that then?"

"Answers, Mister Barty. Answers to the questions that drive you—though I admit, I do not yet know why they drive you so thoroughly. I can guess, but I do not know." He settled deeper into his seating. "You will, inevitably, get the answers you seek, if you survive our endeavors. Adam will probably tell you. Questions are something that they are absolutely fascinated with, much like you. Almost as much as talking about them. You can ask them about it, if you can muster up the courage."

Barty was silent, awkward and withdrawn. The carriage rattled and wobbled, and neither one seemed inclined to break the silence. Jean continued to stare out into the darkness beyond the window, as though he might eventually pierce it and find the answers he yet sought.

Surprisingly, it was Jean who spoke first. His voice was far away, still staring out the window, looking at something else as he spoke. "We are not friends, Mister Barty, nor shall we ever be. We are an alliance of convenience, a transaction where one of us gets what they want out of the other. But we will never be friends. As I said, friends are a liability. Something that weighs you down until it drags you by the throat into the muck and drowns you." His distant tone was empty. He didn't continue, though some part of him seemed to want to say more. The carriage continued onwards; there was no sound from Crook whatsoever. The pair of them were all alone in a darkened world.

Barty's voice was small when he finally spoke. Forcing himself to speak to this man who frightened him, whom he did not like very much, yet did not know how to turn away from. "If I survive, you said." He stared at the floor, not at the hunter. "Do people tend to die in your company, sir?"

There was no answer. After a long moment, Barty dared to lift his gaze to see Jean still staring out the window. The silence hung on, choking and thick, crawling out of the corners and darkness to drown out the carriage rolling along, leaving only the pounding of his heartbeat, before it ruptured and broke as Jean finally replied.

"I did say that I have no friends, Mister Barty. It should not be difficult to understand why."

Barty said nothing. Letting the full realisation of what had been said, coupled with his earlier observation back at the manor, sink in. This man *was* lonely. Devastatingly so, perhaps. And he wanted it no other way. How long before he tired of Barty's company altogether? How long before that convenience ended? Should he run now?

Could he run at all?

There were no answers, as they continued swiftly towards the great city, borne by the brisk, steady trot of the horses. Somewhere above, Crook began to sing, soft and low without words, and that haunting tune followed them as they sped on into the night.

Barty woke suddenly as the wheels clattered over cobblestone. He did not remember falling asleep, but as he startled upwards he could hear sound, thick and fierce and coming from all directions. And with it came the smell.

London was, at the best of times, a place with a unique aroma to it—horse manure, wood and coal smoke. Sewer emanations and street cooking. And people, thousands of people, who never really slept. It was daylight again, though the sun was not far risen, and steam rose from grates below the cobblestone streets as the masses of souls trudged on already weary feet this way and that.

Jean was still staring out the window, his jaw set in a grim line. He did not look tired, but it was hard to read him at the best of times, and just waking-up-Barty lacked the clarity of discernment. *Has he even slept?* Barty could not tell. But something told him he had not.

"Just in time," Jean said, without looking at him. "We are almost there."

"There?" Barty replied groggily, stretching. But Jean did not answer him, and left Barty to stretch his way through his stiffened discomforts. This was the second night he had slept upright in a carriage, and he had not enjoyed either experience. Aside from a short stopover on the way back to London, they had not paused in the journey; Crook had nevertheless saved the horses, unlike the furious journey to the manor that Barty had undertaken in his first meeting with Reynard. He showed more care to the animals that bore them, it seemed, than he showed his passengers; during the stop at a roadside inn, he had not gone inside. Instead, he had kept well away from other travellers and spoke soft words of comfort to each horse in turn. Barty had watched in fascination before his body demanded he head inside himself and see to its needs. Not long after they were back upon the road, his stomach filled by a hot pie and some ale, after which he had fallen asleep, now waking to this familiar, yet tumultuous, cacophony.

He knew where they were immediately. Tottenham Court Road, heading southwards. A familiar sight to him, and this was all well and good. But before long, the carriage began to turn down narrow, quieter streets, that seldom saw the tread of feet even in the depths of London. A turn left and right, and then more and more of the same, and before long Barty was quite turned around. This was unexpected—especially in a place that he liked to think of as his home. But as he looked out into worn, nameless streets with older houses, he was not entirely sure where he was. All he could say for certain was that he was still in the city itself.

The building they stopped at was not exactly unique from its exterior. High and tall, it was built of grey stone. Like many of the other buildings in the place, it had a claustro-phobic air to it—built high, and tightly, rather than outwards. The front door was a heavy thing, black and forbidding, with an ornate door knocker upon it of weathered brass. The windows also were barred and reinforced. It had the odd look of a fortress, or a vault of some kind, a feeling that Barty could not quite shake. The carriage halted. Jean got out without a word. Not knowing what else to do, Barty followed him.

"This is the Lodge." Jean waved a hand idly as he said it, gesturing to the building. "Now help—" he paused, looking to Crook for a moment, who was already removing luggage from the rack and rear compartment of the carriage. The carriage drive saw the look and grinned, and Jean remembered. "Crook, as you call him, get things inside."

Unable to argue, all Barty managed was to mostly stand there as Crook threw things at him. The first thing, a decent sized case, was in his arms before he could say a word. He wobbled in place as Crook effortlessly tossed suitcases and boxes into his outstretched arms, piling things up gradually and balancing them easily, even as poor Barty soon found himself teetering. Eventually, he had it under control, while Jean watched impassively from the side.

Finally, it was done. Barty tottered about helplessly under a mass of luggage that he could barely carry, the rest of it upon the ground around him, placed there when Crook could not simply throw it at him.

The catlike Crook slunk up into the carriage seat, and gave a mocking salute. "I'll have the carriage put away, and these four and I will be singing songs and biting fingers that don't bear apples until you need us again. Give Adam my love, and be sure to look them *dead* in the eye when you see them, won't you?" He grinned that toothy grin, eyes a-glitter with a joke only he knew, and trilled a note. The carriage took off, smooth and swift, soon rounding a corner out of sight as Barty wobbled, unable to put anything down.

Jean was already opening the door. There was the clank of a key that sounded like the settling anchor of a ship as the lock turned, heavy and buried. More clanks followed, as bolts and chains shifted, and the door opened inwards. Barty, balancing the mass that was threatening to cause his spine to fuse together into a solid lump of compressed bone, did not so much as walk towards the entrance as stumble towards it by sheer chance.

A shadow loomed in the doorway, then out of it, then further upwards still as it blotted out the building and, seemingly, the street and sun. It bent down, and down, and down, speaking in a voice that was the most exquisitely refined, beautiful baritone Barty had ever heard, deep and powerful, and as unexpected in its rumble as it was in its kindness.

"You poor fellow. Please, allow me to assist."

Hands scooped up the collection of bags and cases. Just two of them, but each of them so large that they made what Barty had been struggling with seem but the toys of children. Barty found himself looking up, craning his neck, to spy an enormous figure, with long dark hair, taller than the tallest man he had ever seen.

And they were dead. Barty could very clearly see that this thing, this being, was dead. Their skin was pale in places, the colour of a bruise or the bloodless yellow of a settled corpse in others, his eyes the sunken, bloodied eyes of a dead man, and the lips partly pulled back from the teeth already, bearing marks of withering. The features were masculine, but misshapen in their appearance, and there were many scars of stitch marks, however fine, across the entire visage, of some-thing *put together*, and made.

Despite that terrifying appearance, they gave what could only be called a polite smile, and in that same beautiful voice, more courtly than any king, they inclined their head to Barty respectfully. "A most sincere pleasure, sir. How do you do on this fine London day?"

His response, unfortunately, would have to wait. For at that precise moment, Barty chose this as the foremost time to faint, the world turning dark as whatever candle of conscious-ness that kept him afloat was snuffed out.

CHAPTER 6

THE LODGE OF THE HUNTERS

Barty felt everything swim into focus gradually. It took a moment. He had to admit he was getting altogether tired of coming into events in this way, but his constitution was fragile after so many shocks.

His surroundings were unfamiliar, but he was laying upon a dark red fainting couch, covered in rich velvet and rather comfortable. Around him was a well furnished room with a high ceiling, with polished wood panelling and smooth white walls, paintings set here and there in a tasteful fashion. The windows were high and open, letting in what little furtive London light there was to be found. Nevertheless it was bright enough to wince as the light and, what at first was a hazy buzzing, turned into sound that grew in volume.

"—assume that that police have already made a dog's breakfast of the situation." Jean sounded sourer than even his acidic tone normally managed. A deep, measured chuckle answered him.

Barty swung his gaze about from his supine position. Jean Reynard was sat at one end of a table, sitting at ease upon a cushioned chair, one leg crossed over the other as he propped a newspaper before himself. A cup of tea steamed before him in the faint rays of daylight. His coat was put to one side, which surprisingly showed him to still be armed; a holstered revolver and a sheathed knife were present at his belt. Even here he very clearly did not believe in forgoing precaution.

But it was the other figure that caught Barty's attention once again. He felt dizzy once more, as he had the first time, his mind simply failing to account for how *big* the figure was; too large to be believed at all. They were sat cross-legged upon the ground at the opposite end of the table, and yet comfortably rested their elbows upon the surface of it. There was no chair because there simply was no possibility of there being one that they would not destroy.

The coat they wore was a patchwork, and thankfully not leather because there was simply no cow large enough in the world. Perhaps one of the elephants that Barty had once witnessed in an enclosure… but in his addled state he doubted even that. The same could be said of their boots, which were ruptured at every possible point and repatched, repaired, and rebuilt as to be barely described as such any longer. Their long dark hair was tied back, and this, unlike the rest of them, was a lustrous dark colour, healthy and vibrant.

They would have been absolutely terrifying if not for the fact that they were handling what, in their hands, was a very small teacup, comically appearing no larger than a thimble in their enormous pinched finger grip, as they took a very careful sip. Delicate and precise, and despite it all, looking entirely proper about it. They glanced over to Barty, and that hideous visage broke into a smile then. They raised a hand the size of Barty's entire torso and waved in a friendly fashion.

"I see our other companion is awake again! Forgive me, friend. I hope the couch was not too uncomfortable. I admit I was rather excited to use it for its namesake, though I heartily admit to being amused at the fact that it proved useful for either gender." They winked one bloodshot eye, and took another sip as Barty struggled to sit upright. Things were very confusing, not least because the giant spoke with perfect eloquence that might make any lord or lady envious. Their voice was completely at odds with their appearance—rich and melodious, each word spoken with care and precision as though the sound they made was to be savoured. Privately, it was impossible to deny that they *were*. Barty had never heard such a voice before, warm, rich, and utterly comforting as a warm bath and hot wine.

He had to respond, though his heart was racing with panic. "Ah, do forgive me." He could not keep the shaking out of his voice. "We… we were not p-properly introduced," he stammered along, trembling. The massive figure appeared to take this in stride, but Barty saw their gaze lower, a flicker of sadness in those ruined features.

"You are Mister Barty, I am told." They nodded, before going on as that name once again caused other thoughts to jostle in Barty's overburdened skull. "You can, if it pleases you, simply call me Adam. Welcome to our little troupe, Mister Barty! We have been far too long without fresh and lively company." They gestured with precise movement to another chair, set in the middle of the table between the pair. There was another steaming teacup, and a plate set with a neatly quartered pair of sandwiches. "Here. Please, refresh yourself. I trust your journey here was not too taxing?" That rich voice turned to concern, genuine and gentle. Barty, still shy, approached the table carefully, shaking his head, but it was Jean who was speaking for him at this point, still irritable.

"He slept most of the way. You would think he would have had enough of it to not keel over the moment he got here."

His tone was moody. A single finger pointed then at Adam, accusingly, from the hand that held the newspaper. "Upon that note I must raise another, how did you even come to *be* here, Adam? I do not need to point out how risky this is for you, surely."

Adam shrugged, a movement reminiscent of a mountain being born of the sea but sped up to an impossible rate, and sipped at his teacup before answering. "To answer the complications of your question, I have had more experience than you can imagine at going where I need to go, Reynard. You know better than anyone that people are prepared to disbelieve their own eyes, and I have learned to give people little opportunity to see me with them in any case." One huge hand loomed over towards Barty as he finally sat himself down at the offered chair amidst the conversation, who could not help but flinch as they drew closer. This caused a slight pause, before they delicately picked up a sandwich quarter between thumb and forefinger.

It is not simply that they are frightening, Barty realised. They *were* frightening in all things but their manner. Normally, he could get used to that—but Barty had grown up in the orphanage. St. Mary's, the humble name for the hunting ground that he had survived, had been a place where the strong fed off the weak, and the strong were larger, more brutal, and merciless. Barty had never been one of those. He had always been smaller, always been the one to run, to hide. He had gotten good at it, at being where others would not find him, but Barty remembered days and nights spent trying to avoid the eyes of such dread terrors, and now those memories, blended with the shocks of the last few days, were merging together. He tried to shake them off, and tried not to stare at the figure to his right.

When he finally did look, Adam had their gaze lowered.

There was a quiet regret in that posture as they went on, speaking to Jean while keeping their gaze upon the tabletop. "The telegram regarding the death of Doctor Heathwood came while there was no one else about. The circumstances were mysterious, and I felt it necessary to make myself available at the first opportunity. I knew you were thoroughly engaged already, and endeavoured to help how I could, since everything that—"

Silence. Adam stopped talking, as though embarrassed, covering the awkward moment as they rubbed at their chin with one careful hand, still looking downward. Barty, his urge to fidget overwhelming him, rubbed at the back of his head—and paused at a realisation then.

Barty had unfortunately fainted once or twice before, and recently. Each time had been a painful debacle—but not this time. He could not feel any aching, ringing pain in his head from where he would have struck the ground. He felt, nominally at least, perfectly fine. A deduction formed swiftly, and he turned his gaze back to Adam, but after that lapse of their tongue they had fallen silent once more.

Jean snorted, folding the paper and tossing it to the tabletop where it partly scattered the sandwich plate. "I do not need help, Adam. Not from you or anyone else. I especially do not need presumptions of it." His tone was cold as he glared at his teacup. The tension was sudden and palpable in the room.

But it was Barty who broke it, coming to a decision. Ignoring his tea and sandwiches despite his grumbling stomach, he spoke up. "I presume that this will be where we will be staying for the time being?" Jean grunted, nodding without looking up from his teacup, sitting hunch-shouldered and leaning forward. Barty stood at that affirmation, and turned to Adam. "If you do not mind, Adam, could you show me to where I will be staying? If you have a moment."

Adam blinked at that, and that massive head lifted up, craggy brows furrowed a moment before the expression eased. A flicker of a hopeful smile, as earnest as that of a child, formed, and the giant picked themselves up off the ground, pushing up and up to tower in the room, even with the high, vaulted ceiling. "Of course, Mister Barty." That smooth baritone pleased the ear once more, as Jean grunted again, staring at the newspaper with his brow furrowed.

"Do not be too long. I want to be heading out to the Doctor's residence shortly."

Barty did not argue. He simply followed the enormous Adam, who had to bend down to push through the doorway, even though the top of it was well above Barty's head. They exited out into a richly panelled and lit corridor, with stairs leading up and down—the door leading out of the building to Barty's right, the depths of its mysterious interior to his left. Adam was climbing up the stairs, taking them very carefully and precisely one at a time, though with their enormous gait the straight stair would have been cleared in but two or three steps.

"Thank you, for that." The rumble of that musical voice spoke quietly, but it yet bounced off every surface. "I fear I overstepped for a moment there."

"Actually, I wished to apologise," Barty replied awkwardly. This caused the giant to pause, the step creaking beneath them as they turned to look questioningly downwards at Barty.

"For my behaviour, when we first met," Barty went on, abashed. He held his bowler hat in both hands, anxiety in his every gesture, but his time spent observing this enormous being had made some things very clear to him, and he had no alternative but to respond to it. "You were being most helpful. I have not thanked you yet, and that is extremely rude of me." He rubbed the back of his head, chewing the inside of his cheek, before rushing on, "I do not have a lump on my head or any soreness at all, so I presume I was caught before I hit the ground. I do not believe sir Reynard would have bothered with doing that, so that leaves in conclusion—it had to be yourself."

A hum of contemplation then. "You have fainted before, I take it?"

Barty nodded. "Only rarely, and only recently has it been an issue," he replied apologetically. "Each time I have woken with a very sore head, and many regrets. That did not happen this time." He paused, then took a deep breath and looked up at Adam properly. "You have not mentioned it. But I have noticed it. And I was very rude to you just now, and thus, I wish to apologise." Another stumble in his words, his tongue sticking in his mouth a moment, as polite correspondence failed a moment. "These past few days have been, well, exceptionally overwhelming for me I fear, but it is no decent excuse to have bad manners." He said it earnestly, honestly, and with more than a trace of anxiety while being unable to keep the slight catch out of his voice. Barty had told not falsehoods. He *was* feeling extremely overwhelmed.

Adam watched him for a moment, before those scarred features quirked into a lopsided, but genuine smile that somehow did not look at all frightening. They nodded. "It is quite all right, Mister Barty—and you are correct. I was the one who caught you before you fell. I fear it is not the first time it has happened, but it is the first time I have been thanked for it. You are most astute in your deduction. Quite well done." They chuckled softly, a low sound that set the dust on the steps to bouncing. "I think I can see why he is keeping you about. Please, let me show you something." And with that, they resumed their ascent, with somewhat more verve in their step than before, apparently pleased at the interaction.

They rose up past various paintings and other works of art. Barty glanced at each, often doing a double take. Most of them depicted people in some fashion out of various periods in history going back centuries, but others showed fantastical and terrible creatures as well, and scenes out of dream or nightmare. A great antler horned creature with a gaping muzzle, clashing against a knight on horseback. A massive beast that could only be a dragon, coiled around a hilltop, and a gathering of small figures standing before it with one in front of the others, a hand outstretched. Below it was a small brass plaque with the description *The Accord of Yr Wyddfa, 1648*. There were plenty of others, each with their own odd story to tell. Adam, however, while unhurried in their gait, could cover a great distance with a single step, and thus Barty could not linger.

They were in another corridor at this point, similar to the one below in terms of its artworks and doors lining its sides. Adam, still ducking somewhat despite the high roof, stepped surprisingly lightly towards one door, and opened it, standing to one side. Barty could already see that his various—and meagre—belongings were inside, the phonograph in its heavy case placed upon a chest at the end of the well-made bed. The room was hardly large by the standards of the wealthy, but Barty had never been that. To him it was cavernous, extraordinarily and wonderfully so. It was certainly comfortably furnished, and better so than his comparatively dreadful home, a place that held no significance and no decent memories. Even if this was but the offer of just a few nights, this new abode was infinitely better than he expected.

"I fear I have not aired it out properly. I am sure you

understand, Mister Barty," Adam said apologetically. "This was an unexpected meeting for us both."

Barty could only nod, his heart beating a little faster out of sheer happiness. The bed was twice the size of any he had ever slept in. There was, to one side, a bathtub with water from pipes! It was a simple thing of cast iron, set on the floor just near a fireplace. His own bathtub! His own fireplace! A proper one too, that even let the smoke out via an actual chimney rather than just having a hole in the roof. It hardly seemed real. Despite everything that had happened before now, this was undoubtedly something that came close to making it all worthwhile.

"If you will indulge me, Mister Barty, I still wish to show you something." Adam's tone was understanding as they gestured down the corridor. "I am going to assume that Reynard has refrained from elaborating on where we now stand?" Barty shook his head, falling into step alongside the giant, under whom the solid floor creaked.

Barty then remembered. "I believe he called it the Lodge, in passing."

Adam nodded, and sighed. "Jean Reynard is a great many things. Without doubt the angriest man I have ever met, and the most brilliant and terrible in his field, but patient with explaining things, he is not." They sounded just faintly exasperated. "However, that is indeed the name of these hallowed halls. The Lodge of the Hunters, the Halls of Record, and the Home of the Association. The Society of the Hound." They said the titles slowly, reciting them. "In short, this is the London office of the monster hunters of Britannia." They pointed down the hall. "This floor has most of the residences, and down there is the library. Above us is the sun room and observatory. Below us, we have the armoury, the laboratory, and, well..." They paused, then halted, looking at the mystified expression of Barty, who was quite overwhelmed. "I trust that he at least *explained* what the Hunters are, did he not?" Barty shook his head again, as the giant pinched the bridge of his enormous nose delicately with fingers larger than the largest sausages Barty had ever laid eyes upon.

"I might have known. He was probably testing you to figure it out on your own—but it is a method that I, for once, disagree with. That, or he fully expected me to tell you." They made a face, that twisted visage twisting further into something that would make any normal person shudder, but Barty remained stoic as he could. It was getting easier to be in Adam's presence. Despite how they looked, the sheer size of them, they had a manner to them that was gently reassuring, and a voice that was utterly soothing. Kings would have upended their kingdoms seeking such a voice. Every ear turned to it and listened gratefully.

Still, Adam was unambiguously irritated for a moment before getting the faint display of emotion back under control. "The Hunters are a society tasked in antiquity with a simple mission, Mister Barty; to hunt down those that would otherwise prey upon people while being of a supernatural and unnatural nature. This is where the hunters occasionally reside, stage out from, and otherwise correspond with the wider world as is necessary. They have done so for a very, very long time, as their records will show if you take the time to peruse them. I recommend you do. They are fascinating reading."

Barty looked along the hall, baffled as he peered at the various paintings, portraits, and more besides. He looked up to Adam then, frowning. "Why… how have I never heard of this? Forgive me if that is a foolish question, but it is in fact my job to discover things; or at least it was, before all this." He waved a hand. "But I have never heard anyone speak of this."

"That is because outside of this building, they, the Hunters, do not speak of it. That which is not known cannot be spread further. And there are other means, if they become necessary." Adam's broad, twisted teeth bared in a wide grin that flashed and was gone. "You have done well to be part of a secret society, Mister Barty, at such a young age."

"And here I thought they were all like that Golden Dawn thing with those madmen like Aleister Crowley," Barty mused, wryly, but he felt a bit of a twist inside him. *Part of,* Adam said. What had he volunteered himself for in that graveyard?

"See here now," Adam said cheerfully, standing at a large portrait painting of a stunningly beautiful woman. She was dressed most unusually in a man's attire that was tight upon her frame and left absolutely no doubt as to her gender, while wielding a stunningly crafted rapier in one hand and tipping the brim of a large, feathered hat with the other. Little of her face was visible beneath the hat but, that which showed was a knowing sort of smile and an eye that was clear and ready for an easy wink. "This is the Comtesse Regine Delacourte. She was a Hunter, and one of the finest. In her time, she was a lover of both King Louis XIV of France and the famed and magnificent Julie D'Abuigny. At the same time, would you believe. She also defeated an infestation of ghouls in the Paris crypts, cleared a curse from Pope Innocent XII and uncovered a cult of dark wizards in the court of Hungary." They sighed regretfully. "I wish I could have met her. She is certainly one of my favourites."

"I regret to say I have not heard of her," Barty replied in a tone that held true to his words, however unhelpfully.

But Adam nodded, as though this was entirely to be expected and continued on, gesturing to a side portrait of a grim looking man with a large moustache that went down to his chin and beyond. "This is Luther Richter, who was also known as the Luther the Bitter. He created similar headquar-ters to this in Berlin after a schism took place within the Hunters, when a member of the royal family here was afflicted by a transformation that turned them into a monster. Luther slew them and was cast out, but never gave up the cause. This portrait was erected as an apology to Luther and his bloodline after his death, a regrettable incident that would have been avoided save for a crucial mistake and a failure to pass certain records to him— ah… But I am sure you will learn about this later."

Barty listened, fascinated. It remained easy to listen to Adam, but the subject matter was intriguing. The idea that each painting could have so much history behind them stirred the interest of his investigator's heart, to learn, to *know*. To see each portrait and hear the story behind them. He looked around, looking to see one that would catch his eye so that he might ask to learn its story, and his eye alighted immediately on a most unusual thing.

At the end of the hallway, with a door that lead to the library as Adam had pointed out before, was just a frame. More than that, it was charred black, burnt by fire, and, even more disturbingly, the wall behind it was similarly scorched. It had been set ablaze, but not recently. Which made it even more strange, since it had not been taken down. He could not help but point to it.

"Could you tell me, perhaps, about that one? I mean, it looks very out of place here. What happened to it?"

Silence fell. Heavy, thick silence, the sort that choked words from the air and smothered out any further. It flattened out over Barty like a blanket of lead as Adam went as still as a stiffened corpse for a long moment. It made Barty shiver with a sudden rush of fear, as he was reminded that there was much he did not yet know—and was not meant to know, either. But nevertheless, he could not help but draw closer to that burned out frame, his eyes drawn to the brass plate at its base, even as the silence grew ever heavier. It drew him on step by step, that same feeling that led him to asking questions no one wanted to answer.

"I would request that you do not," Adam said very softly. There was not much strength in it, however, nor any sort of threat. It was a plea, gently given and plaintive. But Barty did not hear them.

Most of it was blackened by soot. It was a large frame, very much so. Room for a significant portrait, and the brass plate spoke to the same. He reached up and, with a thumb, brushed some of the soot away, to read what lay beneath.

The Reynard Family, 1892.

Family. The Reynard *family*. And yet here, in this place and time, there was only one, who sat alone downstairs. Barty felt his stomach churn, and his mouth turn dry. He stared at the blackened, empty frame, wondering what it might mean, drawing what implications he could from it. Plenty came, and swiftly. None of them were good.

There was another portrait, on the other side of the door-way. His gaze was dragged to it, away from the burned horror of things unsaid. There were two people in this frame. One was a seated man who had a look about him of a sort of contained, frustrated annoyance, set in a library of some sort. He was somewhat more than middle aged, with one eye covered by an eyepatch and with his hair tied back, the single remaining eye squinting out from behind a monocle. Standing at his shoulder behind him was a young man, standing straight and tall with shoulders back and with a bright, shining grin on his face that spoke eloquently of mischief. One did not have to look long to guess that the portrait was their idea, and the older man was not at all enamoured of the notion from the way they glowered at the painter. Barty, pulled by a sort of sick fascination approached it to see the names below. *Theodore Locke, with Apprentice J. Reynard, 1874.*

If the plate had not said it plainly, he would not have believed it. A picture of a young Jean, full of life, a cheerful smile that seemed like it could never be quenched, alongside his old master and teacher. And to the right of it, that burned out frame, that promise of nightmare and stories that would never be spoken.

He tried to change the subject, to drag them away from this gulf of realisation, of the recognition of that which was no longer there. Not looking at Adam, his voice faltering, he asked a question that had been nagging at the back of his thoughts.

"You… you speak of the Hunters as 'they'. Not 'us' or 'we'" Barty said slowly. He tried to rub his thumb with his forefinger to banish the soot there, feeling distinctly uncomfortable at its presence. "Are you not part of the Society yourself?"

Adam had approached, and stood just behind Barty, hands at their back, shaking their head with a sad, soft chuckle. "Oh, no. Though it was not my choice, I fear I am very, undeniably not, nor shall ever be." They shrugged, as Barty tore his gaze from the pictures, craning his neck to look upwards. Adam wore a rueful expression on that ruined visage. "You see, Mister Barty, a monster cannot become a hunter. That would create what we call a *paradox*, you see."

This caused Barty to swallow. It made his thoughts race a moment, and while it confirmed his suspicions, it absolutely led him to question *how* this was the case. There was a story here, not simply in how Adam had come to be in this place, but how the situation could exist at all. He stammered, acutely aware of how close he was standing to what was, to all intents and purposes, something in the same classification as Clicker-clack. But how could have it been otherwise? That inhuman appearance, size, and the terror of that visage—but yet… the voice. All of it was at odds with the melody of that voice.

"But if that is true," he finally managed, "then why are you here?"

"Ah," Adam said with that sad little smile, straightening up a touch—greatly exaggerated on that vast frame—and nodded. "That is because I *can* choose to be here. And because I *do*." This had a note of firm finality to it, and pride. A decision, and a choice, made completely and entirely. *It was not my choice*, they had said, on being a monster. But being here, being part of these halls, and showing a poor lost youth some measure of kindness and comfort, this was their choice. And one they apparently made gladly.

Barty was about to say something else when a voice barked from downstairs, harsh and final. "Barty! Get down here. We are leaving."

"Ah, the call of the hounds to war," Adam said brightly, turning away from the two paintings, one destroyed and one unanswered. "The weather is a touch chilly today, so do not forget your coat. And please, make sure to take some of the sandwiches on your way and put them in your pockets, they will keep well." They were cheerful, the moment of darkness fading in that almost motherly guidance. Barty did not even think to object; he was down the stairs, getting his coat from the room where he had awoken, and taking the advice to pick up some of the quartered sandwiches and stuff them into one pocket, wrapped in a napkin. *Ham and cheese*, he noted absently, *with a light amount of pickled relish.*

Jean was waiting at the doorway. Though he was still and

silent, he exuded a sort of air of menacing impatience that was more effective than any sort of gesture or command. He watched Barty the entire time, saying nothing, but that baleful glower was its own admonition as his charge returned from the sitting room stuffing a sandwich into his mouth. He was dressed once more in that long coat, hiding the panoply of war that he concealed beneath it. He squinted briefly at Barty, turning away from him to leave, making no gesture but commanding that he be followed regardless. Barty could not help but remember the painting above, destroyed but lingering. Had they followed him, as he did now? What had happened, that was not said, for the burning to take place?

The door opened, and Jean paused while Barty jumped and nearly choked on his sandwich quarter, pounding on his chest as the tableau paused for a moment. A large, broad man was standing at the door, with one fist paused in the midst of descending. He was of middle age, grey in beard and hair, weathered of features, and he was a policeman.

This was not something noted by his clothing, which consisted of a buttoned coat and waistcoat in a sober dark grey. Nor by the pocket watch hanging from breast pocket. The sturdy shoes and the bowler hat, the curved smoking pipe in one corner of their mouth, these too, while adding to the picture, did not complete it. Truth told, if the two uniformed officers behind him, with their carefully trimmed moustaches and sturdy hats had not given it away, it was the *look* of him; not what he wore, but how he looked at others.

He had seen Barty immediately and squinted at him, looked him up and down, and gauged him. Considered the crimes he had committed and catalogued them. Looked for what was written on his face and guessed at what was not. It was the look of a man who knew no one was innocent of anything. But he did not look at Barty long.

Jean, if he was surprised, recovered magnificently from this unexpected crossing of paths. "Inspector Creek," he said in a level tone, as though this was completely normal and not at all a surprise. "What fortunate timing. I was just coming to inspect the scene now."

Inspector Creek blinked, his bullish jaw opening and closing once, twice. "Yes. Of course you were." The man was gruff, his tone also even, as though he too fully expected this to happen, as he carefully lowered his useless hand, perhaps hoping it would not be noticed. Barty noticed, of course. The two uniformed officers noticed, and Jean and the inspector noticed everyone noticing. No one had the courage to say one word about it and worked instead very thoroughly to pretend that they had not noticed. Which made it worse.

"If you do not mind me asking, Reynard," Creek said, shifting his pipe out of his mouth. "How the bloody hell did you know? We only found him an hour ago." Brows like a horse brush beetled down, the jaw jutting so that it and the large nose almost touched.

Jean paused at this. He tilted his head. "There has been another one? Already?"

Creek's beard and broad moustache wobbled as he ground his teeth in consternation. He nodded, exhaling. "We better get a move on. Chief will be there before too long, and you know how he is about this sort of thing."

Jean nodded, clearly knowing precisely how they would be. Barty did not. He had no idea, but he could guess easily enough.

"What makes you believe it was connected, Inspector?" Jean was already moving out, striding past the inspector and his officers as he stepped to the curb of the street and brought two fingers to his mouth, whistling sharply—a low to high, then low again, then continually ascending high before sharply cutting off. There was silence in the aftermath, then the clattering of hooves and the roll of a carriage, and the four horse draw of Crook appeared from around a crowded street corner, the driver seated and grinning brightly in the dim London daylight.

Barty was pleased to see him, but the inspector clearly was not. He glowered at Crook as he drew closer, as Jean turned on the spot, brow raised, and clearly waiting for an answer. His aggressive waiting eventually overcame Creek's desire to glare and he puffed on his pipe before answering in a grumbling tone. "You'll know when you see it, Reynard. Just know that it has me damn well stumped, and the rest of us too."

"Fascinating. Something to confuse the London police department. I would never have imagined," Jean replied in utter deadpan, flat and unimpressed.

Crook brought the carriage alongside, and then released the reins to lay flat along the seat to grin widely down at the inspector from above. "Dear, beloved Creek! It has been too long." He sounded overjoyed, but his grin was entirely, unmistakeably spiteful.

"Not nearly long enough," the inspector growled, refusing to look at him.

Crook gave a high pitched laugh as he twisted himself back upright. He appeared to have a bright thought. "Oh! We are named Crook now, and you are Creek! Crook and Creek! We are like brethren. Brethren unto the end of time and fancy, lovely Creek!"

He continued laughing as Inspector Creek's face darkened to purple. He glowered up at the out-of-sight Crook, then turned to Jean, who simply jabbed a thumb at Barty dismissively. "Blame him, for t'was he that named him thus. Now…" He pulled himself up a step, climbing into the carriage as he continued to speak. "Get rid of your escort. They can walk. There is not enough room for five."

Barty opened and closed his mouth as Creek now looked at him once more, taking far more notice than before, and his expression was one of deep, abiding resentment. He scowled, grunted, and waved to his stoic officers, who nodded and touched their helmets in salute before turning away. Barty could not help but notice they had a swiftness to their step that indicated they were glad of avoiding being involved.

Creek turned back to Barty, and then spoke in a disgruntled tone. "Well. Get on, whoever you are. We are short of time already."

Barty all but sprinted into the carriage to avoid the glowering of his stare. He glanced over one shoulder briefly as he went, to see the shadow of Adam, closing the great door of the manor. He wished he had said goodbye to them. He would have to apologise later; it felt important to do so, even if he feared that Adam would soon grow tired of endless apologies.

In the carriage, it could not help but be noticed that there was indeed room for five, and a sixth if one proved necessary. This would be the case if Jean did not take up an entire side of seats by himself—not out of bulk, but because he wished it that way. So it was that Creek and Barty were sat at the window on each side opposite, Creek glowering at Barty and working his jaw around his pipe, which glowed in time with his irritation. He was gauging Barty, who was doing his very best to squirrel himself into a corner and away from the glare, which only drew it closer.

It was not that Barty was guilty of anything—nothing that the inspector would know about anyway. But Barty was a part of an animal kingdom where people like himself lingered at the bottom. Orphans, even those that had worked their way out of the poor houses and found ways to scrape and claw into something with a modicum of respectability, always knew where they came from. They were at the bottom of the ladder where police stood only one rung below the rich and powerful, those who could decide the law suited the ends they wanted. And people like Barty were the sort that the police were able and willing to bully, to coerce, and if need be, remove. He was never allowed to forget that. He had seldom, if ever, managed to get information out of any of the constabulary either, because even the slowest street-prowler had a nasty habit of turning the conversation around and making him feel like he was a criminal when he was no such thing. He never liked the feeling, and he remembered it now as he adjusted his hat.

It was precisely then, as he realised that his entire wardrobe at present was one stolen from a house looted on Jean's orders, that he broke out in a cold sweat, and Creek spoke in a bark that made Barty nearly jump out of his skin. "So who are you then? What is your story, hrm?" The pipe wobbled in his mouth, before he plucked it clear. "Speak up!"

Barty felt his tongue stick in his mouth, but it was Jean, sat with one leg crossed over the other and hands resting in his lap who answered. "He is my assistant, moving forward. Inspector Creek, this is Mister Barty," he said dismissively. Nothing in his posture showed the slightest hint of the crime that not two days he had been implicit in, of emptying a house of goods and paying off kidnappers with the proceeds, holding people hostage, burning down a church, and more besides. It was not that he was trying to hide it. He simply did not care.

Creek glowered, looking from one to the other. He gave Barty one more suspicious glower. "He does not say much. Something wrong with his tongue?"

"Nothing at all, unless he speaks out of turn," Jean replied dryly. "Now. Speak to me instead, Inspector. Give me the details that you have."

He sounded different, in this moment. Before, Barty could see that Jean was irritable, even anxious. Caged and contained, a lion pacing endlessly in the confines of his enclosure, wanting to be let loose. This was different. Now, sat here, there was a calm air to him, but despite the lack of anxious energy there was now an undercurrent that spoke of determination. *He needs this*, Barty realised. *He needs to do this, to focus on something. On anything.* A burned frame and a brass nameplate loomed large in Barty's mind. Lonely, he had thought him. He was beginning to suspect he had no idea just how much.

Creek did not look pleased, but he finally ground out his pipe and started to speak. "We've a body on a rooftop across the river. Unusual enough, but not the most strange part of it." He made a face. He was angry, but it was not just at Barty. Creek did not want to be here, Barty could see it. He did not want to be speaking to Jean. Did he not like him? Or did he not want to for other reasons?

How many know of that burned frame, and what is in it? Cosgrove, Barty now guessed, had certainly known. But it hovered, unspoken. Some things could not even be inferred.

"Do not leave me in suspense, John." Jean's reply was dry. The inspector grimaced at the use of his first name, but let it pass.

"Very well. You ever see a man who looked like he learned to fly? And then forgot?"

Jean raised a brow. "I've seen it once or twice. The learning is quite brief and the forgetting quite terminal. But you wouldn't call me out for a broken heart departed, Creek. They tend to find the depths of the Thames, in any case."

The inspector shrugged helplessly. "I honestly do not

know how to describe it, except to show you," he said wearily. Barty felt a twinge of sudden, unexpected pity for the man. He had clearly been wracking his brain about this for a while now, and the questions he could not answer had long since tired him into frustration.

It nevertheless spoke more to his character than Barty would care to admit. Simple answers were easy. Simple answers closed cases. Simple answers got things out of the way and out of mind, so long as no one cared about the blood it cost. You could explain anything difficult with simple answers, such as a madman killing five women in Whitechapel, when it had been anything but a human doing so, as Barty now well knew.

But the correct answers to hard questions were something else. They were things that kept men awake and made them grind their teeth to dust and look at the world with a steady gaze of blazing suspicion, because letting go of the question that could not be answered meant giving up, and they did not know how. Creek was not here because he was a fool. He was here because whatever held him back from being in Jean's company was not enough to stop him wanting the truth. Barty understood that. It made him relax, just a touch.

Jean swore softly, leaning back as he closed his eyes. "Wake me when we get there, then." His tone was soured, his interest forcibly quelled for the time being.

How long has it been since he has slept? Barty wondered. The shadows of his face made it hard to tell if he had ever done so with any degree of certainty, and certainly not with any measure of peace. He did, however, realise that in the days since they had crossed paths, he had not seen the man rest once.

The carriage rolled on. Somewhere above them, as Creek grumbled and glowered out the window, Crook started to sing softly. It cut through the sound of the street and the bustle of London, the criers and callers, the vendors and the doom criers, the religious street zealots and the bawdy who never knew solace. The beating heart of London, full of sound and fury, mindless and yet terribly aware. Crook's song wove with it, a discordant note that only those on the carriage could hear, and Barty felt his mind drift without thinking on it, the tune reminding him of things he could not clearly remember, disjointed and strange. A song in a courtyard over a high wall, sung in his voice and joined with another. A shouted cry in a dark alleyway, panicked breathing and breaking glass. A woman's dark eyed-gaze that he could fall into forever, over and over and unblinking. He shook his head, startled a moment at the strange lapse. Across from him, Jean's face flickered a moment, then went still as behind that closed gaze an iron door shut. Whatever it was that Crook's song had showed him, it was not welcome. Not for the first time, Barty wondered if he wasn't either.

It felt like even more of a mistake on the rooftop, as Barty lurched to the edge and hurled up the contents of his stomach into the alleyway void beneath. The remnant of sandwich tasted far less appetising coming back the other way.

Jean stood with his head tilted, hands clasped at his back, his expression merely curious. He paid absolutely no attention to Barty whatsoever. Instead, he gazed at the wreckage that had once been human life with an impassive expression, while Creek looked at Barty disgustedly and the half dozen members of the constabulary looked a mixture of amused, puzzled, and even outraged.

They were on the roof of a gallery, a solid structure built in a style more akin to fortification. The roof was flat, crenelated like a fortress wall at the edges, and the expanse of the roof itself was reinforced from beneath extensively. Rather than sloping edges, the entire thing was levelled out, save for a glass section that protruded upwards and dominated much of the roof itself. But surrounding it was an area level enough to walk around on safely and easily, and in the midst of that space was a body.

It was, most assuredly, a corpse. No living person could look like that. A living person was altogether less *flat*. They also had substantially more blood in their body, rather than pooling around them, though even the famed London weather had not stopped it from drying somewhat, and certainly had not prevented it congealing, turning thick and dark.

Jean had not moved. He simply listened as Creek finally started to explain. "Found them this morning, after blood started to drip through the cracks in the roof into the hall below. Gave the staff a terrible turn."

Jean made a slight hum sound, then walked closer to the body, crouching down beside it, as Barty made his way up on shaking legs.

It was a man, dressed in a suit and torn coat that had both ruptured at the seams. From the wrinkling of the skin and the white hair, they were clearly an old man in the twilight of their life. From the extent of their girth, they were one who lived a fortunate life at this stage as well, that had time and wealth enough to enjoy the finer things in life—in particular rich food. It was hard to make out the face properly, crushed by impact, presumably with the ground. The limbs were spread askew in directions, the body face down. Jean did not touch them, but remained crouched alongside before he finally spoke.

"What have eyewitnesses said so far? Anyone report seeing a man flapping his arms and trying to fly?" His tone was sardonic, but he glanced skyward and over his shoulder a moment, before looking back to the body.

Creek shook his head, walking a circle around the body. "No. There were screams around"—he paused to peer at a notebook—"midnight. Loud, and panicked, they said. Then cut off." He shook his head, lowering the notebook. "They rung the bell, and a patrol had a look about but found nothing. No one was looking on the rooftops after all, and all the doors leading up here were locked."

"Of course they were," Jean said absently. He reached down to touch the ground by the dead man's feet, then absently lifted the lower limb, shifting the pants leg to look at the covered lower leg, grimacing as he set it back down precisely. "So, Barty, let us see if you can ask the obvious question. We can follow up with the answer afterwards."

Barty swallowed. Anxious, he scratched the back of his head. "Who is he?"

Jean sighed, and shook his head. "We can find that out. Someone will miss this man. This suit is fine cloth, expensive. People with money always get missed." His tone turned sour. "Not the question I wanted. Keep trying. Think both less and more obvious."

Barty found this very unhelpful, but struggled to understand. Creek was staring, first at him, then at Jean, his expression decidedly unimpressed. Jean shrugged, a flicker of a cold smile on that weathered face. "His first day, Creek. We all start somewhere."

This made Barty's cheeks redden, so in frustration he

asked the answer he felt would be the most irritating. "How did he get here?"

Jean lifted a single finger upwards. "Correct." Barty blinked in surprise, as Jean looked towards him with a serious expression. "All questions need answering, for the picture to be complete. The simplest ones, and then on to the most complex. In this case, they conflate." He gestured. "A man is dead on a rooftop. And yet." The uplifted finger pointed upwards slightly. Barty looked skywards to see just that—sky. There were no taller buildings above. Across the other side of the street, some fifty feet away, were similar structures, but they were much too far away—and not much higher besides. "Here we are. Four floors up, or thereabouts, and a man has managed to take a step and miss the ground." He tilted his head again. "How hard do you think he hit, Barty?"

The young man swallowed back the bile that threatened to vent forth once more. "I could not… I mean I do not see how I could tell—"

Jean was unhelpfully helpful in making it clearer. "A human body is not made to *bounce*, as it were. It is more liquid in nature. Thus, it is akin to dropping say, a thick custard tart, or a sack filled with jelly from a kitchen counter. Instead they *flatten* outwards—over the side, Barty," he said in irritation as Barty fled to heave once again over the rooftop edge.

Jean sighed, and went on, staring down at the corpse. "Too high, and the sack ruptures. Too low, and it tumbles about. Has to be just right." There was a clattering of carriage wheels then from below, loud and a shouted voice to clear the crowd of onlookers below. Jean did not look up, but continued speaking. "So they were high, but not too high, and not too low. There was *force* behind it." He glanced up, tearing his gaze from the body, as Barty drew closer again, to speak to the suddenly anxious Creek. "Go and slow him down for me, Creek. I need all the time I can get."

The inspector grumbled, but astonishingly, he did exactly that, heading from the scene with a quickened stride. Jean looked down at the body, and spoke then in a tone of muted urgency, his gaze distant as he looked upon the man.

"Look past the gore and horror, Barty. Look close and look hard. All the answers are here if you know how to look." Barty swallowed, and compelled against his will, stared at the ruined body as Jean went on. "You wanted truth; this is where it all starts. This is where you learn the truth of the one who did this. Because someone *did* this. Someone took this life. Maybe he deserved it, maybe he did not. Maybe he did a terrible thing, or the right thing, and the wrong thing happened." He was intent now. Barty could not help but stare at the body, but his attention shifted to Jean instead, to see the look on his face.

The look in his eyes was bright and somehow searing. Barty would almost call it rapturous, but that did not feel right either. Jean's unblinking gaze held the corpse like it had the answer to every question he might ever have as he went on. "It all begins here, in any case. In the *modus mortifico*—the method of the kill." Those lips flickered into a lifeless smile as the expression remained rigid. "The how, that tells you why. The why, that tells you who. It all starts here, in this darkness, if you just look hard enough."

Barty did not understand. He did not know how to express that ignorance, but he also did not have time either. For at that moment, a man stormed up onto the rooftop, Creek looking awkward in his wake. He was young, well dressed, and wore a prominent medallion of office around their neck. Barty knew them from his work with The Times; the chief inspector of the police, Lord Howard Montague, a young up and comer who—spurred on the Ripper case—had used his lordly connections to have his career fast-tracked in only a few years to become the commander of the Criminal Investigations Division at Scotland Yard. He claimed to bring vigour, integrity, and new thinking to the police force. What he had mostly brought was shouting.

"A pleasure once again, Chief Inspector," Jean said in a pleasant tone without looking at him. The youthful chief inspector was already all but howling with rage.

"You… you *bastard*, Reynard! What have I told you about getting involved in these things, what? I thought I already told you!" He stormed over, arms waving in his unbridled fury. Jean remained where he was, his lips turned into a faint, hard smile, glassy in that it could break into a snarl at any moment.

"I am sure you did, but I fear I must have forgotten in my slow, ignorant, outdated way," Reynard replied pleasantly. "Do not fret, Montague. I've left everything as it were. Nothing has been touched, and nothing has been altered. It is all here in place for you to cock up good and proper."

The young lord stormed over to Jean, heedless of where he went, and stood over him. "You get the *hell* out of my crime scene before I throw you headfirst off this roof myself, along with—" He paused, pointing suddenly at Barty. "Who in the hell is this?" He stood there quivering with fury, his moustache twitching so violently as to be nearly leaping off his top lip, pointing with an accusing hand to the shrinking, vomit-stained Barty, whose imagination betrayed him once again in his stolen clothes.

Jean said nothing for a moment, then slowly straightened up. He stood to his full height, which, now away from Adam, Barty was reminded that was quite tall indeed. Without backing away from Montague, standing but inches apart, he looked down his nose at him with a nonplussed expression. He did not look bothered—indeed his expression spoke only of contempt, and the young lord blinked a few times, wavering in his stance a touch before Jean finally replied.

"You walked through the blood, Chief Inspector. Best get it off before it ruins your boots."

The young lord blinked, then looked down and swore. He had indeed trudged through the pool of thickened, sticky blood in what appeared to be expensive riding boots. He started hopping in place, trying to scrape the foul red stuff by scuffing his boots on the rooftop, but it clung like glue. Jean turned away, ignoring him as he walked towards Creek. He did not beckon, but Barty followed him, wanting to get away.

"He had the bit 'twixt his teeth on this one, Reynard," Creek muttered as they drew up. "Could not hold him off for long."

But Jean was shaking his head, untroubled. "I have what I need from here, but I do need the autopsy reports of the other victims. Tell Judith that I will have a bottle of wine sent, if she can get me the unabridged ones."

Creek snorted. "She's always had a soft spot for you, Jean. She'll do it even if there was no wine on offer. Where do you want me to bring them? The Lodge?"

Again, Jean shook his head. "No. Heathwood's. I need to look it over."

Creek's face darkened as Montague continued to swear, then started shouting orders to uniformed officers to get the body taken care of. He glared at his subordinate and Jean, but kept where he was for now.

"You sure about that, Reynard?" Creek asked. "It was a bad one, worse than this. I know you and he were friends."

This made Jean lift his chin, a smile forming that had no humour in it whatsoever. "I thought you knew better than anyone, Creek, I do not have friends. This will be no different than anything else I deal with." He moved to take the door and steps that led down into the building below. "Those reports promptly, if you could, Inspector. More lives will depend on it. Because this one is not done."

Creek made a harrumph sound, an unhappy one, as Jean disappeared. He remained where he was. So did Barty, who was running those last statements through his head and bringing his imagination to bear on what they meant. As all things, when given a chance to think on matters, the meaning and implication did not bode well for him.

Creek seemed to read it on his face, and the aged inspector shook his head regretfully. Putting out a hand, he gave Barty a firm pat that gave way to a shove. "Go on with you, get after him. Try and keep the devil in check." With that he turned away, likely to face further beratement from his furious, but inexperienced, superior. Barty hurried after Jean, who was taking the steps three at a time.

"So, Barty," he intoned as they carried on, passing officers and two men carrying a stretcher, "we have a man who did not learn to fly—but one who had help doing so. Let us go and see the other side of this story, shall we?"

Barty made no sense of this, and his response was a baffled note of confusion. Jean exhaled, and continued on. "The right leg was broken, by crushing. The right knee, twisted around so badly that the lower leg had been nearly torn off. So what does that tell us?" They strode through the plaza, past murmuring clusters of frightened inhabitants and workers. Some sort of financial trading house, Barty noted absently. Not the place of violent crime, and the various clerks and secretaries all looked terribly lost and unsure, unable to work but unable to do anything else. Despite the intention of his travel and the veracity of his guide leading him on, Barty felt as lost as they were, if not more so.

Jean continued to speak as they went. "I remember when I was a young boy, learning the trade, I would occasionally lose my temper during my lessons." He pushed the double doors open and strode on through as Barty hurried in his wake. "When things grew frustrating, I would go down to the loch upon whose shores we lived and throw things into the water." There was a small crowd outside, who Jean ignored. He kept glancing up as he went, as though fixing a position in mind. The road was a wide one in this place, a double laneway with a centre parting, where carriages and carts carried this and that and generally had the right of way. Normally. There was a great deal of swearing and pulling on brakes as Jean strode through the middle of things, his coat collar high and his eyes straight ahead as he focused on a building before him. As a coach driver swore incoherently and Barty hopped along with his heart in his mouth, Jean stalked along, still speaking. "Stones, branches, whatever I got my hands on. I took great pleasure in throwing something significantly far. Felt satisfying to do so. A sort of release, as it were."

He pushed open a door in front of him without pausing. A shop of some sort, Barty could see as he entered. What appeared to be tinctures and other various bottled liquids for the treatment, as far as he could see, of any ailment whatsoever, be it a cold or pox, or an itch between the toes—usually all of them at once. Jean did not slow. To the great shock of the attendant, a middle aged man with a pouchy, droopy face, he set one hand to the counter and vaulted over it, stepping past him and his outraged surprise to push a door open behind him and start climbing stairs two at a time. Barty scrambled after him, croaking apologies to the owner, who was red in the face with anger and confusion. There was no time to linger though.

He followed Jean up several floors until they burst out

onto a rooftop once more through a ceiling door. This one was not like the other roof in that, despite its opening here—festooned with a collection of clothes lines, Barty noted—it was far more cramped and tight, with the roof lined in lead and slate slopes. Jean crouched briefly, then continued on, to come to a torn section of clothes line, the strings languishing in the dirt. Barty, breathing a little hard after the pursuit, stopped on wobbly feet as Jean glowered at things for a moment, before he crouched down, and picked up a loose bit of roof tile, a few inches across. "Down the road from here is a place called the Aurelius Club. It is a place where rich old men like to gather and speak of their glory days, and discuss matters they know little about, in a manner that leads the ignorant to think they know much more." He could not keep the contempt that burned at his every syllable, as he tossed the tile up and down, weighing it. "A man might attend that club, then decide to walk home. But then, someone might walk from anywhere to anywhere." He gripped the tile tighter. "And this is a busy street, even at that hour. People heard it, and yet saw nothing. But why not someone else?"

He tossed the tile a little higher, staring now across the way. Directly opposite them, Barty could now see, was the rooftop they had just left. The body was being lifted, with difficulty. A third and fourth officer was assisting while the chief inspector gesticulated and pointed his finger at Creek, who even from this distance seemed unimpressed.

"I do not understand. How does all this help us figure out how he fell from the sky?" Barty could not help but answer.

Jean was taking practice throws now, slow and thoughtful as he continued to gauge distance while holding the bit of tile. "By realising, Mister Barty, that he did not fall. Much as it was when I threw my stones, and my branches, he was thrown." Barty blinked. A grim smile formed on Jean's face. He tossed the tile in his hand, and then arched back and hurled it as hard as he could towards the opposite roof. It sailed through the air as Jean straightened up and went on. "He was thrown with enough force to spray blood and shatter his leg." The tile piece landed near the chief inspector, who paused in his ranting to hop about in confusion, looking left and right but failing to understand what had happened, or to look in the direction of Jean and Barty. The hunter went on smugly, upon seeing the reaction. "Blood, right there." He pointed, and Barty followed his pointing finger to a line of spattered dark red blood a few feet away. "They brought him up here from the street below. Without going inside the building, up several floors, and then stood right here"—he pointed down where he stood, to where the roof had been dented inwards as though from an exertion of weight or pressure, enough to cave it in somewhat—"to hurl a man weighing more than two hundred and fifty pounds, with enough arc behind the throw to hit that roof there, around a hundred and twenty feet away, by taking him by the leg and hurling him. And it was done in *anger*." He said it with a grimace, then put his hands back in the pockets of his coat, turning away, back to the door. "This is why I am here, Mister Barty. Because this is something I understand."

Barty swallowed, following him. "Something like… monsters, mysteries?"

Jean shook his head as he stalked down the staircase. "No, not in this case, Mister Barty. I am here because I understand anger." His shoulders tensed up and bunched as he continued on. "Now come on. I have to see to an old friend."

CHAPTER 7

WALLS WITH AND WITHOUT DOORS

The journey to Doctor Heathwood's was undertaken on foot. Jean did not bother to explain if it was near or far, but simply started walking, and Barty started following. At this point, Crook and his well kept coach was nowhere to be seen, which only added to the worrisome nature of the man. But Barty had other things on his mind.

Jean had his collar high, hands thrust into his pockets as he stalked along. At one point he fished a cigarette and match out of the depths of his coat, lighting it and glowering as he puffed. Barty watched him, much as one might watch a snake about to bite.

"You continue to stare at me all the time, Mister Barty. I grow very, very tired of it, and find myself questioning your motives. Are you seeking to find a way to proposition me?" Jean's tone was acidic with his irritation.

Barty was mortally offended. "No, thank you," he replied sharply, tearing his gaze away.

Jean grunted. They continued on in silence for a while, weaving through the crowds of the street and avoiding street vendors, displaced goods and barrels, or forgotten souls not sure where to go in the mess of the streets, before Jean spoke in exasperation. "Speak, Barty. You were bold enough to follow me in this whole endeavour. We have time now, so if you want to ask me something, ask it."

"I do not even know where to start," Barty responded with a grimace. "I feel like I'm being dragged along by the collar like a stray dog in all of this for the most part."

Jean gave a short, sharp laugh at that, shaking his head. "You are more akin to one than I think you would care to admit. But go on. You have questions."

Barty scratched the back of his head, adjusting his bowler hat afterwards as he formed questions. "Are they all as strong as that? Strong enough to throw a man as though he were a cricket ball across a street? The… the things, I mean." He felt awkward saying it aloud.

Jean shrugged. "Some are. Some are stronger still. Still less dangerous than some of the others—but you will learn about those, as time goes on." His shadowed eyes shifted, looking out of the corner of his gaze down at Barty. "Does knowing that dissuade you?"

The young man shook his head immediately. "No. I have always been weaker than everyone else regardless." He did not like to admit it, but he could not deny the truth either. This made Jean grunt in a non-committal way as they continued, pausing to make way for a loaded cart rolling from an alleyway.

"And yet you continue on this road. Your ever going search for truth. Why?" Jean was off again as the cart passed, his head shifting as he looked around. Ever aware. Always searching. Always looking for the threat.

Barty shuddered and responded haltingly. "Because it is the right thing to do. At first it was because of the Ripper story, wanting to know what happened to him. But..." he stopped, trailing off, his tongue sticking a moment. Jean said nothing.

"Truth told, sir Reynard... I was hoping he was not dead. The Ripper, I mean." This prompted the hunter to look back with a brow raised sharply as Barty went on. "Not because they did not deserve it. It is because I wanted to know something for sure." He fidgeted, removing his bowler hat to wipe at his brow with a handkerchief, to cover up the pause more than anything else. "You know of my upbringing already. I was a ward of the state, as you said."

"A fancier title for orphan, yes," Jean said dismissively as they continued on. "At St. Mary's, no less." He cast an eye back to Barty, and for the first time, there was a flicker, however faint, of something that wasn't irritation. "There are worse places to grow up, I am sure—but not many of them."

Barty grimaced and continued on. "The orphanage is separated into halves; one for the boys and the other for the girls. We were kept entirely separate from each other." He sidestepped a cluster of small dogs being led by a harried servant, but by the way the leads were being pulled, it was safer to say it was the other way around. Hopping a touch before getting his pace again, he continued.

"That was the goal anyway. But they never quite pulled it off." He could not help but sound a little smug about it. "There was a yard where we could go to, with a wall down the middle of it that separated our two halves. That's where I first met Charlotte." At that name, the tone turned to wistful instead. "She and I used to speak to each other through the wall. Rest our backs against it, and speak through the stones. Sometimes she would sing. Sometimes I would try and do the same, but mostly to make her laugh."

"That bad, I take it?" Jean's tone was dry, and despite himself, Barty chuckled and nodded.

"Far worse. During choir they would only let me hum." Jean snorted, but it was to cover his own chuckle as they started to cross Blackfriars Bridge going north. "She was the only friend I had in that place. We would meet when we could, talk about anything. Stories, gossip… anything."

"Sounds like a match made in heaven to get oneself out of hell," Jean replied with a shrug. "What happened to her?" He continued on a few steps before he realised Barty had stopped. He turned in place, puffing on his cigarette.

His young companion, if that was the right word, had come to a halt, hands in his pockets and was staring at the ground. "She got out of there a few months before I did. Before she left, we met like we normally did and promised that when I was of age enough to leave, we would meet outside St. Mary's." He shifted awkwardly. "When I was shown the door, I waited, but I never saw her there. I never saw her again. And no one knew where she was." He scuffed his feet, then moved to the rail of the bridge, staring down at the water.

After a while, Jean joined him, standing there in silence. Whatever hurry they were in had paused, just for a moment. "I could not tell you where she is now. I still do not know." He made a face. "But I got it into my head, that maybe the Ripper was the one who found her." He said it sourly, doubting. "That somehow he was the one who… who made her disappear. I used to tell myself that I would ask them and find out." He exhaled, straightening up. "And then I found that he was dead, killed by a man no one would name. So I had to find out what *they* knew, so I could know too." Barty shifted his gaze to Jean, who was not watching him, but instead looking at the rolling brown mass of the Thames below.

"I do not expect you to find out, or even know, what happened to Charlotte. She vanished some six years ago now," Barty said quietly. "But she was the only friend I have ever known. If she said she was going to be there waiting for me, then she would. Something happened to her, and someone knows what it was. Maybe the man no one would name would know the answer."

Jean's expression flickered with a conflict of emotion, but he said nothing for a time before, finally, his rusty growl formed into words. "Monsters are not the only ones responsible for the questions that cannot be answered, Mister Barty. I trust that you know that. These very waters you look at claim far more than any beast in the skin of a man might ever do." He gestured to the murk below.

"If you say it to be so," Barty said in a resigned voice, shrugging. "But I do not have anything else. At least, I did not before a few days ago. Up until now, each of my investigations and studies have been towards that end, in one fashion or another. I've learned about a great many things, and answered a great many questions—but none of them about the girl on the other side of the wall."

Jean said nothing, but then frowned. "From the way you spoke, you never got to see what she looked like, did you? With the wall between you, you would have no clue as to how she appeared." Barty shook his head without speaking. There was silence, and then, a snort. The snort gave way to a chuckle, and then a harsh, bitter laugh, Jean wiping at one eye as he roared with laughter. The wandering crowds paid him no heed. Barty, however, could have scorched rock with the offended, but puzzled, glare he gave.

Jean remained unscorched. "Ah, but a rare fool I have found. Not the most pious priest seeking the grace of God could admit that they had not a face or feature to picture in so doing, be it carved from stone or painted upon canvas. But here you are, seeking truth, seeking answers, finding stories, all in the hope that one day the answer will be the one you want but do not expect." He shook his head. "I know of hope, Mister Barty. But even at the best of times, hope is a thing of fools. This is so faint as to be invisible and all but inexplicable." He snorted, flicking his cigarette with two fingers letting it spin into the water below. "People die, Mister Barty. There are never enough answers to make it make sense. These streets ran with blood far before Jack decided to add to the mixture. People die and are forgotten all the time, your friend amongst them—and many others." His voice was harsh and bitter, and it spurred Barty in that moment.

"People die, it is true," he said flatly, still glaring at the hunter. "People like in that burned painting at the Lodge?" He let the question hang as Jean froze, in the midst of pulling out a cigarette to replace the one he had discarded. Those grey eyes turned to Barty and his anger quailed. He became acutely aware of how close he was to the rail. Close enough to be hurled over it into the cold, sucking depths of the river below, where he could not swim. The moment hung in deathly stillness, before Jean moved stiffly, removing his hand from his coat, his gaze unblinking.

"No, Mister Barty. You do not get to ask about that." His voice was soft, silken, but razor-edged. "Now come. We have wasted enough time talking about a dead woman." With that, he turned away, striding along the bridge.

For a moment, Barty stood there, still stung by the knife of those comments. Despite his pledge, despite the agreement, in that moment he felt that he could walk away. That he *should* walk away, collect his things at the Lodge, leave that comfortable chamber he had been shown and go back to the miserable cramped room he had lived in before. Find his answers somewhere else, find someone who might care about that small, broken hope. And to stop following a man who clearly cared about nothing, and no one, and himself least of all.

But the crack in the hunter's armour had been there. The slightest hint, under all the bitterness, of something else. It was faint and it was dying, but it was there. Barty had to know. He always had to know.

He hurried along after Reynard. But the rest of the journey to their destination passed in silence.

THE HOME of Doctor Ulysses Heathwood was on a well-kept street, with tidy, well-built houses lined up tightly side by side. Each of them were built precisely the same; narrow and tall instead of stretching out wide. They had front facing windows and the stones that built them were grey, with steps leading up to each entrance. Barty had trouble telling the differences between each, and would have missed the doctor's entirely had not Jean stopped at it. He glowered up at the building, then strode up the steps to the door.

The front door was a heavy, solid thing, painted black and set with a brass knocker. In the same hue of metal there was a nameplate, bearing the name of the occupant, alongside a slew of initials to denote things Barty did not have the time to decipher before Jean kicked the door in and marched inside.

Barty scrambled in, closing the door behind him with difficulty and hoping no one noticed. "You did not have to do that," he hissed, sweating suddenly. Try as he might, he could not get the door to close properly.

"The police had to break it down to get it open. Whoever

closed it since had jammed it shut," Jean growled over one shoulder. He was already heading upstairs, ignoring the living room to one side and the hall leading down to the back of the house. Barty did his best to balance the broken door, and headed up after him.

Reynard paused at the top of the stairs, sniffing the air. There was a thick scent on the air, copper and rot, and his gaze flicked to each closed door before he saw the one he wanted. A double door overlooking the stairs to the right, and beneath them, a rich carpet, stained black from where something had leaked from the other side of the doorway. Realisation dawned on Barty and he felt his gorge rising.

Jean paid no such delay. He strode to the door and opened it with both hands, standing still for a long moment as he took in the scene, before in a distant, absent tone, much as the one he had held on the roof with the corpse, he began to speak.

"Ulysses did not have any family. His passion for his work drove such things away and out of his mind." He stepped into the room, walking around something on the floor—a marked outline, of something the size of a football. "He was not an angry man, nor an impatient one. In truth, he had an excellent character, and listened avidly to someone as they spoke. He gave an excellent impression of being a very, very good listener, in that he endeavoured to make sure you felt heard."

Barty peered around the corner, feeling queasy. The room had a terrible smell to it that open windows and efforts to clean had not eliminated even slightly. It was the smell of old blood— a lot of it, the stench of metal and decay cloying in the air despite the excess of it being removed by half-hearted efforts to clean the room.

It was a study, that much was clear. A wide desk with a broad chair sat behind it, facing the door through which they had entered. A fireplace to one side, an open window to the other, and a multitude of bookshelves set above closed cabinets. The desk itself was ruined, covered in a thick layering of blood, which had caked over notes and books and other things that had once belonged to the late doctor, all for the purpose of his work. A long couch, much like the one Barty had woken on when he had fainted, was to one side, with the open window behind it. If it was not for the blood and the horror of the place, the room would have been welcoming, even satisfying in some way. But not now. Not any more.

Barty staggered, covering his mouth and nose with his sleeve. The smell was crawling *into* his nostrils, clawing its way down his throat. Jean showed no sign of distress at all. Indeed, his nostrils flared, sniffing the air, for whatever reason Barty did not dare to guess.

Regardless, Jean stood there for a long moment, silent in the middle of the room before he went on. "Doctor Heathwood was one of the few whom I felt comfortable talking to about this sort of thing. He was a great believer in hypnosis, and inducement to… understand trauma." A grim sort of smile formed on his lips, as he stared at the heavy chair. It, and the desk, had definitely taken the brunt of the gore, with blood painted up the walls behind it as well. "He felt that the root of all ills lay within the mind, and that all sickness in some fashion could be linked to the weakness of the mind—and the agony as well." One hand touched the desk lightly, as Barty stepped into the room. "He always liked to inflate the importance of his work." He shook his head. "Ahh, Uly." He sounded genuinely regretful. "What did you go and do this time?"

A new voice, a woman's, spoke then from behind them, making Barty jump almost as high as his heart, which leapt into his throat in a furious attempt to escape his body. "If I had to guess, he made an enemy of a gorilla. Perhaps a bear."

Her tone was as dry as her appearance. A woman of advancing years stood at the doorway, dressed in a businesslike gray dress with her hair pulled back severely. Glasses were balanced upon her nose and she held a satchel brimming with documents and tools to one side. She looked down those glasses now at Barty, her inspection the least dismissive he had received in days and easily the most uncomfortably perceptive. "Creek told me you had a new assistant, Reynard. Have you been feeding him at all?"

"There have been attempts," the hunter said offhandedly, turning to face the woman. He didn't seem surprised to see her. "He keeps getting upset and finding ways to spit it all back out again in the most uncouth manner possible." Despite this, a flicker of a smile formed, however sad it was. "It is good to see you again, Judith."

"That is Doctor Burrows, Chief Coroner of the Yard to you, young man," she replied with a complete lack of amusement, fixing Jean with a calculating stare that quickly assessed and filed away whatever findings it had made for later use. It did not linger long, however, as she looked around the room after a moment and shook her head. "Dreadful business this. And I've been looking at dreadful business for years."

Jean did not answer, but crouched down beside the chair. It was covered in a darkened lacquer of blood, roughly cleaned like most of the room but certainly not enough to get the stains out. The sheer amount that remained spoke of how much had been spread about, and Barty followed Jean's gaze up to the ceiling, quailing at the sight of dark splattering even there on the pale painted roof.

"He was alive when it happened," Jean said quietly. "Had to be quick for this much."

The coroner nodded, stepping adroitly into the room with an energy that was quite at odds with her years. "You can see it too, then. I thought for a moment that it had been a sword, or an axe perhaps. But no. No sign of it on the… wound, if you can call it that." Her face twisted in distaste as Jean raised a curious brow in her direction.

Barty did not want to ask. Of all the questions he had— and they were amassing in greater numbers by the hours— this one was one he did not want to delve into, but instinct overwrote reason. "Begging your pardon," he said in a faltering voice, staring with sick fascination at the splatter of blood on the ceiling. "But how do you know how… how fast it was? I mean…" He trailed off, unable to finish the sentence.

The coroner, Burrows, looked down her glasses at Barty a moment, before she spoke in the clinical tone of one reciting. "When a man is decapitated as Doctor Heathwood was, there is an enormous amount of blood exiting the corpse. However, if the death is sudden, then the pressure of blood within the body gives it excessive force in leaving it before that pressure subsides." She gestured to the roof, then, in a sweeping gesture that followed a pattern of blood from the ceiling, across the room, pointed at the ground beside Barty, one finger extended. "Hence the pattern we see here." Barty went white, and looked down to the outline denoting a ball-like object upon the ground, just near his foot. Burrows nodded dismissively, and moved to stand beside Jean, looming over him. "There was, as noted, no sign of a blade being used. His head was removed by force. Partly crushed in the process— there were fractures around the cheeks and eye sockets. Jaw was nearly torn off as well." She may as well have been discussing the weather, but then her expression flickered and her jaw tightened. "Ulysses did not deserve this." Her voice did not tremble, but there was a hardness to her gaze.

Jean ran one finger across the old, blood-soaked arm of the chair before him. "We never get to decide what we deserve, Judith. Least of all how we deserve to die." His tone was empty, dulled. Judith's expression shifted at that, looking down to the man in silence before she straightened up and stepped away, reaching into her satchel and pulling forth a cluster of typed out sheets with detailed notes scribbled upon it.

"Heathwood was the fourth. The rest were strange, but it was Heathwood that we really started to notice that something was going on." She began reading through each one. "Doctor Maximillian Stringer, Mr Joseph Crow, and Mr Eustace Thurston." Jean straightened and listened, his eyes on the ground, staring at seemingly nothing. "Stringer was found crushed under what looked like a masonry collapse at first. Crow was in a burned out house, but even a cursory examination showed that his bones more closely resembled crushed gravel. His head had been mashed flat." She shuddered. "Whoever it was that did it, they did not like him much."

Jean simply nodded, moving towards a wall behind the chair where Ulysses's body—most of it at least—had been situated. "And the last one?" he asked absently, even as his eyes moved rapidly, something Barty was sure only he noticed.

"Thurston," Burrows said with a grimace. "Impaled on a street light that came through his window and pinned him to a wall." She winced slightly. "They tried to write it off as a 'freak accident' involving perhaps a strong gust of wind." Her distaste was as palpable as her contempt.

Jean paused, his expression twisting into disbelief as he tilted his head to stare at Judith. "I would think *that* would attract some notice, Burrows." His tone was scathing.

The coroner rolled her eyes, huffing in annoyance. "Montague. He believed compartmentalising the cases would lead to 'improved focus' or something asinine like that. Made sure different sections handled different things, different cases, and we do not talk to each other." She shook her head. "The truth is, the same as it has always been with him. He does not want another Ripper case. If coppers start talking to each other, joining the dots, they would have seen this was all connected pretty damn fast. We would have seen that there was something bringing this all together."

"Ignoring the facts does not make them go away." Jean scowled.

Burrows nodded before she replied. "They do not, no. But try telling a politician that. Especially one wanting to be Prime Minister before he turns forty."

Jean grunted. He stood at the window, staring out into the daylight of the street, the sounds coming in from below. The ringing of bells to signal the hour were pealing off in the distance. He let them ring out before he started to speak.

"Whatever they are. Whoever they are… they're using the rooftops. They cannot move on the street, they cannot be seen. They do not want anyone to see them." He touched the window sill with one finger. "They're strong. They can climb rapidly, and they can tear a man to pieces with just their hands." He lifted the finger, rubbing thumb and forefinger together. "You know how much sheer torque is needed to pull a man's head off? That sure, that fast? Thousands of pounds of pressure. And Ulysses was a tough old bird." He frowned, turning back to the chair then. "Was there any sign of injury apart from the ones that killed him? Defensive wounds? He was seated right there, after all. Was he forced to sit?"

Burrows frowned, flicking through her sheets of paper before she answered, shaking her head once. "None. There were no other wounds on him, save some abrasions on his shoulder. The left shoulder."

Jean grunted. He stared at the chair where the corpse had once sat before speaking sharply. "Barty, get over here."

Numbly, the young man stepped over, and when standing close enough, Jean levelled a finger at the chair. "Sit."

Barty went stiff as his stomach turned a backflip in his belly. "Sit? On that? In *that*—" He was cut off abruptly as Jean seized him with inexorable strength and forced him to sit in the chair. It was heavy, high backed, and barely shifted as Barty sat on it, his entire body crawling as the thought of where he was sitting and what he was sitting *in* made him want to scream and pass out at the same time.

Jean stood over him, his right hand on Barty's left shoulder as he looked down at his charge. He looked down at Barty with an expression that made Barty quail. There was no mercy in that expression, nor was there anything resembling understanding. He did not even look fully present, his eyes focused not on Barty, but on a somewhere else that only he could see. Quietly though, his voice distant, Jean began to speak.

"He was sitting here. He was a thorough man. Tidy, like many men of his age are. Fastidious. He was going over the last notes before some other task, in all likelihood. Perhaps the last before going to bed." He closed both eyes, inhaling deeply. "He liked to keep the windows open. The restaurant across the street might have been cooking. Maybe it was a warm night and he wanted to let in the cold a little, breathe a little clearer. No need to worry, after all. High enough that it would not be a problem."

The grip on Barty's shoulder tightened and those eyes opened, gray and glittering with terrible intent. "Except this time it *was* a problem. They came in through the window, fast, too fast for him to react and run. They were on him quick, and enough to make his heart race. Something that he did not expect. *Someone* he did not expect. But—" His eyes widened. "He does not scream."

The coroner was shifting, seemingly uncomfortable at this, but she offered words regardless. "You think he froze up? Unable to react in time?"

"Perhaps," Jean said, but there was doubt in his tone. "Or maybe he knew them. Just did not expect them. Surprised as well as afraid, unable to get the words out. But there *was* something said. There was a moment, just a moment, where words passed between them. They spoke to one another, before…" He trailed off. Then his head tilted, and his expression changed. Clinical, calculating, with something else that made Barty's blood run cold. Jean's left hand closed over his face then, that iron grip closing in and squashing his nose down, painful but not yet crushing. Jean mimicked a wrenching motion, pulling his hand clear—a sweeping gesture that followed the spray of blood that had been pointed out before; recreating the moment that the unfortunate doctor had been murdered, with Barty as the unwilling participant in the display.

Barty sat there, gasping, his breath choked from him as he sat frozen in fright and unable to scream as Jean went on, his tone clinical. "Heathwood said the wrong thing. Whatever it was, the response was immediate. He never got the chance to correct his mistake." He stood there, with that dark look in his eye, the expression oddly speculative. He could have been imagining the scene or contemplating how to recreate it, but the way he looked *through* Barty without actually seeing him made his heart race in terror. For a moment, he wondered if he had said the wrong thing. Something about the whole situation filled him with fear, and he could not move as his heart threatened to rip its way out of his mouth.

"Enough!" Burrow's hand moved in a swift, sharp *smack* over Jean's wrist to punctuate her cry. He did not flinch, and with a seeming reluctance relinquished his grip and stepped away, as Burrows moved over to Barty, real concern, even anger, in her tone as she put a reassuring hand on Barty's back, causing him to flinch violently before he settled again. "That was not necessary, Jean. You did not have to do that and you know it." She helped the wobbly-legged Barty to his feet, as Jean shrugged, his back to the scene as he looked out the window once more.

"It helps me think like they do. Such things make my work much simpler. But spare Mister Barty your sympathy. He desired this, he just has not yet learned what it will cost."

Barty could not find the words. There was no space for anger, not yet. Too much conflict of feeling was seething inside him as his skin continued to crawl from the whole horrible experience. The coroner, no longer as reserved as she had first appeared, responded in a heated tone.

"Thinking like a monster is not a step removed from being one, Reynard. It makes you no different at all." The huntsman snorted at that, but he did not turn, his shoulders bunching tightly. Burrows glared at his back for a moment, as though wanting to say more before she let out her breath in exasperated anger, and helped Barty to stand properly, turning his head to face hers with a firm-fingered grip. "Breathe, young man," she said gently, holding his gaze until she felt satisfied that he had done just that. "Your name is Barty, correct?" He nodded. He did not trust himself to do much else at that moment, as she led him to a stool in one corner for him to sit himself down. Gratefully, it was one of the few things clear of blood in the place. "A pleasure. Doctor Judith Burrows, at your service." She placed the back of her fingers to his brow, and then moved them to his neck, touching the vein and counting. "Your heart rate is slowing. How is your breathing?"

Barty simply nodded, taking a shaking breath and letting it out. The whole thing had been simply disturbing.

"Good. Now sit here so I can berate this bastard of a man a while." Her tone was kind, at odds with her most unladylike speech, as she rounded on Jean, who stood like a man knowing it was coming but with no patience for it.

"I am sure you have a great many words to say to me, Judith, but this is not the time for them, and nor do I care." He cut her off sharp and cold before she got a word out. Whatever familiarity he had with her upon arrival was withering, and fast. "Instead of wasting both our time with advice I am not going to listen to, tell me something useful instead. What connection do the four men have? Tell me about them."

Burrows closer her mouth tightly. Her eyes flashed, then narrowed as she took the contents of the satchel that she was carrying and thrust it out to Barty, all the while keeping her eyes on Jean. He took the sheaf of papers, of reports both typed and handwritten, and held them in his hands dumbly as she went on.

"All the information on the victims is there. You can read it yourself, while I go off to think why on God's earth I thought to help you at all, if this is what you are doing to those under your responsibility." Her tone was flat. "You would think you would have learned *something* by now, Reynard."

Another man might have flinched, but Jean wrought himself of stone as those words were spoken. Burrows continued, her tone still scathing.

"I thought coming here myself would prove useful, I thought you *deserved* that much. But you have not changed at all, save to become worse. Now if you will excuse me, I have to learn the identity of the new body in the morgue."

"Lord George Foxgrove," Jean stated flatly. "Member of the House of Lords." He did not turn, but Burrows froze in step, her face going pale and her eyes wide. Barty wobbled.

He knew the name. But more than that, he realised something.

"You *knew* who it was the moment you saw him," Barty said in astonishment, surprise forcing the words out of him.

Jean nodded, still staring out the spacious window to the world beyond. "I did. Foxgrove was known as something of a hedonistic sort, for his attendance of parties and other indulgences." His tone was contemptuous. "Much like the rest of the House truth told, but yes. They likely do not yet think much of his failure to return because it is quite often expected." He turned from the window and walked over to pull the stack of sheets from Barty's unresisting hands. "Before you ask, I did not say anything because…" He raised a brow to Burrows, as he turned pages.

She wavered, then pinched the bridge of her nose. "Montague," she finally admitted bitterly. "You needed more time. When they figure out who it is…"

"If they cannot paint it as a suicide or misadventure, then the streets will turn to chaos," Jean said sourly, pausing on a page. "The police will come down on anything and everything. The lords dislike it when they are the ones bleeding."

"The one solace you have is that Montague may yet still refuse to treat them all as one case," Burrows muttered. She fixed Jean with a stare. "You know I need to go and report this, regardless. When I inspect the body, if I hide who it is…" She trailed off, but the meaning was clear. Jean, for his part, simply nodded and turned away once more.

Burrows slowly clenched and unclenched her fists, her jaw working. "I will return to my work then, Reynard. I hope you have all that you need." She went to walk away, but paused at the threshold. She did not look back. "I truly wish that I was glad to see you again. And I am not the only one." With that she moved on, and in a moment her purposeful stride had carried her from sight.

Jean said nothing, but Barty could see the comment stung him in some way. The room lingered in silence for a while. The hunter had stopped reading his notes, and stared at the floor for a while.

"I would ask that you never do that to me again."

Barty had trouble saying the words, but forced them out anyway. "I do not even understand the point of it." It got easier to speak, as he remembered the look on Jean's face as he had looked through him. It reminded him of the look the hunter had given the burning body of Clickerclack. He shuddered at the realisation, nauseated.

"That is your own shortcoming, Mister Barty. Not mine." Jean's voice was cold as he moved then to the wall behind the desk, as though examining the trail of blood once more. "It is my task to see what others either cannot, will not, or simply do not know to look for. And that means looking at things others do not have the stomach for."

Barty pushed himself to his feet, feeling heavy as he did it. "And what did making me feel like that achieve then?"

"A few things," Jean said absently, still with his back to Barty as he inspected the blood-marked wall with an intent gaze. "I know how our killer gets around. I know his targets are not random, though I do not know how they are connected. I know they knew who Doctor Heathwood was, and I know they are likely left-handed and probably around the size of an average person." He gestured idly to the window. "There is a mark on the window where a foot stood. Pressure from a strong movement marking the wood, but if they were much larger they would not have been able to fit without causing excess damage." He waved his left hand in the air. "The blood pattering shows that most likely the body was facing the direction I sat you in, and if it was, from where it was facing then the killer used their left hand—likely the dominant one. This was something they did quickly, without thinking." He paused then. Barty said nothing. He could not help but feel like it still had been unnecessary.

"Doctor Burrows is brilliant," Jean went on, as he crouched at the wall, gazing down at the floor. "Absolutely, inarguably so. She fought to the top of her field when it was dominated by men who, while being very clever themselves, were too stupid to see just how much better she is than all of them." He ran one hand over the floor, barely touching it as Barty drew closer, and continued on. "Even if she does not have the respect she yet deserves, she certainly has mine. She does not need it, nor would she ask for it, such is the determination of her character. But she shall always have it, regardless. Her brilliance is that she will always find what is there, no matter how hidden. She is able to see the most insignificant of details completely. But"—his fingers stopped moving—"she is like most people, in that she is trying so hard to see what is *there* that she misses what is *not*."

Keeping the fingers of one hand in place, the other hand slid up the wall with a faint sound, until he pressed inwards firmly. There was a loud *click* and then a line that was not previously visible appeared, and shifted. As Barty watched in astonishment, the wall itself swung outwards smoothly with barely a sound, opening up into a small, narrow antechamber. There was a small counter, upon which were piled what looked like books and gathered stacks of paper and notes. The whole space, if it could be called that, was only three feet deep, and about as much across.

As Barty gaped, Jean went on in a distant tone. "The blood did not pool here, against the skirting." He gestured idly to his feet. There was a spreading, dark stain of congealed blood. "There was a gap in the seam that ran through, but there was no blood soaking through downstairs. It had to go somewhere. And despite efforts to clean things, the smell remained." He stepped forward, running a hand through his hair as he sighed. "Canny old fox, Ulysses. What were you hiding this time?"

Barty drew alongside, and after a moment, both of them reached out to grasp the simple folders that contained whatever documentation the doctor had been concealing. Barty flicked through handwritten notes as Jean slowly turned pages on more official looking, typed out documentation, found laying next to the typewriter that they were clearly processed by.

"This appears to be notes on hypnotism," Barty said with confusion, reading faster. His shock was wearing off fast. Something about this revelation had galvanised him, instead making the adrenaline useful. "Hypnotism with an induced chemical effect, and the result of it." He could not keep the confusion out of his voice as he continued to read. "I see a great deal of initials that he references to… other researchers, subjects, I think. He does not use names."

"Same here. Both his own shorthand in, perhaps, an effort to keep things hidden." Jean's frown deepened as he read. "Some of these notes go back over a decade and more. He was working on this for quite a while."

Barty nodded, turning another page. "Clearly. But I cannot make any sense of it. Listen to this… 'Subject B.W. shows promise of addressing regressive behaviour changes becoming less commonplace, exhibiting self control of the *lupis canis minoris* that otherwise would become untenable during the height of the lunar cycle'—" Jean cut him off by snatching the piece of paper out of his hands, his expression turning rigid.

Barty bristled, but bit down on his tongue. "I assume you know something? Or had you gone too long between doing something rude and just had to do *something* about it?" He could not keep the acid from his tongue, but Jean paid him no mind, his words coming from between clenched teeth.

"*Lupis canis sapiens, minoris* refers to bastard offspring of werewolves." He nearly snarled the words, biting back rage. "B.W… B.W, if it's him…" He trailed off, and started going through the typed out sheets, discarding ones as he went, furiously searching for something. Barty was shaken, but he was not sure he had heard correctly.

"I beg your pardon, but did you say *werewolves?*" The disbelief was total in his voice as he said it, and he even wiggled a finger in his ear to make sure he heard it right.

But Jean was *angry* now, as though the mere discussion of it had set him off. He kept talking, striding and discarding paper as he went. "I can see it now… Ulysses, why you did not tell me about this, you bloody fool. How long have you been at it, I wonder? Did *he* set you on this?" he snarled, then wrenched out a piece of paper, and glowered at it. "There you are. I knew it, I *knew it.*" His eyes flashing with fury, he shook the piece of paper. "B.W. I know who you are, you little *wretch.*" He shoved it into his coat. "We have what we need. We are leaving." Spat out, and striding away, as Barty futilely tried to gesture to the hidden filing room and the discarded paper. But Jean was already moving, heading to the stairs and on, that relentless force of momentum which drove him putting fire to his step and hate in his breath.

Barty stood, torn for a moment. Caught between wanting to remain, to follow… and to leave. The room felt darker now when it was just him in it, and for a heartbeat that seemed to drag on forever he trembled with the desire, once again, to just *leave.* To get clear of this madness and this terrible man.

You have to know, the voice told him again, and he shuddered. *There's so much you do not know yet. About all of it.*

There was no time, but he acted regardless. Crouching down, he gathered up every note that he could, shoving them together quickly. As he was scooping up the sheets that Jean had discarded, he noticed something peeking out from between a cluster of pages.

It was an old photograph, with people he did not know. They were gathered as though in discussion, gesturing towards a figure that was strapped into a chair. The figure strapped down was blurry, indistinct, clearly in the midst of frantic movement that the photograph could not cleanly capture; the time of the exposure was long enough to turn them into a blur of silent, frenzied effort. Barty could not explain why, but it made him feel incredibly uncomfortable.

He shoved it into his vest, picked up every piece of disordered paper he could carry, and hurried out of the room, leaving the crawling scent of blood behind, knowing it would follow him, and in the quiet of solitude, it would catch up with him eventually.

Jean had not waited. Barty was only able to tell the direction he had gone by seeing a well-dressed, middle-aged man sat dazedly upon the ground further up the street holding his nose, blood streaming between his fingers. He looked completely confused, while people pointed further along the street. Hoping he was not about to lose his grip on his papers, Barty took a chance and sprinted on after the pointing fingers.

He found him stalking along, filling the air around him with growled out muttering. Barty scrambled after him, and seized Jean by the shoulder. He spun like he'd been burned, teeth bared, and his fist raised up quick as a whip. For a moment, the heart-stopping instant before that hammer blow fell, Barty did not think he even *saw* him, from the way his eyes burned. But then Jean blinked rapidly, and settled, sagging. His expression shifted from rage to confusion, before he looked to his clenched fist, opening it and shaking his hand slightly.

He started to say something, closed his hand again, and shook his head to clear it. Then he began to speak, but his tone was uncharacteristic in that it was suddenly subdued, veering wildly from rage to sombreness, even regret, before Barty could understand it.

"I will explain later. For now, we shall need to be off." There came a whistle in the distance. The man with the bloodied face had alerted the police. "Now would be *most opportune*." Jean started striding away in an instant. Barty once more wondered why he was following him, even as he set off after the huntsman. He was starting to wonder if there even was an answer.

CHAPTER 8

REAL AND UNREAL

Barty was worn out by the time they made it back to the Lodge, passing again through a series of alleyways and narrow streets that soon turned his head around; despite his belief he knew London fairly well, this was proven thoroughly wrong with how much difficulty he had keeping track of the way. Jean, for his part, had no such qualms, and had kept the path easily, until they once more passed the horseshoe doorknocker of the Lodge and headed inside.

Barty had managed to get the documentation into a fairly compact stack by the time they reached the door, but he worried just how much work it would take to reorder again. Jean paid no attention to it. As he strode inside, he started speaking again as he moved to the stairs, this time descending, where Barty had not yet gone.

"*Lupis canis sapiens*," he growled out, and then counted off three fingers. "Ranging from *minoris, majoris,* and *extremis.* Easier to call them werewolves, though." The descending stairs led to darkened corridors below ground level, the sounds becoming muted as Jean went on, continuing to *another* descending stair that promised to go significantly deeper. "Shapeshifters, for the most part. Part human, part wolf, all dog." He spat with contempt. "And all of them deserving of a bullet."

Barty listened, but could not help but notice that Jean remained furious. It was as though the very mention of these beings—though admitting such creatures existed made him question his sanity—filled Jean with a towering fury. Barty said nothing. He was afraid of what would happen if he did.

"They have existed in society for a long time. Difficult to ascertain how they originated, but the first legends are undoubtedly French. People who turn into wolf monsters during a full moon. They have nearly been eradicated, and then returned, several times in history." His expression flickered, a snarl forming. "Unfortunately, over time they formed into a more rigid society. Clans and the like, trying to work in human society, or so they claimed."

"Claimed?" Barty could not help but ask. Jean did not answer.

Upon reaching a metal double door, he opened it sharply, revealing a rather cramped metal lined chamber with a strange, gear set crank in the centre. He stepped in, pointing for Barty to take a corner.

As Barty apprehensively stepped inside, Jean slid the door shut, and inspected a panel on the crank. To Barty, it looked like a hand crank of some sort of larger mechanism, as Jean flicked a glass panel set to one side of it, nodding. He then gripped a handle of the crank and yanked on it.

The floor lurched, and Barty felt his stomach rise as a loud mechanical grinding filled the room, and then the chamber began to move. He could not see outside of it, but could tell what was happening—they were in an elevator, and descending downwards, a fact that left Barty blinking and looking around in astonishment. He was familiar with such devices, even though they were rare, but this was entirely new. Normally they were something that went *up* but not in this case.

Watching the gauge and a descending number set into it, Jean continued. "They are the product of a curse. It has spread and warped as the centuries have passed, but it is a curse nevertheless, passed in bloodline or afflicted infection. It warps the mind and the body both, changing them and their perspective completely. And in the case of many, the curse drives them insane." He stopped then, his jaw working.

Barty swallowed, and tried to volunteer. "I... growing up, there were fairy tales about such things." It was not much, but he had to say something, to drag the hunter back. He had seen that distant look too many times today already.

Jean started, blinked, then nodded. He did not speak at first, but it soon became apparent that it was because they had reached their destination as, with a firm push, he set the crank back into place.

"They are very dangerous. Very strong, very fast, and all but invulnerable to practical weapons. But yet they *are* vulnerable. And to exploit that vulnerability"—he stepped to the double door and pushed it open before continuing—"we need armaments."

Well, thought the stunned Barty as he blinked. *They certainly have that covered.*

The chamber they had opened up to was lit by glowing bulbs, set into the walls, each humming faintly. It was massive, easily twice the size of the house above and extending from the elevator off into gloom. The walls were solid brick, the roof reinforced and high. And it held enough weaponry to outfit a battalion, in the most bizarre arsenal Barty could ever imagine.

There were racks set with what appeared to be suits of armour, most entirely antique, but many others seemed almost modern in their application. There were firearms; various forms of pistols and long arms, from revolvers to flintlocks, muskets, rifles, shotguns, and crossbows. Other things that Barty simply did not know how to name—there was one exquisitely crafted weapon that appeared to have the rotating chamber of a revolver, but the bullets it held looked to be the size of a shotgun shell, and the handle and form of the weapon was closer to an old, heavy flintlock with a long, straight grip. To top it off, underneath the barrel was a shining silver axe blade. It looked both completely impractical, beautifully made, and terrifically murderous at the same time.

And it was far from the strangest thing to be found. Swords, axes, maces, daggers and more besides, from all periods of history and all forms of make as well. Delicate, thin-bladed rapiers sat alongside German zweihanders, massive blades designed to break pike formations.

There were also various apparatus and devices akin to what might be found in a laboratory, some of which were holding slow moving liquid, and some boiling under direct, gas lit flame, giving the place a chemical scent that blew up into vents above. There were stone slabs with, what Barty realised with discomfort, were drain gutters around them, for the examination of corpses, as found in a morgue, save that some were much larger than he had ever seen before. There were diagrams on the walls of human anatomy—and other things that were most certainly *not*. Books, devices, machines, and weapons, over and over again, more and more of them, ones Barty could recognise and ones he most certainly could not, that nevertheless filled him with disquiet at the sense of menace they projected, despite how innocent some could appear. If it was not for the fact they were behind lock and key in heavily barred cabinets, he might not have thought much of them; a blackened mirror, a locked book, an archaic metal gauntlet lined in gold. All in all, this place was full of fantastical mysteries, ones which he could spend a lifetime investigating.

Jean watched his reaction, a grim look on his face that held a touch of a knowing on it, and perhaps even a smile, however bitter it might have been. He nodded in under-standing at Barty's stunned expression, then stepped within and raised his voice. "I see you've made yourself at home already."

Barty had not seen them, but the giant Adam loomed out of the shadows at the opposite end of the chamber. They raised a hand in greeting, cheerfully, while at the same time, even from the distance they were at, Barty could see that they held a rod of metal in their other, bare hand. Metal that was glowing red hot, to the point it was visibly sagging under its own weight.

"Are they…" Barty could not keep the shock from his voice as Adam turned away to whatever he was working on, obscured in the racks and rows between them.

Jean continued on, keeping his voice raised. "What are you working on now? A toothpick?"

A rumbled snort answered him as Jean and Barty both drew closer, before Adam called back over their shoulder. "See for yourself, Reynard. I would be happy to explain it, if I thought you could understand a word I was saying."

The area Adam was working in was hot, significantly more so than the rest of the armoury and it was immediately obvious as to why. A forge, heavily reinforced and yet putting out great heat was before Adam, who stood before it unphased in their massive, stitched together coat, turning the metal rod in their hands in an opening into the fire itself.

There was an anvil and work table, both of them festooned with tools. Beyond the forge, the chamber continued on, but on into darkness, without lighting. Barty could not tell how far the tunnel went, but from the way the voices of his two companions echoed and bounced off the walls down into its depths, he wagered quite a ways.

"I have been working on it for weeks, but it was mostly theoretical," Adam went on in that rich voice of his. "Much of it is using Gavric's principle of thaumometallurgy from the 13th century, combined with Hephaestus' theory of unmaking, designed by Ullios in 600BC. Or thereabouts." Barty did not know about Jean, but he *certainly* had no idea what the giant was on about.

"Interesting," Jean said slowly. He eyed pieces of already shaped metal lying on the anvil. "Correct me if I am wrong, Adam, because it has been some time… but both of those theories laid out that it is in fact impossible to create alloy out of the real and the unreal. And yet, you appear to be attempting that."

"Quite so!" Adam said cheerfully. Within the forge there was a glow now, that was not the red-hot glow of fire and melting metal. There was an odd mixture of blue, white, and green in there as well, flashing into one or the other quickly. "I created a cage around a foci, and now I am attempting to—"

The glow flared suddenly, and there was a *thump* as air pressure suddenly, and violently, shifted. The forge suddenly— impossibly—went completely and totally dark. All heat was robbed out of the air instantly, as the forge itself went entirely cold. There was nothing save for a faint hissing sound, and the *plink* of rapidly cooling metal.

Adam sighed. "Well, I certainly was not attempting *that*." They carefully eased the metal rod out of the depths of the forge. At the end of it was a point of light that seemed to *vibrate*, nearly obscuring the webwork of metal surrounding what Barty thought might be a gem of some kind. It was dim at first, but as he watched, it started to glow brighter and brighter, gradually but with increasing speed.

"Gentlemen, please excuse me," Adam said cordially, but Jean was already moving, stepping sharply back several paces and behind what appeared to be a conveniently, but worryingly, placed blast shield of heavy iron. Barty did not question. He simply followed, as Adam cast a speculative gaze on the vibrating glowing stone at the end of the rod for a long moment, and then, as a whining sound was heard as of pressure reaching breaking point, they tossed it down the tunnel.

Adam's movements seemed almost nonchalant as they performed a flicking throw from their shoulder, as one might do to throw a small stone or other playful, lazy gesture. But the glowing rod shot from their hand with enough force that it created a *tearing* sound in the air, faster than an arrow, as it plunged into the tunnel with the velocity of a gunshot, almost vanishing out of sight into the tunnel depths, where it exploded. With extraordinary force.

The entire tunnel, Barty quickly realised, was heavily reinforced for a reason. The noise was catastrophic, and the walls and roof shook with the power that had been unleashed. The thump of the blast shocked him so much that he gasped all the air out of his lungs, as the tunnel flared as bright as daylight for an instant, before it winked out into complete darkness, the air full of dust. All of the glowing globes lining the wall went out.

Over the ringing in his ears, Barty faintly heard Adam sigh. "I truly believed I had it that time."

Jean pushed himself to his feet, coughing through the falling dust, and the lights on the walls flickered and came back to life. "Evidence, I fear, speaks directly to the contrary."

Barty could not manage words as he sputtered the thick brick dust away and shivered in fear. Jean helped him to his feet by dragging him upright and pounded on his back with one hand until the dust cleared. "However, it did not kill us all, so that is progress, at least."

Adam made a sound at that, not quite a chuckle, not quite a sigh. They shook their head and turned back to the pair, a fearsome figure looming out of the cloud of dust. Adam straightened themselves and their coat, speaking in that rumble that bounced off walls and carried on forever. "So, I assume you did not come here to witness my failures. What have you learned that the police could not?"

Jean grunted, and pulled out the piece of paper he had kept—the only one, in fact—while Barty carefully put down his collected files to one side on a bare spot of table. "The night of the murder, Heathwood was meeting with a special client," Jean explained. "He was treating non-humans, in secret, using hypnosis as a method for them to control their impulses." He gestured with contempt to the piece of paper. "He believed the application of such treatment and perhaps the use of drugs could control the bestial instincts of his subjects, and allow them to function normally in society." He growled, angrily. "In effect, I would say he was simply making it easier for them to hunt."

Adam raised one brow slowly, their entire misshapen face twisting weirdly as they did so, looking down at the sheet. "This one, B.W? This file says they were trying to become more human in their behaviour, to control it. How would that apply to them 'hunting' in any way?"

"Because it is a werewolf, same as all the rest, Adam," Jean snapped, eyes flashing. "The better they can control their instincts, the better that they can get close to those that they can prey upon. He was not teaching them how to be normal people. He was teaching them to lie better, but could not see it."

Adam made a sound, non-committal, as they read the sheet. It could have been accepting, it could have been disbelieving. It was hard to tell. They paused. "The description of them is here as well, alongside their initials. You do not think it is…" They sounded surprised. Jean barked a laughed.

"I know it is. Of course it is. And that means he is here in London. And if he is in London, I know where he is going. Same place as I am."

Adam put down the piece of paper firmly, and stabbed a monstrous finger down on it to pin it in place. "Jean, you *cannot* go down there. You know how they all feel about you. About us." Their voice was firm, harsh even.

Jean simply shrugged, and turned to start walking through the racks. "I know the mongrel will not come to me. So, I need to go to him, and that means going to the Under." He opened a case, frowned, and closed it again. "Have you finished it? You know what I am talking about."

Adam remained stiff, saying nothing for a long moment, before they pointed wordlessly at a black steel case sitting alone on a worktable. Jean strode over towards it, with a sort of eagerness to his step that contrasted starkly to Adam's hesitation, even dread.

Barty had been holding his questions, simply listening before he turned to Adam. "Where is he going? What is the Under?"

Adam opened their mouth, but it was Jean who answered. "*We*, Mister Barty. We are going together. At least us two. Adam I know will have objections I cannot overcome." He was carefully lifting something from the case, consisting of several cylinders. Barty could not see it fully as the hunter continued, "We are going to the place where the monstrous live, so that those who walk in the world do not have to bear their countenance." He moved on, heading deeper into the racks of the arsenal, with an almost cheerful final call over his shoulder. "We are going to the Undercity."

Barty was, to put it mildly, baffled by this, so he turned to Adam, hoping that they would have more answers. Adam's expression was uncharacteristic in its tension, and they gave Barty a warning look. "You should refuse him. Stay here where it is safe." They tried to keep quiet, but Adam managing to be quiet was a thing of tragic fiction.

Jean heard it and barked, "He cannot. Not if he wants what he is chasing after." There was a clattering and clanging in the racks as he went on. "Your first steps to truth are before you, Mister Barty. Turn from them now and you will never have another chance. Of that, you have my word."

Barty was quiet. He then sighed, sagging, and for Adam that was enough. When Barty finally turned towards them, the giant was picking up the pieces of worked metal they had on the anvil, inspecting them sadly next to the dead forge. They did not look at Barty, but clearly felt the weight of his gaze as they spoke.

"Do be careful down there, Mister Barty. Keep close to his side and do not get separated." They set the pieces down and gave him a look that could only be called regretful, as though they saw a future they were afraid to admit to even themselves. "It is rare that I make friends at all. I would not lose a new one so swiftly."

Barty's blood ran cold. Adam said nothing more. They turned and walked off into the depths of the tunnel, where they had hurled the device they had built, leaving Barty alone with his thoughts.

CHAPTER 9

THE UNDER

The sewers of London were an astonishing feat of engineering. Built in antiquity by the Romans, they yet endured, were expanded upon, and shifted. Barty had never made a habit of traversing them, but now, as he did so in Jean's wake, he had to admit they were far more complex than he could've imagined. They stretched off in all directions, a maze of tunnels, cisterns, wells, and more besides. If the place had not borne the smell it did, it might have been interesting to study.

Unfortunately, it did have a smell. It had many, and all of them unpleasant. The smell of tanneries, of factories, of refuse and waste and the stark ammonia of human existence, all flowing together towards the river and the sea beyond. It was more than unpleasant, in all honesty. It was overpowering.

Jean led the way. Barty wondered if he should have felt surprised that he seemed to know precisely where he was going, but at this point the man was surprising him less and less with how he behaved. The outburst of anger that he had displayed back at the murder scene of Doctor Heathwood was now under control again; he moved with that same menacing, watchful purpose he had used before, carrying the bullseye lantern he had used in the church to lead the way with minimal light.

He had offered Barty a gun back at the arsenal. Barty had refused it, which had earned him a look of amusement, bordering on acidic contempt, but Jean had not argued the point. Perhaps he had not needed to, because Jean himself had enough weapons on him for them both.

He had swapped the coat out for another, except this one was much heavier and bulkier. It was armoured, Barty soon could see—fine but archaic chainmail lined the interior of it in select places, as well as metal plates that were part of the shoulders. He had a revolver, a sword, daggers, and what appeared to be a shotgun the size of a rather large handgun, the two barrels set atop each other, the barrel and stock cut right down. In short, Barty was extremely glad they had not taken the open street; they likely would not have gotten far with him as heavily armed as this without attracting attention.

For his part, Jean seemed to revel in this. He seemed more complete, more *real* as he moved swiftly through the tunnels. There was a boldness to his movement, like that of a stalking animal, that even in his most arrogant dayside wanderings would not match. He no longer had to conceal the truth of himself and the nature of his profession. Much like the things that he hunted, he could only be what he truly was out of sight of the rest of the world. The realisation was not a comforting one for Barty.

They were descending, going ever further into both the tunnels and the earth, which surprised Barty. The nature of water being what it was, when they descended past the water-line of London, he expected there to be more of the same.

But the sewers continued to confuse him as they controlled seemingly even the most excessive flow of water from the ever-raining skies of London away from these strange, hidden paths.

It started to get confusing very quickly—a ladder, a narrow path next to an abyss with whistling wind coming from below, a twisting tunnel that turned for seemingly no obvious reason, cycling downwards in a continual curve, and then stepping through what looked like a hole in a wall. He kept right on Jean's tail, taking Adam's advice to his heart. If he got separated here, let alone in the place that they were trying to find, he would never make it out again. A pile of mouldering bones huddled in a pitch black corner in the depths of the earth was the fate that awaited so much as a single wrong step.

Because of this, he walked into Jean the moment he stopped abruptly, letting out a very undignified squeak. Jean stood grimly, staring at what the lantern light had illuminated —the way was barred before them. A seemingly solid wall of blackened metal, crude in its construction but nevertheless heavy and impenetrable. It appeared nothing but a mass, absorbing all light and denying all entrance, save for a narrow culvert at its base to allow water through. Jean stared at it, his brow knitting, before he seemed to get an idea. He turned to Barty at his side, his expression almost entirely concealed in the gloom. "Do me the honour, Barty. Go over there and knock, could you? I shall wait here."

Barty looked baffled. "Are you sure? There is no door that I can see—maybe it is just blocking the way? Should we keep looking instead—" His arguing was cut off as Jean lost patience and pointed the lantern's beam into Barty's face, causing him to wince and blink as he was blinded by the change in light.

"Barty," Jean intoned, his voice flat. "Cease the prattle.

Get over there. And knock." He said each word clearly and steadily, then pointed the lantern back at the black blockade.

Barty had to bite his tongue as he squinted, his vision so distorted by the rapid change in light that he struggled to make anything out for a few moments. Eventually he staggered forward, balled up one fist and, imagining that he was instead pounding on the face of the man who stood behind him, thumped on the black iron.

He immediately regretted putting so much force into it. The iron was much stronger than he was, and his hand hurt. The knock created a hollow, clanging sound that echoed on the other side, and then there was silence. Barty was about to turn away and demand Jean do it when he thought he heard movement—and a few heartbeats later his suspicion was proven correct as, around his waist, a metal slot slid open with a sharp, ear-piercing screech of metal scraping on metal.

A nasal voice rang out from behind it, irritable and no nonsense. "Hand up." It was high in tone, but there was a growl to it. It did not sound like it came from a person.

Barty was confused and more than a little frightened. Without knowing what else to do, he put his hands up slowly. This did not seem to have the desired effect as, for a good handful of seconds, nothing happened.

The voice spoke again, slowly, as though talking to a simpleton. "Hand. Up. To the slot," they recited clearly. "But I can already bloody well tell you, you are not going to get in."

Barty smarted at this, but did as he was told. He brought his hand up to the slot, but hesitated as he got closer. He was not sure he liked this.

It turned out he did not need to, because something was poked through the slot. It took Barty a moment to realise it was a nose—an extremely long one, akin to the snout of a rat more than a human nose, some six inches long, pointed and narrow. It was girded by whiskers, and snuffled at the air, the nostrils twitching and flaring. He flinched away, but the being retracted its nose and snorted in disgust. "Bugger off, topsider," spat the voice, before the door slammed shut with a screech.

Jean was grinning. Barty did not even need to see his expression to know he was, a nasty, knowing grin that enjoyed watching him make a fool of himself. As Barty retreated, shamefaced and frustrated, Jean strode forward and, with a much louder sound than before, pounded on the wall again. There was curses in response to this on the other side of the wall, and then the metal slot wrenched open. "Hand up to the slot, but if it is the same smell as last time, I'll make a meal of your kneecaps straight after."

Jean said nothing, but held his hand out, as Barty had before. The nose snuffled again, the ritual performed once more, then froze mid-sniff.

Quick as a snake, Jean's hand wrapped around the nose and *pulled*. There was an agonised squeal on the other side of the wall as Jean, still holding the long nose in an iron grip, squatted down and pulled a revolver free with his left hand. He stuck the barrel through the slot, cocking back the hammer with a click. Everything went very quiet as, whomever the sniffer was, they now had a black barrel sticking directly at their eye socket.

"You should not be here." The voice on the other side of the wall was small now. The threats of devouring parts of legs were long gone, the irritation also, all swallowed up by dread. "Please…. I… I didnae mean it, Reynard." They were pleading, clearly knowing who it was that they were being held by, and knowing, quite a bit better than even Barty it seemed, just how bad a situation this was to be in.

"Open the door, Wickermont," Jean said slowly. He did

not move. "Or I will find another way in. You know I will. Save us both the trouble." There was a grinding sound as he closed his hand holding the long nose, and a whining, sobbing whimper was the response.

Barty could not help but shudder. He felt sick. The agonised sound was piteous, and Barty could clearly tell that they were not very large. A small, and in this moment, helpless figure caught in cruelty.

There was a clank of metal, and then a grinding sound of the metallic kind. A seam appeared and then moved, and the door swung outward a fraction. Jean did not let go of the nose whatsoever, and jerked his chin towards the opening. "Get that, Barty. And do not let it from your grip."

Numbed, Barty stepped forward, and seized the door frame. He felt the door shift, along with a sudden cry of agony, and then the door shifted open in a jolt as whatever tension was holding it in place released. The great black iron door swung easily, and Barty could see beyond clearly.

The tunnel continued, but then dropped out into an open expanse a short way beyond where they now stood. Crude wooden scaffolding had been put in place with steps at the edge, lit by a melted down candle. Before them, huddled in the gap between the barrier and the descent, was a little makeshift shelter, made of debris and ragged cloth, keeping a small fire concealed. A figure was sat upon the ground, and Barty could not help but stare at them.

They were as tiny as Adam was enormous. A short figure that was barely three feet tall, that would have been thought a child if not for the fact that their appearance was very clearly not that of one. It was not that of a human at all.

They had large, pouchy eyes that were almost too large for their face, and ears that were long and upswept, twitching as Barty watched. The nose, as promised by the sight at the slot, was incredibly long and dominated the face. Their torso was small, the arms and legs gangly and more substantially built, to give the entire form a very twisted appearance. The skin was pale, but black hair sprouted wildly from their head, and they were dressed in crude clothes. Those huge eyes were bloodshot and wet with tears as they sat on their rump on the ground, clutching that gigantic nose with both hands, crying softly.

The tears cut off as Jean pushed Barty within and strode into the tunnel, closing the great iron door with a clank behind him. The pained expression twisted into outright fear instead as they scrambled back. Jean gave them no chance to escape, but strode over to the figure—Wickermont—and squatted down in front of them, to bring his head more level with their own.

"No running now, Wickermont." Jean's voice was quiet, but menace rang from every syllable.

The figure sobbed, shivering as it rocked back and forth. "Please, Reynard, I didnae do nothing, please donae be hurting me!" they babbled, terrified. Jean snorted, shaking his head, but Barty felt a great well of pity for them. More and more, Barty wondered just how many deserved to be on the wrong side of Jean.

The hunter carried on, regardless. "I am not making that promise. But I can make you an offer in its stead—in fact, if you do not run, do not go tell anyone we are here, I shall well make it worth your while." He held up his right hand, showing something small and glittering clutched between thumb and forefinger, reflecting the faint firelight.

Wickermont froze, releasing their reddened snout, which twitched as it sniffed the air. Once, twice. "That's topaz," they said, a note of confusion beyond the dread.

Jean nodded. "Good cut. Clear. Holds the light well—I

know you knockers have your tastes." The knocker also nodded, wringing their overly large hands together, trapped between fear and naked greed, leaning forward as their nose sniffed eagerly. "Let us in, raise no alarm, and when I come back I'll have another two of the same, Wickermont. What do you say?"

The knocker struggled with it a while, then spoke in a pouting, hurt voice. "This is never going to come back to me, is it?" Their gaze remained on the stone Jean kept clearly in sight, their large eyes glittering with a want that was almost hunger. Jean nodded. Wickermont sighed, rubbed his nose, and seemed to relax a bit. "You know, you could have led with that, Reynard."

Jean nodded pleasantly, holding out the gemstone. Wickermont reached for it, but instead of simply placing it in the knocker's hand, he grabbed them by the wrist and dragged them close, the pleasant tone turning harsh.

"If anything goes awry, and I think you are to blame for it, I *will* make my way back to you eventually, Wickermont. And when I do, I will bring something far less to your liking. Are we clear?" His grip tightened with an audible grinding of the leather glove, causing Wickermont to cry out in pain again, huddling down like a whipped dog. Jean watched him for a moment, then released his grip. The tiny Wickermont clutched the gemstone he had been given and, with a hurt, frightened expression, scuttled backwards into their shelter. Looking up at Jean in trepidation, their gaze tore from him briefly to Barty, then back to Jean, as they huffed anxiously.

"Mind yourself down there, mister," he said in that growling whine of a voice, massaging their wrist as they stared up at Jean fearfully, speaking to Barty. "There's all sorts down there. And you're with the worst of them all."

Jean gave that barking, single laugh that was no humour

and all bitterness as he straightened up, walking away. "He is well aware, Wickermont. We shall be back." He strode off to the scaffold staircase, and started making his way down it quickly.

Barty looked after him, then back to the huddled knocker, who returned the gaze. He tried to say something, tried to apologise, but the hurt look on the little creature's face told him it would not matter. Then Jean shouted his name, impatient, and he shook his head to follow.

At least, that was his intention. For once he reached the scaffold, and was able to see out to the expanse it descended into, he was unable to stop himself from gaping.

The cavern was enormous—hundreds of yards across, a great circular chamber, it was lit with fires and other glimmering lights. Though they were about a hundred feet above it, they were not the only opening into the place; there were other tunnels leading into the chamber, some with similar staircases and some pouring water into gaping boiling cisterns beneath them.

And the chamber itself was far from empty. It was overflowing with crude structures, layered on top of each other and built in a ramshackle network of walkways and paths, a great connected warren more akin to a rat's nest. There were fires all over the place, lighting interiors and exteriors, with dark moving shapes that scuttled from one to the other and kept to the shadows. Some of the dilapidated constructs seemed far more permanent, and far more solidly built; others looked to be put together by any sort of means necessary. There was no rhyme nor reason to it, and it was as close to chaos in design that Barty had ever seen.

Jean was not slowed by Barty's gawping. Remembering Adam's advice back at the lodge, Barty put his astonishment aside and raced down the shaking, wobbling steps to catch up with him. If Jean went into that maze, out of his sight, he would lose him in a heartbeat.

Falling in beside him at the bottom of the staircase, Barty kept in step while looking in every direction. He could make out figures that slunk deeper into the shadows at their approach, some of them normal shaped, or so it seemed. Some small, like Wickermont, or in between. And some large… too large. They passed a crude alleyway where Barty heard a sound like sand being poured, and a great form—large as a cart—shifted in the darkness, moving vast bulk as it set a pair of blazing eyes glowering out from the gloom, giving a volcanic hiss. Barty hurried on from it, not wanting to see the rest of whatever the thing was.

"What *are* they?" It was a stupid question, but in the shock of finding out there was an entire town beneath the city, stupid questions were all that he had.

Jean shrugged, his stride impatient as he strode down the twisting, winding street like he owned it. Slinking shapes vanished from his path, to reform behind him akin to the wake of a ship. He grunted in response to Barty's question, before answering.

"Kobolds, goblins, knockers. Fae and stone kindred. And of course, half-breeds and freaks, and other things with names you will not recognise." A couple of small individuals with heads too large for their small frames scuttled past, giggling in high-pitched shrieks. Barty followed them with his gaze to see them dash down an alleyway, and glimpsed a figure leaning against a wall, hidden in shadow. He briefly made out a hooded, slim form with a cloth mask covering the lower half of their face, their eyes visible—normal eyes, human eyes. She —and he was able to tell immediately that they were a she— looked puzzled about something. Her head tilted and brow furrowed in a cockeyed expression of bewilderment, an expression so pronounced he could understand it clearly in even a brief glimpse. But the pace of their passing did not slow, and in a few steps she was gone from sight.

Accepting the information he had been given without comprehending it, he tried again with a different tact. "And where exactly are we going?"

"We are going to where all hard working Londoners go after a long day at whatever job that men whore themselves out to do, Mister Barty," Jean replied without humour. "The home of libations and bawdiness, and sins far from God's light. We are going to the pub." He pointed briefly in front of himself, forward and up.

The building looked old . It sat atop a raised platform, rather than being built on top of some ruin, like most of the shelters that made up the ramshackle Undercity. It was built of stone and, while not larger than some of the other structures that made up the place, it nevertheless had an air of importance to it in some fashion. The rest of the city appeared to give it something of a berth, a bit of extra space that the others were not afforded. For whatever reason, this worried Barty.

"They will not mind us going on in, I hope?" he queried. "It does not look a very friendly sort of place, is all."

Jean was staring at it, fixated, and the tight, bare-toothed and brief grin that came to his lips matched the glitter in his eyes. "Fret not, Mister Barty. They know me well here. Very well indeed." His pace quickened, the sound of chatter and what sounded like barking coming from within, as well as several raised, raucous voices, growing louder as they got closer. Barty raced to keep up, even as he wondered why he had not yet turned and run. Fear of other kinds were their own chains today.

They crossed the street and Jean reached a doorway set

below a crude sign marked in black paint that simply said 'The Den'. Jean flung it open, and strode on in. Torn between the choice of being out on the street with the shadows that had gathered in their wake, or being at Jean's side, Barty felt he had no choice but to choose the latter, and plunged on inside.

The interior was gloomy, barely lit by a few candles and lanterns that did nothing to really banish the gloom. For this reason, Barty walked directly into Jean's back and bounced off. The huntsman did not move.

Then Barty noticed the smell. It was not a pleasant one, akin to that of wet dog, amongst other scents that also leaned towards canine; a musky, nasty smell that thickened the air… along with the overwhelming, crushing silence.

A pin could have dropped and made a terrific racket in so doing. The hanging silence in the air was dulled by the echoes of sound and the death of dozens of conversations that had perished as soon as they had walked into the pub. And as Barty's vision adjusted to the gloom, it was to see the score of pub-goers staring straight at them.

They were a motley bunch, all different shapes and sizes but, as things became clearer and Barty could make them out, it was fear of breaking the silence that halted the scream in his throat.

None of the inhabitants were human.

They were a mixture of differences, but there were some universal themes; eyes that reflected candle and torchlight in glittering orange, huge, furred ears like that of a hound, swept back and low, and muzzle-like jaws on some, near normal on others, with fur built heavily down the shoulders and backs, on forearms, with long, sharp, rending claws arching from twisted hands. Some were very large and bulky, heavily muscled and scarred. There were men and women both, all of them a twisted reflection of human and hound—no, Barty realised, not hound.

Wolf.

They had tankards and bottles around them, a card game at another table, and one had been chewing on what might have been the thigh bone of a cow or horse, now stilled at their arrival.

Behind the bar was a huge figure, with grey fur on their forearms and a single eye that glowed orange. Their face was wrought into a muzzle, and they had their huge arms folded across their chest. They stared at Jean, unblinking, along with the rest of the room, and everyone held their breath. Violence did not so much as hang in the air as it plummeted down like a comet. All it would take was the wrong word.

Jean held a moment, making sure that he could be seen. He had a smile on his face that had no humour in it, and there was a tightly-wound stillness to him that was reminiscent of the first time Barty had met him. He strode into the room, his coat trailing behind him, his gaze firmly on whom Barty realised was the publican of this nightmarish place—a fairly ordinary job in a place that was anything but. Jean reached the bar and set both hands upon it, with Barty trailing along behind, almost walking into him with every step. All eyes in the place followed them as they went, and, still, no one made a sound.

Dimly, Barty realised, they were dead. These people hated Jean, and that hatred was so profound that it flowed on to Barty by proxy. And yet they had not attacked. For all that hatred, for all that rage, there was something that held them back.

Jean and the publican stared each other down, and it was Jean who spoke first.

"It's been some time, Yarrick." His tone would have been

almost pleasant, but the undertone of menace was impossible to deny. The massive figure opposite said nothing. Jean went on as though the silence was not a warning. "Pardon the intrusion, but I come looking for aid. I am seeking someone. Someone who comes here often enough." He fell silent, waiting, tilting his head a touch.

The bulky Yarrick's brow was furrowed, his upper lip lifting to bare yellowed teeth. "You..." They struggled to get the words out through the growl in the back of their throat, but tried again. "You have a lot of nerve coming here, Reynard. After all you've gone and done."

Jean gave a rasping chuckle. "I am not *done* yet, Yarrick." He leaned forward. "I am *far* from being done." He gave a smile. "Would you like to find out how much? Or would you prefer to talk instead, like civilised..." He paused, his eyes flickering about the shadows, before he went on. "*Men?*" The word brought growls and anger from all around.

There was a scraping behind Jean as someone pushed themselves to their feet. Barty, drenched in terrified sweat, turned his head to see a tall, lanky figure with a head almost entirely in the form of a wolf stand up, hunched and menacing, one clawed hand digging long furrows into the wood of the table they were at. "Y'aint welcome here, hunter." The words were slurred, the long tongue making pronunciation difficult, but the baleful glowering spoke clearly enough. "This ain't your place. Not no more, t'were ne'er was."

Jean did not bother to look at them, but continued to stare up at Yarrick. "Tell your man to sit before he gets hurt," he said loudly, before going on in a lower tone, "I'm looking for Benji."

The barman said nothing, but the standing wolf man gave a low, deep snarl, prowling around the table as they went.

"You better listen, hunter. Y'aint welcome, you or your

man here." He sniffed the air, then grunted, sneering. "You find another to replace your last one? You'd think you'd have learned by now what happens when you bring yours to the wolves, Reynard."

They snorted, and at that comment there was sniggering from the corners—and fresh growling. Barty wondered who they were talking about, but he saw the tension flow out of Jean then, saw his shoulders relax, and, for whatever reason, it filled him with terror.

Jean did not turn his head. He reached into his coat and, in the same fluid movement, a heartbeat after the snort, he had the twin-barrelled, heavy pistol in hand. He pointed it at the great standing brute behind him without looking, and fired. The explosion in the room was deafening, a burst of smoke with a bright flash in the gloom that was blinding. Barty had ducked away from it just in time, but the lanky wolf man did not—seemingly frozen in shock at a gesture which could only be described as suicidal, an action so clearly insane that it made no sense to even contemplate it. With a sound of surprise, they were knocked off their feet as the round struck them with an audible *smack*, and blood burst from the wound, a great hole torn into their shoulder.

Jean didn't stop there. With the gun still aimed and smoking, the shot still echoing, he reached into his coat and wrenched out something else; a cylinder about ten inches long, a metal frame around it and, at the end, a complex device with a ring pull pin, and a latch. Jean wrenched the pin out with his teeth and held the latch, slamming down the cylinder bottom down on the bar.

Yarrick had reeled back, one hand raised to protect his face, his fanged mouth open in shock. But he seemed to gather himself swiftly as he shifted instantly into fury even as Barty huddled on the ground, clutching his knees. There was a stillness before the pub erupted in a frenzy of frantic move-ment, Yarrick giving a snarling howl and lashing out towards Jean, who lifted the cylinder he held and shoved it into his face. Yarrick froze mid-movement, his single eye going wide.

"Before anyone does anything *else* that's stupid, let me tell you what I have here," Jean growled, as the rest of the bar also paused in the midst of rushing the hunter and his luckless lackey. "Take a sniff. Should give you dogs an idea." His voice was harsh with malice, and now there was no hiding his rage; it snarled and snapped in every syllable, a grinding spite that sung with a violence to match that of every inhabitant in the bar—and then some.

Yarrick's nostrils shifted, and then his eye widened. Jean held the cylinder steady, the other hand still holding the gun pointed towards the mob. The shot wolf man was whimper-ing, rolling on the ground, holding their shoulder as blood pumped thickly from the wound. Yarrick was shrinking back, as Barty dared to look closer at the device.

Within the metal frame casing, which itself was bright, polished silver, the cylinder was made of glass. Within it was a pale, yellowish liquid, seemingly quite thick, and inside that a core—also encased in glass—of some gray material. Jean started to speak, his tone now almost cheerful as he went on, his hands steady as stone.

"My inventor built it to my request. Fascinating stuff, really. Silver casing so you cannot even touch it. A reservoir of oil of aconite. They also call it monkshood… or *wolfsbane*. I am sure you know what it does to your kind." No one said anything, as Jean went on. None of them needed to. "That is, of course, not all that it is capable of. The core is what my friend Adam calls a *vaporising agent* that turns all this to mist and gas, spreading it all over the place in an instant as it explodes. It is itself a mixture of phosphorous. And *silver*." There was menace in his words, and now everyone in the bar was cowering back, pushing and shoving each other to get distance. "It ignites with the air, sticks to flesh and burns through it. Silver and fire together, is that a thing that you and yours tend to have trouble with? It is, by my reckoning." Silence fell as imagination filled in the gaps of what terrible things might happen if Jean took his hand off the latch.

"In France, when I was making floor rugs out of the rest of your kind"—the wounded wolf man tried to crawl away, the arm to his wounded shoulder hanging useless and trailing blood—"I once had to shove a thumbful of this stuff up the nose of one of you. I then got the pleasure of watching them smash their brains out on the ground, crying and screaming while they *begged* me to kill them and finish it." Jean leaned forward, his voice becoming a venomous hiss. "I had places to be and things to do, so I gave them a bullet in the eye. But if I had not… I tell you true, Yarrick—I could have sat there and watched them die all day."

Yarrick tore his gaze from the cylinder and stared at him, his expression conflicted. "God's blood, Reynard… what happened to you? You'll die too if that goes off. So will he." He gestured to Barty, who was still huddled in terror on the floor, blinking back fear so thick his guts cramped. "You're a mad dog."

Jean's expression flickered, and his eyes narrowed. "An irony from your lips if I ever heard one." His own twisted into a grin that was closer to a snarl. "I confess freely, if I was to meet my end burning to death in this wretched place, it would yet be worth it to watch every mongrel in here die screaming. Honestly, I will die *laughing*,' he finished with a snarl, letting the moment fester before continuing on, his tone once more level. 'Now, you can help me, then help your man over there get the silver that I put in his shoulder out before he bleeds to death. Or, we all die."

Yarrick paused, looking from one to the other, then back to Jean, his jaw working, trembling, as fear, rage, and hatred warred over his features.

"I implore you. Grant me cause, Yarrick. You would be doing me a favour." Jean"s tone was a growl, soft and furious. The barman stood immobile for a moment, then set both hands on the bar, the talons on his fingers carving into the wood. He fixed Jean with a hate-filled glare and spoke through clenched fangs.

"Go on then. What do you want?"

Jean gave a smile, but did not lower either the bomb or the gun. "I already told you. Benji Wrongblood. Where is he hanging his tail these days?"

There was a moment of pause. And then a scuffling sound, before Barty caught sight of a rather small figure, about the same size as himself, scrambling along the ground before leaping through a shuttered window, which exploded outwards as they vanished through it.

"Looks to me you just missed him," Yarrick growled, as Jean spat words in a language Barty did not know but were most certainly the blackest of curses.

Jean spun back to Yarrick and slammed the explosive down on the bar.

"With my compliments then, old friend." He took his finger off the latch.

Things happened very, very fast after that. Jean raced to the same window their target had burst through. The bomb made a *ping* sound, a cog set into the mechanism at the top starting to turn. The inhabitants panicked, trying to claw their way out of the place. The older Yarrick looked resigned instead, staring down at the thing, and did not move.

But Barty, on the other hand, did something that even he could not explain.

When Jean had yanked the metal pin from the ignition latch of the bomb, it had fallen onto the grimy floor below—a shining metal jewel amidst the muck right in front of Barty's eyes. He'd grabbed it, gotten to his feet as though pulled up by a string, and found himself with his face inches away from the device from which the pin had been pulled.

Barty was, for what it was worth, skilled at things besides simply asking questions and getting to the bottom of things that people wanted to forget. He had gotten his phonograph working after finding it broken, even improving upon its design to make it portable, powered by a foot pedal if need be. He had a knack for such engineering, for devices, that he had never fully explored; he simply made use of it from time to time. Truth be told, in the arsenal at the Lodge, he had been overwhelmed with the possibilities, but had not the time to explore them. He had, however, taken the time to look at some of the fine machines and mechanisms that Adam had wrought, and learned rather quickly that the giant had a strange fascination with clockwork, self-winding mechanisms.

Barty had not realised how quickly he'd worked them out but now, holding the pin, faced with imminent death as another tick of the winding cog signalled the oncoming detonation, his mind turned startlingly clear, and instead of questioning *why*, his instincts instead told him what to *do*—and his body followed.

He clamped down the lifted latch, revealing the hole where the pin had sat, and shifted the mechanism in so doing. There was an interior slide that moved with the latch which almost prevented it coming down—Barty reached in, shoved it down to one side with his finger, and revealed a winding cog, moving steadily. Holding the pin, he looked to the spot where it had come from, and then at this interior, winding mechanism— and shoved the pin into that instead.

There was a grinding of metal, and the arming pin shuddered in his grip as the winding cog crushed itself and pin both, stuttering to a halt. Barty took his hands away. The pinging sound had stopped. The whole thing had taken him no more than three seconds, but only after that did his mind catch up with what his body had done, and he all but spasmed with terror.

Yarrick stood on the other side of the bar, backed into the wall but with nowhere to run. He stared at the bomb, then at Barty. The place seemed to hold its breath as realisation sunk in slowly; Jean was gone. Barty was alone in the bar, with a bomb that he had just jammed. And, though it would have done him no good regardless, he was unarmed.

The barman sagged, leaning forward and breathing out. He glowered at Barty with one eye, as the young man cowered and clung to the bar to stop his shaking legs from failing him, gulping air in his terror.

"Get out," Yarrick growled. "Get out, and take that with you. This is the only warning you're going to get." He turned away, wrenching a small box from a shelf and opening it. Barty saw small metal implements as the one-eyed barman snarled something in a language Barty did not recognise, as the inhabitants of the bar swarmed over the wolf man that Jean had shot, lifting him onto a table as Yarrick approached. He picked an old, thick bone from the floor and shoved it into the maw of the wolf man before pulling out a blade. The injured wolf man was barely conscious by this point, their long pink tongue lolling from their mouth as their eyes rolled in their head.

"Go. Get out," Yarrick grated, putting his back to Barty.

The other denizens glared at him. Somewhere in a corner,

someone was crying. The air had changed and, for all their rage, the atmosphere in the place was now fear. Fear that had nearly seen them all dead, himself included, but the look in the eyes that met his, behind the anger, was something else far closer to despair. Barty suddenly felt sick for reasons he could not understand. He picked up the unexploded bomb and scurried out.

He stumbled clear of the place and realised a new danger; Jean was nowhere to be seen. The shadows were still watching him, and now they seemed larger and more fearsome than ever. Unlike up on the surface, he could not tell where his guide had gone—there were no telltale signs of his passing, no marks of his usual violence. He was gone, as clearly as any hope Barty might have had of returning to the surface.

Panic set in. Barty clutched the bomb to his chest like it was some sort of protection, even though he knew full well it was perhaps a second or two from exploding if the pin worked free. If anyone came upon him now and he dropped it, that explosion would be on them before he could stop it—but if he threw it away, it would still go off, and the aftermath would likely be an inferno in this ramshackle place. Those fractured thoughts tumbled and bounced through his mind, but in this particular moment, he was blind with panic and horror... and the realisation that he had nearly died.

Jean had not hesitated, not even for a moment. He had not tried to bring Barty to the window with him, or warn him of his contingency plan. He was not even sure why he had brought him along, except to leave him to die. The sick revelation of that fact sinking in made Barty nauseous, but there was nothing in his stomach to bring up. In that encounter, Jean had quite clearly displayed his madness, and fury besides.

Barty replayed parts of the scene as he staggered blindly down a lane and into an alleyway, heedless of anyone who might be watching, though he could feel the hairs on his neck standing up in terror, telling him that eyes were indeed upon him.

But there was nothing for it. In this dark place, in this maze of shadows and horrors, Jean had left him to die. It did not matter that the bomb had not gone off. He had killed him anyway. In a place full of monsters, Barty was trapped, and he would be better off letting the bomb explode and having it done quickly, than let it drag out. He slumped against a wall in the midst of a stinking alleyway, heart in his mouth and squeezed his eyes shut.

"Are you just going to sit there then?"

He opened his eyes. He did not recognise the voice that spoke. Light, feminine, and with a trace of an Irish lilt, coming from above him. He looked around in panic, then up. Above him, perched on the guttering and silhouetted against the faint glow of firelight that lit the Undercity, was the same female figure he had seen watching him from an alleyway on his way to the Den. She had her head tilted, letting a strand of curly dark hair spill forth, and her eyes were glimmering pinpoints of light in the depths of her hood.

He did not move, did not say anything. He just sort of goggled for a moment, still in shock after all that had happened. The girl, if that is what she indeed was, stepped off the guttering casually and plunged into the alleyway to land lightly in front of Barty in a crouch, her coat splayed out around her as she met him at eye level. He could barely make out her face; much of it was covered by the cloth mask and the rest was shadowed by her hood, but her eyes did not seem to blink. Without saying a word, she reached out and plucked the bomb from Barty's unresisting hands.

"Something tells me you do not be wanting this," she said, turning it over, humming at the sight of the pin in the detonator. She shook her head. "No, no you do not. We can't be having this here." Her tone was final and decisive, and, still holding the bomb, she got to her feet and marched out of the alleyway, humming as she went. And Barty was alone.

A few moments passed, and then her head poked around the corner. "Well? Are you coming or not?" She clicked her tongue and turned away, huffing in annoyance.

Briefly, Barty considered staying where he was. He was rather tired of blindly following people about, especially since the last person whom he had done so with had just performed actions that had left him in his current predicament. But there was no arguing with that tone—that, and he thought he heard something slither in the further depths of the alleyway, in the darkness that his eyes could not penetrate. He scrambled to his feet and followed.

Whoever she was, she was carrying the bomb in both hands and all but skipping down the makeshift street. At this point Barty was sure she was quite mad—which would have put her about normal for his company for the last few days. This was not a comforting realisation.

"Where are we going, pray tell?" It was not the best way to start the question, but it was the most obvious. "And what is your name? My name is—"

"Barty, correct? That's what *he* called you. And we are off to the Pit," she said cheerfully over one shoulder. "Best place for something like this." She held it out in front of her and sniffed, then winced. "Bit of a shame really. Good craftsman-ship—but too much of a nightmare to keep." She sighed, and then continued on. "Trust *him* to bring something like this. He always likes his dramatic gestures."

Barty grimaced. She had not yet told him a name. "He left me to die back there." He said it flatly, helplessly, the heavy reality still hanging overhead. His new companion paused at that, peering over her shoulder. She looked like she wanted to say something, but seemed to think better of it and carried on. Barty followed her.

He glanced about, seeing figures now that did not simply lurk in shadows. Twisted forms that looked a mismatch of different bodies. Human-like figures that were all the wrong sizes—too small, too large, wrong-sized parts in places and eyes, eyes all wrong and watching. They had come out of the dark, but he wished they would go back into it, if for no other reason than that they frightened him.

"They are more scared of you, would you believe?" her voice said at his ear, and he realised he had been staring even as he jumped in surprise. A giggle came from her then, pleased at his shock, before she skipped on. "Especially since they know who you came in with. Wild and bold, that. Wild and bold indeed."

"Scared of… of me?" Barty stammered, hurrying on after her. "But why? They're all—" he trailed off, as she turned on him, still walking backwards, holding the bomb across her chest.

"Monsters? I think that is the word isn't it?" She mused, turning around again. "And yet here they all are. Hiding as far as they can from everyone on the topside, afraid to look you in the eyes." She hummed another part of the tune briefly, and pressed onwards. "Makes you think, does it not?"

Something about the way she spoke made his mind itch in recognition. "And what sort are you then?" he tried boldly.

She laughed, an unexpected sound from seemingly anyone but her that echoed off the walls, bouncing from them as though the sound shocked them also. "Oh, the worst kind, the absolute worst of them all." She halted. "And here we are."

Her description had been apt indeed. The Pit was precisely that, a great black abyss that stretched into a great void below, with sheer, smooth walls surrounding it. It was enormous, with water pouring into it from the pipes and slipways that came from above, channelling the water that flowed down to this place. They were standing right at the edge, making Barty freeze. There was nothing to denote its existence. The street, such as it was, simply ended at its edge, cut as though with the blade of a knife.

The girl gave the device a turn over in her hands again, sniffing. "Really, not bad work. Exquisite under different circumstances. Could use the silver too, I am sure… but, oh well." With that, she yanked clear the pin and lobbed the bomb into the Pit in one fluid movement, bending at the waist at the very precipice to watch its descent.

It vanished from sight momentarily, and a heartbeat later, there was a concussive *boom* in the depths, and a flare of white light, followed by sizzling sounds and, when Barty peeked over the rim himself, falling clouds of fire, burning and wisping out as they went. There was scuttling around them, and shapes at the corner of his vision fled into deeper darkness. His guide ignored them.

"Looks like it worked. Good thing we got it here in time." She sounded satisfied, then turned on her heel, balancing at the edge of the Pit and, with her hands at her back, fixed Barty with an intense stare. He flinched under it, her dark eyes speculative before she finally spoke. "Correct me for my presumptive deliberations, Mister Barty, but you have the look of a man who has absolutely no idea what he is doing *or* what is going on." Her tone was amused as she took a step from the edge, which made Barty breathe a sigh of relief, as he helplessly shook his head.

"I am indeed somewhat new to this… whatever *this* all is. And I still do not have your name." *New to this*, he thought bitterly. *My so called teacher just tried to kill me.*

The girl made a humming sound, perhaps of thought before she nodded. "You can call me 'Elle', for now." She nodded, then marched on down the street. "Come on then. Let us get you where you need to go."

Always off and going, just like Reynard, Barty thought sourly—but with no other options, even if still unsure, he set off behind her. "And where, pray tell, is where I need to go?"

She shrugged slim shoulders without turning to look at him. "You are looking for Benji. I know where to find him."

Barty was surprised. "But… why should I be the one to find him?"

She did look back at him now, her obscured face not hiding the flicker of sad resignation to her gaze. "Because better you, than *him*. He—Jean, that is—is too consumed to think of anything except violence, and Benji does not deserve that." There was regret in her voice, a sorrow she could not keep from her tone, though she was clearly trying her best.

"Jean was behaving as though Benji was some sort of killer, from what I was seeing. Is he dangerous?"

The response was an irritated shake of the head and an unladylike snort. "Benji is about as dangerous as a terrier and half as bold. He would not hurt anyone, especially someone trying to help him. Too few ever have." She turned down an alleyway abruptly. "You will understand, once you meet him. Benji is a good soul, dealt a poor hand. Like most down here."

Barty could not help but give a frightened, nervous chuckle. "They… you, that is, all seem terrifying to me, if I am honest. I mean…" He trailed off, as something caught his eye. It was an open window of a ragged shack, within which was a small figure—clearly a knocker, much like Wickermont up at the entrance, except this one's features showed them to be female. They were looking through the window fearfully, and holding in their arms two tiny figures that were more eyes than face, that he quickly realised were children of her kind. She tightened her grip on them as Barty made eye contact, huddling down further. Barty, his trail of thought quite unravelled, wondered if he should say something.

Elle drew alongside him. She raised a closed hand to her mouth, tapped the knuckle of her forefinger against her upper lip and then made a slow, sweeping gesture from her mouth while exhaling before nodding. Barty had no idea what it meant, but the knocker did. She sagged, releasing her grip on her children, then tapped below her right eye twice before making a salute gesture and nodded in kind. Elle nudged Barty, and he stumbled along back into her wake.

"Still think that they're all frightening?" she asked dryly. Barty did not answer. He was shaken by the experience; it was the first time in all his life someone had looked afraid of him, and not the other way around. It made him feel disquieted.

He finally found the ability to speak, a bit unsure of himself in the doing. "What did that"—he made a poor attempt to copy the gesture she had made—"mean, anyway?"

"Letting her know that she was safe, but to keep her head down regardless," Elle replied. "Sometimes it is safer not to speak down here."

Glancing around, Barty could not help but agree, without fully understanding the ramifications of such a statement. But he was still struggling with that frightened expression, staring out at him from the shadows. "I thought I was coming here to help track down a murderer. Not help one."

Elle halted abruptly at that, stiffening up as she rounded on Barty in a way that was almost fierce. "He is not. Jean Reynard is many things, but murderer is not one of them," she said firmly, giving Barty a hard look.

He could not find it in him to accept this. "I was nearly burned alive by him only a short time passed. Along with a whole room full of... of..." He struggled, not really knowing the right word. He gave up. "Werewolves, I suppose."

Elle rolled her eyes at this and turned away, setting off again into the maze of alleyways. "By Morrigan's eye, you *really* do not know much." Her tone was sour, and she shook her head. "But I should not be surprised. He is never a good teacher at the best of times."

"How—" Barty tried to ask, finding that statement odd, but Elle continued on as she ducked beneath a fallen beam, cutting him off.

"There are three kinds of them, and all are different. Werewolves, I mean." Barty shuffled in under the beam as well. "There are the pure strains—those are the most dangerous, because they look like everyone else, right until the moment that they do not. When that happens, it is too late for anyone around them. And then you've got the curse bloods." She sighed. "That is what they are... Benji and Yarrick and the others. They've got latent strains in the family. They don't look like us, they don't look like them, and nobody wants them anywhere." She shook her head, going quiet.

"What about the third one?" Barty asked. "You said three?"

She did not answer him. Instead, she halted where she was, hands in the pockets of her coat, and looked ahead.

"Benji's place is just up there," she said, ignoring his question. "He will probably be along shortly, you will see him from here." She gestured; the place was a level above the ground, with other buildings above and around it. It was but a tiny corner, buried away and hidden, the windows boarded up and a crude door made of mismatched pieces of wood, the rest of the structure teetering on the bring of collapse. A sad place indeed. Barty focused on it, then back to Elle, a questioning look on his face that she interpreted before he even opened his mouth.

"No, I will not be coming with you. I brought you because it was the quickest way to get you out of here." Her gaze darkened a moment. "Speak to him. Benji is, like I said; a good soul dealt a bad hand. You can talk to him, I promise. But he is not your killer." She paused, reaching up to adjust her face mask. "Do me a favour, could you? When Jean finds you, don't tell him you ran into me? I will owe you for it."

Barty felt his hackles rise. "Find me? I doubt he wants anything to do with me. And I certainly do not want anything to do with him." He could not keep the anger from his voice, but in the back of his head came the thoughts, firmer on himself than ever. *He is still the only chance you will get. He still is the only one who would know.* "Besides, I doubt he will find me in this maze… me, or this Benji."

"He will." She said it quietly, simply. "He always does, eventually. Even broken as he is, even if he is half as good as he used to be, he is still better than anyone else."

Barty did not like the sound of that at all. Angry, he looked away from her, back to the indicated door. "He is a madman, is what he is. Enraged at the whole world for existing in his presence."

"And at himself most of all," Elle said quietly, but now there was a curiosity in her voice, giving way to astonishment. "But you… you do not know, do you?" She sounded startled. "About James. You… he has not said anything, has he?"

Barty shook his head, his expression as blank as his realisation. Elle sighed. "Then you had better ask him." She pulled her hood further over her face, hiding her eyes entirely. "But best do so gently." Her tone was subdued now, the cheerful nature of their first meeting gone. Now there was an abiding sorrow and grief in her words, and Barty could not help but wonder the question he finally gave voice to.

"Just what is Jean to you?"

She went still, silence falling. Then, she pointed briefly. "Your boy is here. Best go and see to him before he scatters."

Barty snapped his head around to see a figure furtively making their way to the rickety stairwell leading to the crude doorway, only slightly visible in the gloom. He turned back to Elle, but she was gone, the shadow where she had once stood now empty.

He blinked in astonishment, but was also torn between moments, of what to do next. Finally, he swore under his breath and made his choice. Moving sharply up the alleyway, crossing the rough street, he came to a stop at the stairwell. "Benji?" he called up.

The slightly-built figure was a touch shorter than Barty himself. They were crouched in shadow, digging through a sack on a drawstring as Barty approached, while beside them the door remained unopened, locked by a length of chain and a heavy, rusted padlock. But on hearing the name, they shot up suddenly, bringing both hands up. Fingers curled outwards, each with a long, dark claw extending from the tips. They would have looked terrifying—they *did* in fact, Barty had to admit—were it not for their face.

Benji was maybe a year or two older than Barty. He was dark, and would have been handsome indeed if it was not for the fur that lined his jawline and forehead, the pointed ears and sharp teeth. But despite those terrible features, it took nothing to see the fear on his face—real, awful fear, on the verge of panic and tears.

Barty's hands shot up. "Uh… hello?" It was as good a thing to say as any, really.

"Who are you? What'd'you want?" Benji blurted, trying to

growl as he did so, but instead his words came out in more of a squeak, making him cough. Barty felt an immediate sympathy, despite his own panic. There was a kindred spirit here in more ways than one.

"My… my name is Barty." *No it is not, but it is simpler at this point not to argue with myself,* his thoughts interjected as he pressed on. "I was hoping to speak to you."

"About w-what? Spit it out!" Benji looked around even as he asked, as though looking for something else. It did not take long to figure out what.

"Reynard is not here." Despite what Elle had said, Barty doubted the man would find them any time soon. "I am hoping to—" He stopped and thought. What *was* he doing here? He did not want to go back to Jean in any case. Why was he scaring this youth so?

Because, if he did not, then Jean *would* eventually find them. And when he did, Barty was not sure he would stop to ask questions. Maybe, instead, he could reveal what he knew about Heathwood to Barty, and he could relay it to Jean, and then take his leave of the whole thing. Even if it did not bring Barty to the truth he yearned for, it'd be better than leaving this frightened creature to inevitably suffer.

"I wanted to know about Doctor Heathwood, Benji." Barty lowered his hands and straightened up, ignoring his pounding heartbeat. "I wanted to know what happened to him, and what you saw."

Benji flinched. It was a tell Barty had seen plenty before, in those that thought the secret was out. It was a stab in the dark, it was a hand played entirely in bluff, but it worked often enough. All it often took to get answers was asking the right question, and *this* was apparently the right one. Benji sagged. He looked around furtively, before reaching down and picking up the key he had dropped. He gave Barty a suspicious look. "*He's* not with you, is he?"

Barty shook his head. "No. And if we just talk, hopefully he never needs to be." It was the truth, and Barty meant it. Something about that seemed to convince Benji; perhaps it was desperation. Barty wondered just how many friends someone in Benji's position would have, with the hunter after him and blood in the air. At times like that, you learned fast to take even the promise of a friend, because the alternative was something you could not outrun. Benji, reluctantly nodded and opened the lock, sliding out the chain.

"If he comes after you, I'm gone, all right? Just talking, yeah? Just talking." He opened the door.

Two hands came out of the darkness of the room and seized Benji by the collar of his shirt, lifting him bodily off his feet as he gave a shriek of shock. The creature was pulled inwards, bringing him face to face with Jean Reynard, who had his teeth bared in what could not even charitably be called a smile.

"Oh, I am *all ears,* Benji," he growled, and hurled him into the depths of the room. The door slammed shut behind them. Barty stood stock still for just a moment. Then, without thinking, he raced up the steps and kicked the door in, heart hammering in his chest.

Jean had Benji pinned on the ground with a knee on his chest, the youth covering his face protectively with both hands. Jean had already drawn his gun, grabbed Benji by the chin, and maybe was or was not about to shoot him—Barty did not wait to find out. Fuelled by his fury at the man who had almost gotten him killed, he threw himself at Jean to knock him loose.

It was like running into a brick wall, but it worked. Jean was dislodged, though his reaction to the blow was ferocious.

He rolled, bringing Barty with him, and lifted him completely off the ground to pin him, with one arm braced against Barty's chest, against a wall that buckled under the impact. Barty had the air smashed out of him and his ribs creaked as he saw stars. Jean's face was inches from his own, staring at him with teeth bared, but in that dazed moment Barty did not think Jean even *saw* him, let alone realised where he was, or what he was doing. The man looked demented, tortured, and on the edge of a furious breakdown.

Benji was scrambling, huddling away in fear. Too frightened to even run, to do anything but cower. Barty got air into his lungs with difficulty, and desperately tried to figure out what to say.

Ask him about James. But do it gently.

Elle had said that. And while it was hardly not as gentle as circumstances would normally allow, this was possibly the last chance he would get to say anything at all.

"Who… is James…" He managed to barely grunt it out in a gasp, screwing his eyes shut against the expected retaliation, but instead, the pinning weight relaxed slightly. When Barty opened his eyes again, Jean was blinking rapidly, his features slacking. The pressure vanished abruptly and Jean stepped back as Barty crumpled to the floor, Jean standing over him.

He opened his mouth to speak, or tried to. "I…" He fell silent again, looking lost. It was such a completely out of character moment for the man that Barty, too, did not know what to say.

"I didn't kill Doctor Heathwood," Benji said then, in a voice filled with tears. "I would never do that. He was… he was my friend." He huddled inwards, hugging his knees to his chest and rocking back and forth as both Barty and Jean turned towards him, their own conflict fading in that moment.

Barty looked to Jean, who pushed himself to his feet and

looked straight back. An unspoken understanding passed between each. They would return to this—but not now. For once, Jean was the one who looked away first.

"I'll get the door," he said quietly.

Barty let out a shaky breath, sagging further onto the floor as he looked over at Benji. Despite all the youth's monstrous features, in the end he looked exactly like what he was; a frightened boy, too young for all that the world had thrown at him.

"Hello there," Barty said wearily from his crumpled position. "So... I am Barty. What do you say we start from the beginning?"

CHAPTER 10

THEY WHO DARE TO HOPE

The situation was still tense. Jean's very presence lent to that, as he loomed over the scene, banished to a corner from which his menace emanated from the shadows. Barty sat with Benji upon two upended crate boxes, the best that could be managed for chairs.

It was a common theme; Benji's home was a collection of repurposed junk. A shovel blade used as a frying pan over a brazier. Planks of wood leaning together to create the most basic of furniture. They were cast offs, the most unwanted of the unwanted refuse. Just like the one to whom they belonged.

Barty had come looking for monsters. He never expected that he had been with one the whole time but now, seeing Benji up close, it was all too clear. The subject of the 'hunt' was small, part-starved, and terrified. He would not make eye contact—he tried to huddle in on himself, as though it would let him vanish into the ether. His clothes were worn, but had once originally been quite good in terms of cut and quality. Barty noted that and set it aside; he had either stolen them at one point, or someone had given them to him. He was leaning towards the latter; if theft was more what Benji was inclined towards, he would have stolen fresher ones if good clothes were so important. He was the first of the creatures—the *people*—that Barty had seen of the Undercity that, despite the inhuman features, displayed the most humanity in his countenance. He was frightened. He was alone. He was confused. Barty could not help but feel a kindred spirit.

It had taken a few drams of rum to settle Benji's nerves even a fraction, from a dark bottle with a broken neck. Barty sympathised with it irrationally; his own neck felt like it had little pieces of bone splintered off after Jean had pinned him to the wall, swimming in his flesh and spiking out shards of pain.

He paid it as little attention as he could—he had something else to focus on at this moment. Benji had his breathing under control, but refused to look at Jean. For the hunter's part, he remained dead quiet, his eyes glittering gray in the gloom from the faint glow of the cigarette he smoked in the corner. For once, Barty was grateful of the smell; it at least was not as bad as the rest of the smells of the Undercity, and it drowned them out with the thick tobacco scent, mixed with some others that Barty could not make out at the best of times, let alone now.

"So…" Barty began slowly, his voice subdued. "Let us start from the very beginning. You said Heathwood was a friend?" Benji nodded without looking at Barty, who took a moment to continue. "Can you tell us of your relationship?"

Benji's dark-eyed gaze flickered upwards, and then he reached up and scratched awkwardly behind one ear. "He was helping me." Barty did not say anything, just nodded expectantly. It was an old trick of conversation and—he hated to admit it—but the nervousness of Benji would help. Once the silence was broken, an anxious person would often race to fill it, to stop that silence from coming back. The silence had questions in it. The silence allowed imagination to creep in. Silence was frightening.

"He knew me from… from before," Benji went on awkwardly, fidgeting a touch more. "I was part of his research. Into hypnosis. Into…" His mouth worked. "Into 'manifestation of physicality', that was what he called it."

"What did that involve?" Barty asked curiously. He had to resist the urge to lean forward, as the fascination of learning a new secret started to take hold. He did not want to crowd his subject.

"He would make me look at a watch, counting the seconds while he said… things," Benji mumbled. "Things I did not understand, just nonsense things, but they made everything go quiet, slowed down." He shrugged. "He called it hypnosis. Felt like a bit of old nonsense really, but he said it was helping. Said it was working." Benji fell quiet again, his gaze lowered once more.

"What was working? Did he tell you what he was trying to do?"

Benji's gaze flicked up, his expression twisting. "What does that have to do with him getting killed? I told you—"

Barty took a chance and held a hand up. "I am sorry, Benji. I just want to know what you were doing there. If I get all the pieces, then we do not have to keep going back and forth. It is better… believe me."

The wolfblooded youth grimaced, rubbing one eye with a twisted knuckle. He cast a dark, wary glance to the shadow Jean was lurking in, then wrenched his eyes away as if stung before he went on again. "He was trying to see if… if he could make me normal. Make me… make me like I used to be."

"Used to be?" Barty was confused.

Benji slunk inwards, and didn't answer, so it was the cold, hard voice of Jean that spoke. "The change strikes around adolescence, Mister Barty," he said flatly. "All the curse-blooded look like everyone else—until the change sets in. It goes on, then stops, and they never go back." Benji flinched but said nothing. "Is that what Heathwood was doing? Trying to cure physical symptoms by treating the mind?" Jean's voice went harder still, and the cloud of smoke from his mouth became larger as he leaned forward out of the gloom, the gesture making Benji shrink further even though Jean was on the other side of the dingy, foul room. But it was Barty who responded.

"*Thank* you," he said pointedly, glowering at Jean from where he sat. The hunter caught the look and raised a brow, meeting the stare for a long moment before he grunted and retreated back, casting himself once more into shadow. Barty returned to the matter at hand. "So you were meeting him for treatment then." Benji nodded wordlessly. "Did you feel it was working?" Barty had to get him talking again after Jean's interruption.

It took a few long moments, but eventually Benji shrugged. "It might have. I felt better about things. We were going to try something different when I—" He abruptly went quiet again, then sniffled, wiping at his nose.

Barty let the moment hang, then reached into his coat, seeking a handkerchief. He found one in his interior pocket—and something else as well. A piece of smooth, thickened card; the photograph he had taken from Heathwood's floor, amidst the paperwork he had collected and left with Adam. He had almost forgotten about it. Moving past his moment of pause, he pulled out the handkerchief and handed it over to Benji. The sorrowful wolfboy stared at it a while, then took it and wiped his eyes, before blowing his nose.

"Are you all right to continue?" Barty asked gently.

Benji's face screwed up, but it was to take a deep breath and harden himself as he nodded firmly. "Yeah… yeah, I'll be all right." He frowned, his eyes focusing on the distance. "It was around ten or so, from the ringing of Big Ben. Doctor Heathwood and I always would meet late because it was easier for me to move around at night. I remember that the streets were very empty, which was good. Made it easier to get around, keep off the main roads, use the alleyways. Everything seemed right as rain, yeah? Everything like normal, tick tock on the clock. There's an alleyway across from his place where you can see his windows. I was there, making my way along, listening to see if the street was clear enough. That's when I saw them." He shuddered, a full body movement from head to toe. "They were coming in through the window, from the rooftops."

"I take it that surprised you somewhat," Barty said a bit wryly, glancing briefly to the shadow of Jean, remembering that he had come to the very same conclusion.

To his surprise, Benji shook his head. "I knew there were others he was seeing. Others he was trying to help he said. I was just one of them. I guessed that was one of the others, you know? Thought it was strange, but not as strange as some might have seen it." He paused a moment, and sniffed again. "But something was *wrong* with them."

"Wrong? Wrong how?" Barty asked.

Benji shrugged. "Can't explain it, not really… no. There was something about them that did not seem right. Something about the way they moved, it felt off. Like they were off-balance, all… jerky-like. Twitching like a skeever from the Poppy Lanes, you know?"

Barty shivered. He knew the Poppy Lanes and houses, where people would go and smoke opium to kill themselves slowly, day by day. He nodded to Benji, leaning forward. "Did you recognise them at all?"

Benji shook his head. "Didn't get a good butchers at 'em," he said, which Barty took a moment to understand, but Benji was continuing. "They were fast, and big." The furred brow bent down. "I wondered for a moment if I had the time wrong. Like I had gotten things mixed up, but..." He shook his head. "It is like I said. I didn't know them. And everybody knows everybody in this business."

Jean leaned forward at that, out of the shadow, but Barty paid him no mind and went on. "They weren't from the Undercity?"

"If they were I'd have known 'em. They're a topsider, sure as sunshine," Benji said firmly, then went back to recollection.His expression shifted again, sorrow on his features. "I stopped in the alleyway, across the street, and waited a spell. I was trying to figure out what was going on and then..." He swallowed. "I heard a scream. Strangled, and then it stopped, sudden like. I knew something was wrong, real wrong, but I..." He trailed off, and lowered his head, shoulders slumping. "I ran away. I ran home." His voice was small now, and he refused to meet Barty's gaze.

"You did not go to anyone about it? Did not talk to anyone, let the police know?" Barty asked gently, trying to avoid that topic further, seeing clearly the shame on Benji's features.

The question was met with incredulity, Benji looking at him with a conflicted look of astonishment. "You think anyone would have listened?" Surprisingly, at that moment, he flicked a gaze to Jean—accusingly so. He grimaced, biting on his tongue, and lowered his head again.

Before Barty could speak, Jean's growl came out of the

gloom once more. "Go on then, Benji. Something is on your mind there. I can practically smell it."

"Reynard," Barty said, "you are not helping—" But Benji interrupted.

"Yeah, you got that right, Mister. He's not helping. He's not but he should be," he said heatedly, anger rising above shame and even grief. "You should be out there looking for who killed the doctor, not coming after me. You were supposed to be on our side! That's what you told us! You and him!"

Barty was mystified, but even more so when he saw the effect that the words had on Jean. The man had visibly paled. His jaw worked, grinding over and over before he got abruptly to his feet and walked to the door. As he reached it, Benji shouted at him, "He was my friend too!"

Jean stopped dead as though struck. And then, dragging himself through it, pushed the door open and stepped outside. Barty heard his steps descend, and he was gone.

"What was that about, Benji? Doctor Heathwood?"

But the youth was shaking his head, wiping his eyes with the back of his hand. "No. It's about James. Jean's son." He blinked, looking at Barty in astonishment. "You've been running around with him and he's never mentioned James? Not even once?"

The burned picture in the lodge loomed large in Barty's thoughts, crawling up his spine with frost-covered fingers. He shook his head. Benji looked disappointed, and sank dejectedly on his crate.

"What... what happened to him?" Barty asked.

"He died," Benji said bluntly, staring at nothing. "And *he* was the one who did it." He gestured to the door, and Barty felt the world wobble a bit at that statement. Simple, and yet horrible. Jean had killed his own son?

"You know, it's strange," Benji went on as Barty struggled to comprehend the enormity of what he had just been told.

"What's that?"

"You remind me of him. Of James. He always kept his old man in check, you know? I mean, clear that he did now. Look what he's gone and become without him." His tone was bitter, regretful, as he scratched his claws through his thick, matted hair. "Way you was acting, I thought you might have been friends or somethin'. When he was alive."

"How did Jean kill him? This James?" Barty ignored the statement, but out of necessity, this burning question needing to be answered. Why had no one said anything? He realised now that over and over again people had gotten close, so close to bringing it up, but had always stopped at the last moment. Be it out of fear, or the Old English way of never addressing the wounds, even if they were bleeding all over the place, no one said anything. So many people who wanted to speak, but didn't, and one man who refused to speak about it at all. And as he asked the question a spiteful, bitter part of his brain wondered just *what* Jean had done to get his son killed. Had he been as reckless, as mad, as he had been with Barty? Worse?

Benji grunted at the question, and said nothing. More silence of fear, Barty wondered, before the youth found his voice. "You're going to have to ask *him* that. He knows. But..." He trailed off, then rubbed his face awkwardly. "Sorry. These last few days haven't been good." His tone was apologetic. Barty wondered how the hell he had remotely earned an apology for anything, after all the disruption to Benji's life he and Jean had caused.

Benji fished out the broken bottle and, with care, took another sip from it. He held it out to Barty, who wisely, but politely, refused. The little wolfblood shrugged and after a moment, all unprompted, started to speak.

"James was like the doctor, you know. Trying to help. He did it different, did it in different ways. Doctor tried to treat us —me, and a few others, to try and make us normal topsiders maybe." He sniffed, growling a moment, a regretful, worrying sort of sound. "That's what he said anyways. We'll never know now, right?" He asked the question expecting no answer, sounding resigned.

"And James? How did he try to help?"

Benji sniffed, and took another sip from the bottle. "He would treat us like people. Simple as that, really. Used to come down here and talk to us, find out what we was needing, what we was wanting. Got us food, got us clothes, medicine, you know? Made things bearable. Bit easier." He sounded wistful. "He was young, like me. I used to help him out. Told him about things going on. He had an idea… more a dream really." He fell silent again. The bottle had become empty. Benji sat quiet for a long moment. The silence turned heavy.

"What did he dream about?" Barty asked, subdued. Benji startled, then shook his head. He blinked a few times, dragged out of his memories, blinking myopically at Barty until he recognised him again.

"He wanted to get us out of the dark. Wanted us to have a place that wasn't down here in the mud." He slurred his words as he spoke, and Barty wondered just how strong the liquor in the bottle was. But then, Benji was not a very big person. "He wanted to make us people again, without changing who we are." He shook his head. "And then he died. Just like the doctor died. Anyone who tries to help us out dies."

Barty didn't know what to say. He tried, aiming for hope. "I'm sure Jean will find who killed the doctor."

He missed. Benji gave him a bloodshot look, flat and empty. It was the look of someone who had seen too much, and none of it good. It was the look of someone who had been promised and denied by the world itself, on every level it could be denied. The change had set in at adolescence, Jean said. Before that, they looked the same as everyone else. Who had Benji been, before he was the Wrongblood? What had the world taken from him? What had he lost?

"I'd like you to leave now, Mister Barty," Benji said quietly. "I don't want to talk to you anymore." He turned his back to him, hunched over and, despite Barty being nearby, was entirely alone on his little wooden crate.

Barty stood slowly, then paused. "If you remember it, my old home is on Lancashire Lane. 15b to be precise," he said. "I do not know if I will ever be going back there, but if I do, and if you remember something..." He shook his head and tried again. "If you need *anything*, leave word."

He left it at that. Benji did not turn. Barty, seeing no point in further farewells and simmering in guilt, made his way outside. He did not want to admit what Benji's anger made truth; even if the killer was found, even if Jean managed to stop a creature that could rip a mans head off, it would not change anything for Benji. Or anyone else in the Undercity. His gesture was as empty as Benji's hope.

Jean was sat at the bottom of the stairs. The street was barren. The man was staring at nothing, with a gun in his lap, eyes on the ground.

He killed his own son. The realisation halted him in place, robbed his breath from his lungs and left him staring. The enormity of it was too much.

What sort of man could do that? What sort of man was he?

Whatever he was, he was also Barty's only way out of the place. This fact sat uncomfortable over him, but there was no way to avoid it. Elle was nowhere to be seen, and he did not count on himself to get that lucky twice.

The hunter was silent, and though Barty felt the quiet pressing in like a hammer, he felt no urge to break it either. Eventually, Jean got to his feet and, saying nothing, started walking away. Barty fell into step behind him. The wordless shroud followed them, as they made their way back through the hovels and lanes, the wretched Undercity in all its foul glory, back to the world above. And as they went, every step of the way, Barty was asking the same question he had been asking for days on end now—just who *was* Jean Reynard? But now in the context of a new name. A name that would not be forgotten or buried. The name of a son to a father, and all that entailed.

I have to know, he admitted to himself, as they passed the wordless Wickermont. Jean tossed him two sparkling stones without looking. Wickermont caught them deftly and retreated into the gloom, trilling happily as he went, untroubled by explosions and shootings and other horrors that had gone on in the city below; he was with his gems and that was all he needed, all else was naught. Barty, trapped in a prison of his own making, his own curiosity that now dragged him along, could have envied him for that.

The silence followed. The journey continued.

CHAPTER 11

A DEAD MAN'S NAME

Back at the Lodge, in his rooms, Barty wondered about his next step.

He was tired at this point. Between the murder scene, the doctor's office, and lastly, the Undercity itself, it was now quite late, and he was rather hungry as well.

Jean had not said a word. The whole time he had remained stubbornly silent, his eyes hollow and glowering out at the world, his lips set tight. He had vanished upstairs and into what was presumably his own quarters immediately upon arrival. He had not come out. Part of Barty wanted to see if he was managing, but it was overwhelmed with his dislike for the hunter. He was not simply angry at him for nearly getting him killed; it was an anger that fermented and remained thick after seeing how he treated Benji. He himself had been on the wrong end of thugs and bullies most of his life. He knew how they acted, how they worked, and what they looked like. Jean had looked too much like one to be thought of as anything else.

Barty had cleaned himself up. It was either that or stink,

and he was a little tired of stinking for the time being. He had despaired of alternative clothing until he'd opened a wardrobe and found a variety of clothes that were both terribly out of style and smelt powerfully of mothballs, as well as being made for an individual about a good foot taller than he was. But he had worn clothes too large for him before and he had learned to make do, folding up his sleeves and trouser legs. It was ludicrous looking, but he was not going anywhere for the time being. No, right now he was looking for only one thing, and that was something to eat. Leaving his room, he was about to head downstairs to find the kitchens when he heard a curious thing above him, from the stairs leading to the next floor.

Adam's voice was the sort that carried for quite some distance and time, bouncing along walls and squeezing through crannies to get where it needed to go. Barty recognised it instantly, but not the words being said. Though what he most certainly did *not* understand was the harsh cry of what sounded like a raven that came amidst it. *This is something worth noting*, his mind told him. His curiosity piqued, he decided to find out. What could the harm be? Questions needed answering.

He approached the stairs, moving carefully, his feet nevertheless causing faint creaks as he went. The house was old, and it protested at every movement, however faint—much fainter than the shrieks that Adam awoke in the ancient timbers. But emboldened, Barty crept up, until the rich, warm voice of Adam became legible to his questing ear.

"I am worried about him, but that is all I can say. He is alive—but I am hardly a good judge of human character, old friend." Their tone was exasperated. Another harsh raven croak. "You are well aware of the arrangement he and I have," Adam chided in reply before they went on. "And how it does not lend terribly well to an engaged conversation between us at times. It is a business arrangement. And he is a recalcitrant man to say the very least." A pause, as a muted raven croak came out, and a thunderous sort of sigh. "This young man he has taken on is a strange thing however. Not like him, especially after—"

There was a chorus of raven croaks and cries now… more than one bird? Barty took another step up, carefully, as Adam made a tutting sound with their tongue and rumbled in gentle rebuke. "Now then, there's no need for that. I know it is unusual, but if you will just let me explain—"

Barty had risen up the stairs enough to see the uppermost floor. What he bore witness to was not quite what he expected —in truth he was not sure what he could have expected, but this was different enough from that nebulous image to surprise him regardless.

The upper floor was more akin to a loft than anything else. It was huge for a start—one massive room, with pillars holding up a high roof. There was a glass panelled rooftop as well that dominated much of the place, letting in the gloomy sky of London above. A panel was propped open, probably by Adam's own hand. They had, it seemed, some guests.

The giant was standing in the middle of the room itself. There were bookshelves, bookshelves everywhere, and tables stacked high with even more books. Barty noticed that the floor fell away at one end of the room – leading to double story room that had floor to ceiling bookshelves, as well as comfortable couches and a great round table strewn with notes. He realised that the door at the end of the hall in the floor below, the one with the burned painting on one side and the one of the younger Jean and his mentor on the other, led into this great library. It was startling. Where the bottom of the Lodge was a place of weapons and armament, this was a hall of knowledge. It was of some concern of Barty however, that some of the books appeared to be chained shut, something he could not recall ever seeing in a conventional library before.

Adam had fallen silent, as they were looking at Barty curiously, having beheld him instantly upon his head coming into view—Barty wagered they had been facing directly towards him. And they were, as previously noted, not alone. Four more pairs of eyes also stared at Barty, but due to the nature of those who they belonged to, only one at a time was usually directed towards him.

The four ravens were huge, their feathers glossy and ruffled, their beaks long and shining. They were gathered together in a row upon a table before Adam, except now they each had their eyes turned towards Barty, affronted at this interrupting spectre. Barty could not help but feel he had interrupted a conversation. Which was mad, as they were birds. But they had such an uncomfortably *knowing* look about them.

"I have been alone in my conversing for so long that I forget that they can be overheard," Adam said wryly. If they were irritated at being overheard they certainly did not show it, instead beckoning Barty upwards with one enormous hand. "Come up. Do not mind this gathered unkindness." A harsh shriek of four voices at once, four beaks turning towards him with vindictiveness. Adam held up a hand, mildly protesting. "Forgive me, I was not the one who invented the noun for your gathering." Beaks clicked with irritation as Adam gave a rumbling chuckle, and Barty continued up the steps, nervous and slow.

"These are companions of an old friend; a very dear friend at that," Adam went on, waving a hand idly. "I was just evaluating them of the situation." A raven to the right croaked warningly, and Adam shook their head as Barty drew close. "He probably does not understand, no," he replied cryptically to the croak. "But give him time. All things become clear once one has enough of it."

"I am sorry, but are you *talking* to them?" Barty said in astonishment. Beady eyes swept back to him with dark suspicion. Then, without warning, all four spread their great black wings and, with a furious flapping that spread pieces of paper and rattled the windows, the small flock of ravens flew one after another through the open window and into the night sky above, leaving a single black feather falling to the floor in their wake.

"Well, I *was*," Adam said with exasperation. "I am afraid they were in little mood to listen. Their mistress is in a spot of a vexation, I fear." The giant turned their head to Barty. "The four—remind me to give you each of their names next time—are a means for… someone very important to Jean to communicate with the household."

"Strange that they do not come themselves," Barty said with a frown as his gaze shifted around, taking in the expanse of the library and loft. Adam rumbled a sad sound, which might have been a sigh or a precursor to a chuckle. "They have their reasons that are their own, but it is one that both Jean and they are united in, even if they are coming at it from completely different and yet very similar perspectives."

It was delicately said, as Barty picked up the large black feather from the floor. It glimmered darkly at its edges. He reached into the shadows between the giant's words, and took a chance. "Does it have something to do with James?"

Stillness echoed in the wake of that statement. Adam was staring at Barty, their twisted features giving nothing away. Finally, they spoke slowly. "Have you yet taken dinner, Mister Barty?" Barty wondered if he had overstepped. Hesitantly, he shook his head. Adam nodded, then gave a beckoning gesture as they moved with great, smooth steps to the stairs. "Do accompany me then. I shall endeavour to reckon with that." Their expression twisted into a grimace. "I am reminded that myself and Cosgrove both have to fight with Reynard to get him to eat anything these days. I am not surprised that he forgot your obvious needs."

Barty wanted partly to protest, but it was a foolish notion. His stomach snarled at him in no uncertain terms that he was to make use of food and to do so *promptly*. So he simply nodded and fell into step, following Adam as they made their way down the pair of staircases to eventually find themselves sat in a sturdy, stone-walled kitchen at the bottom floor at the rear of the lodge.

Adam ushered Barty into a seat at the kitchen table, which he took up gratefully. Though it was but dimly lit for the time being with a single candle, Adam had no difficulty in finding what they needed. The kitchen was well tended, but goodness knew how Adam had secured everything; the notion of them going out into the street to fetch what they required was a ludicrous thing, and as terrifying as it was comical. Yet there was no denying the fresh bread, the cheese and ham, the mixed chutneys and relish that they carefully mixed together to make more of the same sandwiches that Barty had eaten that morning—and thrown up too, he was ashamed to admit. This time he would endeavour to keep them all down, but with how staggeringly hungry he suddenly felt, he did not think that would be a problem.

"Now then," Adam said quietly, as they sliced through bread carefully and slowly. "What exactly do you know about James?"

Barty considered his words for a moment. He noted that Adam did not ask *how* he knew about James. He nevertheless spoke carefully, at least at first. "I know that he was the son of Jean. That he had contacts in the Undercity... no, he had friends there." He frowned, remembering Benji clearly once more. "He was trying to make things better for people down there."

Adam gave a sad chuckle. "James always had a heart about three times too big for him. I say that as something of an expert in the matter." They sighed, pausing a moment. "Go on." The tone was gentle, but there was a firmness there. Barty might normally have argued that he was giving more than he was getting in this conversation, but he did not have the strength to do so, and so instead struck out for boldness on the matter.

"I know that he died," he said bluntly. "I know his father is the one who killed him." Stillness echoed. "I do not know why. I cannot *conceive* of why. I cannot imagine how any father could do something like that. All I know is that he did so, and that everyone down there hates him for it."

"They do not hate him just for that. They hate him for what he did afterwards," they corrected quietly. "They hate him for the massacres that followed. They hate him for the blood he shed and the war he brought." They wordlessly brought the plate of sandwiches over, then sat down upon the ground—carefully, bending one massive limb at a time to sit on their rear upon the tiles, slumping down to bring themselves somewhat eye level with Barty. Adam's expression, as difficult to read as it was, was undeniably pensive. Barty felt the conflicted churning of anguish in his gut drowning out the growling of his hungering stomach. He could not help it.

"Why do you follow him? Why does anyone, knowing what he did?" Barty said in a hushed, furious whisper. "The man is a brute, a thug, and he murdered his own child. What sort of man does that? Regardless of his talents and abilities and everything else that people apparently admire, with everything else he has done, *why do you serve him?*"

Adam would not look at him. They stared fixedly at a wall past Barty's head, and when they finally started to speak, it was as from far away. "The dream James had was to bring an end to the need for the hunters. At least, as they existed. To establish that men and the monstrous were, in many ways, not so different. That actions defined what we truly are." Unblinking, the corpse gaze of Adam looked all the more inhuman, and there was a chill to his tone now that Barty shivered to hear. He had crossed a line.

Adam went on. "Jean? He supported this. He was *proud* of his son. How proud you ask? As proud as any father could hope to be. He supported his son, he helped with his dream, he let go of his conceptions regarding the inhuman, he listened to the inspired teachings of his son and accepted them as his own. It would have been impossible, were it anyone else. James made his father *believe*." That still expression flickered. A hint of pain. "Jean is brilliant—or he was, perhaps—but his son was incandescent. He was born to lead. He was born to inspire. He brought out love in those around him of a kind that no one else dared to imagine was possible. He saw people as they were, and most of all, what they wished they could be, and saw how they could do so." Finally that gaze lowered, and now genuine sorrow entered his voice. "He was my *friend*, Mister Barty. One of very few I have ever had, and one of the only ones I ever allowed myself to have. We all loved James. We still do. The memory of him hangs over this place, even though there is no face to put to them any longer."

Barty swallowed. The burned painting. Were there more? Had there been others? What was left of him now? What remnant of this spectre yet lingered? But this story still did not make sense. His mouth dry, his rage conflicted now with this image—Jean, proud of his son?—and yet, it had all come to pass in a way that Adam did not deny.

"Then what happened? Why did..." Barty trailed off.

Adam grimaced. "I... cannot," they finally exhaled. "I am sorry. But it simply is not my place. I wish that it was, but I cannot. I owe Jean much, but I cannot speak for him. Not in this." They sounded weary about it, defeated. Barty felt his own frustration grow, but bit it down and forced himself to nod. He tried another question instead.

"That does not answer why you follow him however. At least, not that I can understand." He reached for one of the sandwiches and took a bite, unable to stop himself any longer.

At this, Adam gave a smile, showing crooked teeth, a gesture that was nevertheless sad and yet bitterly amused. "Ah. Well, the reason for that is that he alone can offer me a service that no one else possibly can, and I have searched, believe me."

Barty chewed and swallowed before responding. "Oh? And pray tell what that might be?"

Adam gave one of those gigantic shrugs, sighing. "He is going to answer a question for me that has plagued me since the dawn of my first day, when I was first created. He is going to learn if I have a soul. And then he is going to find a way to end my existence."

Barty would have choked if he had not already swallowed the sandwich down—despite that, he yet coughed and came close. "I *beg* your pardon?" On top of everything else that the day had brought to him, this was yet another unexpected occurrence to say the least. "Are you telling me that he will one day *kill* you?" *They also said, 'created', not born.* It was something he would have to find out about later.

Adam nodded. "Oh, yes. I am quite confident he will figure it out some day. Jean is more accomplished at knowing how to end the lives of the unnatural than anyone I have yet met. Once he meets that certain other condition, of course. I admit I am quite looking forward to it. Some nights it is all that gets me through the endless silence." They gave the obviously stunned Barty a very, very faint pat on the shoulder, barely a brushing with that gigantic hand, and then pushed themselves to their feet once more. "Enjoy the sandwiches, Mister Barty. Crude fare, I am well knowing, but future meals shall hopefully be more forthcoming." They started to the door, pausing at the threshold to look at the still dazed young man in clothes too big for him, clearly overwhelmed by what they had heard.

"Jean is someone I trust with this task, because he is a man who will, nearly always and no matter what it costs him, try to do what is right. He may lie to himself and others, but it is what he is. The fact his way has become lost does not change that about him." They paused a moment, hesitating, before going on. "I will leave you with this, Mister Barty. Were you aware that James had a sister? A twin?" Barty blinked, turning in his seat to look back up at the giant, and shook his head mutely. Adam nodded. "He still does, for she still lives. Because of a choice no father should have ever have to make. But as I said… the right thing, no matter what it might cost him." Barty stared at the giant for a moment, who gave a sad nod. "Goodnight, Mister Barty."

They turned, bent double to exit through the doorway, and passed from sight, leaving Barty alone with his conflicted thoughts, wrestling with this new revelation—and what it all meant.

BARTY WAS EXHAUSTED when he finally went back to his room, having spent time lost in thought, the candle that lit the kitchen burning down. It was a difficult journey with that now faint, sputtering light, clutched in one hand to guide him on his way. He had long thought over what Adam had said, but had been unable to wrestle his way through it, save to once again acknowledge that he did not know enough.

When he reached the door to his room, he paused as a sound of movement came from his right—that fated door, with the two paintings on each side of it, leading to the library. There was the slight alcove to each left and right at the end of the corridor which he had noted the first time he had gone down there, and thus he could not make out anything present, but the candle light did not lend much. He waited a moment, but hearing nothing else, supposed that he had only imagined it.

But he did not go into his room just then. Instead, he took the faltering candle and walked towards the paintings, in his tired state wondering if there was something in either picture that he had missed. Some sign or clue. Perhaps a name, or more than one, that could add some clarity to the empty frame. He drew closer, staring at the blackened rectangle, still hanging despite its clear uselessness. What manner of reminder was it supposed to leave?

"I was not the one who burned it, if you must know."

Barty stiffened, nearly dropping the candle, and slowly, his spine a stiffened lump, he turned on the spot, wondering why he had not expected it.

Jean sat in the corner of the alcove opposite the empty frame, on a simple chair. He was still dressed as he had been when Barty had last seen him, travel-stained and ragged. His expression was still as empty and flat as it had been when he had journeyed and arrived back at the Lodge, but there was an edge to it now. A sort of wavering. At his sprawled feet, there was a bottle without a cork. Barty could not see if there was anything left in it. Something told him there was not.

"His sister set fire to it. Masterfully done, really. She used a sort of fuel to make it burn so quickly that it did not bring the rest of the house down. She always was adept at that sort of thing." He was not looking at Barty, his unfocused eyes staring at nothing instead. Not at the empty frame, but at a somewhere that no one else could see. Haunted and distant. It was a look that kept clawing its way back to the hunter's face in their time together but now, only now, did Barty recognise it not as aloofness, but instead as a sort of agony that had depths yet unplumbed.

Barty wanted to say something, but was not sure of the right words. Jean, however, seemed for once to have a few of his own to say, all unprompted. He lowered his gaze, rubbing his palm with the thumb from his opposite hand as he went on.

"She hoped in so doing, I would cease finding myself in this very position we find ourselves now." A bitter, humourless chuckle. "That if I could not see him, I could imagine a world better without him somehow. She always did like her dramatic gestures." He fell silent again, going still as the dead.

His sister, he had called her. Not his daughter. Had he rejected her? Cast her out? Or was it something else? Barty felt his anger towards the man wavering. He dared to delve deeper.

"You overheard Adam and myself, I take it." He did not frame it as a question, and yet said it cautiously. He did not trust Jean not to snap to violence in an instant. He knew how quick the man could be, and still bore the bruises from when he had pinned him to the wall. More than that, he remembered the look in his eyes when he did it. As still as he was, this was a man a hair's breadth from rage at any moment.

Jean snorted, his gaze lifting once more. "I hear everything that goes on in this house. Everything. And Adam's voice carries well." Another pause. "I have not seen her since she burned it. I have not seen her mother since I came home to tell her."

Barty swallowed. "Tell her what?"

Now Jean did make eye contact, his gaze resting fully on Barty. "That I had shot our son."

Barty's tongue froze up. Jean, his dark gaze holding Barty now and, not blinking, continued on inexorably, inevitably, with the grim determination of a man driven to confess. "I believe I told you that there were three kinds of werewolf, Barty. *Minoris, Majoris, Extremis.* You have met the *minoris* aspects, but James… James met with the *extremis* as well. The purebreds. Mostly in France, they were. Pureblooded were-wolf families who had existed for centuries, mostly in opposi-tion to my kind."

He closed his eyes then, leaning back. "The hunters have been in decline for more than two centuries at this point. There are so few of us left; James wanted to end the need for us at all. He sought to unite monster and hunter, and then the rest of humanity eventually as well. I used to call him mad, to scold him but he would never, ever let go of it. Like a hound with a bone, worrying at it, over and over." He sighed, hazily, and continued on.

"Eventually he started making sense. Either that or his passion for it consumed me as much as it did him. So I listened to him, guided him, and helped him make it happen. He lifted up those in the Undercity. He showed me things I did not know were even possible. My son. My brilliant fool of a son, showing his father what was possible by simple words, when all I had known was how to end things." He snorted, going quiet, regret echoing from his stillness.

"He must have been extraordinary," Barty said quietly. And he meant it. He found himself missing this person whom he had never met; when he had started this, to find the man who had killed the Ripper, he had been looking for an unspoken hero. He had not found one, not that he could see, but it was clear that there was one that had existed. One he had missed.

Jean nodded once. "He used to tell me about Benji. That was how I knew him; he told me his story and that of others, of those who lived in the Undercity. What they were capable of when they were given a chance. Benji could sing birds out of trees, he told me. I used to laugh at the thought." He shook his head, and then his expression twisted, struggling under the surface. "When he told me that he had made contact with the clans of France, I had long forgone questioning him at that point. I was proud to help him. We met with those who had been our hidden enemies for a millennia. We broke bread and shook hands. Hunters and monsters, finding common cause, common ground, learning the common truth—that man, or monster, there are beasts in either blood, and together, we can stop them from harming others." He paused again. His jaw trembled as he went on.

"And then, one night, James changed," Jean said flatly. "There was no warning. No hint beforehand. If there were, he kept them from me, but I doubt he would have done something like that. You see, there are *three* types of the werewolf, Mister Barty." He turned that dead-eyed gaze to Barty. "The third, the *majoris*. The infected. Those who have been bitten, or have taken on the blood of a werewolf. He was not bitten. Not a week after the major meeting with the leaders of the

French clans, he turned, and as all others of the accursed strain, he went mad."

Jean gestured dully to the library, as Barty stood there, rooted to the spot. "In there, there are dozens of cases. Hundreds gathered over centuries. Many of them dealing with the accursed werewolves. They go into a frenzy, you see. Completely insane as the change burns out their mind, and turns them into a killing machine that, in their rage, pain and fear, destroys everything in sight, unable to stop. I watched my son, as he locked eyes with me. I could see his face. He knew what was happening, even if he did not know how it happened. I looked him in the eyes, and I knew, *I knew* what he wanted me to do. Even before he begged me to do it. He pleaded with me until he could no longer form words." His jaw worked, and in the fading light of the dying candle, his eyes glistened. "Can you even imagine what it was like? To have that taken from you? Can you even *begin* to understand what he was going through? I watched my son, my boy, go insane in front of my eyes, as his body warped and changed. As his flesh ripped itself apart and he turned into a monster. I saw how frightened he was, how he knew he had no *time* and I… I…" He stopped, the strength to continue withering into nothing, clenching his hands into fists as his voice shook too much for him to go on.

When he finally found the strength to speak again in the vast echoes of that silence, it was in a hollow tone, each word forced out with an effort. "And I simply stood there. I stood there, and I watched it happen. I could have stopped it early. I could have taken the shot then and there. The gun was there, it always was. I could have put him out of his misery. I could have ended it while something of him remained. But no… I failed a father's duty. I stood there, frozen… useless. Unable to understand it or comprehend it, until he heard his sister scream as she came running into the room to see what was happening, and instinct took over. He leapt at her—and I shot him." He went quiet again, letting the moment sink in. "I do not even remember it. I do not remember drawing the gun, the one I knew had the silver bullets." He reached down, and from his hip he pulled out the twin barrelled gun that he had used that very day in the Undercity, and Barty's blood ran cold with sudden dread that had nothing to do with his own safety. "When my senses returned to me, he was on the ground and the gun was in my hand, still smoking. I can still smell the gunpowder. I wake up in the mornings with it filling my senses."

His tone was dull now, but Barty's heart was racing, pounding in his chest and thumping in his ears. Some confessions were dangerous things. They were laden with guilt and filled with dread, and they waited until they were finally released before the weight of them came crashing down again, heavier than ever, and the sinner who had finally surrendered them to the world could not bear the world knowing. Broken by that burden, a torture that no soul should have ever had to bear, they sought in desperation the only way out they could find. Barty's mouth was dry, and he wondered if he should shout for Adam.

Jean pulled back the hammer, then clicked it back into safety, seemingly without thinking of it. And then continued to do so. Just an idle, repetitive motion, mechanical, teetering on the edge and setting Barty's teeth upon it as well.

"He went quick. I never quite figured out how to miss, you see." Click. Clack. Click. Clack. "It would seem it has ever been the only thing I have ever had any measure of true skill." Click. Clack. Click. Clack. Bitterness soaked in his every word, harrowing and aching. He then looked to Barty, and that bloodshot, glassy gaze brightened. "Do you know what I did then, Mister Barty?" His tone was disturbingly cheerful, as the young man shook his head in mute horror. Jean nodded, and his gaze flickered back to the burned frame. "I went home. I told my wife that I had killed our son. And while she broke under that news, with the echoes of her screams and grief still in my ears, I went to France. I used every piece of information, every bit of knowledge that James had gathered, under promise of peace, of the werewolves living in common society. Information that they had freely, openly given as a mark of trust, the names and identities of whole families, the greater ones who could change at will and had been so hopeful that they finally might have recognition, and I tracked them down and killed each and every one of them. One by one, bullet by bullet."

His gaze slid back to Barty, unblinking as he went on. "I found the adults. The men and women. I found the younger ones too. I went to each, asking which of them had cursed my son. And each time they said they did not know, and each time I killed them anyway. I did not stop until there were no more names left. I did not stop…. I did not know how." He looked back down to the gun. "And I still do not. I never will."

Silence fell. The gun in Jean's lap sat there, his hand around the grip, one finger resting close to the trigger. The hammer was pulled back—and he did not set it back to safe.

"I am sorry," Barty rasped out, his voice hollow. Heavy as God's own weight. Saying those words hurt, but he had to. He *had* to. Of all the stories he had expected, this was not the one he had anticipated. This was nothing like what he expected. The agony in Jean's voice, spurred on by whatever he had drunk to loose the demons on his tongue, was as palpable as a wound. There were no combination of words to make any of it better. There was nothing that could be said to make it easier. Barty knew it was a selfishness on his part to say it at all, to say something like that in the face of that awful truth. But he had to say it.

Jean made a strange sound, and it took Barty a long, horrible moment to realise the man was laughing, a sort of strangled choking that hovered on the edge of madness itself. "You? You are sorry? For what?" He tilted his head, as Barty searched for the words that would not come. "Oh, you are sorry *for* me, I see." The tone changed then, menace once more crawling back into the tone. "Save me such, Mister Barty. Save it, or discard it, burn it or ignore it—but do not *ever* give me your pity. I neither want it, nor deserve it." He straightened, and the hammer of the gun gave one more clack as he set it back to safe. But now his gaze turned onto Barty, who shrank under its burning rage, the grief swallowed up by fury. "I not only slew my son, I destroyed his dream. In my grief, I took all that he had built and burned it to the foundation, to try and satisfy my guilt. I compounded regret upon regret, I all but *drowned* in the blood of those that were innocent of any involvement in my son's death to kill the sole individual who was responsible, and I will never even know who it was. But everything my son worked to build is as dead as he is, and in both instances, they were slain by my hand, and mine alone." His voice was back to that cold, harsh tone that Barty knew so well by now. That grief was buried beneath the frost and fury as he went on, pushing himself to his feet. "If that were but the sole limit of my failures and sins, that would be enough. It is not. So, I would take it as a courtesy that you never apologise to me again, that you never show your *pity* to me again. I deserve everything that happens to me, no matter how terrible you might find it. I deserve nothing less." He started to walk away stiffly, but paused after a few steps. Wavering slightly despite his every effort to remain upright, Jean turned his head to one side. "Knowing all this, I expect you will be leaving the first chance you find convenient. I would not blame you. Especially after today, let alone this."

Barty quivered. He was right. Most of the day he had been trying to figure out a way to get out of this man's company, to renege on the accord made and find his own way, struggling with his curiosity while also dealing with his anger. But that anger now felt meaningless, and empty. He was horrified by what he had heard, and sickened by the story and how the truth had played out. Jean Reynard had finally shown what lay beneath the mask, and it had horrified him. The monster hunter, a beast himself, and all the more successful at his dread task by being worse than what he hunted.

And yet…

"I cannot," Barty croaked. "Because of Charlotte."

Jean turned at that, his shape a shadow amidst gloom, but the glimmer of his eyes yet visible. Barty struggled on.

"I can see her eyes. I can see them, but I cannot see her. Something… something took her from me too." He struggled with it, his gaze lowering in his shame. The confession coming unbidden, coaxed by the bare, bloodied truth he had been rent by. "If I knew what it was—if I knew how to find it— then I would not stop either." He shivered, afraid of admitting what he knew to be true. "I would find them too. I would make them pay for it. I would never stop."

Jean said nothing. Hesitating and unsteady still, the only sign of whatever it was he had drunk in his vigil in darkness. In the end, he simply nodded, turning away, speaking over his shoulder as he went. "I apologise for putting you in such danger today, Mister Barty. I cannot promise it will not happen again—but I will never put you in a position where my actions will get you killed alongside me like that again. Now, goodnight. I will see you tomorrow."

Jean kept his back straight, despite the faint wobble to his step, moving down the hall to his room. Barty stood there, holding the candle that had lit the way until that moment, gripping it firmly in one hand and ignoring the molten wax pouring down its length, even as it burned his skin and piled up, even as the candle burned itself out and the Lodge went entirely dark at last, leaving Barty alone in the crushing void, but for the weight of a dead man's name, and all the blood it had wrought.

Chapter 12

Merry Bethlehem

Barty could not remember getting into the bed, but he certainly remembered waking up in one. Startled awake by a concussive blast that echoed with a thump through the room, he jerked awake, disorientated and dishevelled, trapped in that eternal instant where one does not quite recognise their surroundings, still not nearly adjusted to his new home.

As he blinked away the grogginess, the door to his room opened with a creak, and the figure of Adam—blocking out the entire frame despite kneeling—appeared in the midst of it. They looked apologetic, as much as their features allowed it, and were careful with the door. "Apologies, Mister Barty. I appear to have knocked a touch too hard." They sounded mournful, looking down at their knuckles regretfully before gamely pressing on. "Breakfast shall be had in the study today, just down the hall. I do believe we have much to discuss." And with that, they hauled themselves away, leaving Barty alone, closing the door behind them.

Barty very briefly considered going back to sleep, but his pounding heart made the decision for him. He levered himself out of bed, all elbows and knees and a jangling shape, not yet remembering how to be human. He wondered if he had been dreaming. Something told him he had, a memory of a steady gaze, a knowing smile, and dark oblivion hovering at the edges…

He shook it away. A nightmare of the previous day, and all that had transpired. He hoped that this day would instead be less dramatic; he hoped, above all, he would not have to ask more questions of his fellows. There was much he had learned and much he had left unanswered, but the truth thus far had been more than he could have ever dreaded. He was content to leave things as they were, at least for now.

As he was dressing himself, he went to pick up his stained, purloined coat, and blinked as his hand closed on something in the inner pocket. He remembered what it was instantly— the photograph that he had taken from Doctor Heathwood's home, and pulled it clear to look at it once again. It was a bit more travel-stained now, and his folding had dreadfully marred it significantly, but it was still very distinct. Except now, when he finally turned it over, he could make out words written upon the back, in clear, cursive script. *Bethlehem, 1883.*

Curious, he put it to one side as he continued to ready himself, bringing it with him as he left the room and carried on down the hall. There were smells of toast, of butter and possible marmalade, and most assuredly of tea coming from down that hall, propelling him along with speedier steps. He paused a moment, coming to a halt at the doorway, stealing a glance at the burned frame as though it might reveal a secret yet unspoken, but it remained as empty as it had been since Barty arrived. The bottle that Jean had plumbed to find the depths of his own sorrow was gone as well. Everything was as it had been.

The smell of breakfast pulled him from that dark place. The memories, the things he had learned—they had a place now within him, burned into his mind. But he could not let them overwhelm the now. He opened the door and stepped inside, momentarily blinded by the incandescence within.

The ceiling glass left the loft incredibly brightly lit, bursting with light and life. Dust motes danced on the air, glittering in the sun, reckless and joyful. A fire was crackling in the grate, a pipe chimney shooting straight up to the roof, and before that fire was a round table and chairs. The table was festooned with all the things that Barty had smelled and a few more little things besides in a breakfast he had never had the pleasure of knowing before.

Adam loomed, as was their helpless want, to one side. "I am afraid that I could procure neither sausages nor bacon, despite my best efforts, and unlike Cosgrove I am not prepared to kill a man for them if necessary." Their tone was deeply apologetic. Barty tried to stammer that it was all right, but a snort from above choked the words from him.

"Cosgrove is not nearly as terrible as you portray him, Adam. He would never do such a thing." Jean stood on the floor above, at the head of the staircase leading down to the lower study. He was sipping at tea with one hand while reading a sheet of paper with the other. While more simply dressed than usual, he appeared not the slightest bit affected by his imbibing the night before—but looking at his grim, almost cadaverous features, Barty wondered briefly if that was because he always looked awful.

In regards to the assessment of Cosgrove, Barty was more inclined to agree with Adam, but before he could voice that belief, Jean started to descend. "The files from Heathwood's office paint an extraordinary image, if I do so say," he said sourly. "And I can see why he hid them." Reaching the bottom of the staircase, he placed the piece of paper on the table, which Barty could now see was layered with the many pieces of paper he had retrieved. All carefully laid out and arranged, the correct sheets placed together from the different case files. Someone had clearly worked for some time to get it all properly arranged. He looked up to Jean, who was looking at him directly, one hand on the table, the other holding his teacup.

"You did well to bring all these files, Barty," he stated bluntly. "They will make the process simpler." He took another sip, nodded once in recognition, and moved to the rows of books behind him, apparently selecting one at random and giving it a brief look over before setting it back.

"What does that mean? What does this place have to do with it?"

Jean gestured irritably—perhaps there was some lingering influence of alcohol on his humour—and Adam took it upon themselves to explain instead.

"This is the Lodge's collection of active and closed case files of London, and a significant number of England itself," Adam said slowly. "The accounts of Hunters, their records, their thoughts and observations of various creatures. We use them as references."

"Comparison, Mister Barty," Jean said sharply, unrolling a scroll. "The variations and differences of creatures of the esoterica is vast, and no one hunter will ever witness all of them. But many might." He grimaced. "Based off the description that Benji gave, we now have to search through these accounts of Heathwood and the files we have here, to see if a common thread can be found, that we might pursue it."

Barty let this run through his mind. "You were fairly sure at first glance that it was Benji that did it." He said it carefully, remembering just how unfairly the wolfblooded had been treated.

Jean grimaced. "He still may have. But you are correct, in that my reaction was… shall we say visceral." He hesitated, then rolled the scroll back up and put it into place. "I was not thinking clearly," he said shortly, not looking at the pair.

Adam stepped in, offering Barty some buttered toast. "Reynard is going to investigate the open cases. After all, whoever did this is still alive." They peered up at the stacks wistfully, then gave Barty a knowing sort of side look. "It is a real rogue's gallery up there, to be quite honest. Some notorious entities. The Black Dog of Newgate, Black Annis, the Lantern Man—myself." They winked as Barty jumped at that one.

Somewhere in those stacks, Jean called back at that comment. "Remind me to make a note in yours, Adam—a bloody awful maker of tea."

The giant chortled softly. "My maker did not render me with delicate nostrils to get the right smell for the leaves, Reynard, you know that. She had far different uses for me."

"Your… maker? She?" Barty blurted, but Adam waved it off.

"Eat your breakfast. Jean knows the cases we can use better than anyone. He will find what he needs. Until then we are best suited to wait." They turned away, busying themselves by pouring tea and avoiding Barty's eyes. Whatever that revelation meant, Adam was in no mood to elaborate, and Barty did not want to push his luck further than he already had.

Chewing on a piece of bread wordlessly, Barty looked around the room more carefully as he stood numbly at the table. There were books of various ages scattered about, when he looked closely. The shelves were also carefully arranged, more than he might have thought. There were carefully placed dividers between different collections, each section of books being notes on just one entity, or case, that had not yet been closed. Some were only a single book or file. Some were several. But eventually his eye trailed to an oaken cabinet, with glass windows and key locked doors, that stood all on its own at one end of the room. It was filled with volumes, dozens of them. Some, ancient scrolls carefully bound, others, more modern, leather-bound volumes. For some reason he felt drawn to it, and so, still chewing, he wandered around the room to the cabinet.

There was a painting set above it, as well as a trio of mismatched carven statuettes from different periods. The painting was more modern, maybe a century old at most. It depicted a scene in a darkened garden of thorn bushes and twisted trees, and amongst them was a woman in a red evening gown, her dark hair obscuring much of her face. There was a strangely ethereal quality to the art work, something about it that seemed out of focus. The eyes, however, were startlingly, piercingly captured, staring out of the painting with an intensity that took the breath away. It was as though the artist had placed all the power of their focus and talent into the eyes, and nothing more than that. Dark, knowing eyes that were clear and yet kept everything hidden.

The three statuettes were also each of a woman. They were different in that their period of make was clearly widely spaced apart—one appeared to ancient Greek in its origin, wrought of marble, the woman clad in a gown of diaphanous material that left little to the imagination. Much the same could be said of the others, which appeared to come from the renaissance period and later still, all of a beautiful, alluring woman. She appeared strangely familiar each time Barty looked for long enough, before he shuddered and looked away. Something about her eyes was powerfully arresting.

There was a name, set below the painting, etched into a brass plate. Barty read it aloud without meaning to. "*Carmilla.*"

"Best distance yourself from that one, Barty." Jean's voice came from behind, with an uncharacteristic note of warning that lacked threat. "That one is dangerous."

Barty turned but could not see Jean at all, lost from his sight amongst the rows of shelves. Had he heard him?

Adam was perusing papers on the table, but glanced up and nodded. "I, for once, agree with our esteemed leader," they said dryly. "The Case of the Woman in Red has been open longer than any other on the Hunters' record, and with good reason. She is astonishingly dangerous, and has been for a millennia."

Barty could not help but make an astonished sound at such an incongruous statement. "I am sorry, a *thousand years*?" He blinked, unable to comprehend it, before his mind tried to rationalise instead. "Oh, forgive me. I assume it must be a persona, rather than the same person."

"No, it is just the one," Jean said darkly, as he reappeared from the rows, flicking through a tome. "The same one, who has haunted our order since its conception." He grimaced, snapping the book shut and turning back into the stacks, clearly not finding what he wanted. "Aside from that, I would ask you leave it well alone for the time being." He vanished from sight. Barty made surreptitious eye contact with Adam, who gave a subdued shrug before speaking in their rumbling not-at-all-a-whisper. "The Red Woman is a sore point for this household, Barty. Best leave it alone for the moment."

"Quite," Jean said, returning, slamming a heavy tome down on the table and scattering some sheets of paper. Adam placidly replaced them as the Hunter went on. "Currently I am looking for anything that matches even the vague description that Benji gave us on our killer."

"There was not much that he saw," Barty agreed with a frown. He cast one last glance to the cabinet of Carmilla—dozens of tomes he could see, all chronicling this single entity—and then returned to properly inspect the documentation. "I assume there is not much then to be found?"

"Entirely the opposite," Jean replied sourly. "There is too much. When the details are vague, even tenuous connections can be made with all too much ease."

Barty considered a moment, then stepped forward, setting down his tea cup. "May I? This is something I have familiarity with."

Jean replied with a raised brow that gradually, reluctantly, gave way to a nod.

Taking a deep breath, Barty went through the files on the tabletop briefly before he pressed on. "We need to look here, first. We still do not know what the connecting fact is between the cases. Heathwood is just one out of five after all."

"That we know of," Jean added. "I went over these files myself—a various collection of afflicted humans and other creatures not yet sure of themselves. But none of them caught my eye."

Barty nodded to this, and went on. "That is what we can see, yes. But what about that which we cannot?"

Jean went quiet, as Barty started to warm to the subject. "It is not what is being said, or found in the files, it is about what is *not*. It is what I used to find people, to learn about events, I even used it to—" He cut himself short.

"You used it to find me," Jean finished for him quietly, but there was a hint of agreement to the words. He nodded, then set down the tomes he was carrying. "Very well then, Mister Barty. Impress my sensibilities. Show me what is missing."

Barty took a deep breath, then turned one of the case files about, reading the description briefly before setting his forefinger down on it, pinning it in place. "We know what Heathwood was doing. We know that he was studying the monstrous, or what he called that, and trying to treat the mind to alleviate symptoms in the body. But *where* did he learn that? Was it something he ever discussed with you? You were associates after all."

Jean was frowning, his arms folded as he tapped one elbow with his opposite forefinger. "Ulysses and I spoke at length over the years. I approached him for insight into the workings of the deranged mind, in most cases. He would ask instead about the mind of the monstrous. We would approach both to find a common ground, and thus find the joined aspect of each—where one or the other ended, or became one. It was useful for me to expand my knowledge of perspectives." His frown deepened, those gray, shadowed eyes darkening. "I admit I find it unusual, in retrospect, that he kept his research from me. There was little to no reason for him to do so, considering how long this work of his was going on."

Adam was sat upon the ground at this point, their massive form taking up a whole corner of the room. "They may have sought to keep it from you for the sake of surprise? Something to reveal to impress you?"

But Jean was already shaking his head. "No. He was free with his research and findings, but not with this. He went to great lengths to keep this to himself."

"In my own experience, people conceal such things for two key reasons," Barty put in, his voice subdued. "The first, to protect someone, or something, or themselves. It is possible that this is the case here, that Doctor Heathwood felt compelled to keep the identities and treatment of these individuals secret, or because of the second reason. He was ashamed."

"Ashamed of treating those who needed his aid?" rumbled Adam with a frown, but Barty waved one hand to dismiss that notion as though brushing it from the air, the idea forming and growing stronger as he spoke.

"No, not of that—but of how he came to that point. How did he know how to do this? How did he learn that this might work?" He took a deep breath, and reached into his pocket to pull out the photograph. "I think I might have an answer, right here."

He placed it on the table, a touch embarrassed. Jean came alongside and swept the picture up, scowling as he inspected it. "That is Heathwood at the front there. Where did you get this? From the office?" His tone showed a touch of irritation, which Barty guessed was because it had not been seen earlier, but there was genuine curiosity as well. He nodded, a bit shamefaced, before he went on to explain.

"I scooped it up amongst all the notes. I have been meaning to bring it to attention, but I am sorry to say it lapsed from my mind with everything taking place." His ears reddened, and he held his breath, expecting to be shouted at without realising why, but Jean merely sighed, setting the picture back down.

He stepped away before speaking stiffly over one shoulder. "It was a very difficult day, Mister Barty. Let us be glad you remembered as promptly as you have." He stood, gesturing for Barty to go on before he stood with both hands held at his back. "Continue with your line of reasoning. What is your answer?"

Taking a deep breath, Barty did just that, his heart still racing. "Heathwood kept this picture amongst all his files of his inhuman patients. But he did not keep it prominent. It was hidden away as well, hidden away amongst files themselves that were *also* kept concealed. He did not want to look at it, but he did not want to throw it away either. It was a reminder. A reminder of something he was ashamed of." Adam and Jean both remained quiet, watching intently as Barty pushed on, a little breathless now, pulling the pieces from the air and putting them into place with his words. "Something happened with this picture. Something happened where it was taken." He turned it over, stabbing his finger down on the name. "Bethlehem, in 1883. That must surely mean Bethlehem Hospital. It has to."

"*Old Bedlam,*" Jean said quietly, his grim tone lending a dread weight to that name, and Barty shuddered before, faltering only somewhat as he looked between his two observers, he went on.

"Bedlam hospital has had its name earned a dozen times over. It has had *horrible* things happen inside its walls, over and over again. Something happened there with Ulysses Heathwood, something to do with this picture, something that stopped him from telling you about his work, *and* compelled him to do the work in the first place. Something he was ashamed of."

"Or *someone,*" Jean murmured staring off into the middle distance. Barty blinked as Jean went on. "His killer knew him. And he knew them." He dragged his gaze back to Barty, and nodded. "As Benji said—there were no screams. Not at first. Just the one, when the realisation set in." He went quiet, frowning.

Adam had been watching the exchange before they finally spoke up themselves. "You were right to bring him into this after all, Jean." There was a faint note of respect, and fainter, buried beneath it, a regret as well that Barty did not understand.

"He brought himself into it," Jean said dismissively. "He found *me* after all, despite all my efforts not to be." He stopped at the table, and tapped on the pile of books as he stared down at the files for a moment, contemplating something, before turning and looking at Barty directly.

"How confident of this are you? Truly, I mean."

Barty stammered, floundering for an answer, before giving a helpless shrug. Jean rolled his eyes, exasperated, and tried again. "Spit it out, Barty. If you had to bet a life upon it, would you?"

Barty swallowed. "That is something of a difficult bargain to make, sir."

"One I make every day," Jean replied bluntly. "Answer the question."

The young man struggled with it, then struck out for desperate honesty. "At least half sure. If I knew more about the people in the picture, and why it was there, it would certainly help in the matter."

"Well then," Jean said with a firm nod, "that is easily managed." He sounded quite pleased.

Barty was left mystified. "Sir?"

"Crook, as you have chosen to call him, will be waiting outside with his carriage. He will take you there to ask your questions, since you are so skilled with them. I am better suited to my files here, to see if there is yet something that I might have missed," Jean said with a wave of his hand. Barty opened and closed his mouth, to which Jean raised a brow. "You have talent in this, Barty. I say that without irony nor rancour. If you wish to learn the answers, this is a part you can do." A mirthless smile flickered. "You found me after all. This will surely prove to be less protected to unravel."

Barty could not think of an answer to that, but as Jean turned back into the cases, it was Adam who spoke up. "Forgive me, Barty, but did I hear that correctly? *Crook?* You gave him a name?" They sounded astonished. Even somewhat horrified, which made Barty confused.

"He asked me to."

"If that was but the limit of his foolishness with the Prince of Midsummer," Jean called from amongst the bookshelves. "But Crook is his name now. Let him figure out the rest."

Barty was baffled, but Adam actually looked impressed as they pushed themselves back to their feet slowly. "You are a braver being than I thought, Mister Barty. Come. You appear to have a long day ahead of you."

Barty did not have the strength to argue. Snatching up the photograph, he followed Adam out of the library, leaving Jean alone to search the words of men and women long dead.

When the door opened, the carriage was already there. Resplendent and fresh, unmarked and spotless. The four horses that pulled it along stood proud and tall, larger than most such steeds and, somehow, a bit rougher rather than sleek and carefully presented like other coach horses tended to be in London.

Crook was leaning back against the door to the carriage, grinning. That wide, toothy grin with glittering eyes, his silver hair bound back. Far from crooked, this time he towered straight and rigid, arms folded across his chest. He touched his brow, opened the door to the carriage, and beckoned Barty enter. This made Barty pause.

It was obvious by this point that there was something *different* about Crook. The reaction everyone had to him was telling. Cutter, the brute from when this had all begun, was terrified of him. Adam held him in caution. And his behaviour aside, there were questions to be asked—but now was not the time to slow.

So, he approached confidently. Now dressed in the clean and pressed apparel that Adam had taken care of for him, to give an appearance somewhat more professional for his venture, Barty took some of the courage from earlier and strode up to Crook, tipping his hat in reply.

"If I may, Master Crook, I would prefer to join you on the driver's seat this afternoon instead. After all…" He gestured to the autumn gloom, not yet raining but promising at some point, that hung over all. "It is such a fine day."

Crook reared back at this, his spine curling as his features twisted into bemusement, before he straightened with a snap. Laughing, and with but a single finger, he caused the door to the carriage to slam closed once more, and then *slid* up the side of the carriage, like water running backwards up a hill, to place himself in the carriage driver's seat. Eagerly, he grinned down at Barty and patted the leather beside him. "Well then," he said gleefully, but his eyes glittered strangely. "Far be it from me to deny a fool his delight."

This did not reassure Barty in the least. He climbed with difficulty, a distant shadow to Crook's unnatural agility. The coach seat seemingly had not been designed for a normal person to have easy access to; there was a hint of a ladder, but no foot points for a person to get a step up to the seat. Crook quite clearly did not need them, which made it clear that this coach was his and his entirely.

But Barty was slight and spry and wriggling, and he made his way up. Crook nodded, seemingly impressed, and the carriage set off smoothly before Barty had found his seat. Falling into it at the strange man's side, he gathered himself.

"You know where we are going, then?" A foolish question, but it was one to start the conversation.

Crook gave a genteel snort. "Of course I do. I can find a dream in starlight, a dandelion in rain. I can find a place where the touched by the sky scream into silence and ignorance, for it is a far simpler thing than that."

I suppose that means yes, Barty thought, baffled, as he nodded hesitantly. As the journey continued, he struggled to think of another way to phrase his questions. It had seemed much easier until he sat next to Crook. There was something about his presence, when this close, that was more than a little unsettling, a scratch at the base of the brain that only got worse as time went on, building pressure.

"You know, you sons of lost stones really do need to hide your curiosities better." Crook sighed, watching the road ahead as the coach rattled along. Barty was taken off guard, which, from the sly wink he was given, was precisely the point. Crook gave a high, sharp laugh that descended into giggling. "Oh, sweet lad. You are *brimming* with questions to the point of bursting. It is writ large in your eyes and sings in your ears."

Barty struggled to understand the bewildering speech as the carriage turned and twisted, changing direction sometimes abruptly as Crook gave a twisting gesture with his wrist that might have been the approximation of a bow.

"Go on. I will read your clumsy tongue and pull the truth you mean from it, though I fear I will follow in similar clarity —which is to say, none at all." This was far from reassuring, as Barty could barely understand Crook's speech as it was. He struck out for the simplest.

"I notice you do not come into the Lodge… do you have a place nearby that you stay at? It must be terribly close, since you are able to come so very quickly when called." He pushed his hat down, irrationally afraid that the motion of the carriage would cause it to sail from his head. "There is no coach house behind the Lodge, after all. Is there one close by?" Crook's ever wide grin twitched a touch.

"I keep it between the stones, in the puddles of rainwater that are freshest and cleanest," he replied with a wink. "It is where I am, and I am *everywhere*." A long, pale finger reached out and tapped Barty's temple like the strike of a snake. "Especially in here, I can see." Crook sniffed. "I fear it is a little too barren for my tastes, but it shall do."

"That makes *entirely* no sense," Barty responded with exasperation. The grin on Crook's face faded a touch, an air of disappointment to it.

"Does it? You live in the butchered bones of the world, the dead bodies of the ancients of the wood—vast beings who watched the rise of the first world, and the one after, and the one after that until mankind deigned to name them 'tree'," Crook said sourly. "You craft glittering cages from the corpses of those far worthier and wiser than you. You will have to pardon me that I find such an idea repugnant, and could never bear to be confined in such a horror."

Barty blinked at that. He was trying to digest the strangeness of the statement, and for a moment he wondered if he should make a comment about the coach upon which they now sat, which clearly was a thing made of wood itself. He was about to say something along those lines, but the words stuck firmly in his throat as realisation dawned.

Crook was not steering.

True, he held the reins, but it was completely for the show of things. He gave them no tugs, he made no application to the brake nor made any efforts towards guiding the four horses whatsoever. And yet the coach rolled along at a brisk, fierce pace. They were even now careening over a bridge, overtaking a slower wagon as Crook laid back, stretching idly, and Barty buried the scream in his throat, at war with his fascination.

The horses knew where they were going. Moving as a single entity, the massive beasts were untroubled, unhurried, and yet had a tremendous energy and power to them. Barty had never really paid attention to coaches and horses before. They were a thing in London—the many, many clean up wagons armed with weary men clutching shovels to take care of their passing was sign enough of that, if not the smell—but they were so common, so prevalent, as to be something in the background, not paid attention to. But he was paying attention now. The horses had no blinders, and their tackle was simple, just to keep them secured to the coach. The coach itself was also an oddity. The more Barty looked, he could not make out lock or bolt, no seam nor notch. The coach was almost like it was all a *piece*, singular and yet skilfully set apart. He put his hand to what he thought was the leather of the seat, and it felt *strange* under his hand. It did not feel like leather at all. He could not even begin to explain what it felt like.

"You would not believe the song I had to sing to bring this forth," Crook said with sly humour, bringing Barty back to the world with a startled shock. His eyes were bright, shining, and fixed on Barty like a pair of stars. "But it was a wonder. A skin to be worn in the city of men, a disguise to blend us all forth." He laughed, high and clear, terrifying. "Oh, but I love how blind you all are."

Barty swallowed, sweat beading on his brow. "Who are you, Crook? Jean… Jean called you the Prince of Midsummer. Who are you, really?"

Those shining eyes grew brighter, colder, a glee of the unknown and the abyss filling the world. "Ah, but the Huntsman would place the breadcrumb trail first, would he not? Of course, of course." One eye went dark, a wink to swallow a world. "We are that which was first, dear Barty. We are that which is Eldest."

And then the world came rushing back, sound and fury, light and air as Barty remembered to breathe again, and Crook's voice spoke bright, innocent and friendly. "And here we are!"

The jerking sensation of shock yanked Barty back to the world, tearing him away from the abyss that he was seated beside. He blinked, looking around, before focusing fully.

From the outside, Old Bedlam did not appear so terrible. It had a high iron fence, a tall dome set on its roof, and many high, open windows. It had a wide grounds, and a great, wrought iron gate. It had the appearance of something ordinary at first, and it was not until one looked closer that they could see the bars upon the windows, or realised people did not look at it as they hurried past. There was a palpable air about it as well, a note at the edge of hearing that lanced upon thought.

"Best mind your step, dear child," Crook whispered at his ear, making Barty stiffen. "Take a wrong step there, and they'll never let you out. Best play your hand correct and clear, yes-yes?"

"Thank you," Barty replied haltingly, as he pushed himself from the seat and landed heavily on both feet on the ground, straightening up with a wince. "You will not be coming with me?"

A high laugh, clear and strong and pulling confused stares from passersby. "By the *bones* no. I would set that entire hall to dancing until it fell upon all within, and we cannot have that." He shrugged, swinging the end of the reins around in a pensive circle. "Not yet, at least. I'll be near when you are done. Ta-ta, lost child." And without command or gesture, the carriage took off, going from still to speeding just quickly enough to be disquieting, and Barty was alone.

Alone, but not without purpose. He took a deep breath and drew himself up; he knew what he needed to do, and he remembered how to do it. So, shouldering his satchel pack, he set off.

Vaguely, he remembered his overly heavy, overly obnoxious phonograph. It was still sitting at the Lodge, waiting to be used—Adam had no doubt had a curious look at it by this point—and irrationally he wondered if it would be useful here. He put the thought aside. Eventually it would have its use.

The iron carriage gate had a secondary, smaller entrance to one side as was customary. Barty pushed it open and stepped inside, and no sooner had he done so than a heavy-set man in a white, buttoned up uniform appeared from a small gatehouse. He had a baton at his belt and a no nonsense expression, as he levelled a finger with a cry. "Here now, what d'you think you're doing?"

Barty probably should have knocked, in retrospect. Instead, he fell back on his tried and true method when confronted by such things and lied ferociously instead.

"Oh, how do you do, sir. I am here from the Times. I believe I am expected?" He was not, and he *definitely* was not, but this thug would not know that. *Confidence. Display it, show it. You belong here. You belong here more than he does.*

The guard frowned, wavering. An official voice, an official question, an official name; they made a man used to fearing all three pause. "I will need your name, then."

Barty opened and closed his mouth. He had nearly said Mister Barty, a name no guard would accept. The guard frowned as Barty recovered and, rummaging for a name from his long catalogue of pseudonyms that he had had used in the past, said aloud, "But of course. I am Mister Barty." He blinked. Stammering, he tried again. "Apologies, I am of course *Mister* Barty."

He had not intended this. He had not at all intended to use his name but there it was, spilled from his lips unwanted. And then *again* on the apparent correction.

The guard tilted his head, clearly unimpressed, then spoke sharply. "You best come with me, *Mister* Barty. We'll see to the front desk." There was menace in that tone, and Barty fell into step as they marched along. His attempt at authority had been rent away. But more than that, Barty felt the slow and sickening realisation. There was something wrong with his name. Suddenly, out of nowhere… it no longer felt like it fit.

This made him look up at the entrance to the hospital as they drew nearer, with a sense of apprehension that only grew. A man forgetting what his name was, a man forgetting his own sense of self, was not a man destined to wander freely on the streets. The place seemed to beckon, ready to swallow him up for his falsehoods. Dimly, buried in its depths, he thought he heard a scream, high and despairing, a call to a God that refused to hear or forgive.

He forced it down. He had faced worse, and gone into worse, than this. He would not be dissuaded now. Above all, he was tired of being only vaguely necessary, of being on the outside looking in of this whole affair. He could do this. He had done it plenty a time before.

Entering in through the double front door, the entrance hall of the hospital was a severe sort of place. There were corridors leading off to each side, and high staircases leading to offices and other floors, as well as seemingly more patient rows. There were distant echoes coming from the depths of the building, discordant sounds that rang of desperation and despair, and there was a strong chemical scent over everything, of soap and solvents, acidic on the nostrils.

The nurse seated at the front desk was a woman to whom the word 'acid' was a potent application of character. She was not so much formed as she was *etched* instead, all harsh lines and cold countenance. She had to be in her late fifties, but she had the stiffness instead of a millennia old mummy, as she continued to write in what appeared to be a logbook as Barty approached with whom he could not help but think of as his captor. She did not look up, and the guard said nothing as she continued to write with her pen. *Scratch, scratch, scratch* went the pen nib, scrawling onto rough paper with patient care, seemingly with no intention of stopping. The guard simply waited. Barty got the impression he had endured this more than once before.

Several interminable heartbeats of waiting later, the woman spoke, her voice disinterested to the point of nearly being disembodied from the rest of her. "What appears to be the issue?"

"Reporter from the Times, ma'am," the guard replied dutifully and sharply, even as Barty was opening his mouth. "Said that he's expected, ma'am."

The nurse paused, then carefully placed her logbook to one side, sliding it across her desk with a scrape before shutting it. She then set her hands before herself and looked down her glasses at Barty with an excruciating stare, before she finally responded. "I do not recall any such arrangement." Her tone was silken with its spite, before she went on, "and your name, sir from the Times?"

"Says his name is 'Mister Barty', ma'am," the guard interjected, once more cutting Barty off before he could speak. He was looking at Barty now with a smirk, who could tell he was enjoying the show—whatever it was, but Barty surely was not.

"Let us see now," the desk nurse said slowly, carefully pulling forth another logbook that she opened and started to turn the pages slowly. She went page by page until she found the current date and entry, and placed one pincer-like finger upon the point to tap it twice.

She looked up at Barty, and gave a serpentine smile. "I am afraid there is no meeting here upon this date. I am afraid I will have to reject your entry to the hospital, Mister Barty." There was a note of finality to the statement. The guard turned to Barty, gesturing to the exit promptly, but Barty, tired of being unable to speak himself, cast his dice and pushed forward.

"Please, do check again. My name is Mister Barty, from the Times."

The nurse nodded. "I heard you, yes, and no, it is not here," she replied with false pleasantness.

Barty strove again as the guard put a hand to his shoulder, firmly, a hand used to handling unruly patients in an impatient manner. "Please, it is in regards to the occurrence of 1883, and the work of Doctor Ulysses Heathwood."

The words came out louder than he intended, but they worked. There was a pause as the nurse blinked, flicking a look to the guard, leaning back. The words had struck a nerve. *When you have no cards, all you can do is bluff.* The moment froze for a time, before the nurse frowned, her already pursed lips tightening further. Barty could see she was about to order his removal regardless.

A door opened above and, on the upper balcony, a man stepped into view. Leaning over the railing, he called down to capture the attention of the scene below. "I beg your pardon, but did you say the Times, my good man?"

Barty craned his head back. A pleasant-faced man in his early fifties looked down at him, with a curious expression and a slight smile. It was the face of a man who knew a lie when he heard one, and knew how to spin one of his own making as necessary.

There was no point halting the gamble now. Barty cast the dice again, and put on a smile as well. "Yes, sir. And you are Doctor…" He played the artful hesitation, fishing for a name that was on the tip of his tongue and leaving a silence to be filled.

"Doctor Gaston, of course," the man replied, that smile remaining. "Come up, please." He nodded, and stepped back, calling over his shoulder. "Allow him in, Mrs Upton. He is expected."

Barty looked back to the nurse, Upton, and gave a smile and a nod, embodying the air of a man who is completely expected while, internally, Barty wrestled mightily with the fact that he was absolutely not. She gave him a flinty look, and nodded to the stairs. Released from his captors, Barty took the offered lifeline and soon found himself entering the office of one Doctor Gaston.

The man himself had a bemused expression. His office was well laid out, a study and place of record both, with a secluded corner that bore a complex chemistry set, currently at rest but nevertheless giving the room a peculiar chemical scent. A window was open, thankfully one of the few without bars, that gave the place a much needed breeze to dismiss the worst of it. Doctor Gaston made a gesture to a seat opposite his desk, remaining behind it as he watched Barty sit.

"Now then. Let us get the obvious out of the way," Gaston said with an amused tone. "You are not here at my request—and you are not here from the Times." Barty had expected this somewhat, but he still froze up a touch as Gaston went on. "I am familiar with Bell, the current editor, yes? And he would have sent word ahead. More than that, he would have probably employed someone a little more… bombastic, to the task. Much like the man himself."

Barty mused this over, before replying a bit meekly. "In truth, sir… I *was* employed by the Times until recently. Just not quite directly." He pushed on from that, trying to get some control back into the conversation. "I must confess though—this does not make much sense as to why you invited me up here."

Gaston leaned back, his expression remaining amused. He did not seem the least bit threatening, though his place of work was hardly one to inspire much confidence as to the gentility of his nature. He tapped on his wooden desk a moment with one hand, before nodding as he came to a conclusion and answering, "The sounds from below carry up wonderfully, the best thing about this office, especially since they do not convey back in the same fashion. So when you mentioned Doctor Heathwood, my curiosity was immediately piqued. I had to hear for myself."

"You were a friend of Doctor Heathwood then?"

Gaston was shaking his head. "Not quite. I know of his work, of his studies, and have researched them vigorously. More than that, I have something of a kinship with the man, or… had." He sighed then, his expression changing as he shook his head. "An awful business, what happened to him. I saw it in the newspaper, a terrible shock. Something about a burglar? The details were light in the missive, I admit."

Barty was careful in his response. "There are hints towards that there was more to it," he said slowly, "that it may have been in response to something in Doctor Heathwood's past." He pulled out a notepad, and a pencil. "You said you felt a kinship with him? Something you could elaborate upon."

"Nothing terribly profound, mind you," the doctor replied dismissively, before gesturing around the office. "This was once his office, is all, while he held tenure here. I took it not long after he retired from the position."

"You did not know him then?"

Gaston shook his head regretfully. "I am told he had an excellent reputation here, and forwarded the treatment of the insane and afflicted magnificently. But no, I never met the man." He paused. "Now, I have answered a few of your questions. Would you mind answering a few of mine?"

Barty prepared to lie, knowing full well he was speaking to a man skilled in recognising them by sheer effort of his work. "Please, go on."

"If you were not sent by the Times, who *did* in fact send you here? And what is their interest in the history of the hospital?" Gaston steepled his fingers with a brow raised. But Barty was ready for him.

"The truth is"—he hesitated for added effect—"I am here independently. But I am investigating with the hope of finding my answers to *create* a story. My inquiries so far have led to this place, and to an incident involving Doctor Heathwood in 1883, here, in the hospital. I did not have permission—but perhaps, in this instance, it was easier to seek forgiveness than the alternative."

Gaston made a humming sound that gave nothing away. He might have believed him, he might not have. "And why in particular that date? What prompted *that* in your statement of inquiry?"

"Is that year of particular significance?" Barty countered, but Gaston was dismissive.

"I fear not. As I said, I arrived somewhat past Doctor Heathwood's tenure. But please, answer the question."

"I found a picture amongst the doctor's effects," Barty answered honestly. One part honesty, now for the part of the half truth. "I believed there was a story in it, because there were some noteworthy individuals in it, people who were once part of this hospital, in fact, if I am not mistaken." He reached for his satchel, then paused. Now for the full lie. "I believe this story of the murder is linked in some fashion, sir. I believe if I can bring this to the editor, that the Times might employ me properly as a reporter, that I can continue a career there proper. A man in such a position must be able to show willingness, sir." He had a pleading note to his words, and a very real desperation.

Again, that non-disclosing hum was Gaston's reply as he sat in otherwise stillness. Eventually, the doctor nodded. "Might I see the picture in question?"

Barty was briefly reluctant, but recognised his lack of choice swiftly. He took the picture out and placed it down, passing it to Gaston by pushing it across the desk. The strange scene with the blurred man, and the various doctors and orderlies. Gaston tapped it twice, then spoke distantly, his expression subdued. "I know that this man here is Doctor Heathwood. The other is a Doctor Stringer, whom I recognise from his portrait. The other four I do not know." He frowned. "I believe Stringer was slain a month ago, by a weak foundation collapsing a wall atop him at his home," he said in a wary tone, casting his gaze back to Barty with a speculative look on his face.

"And the last? The one in the chair. Do you know who that is?"

Gaston blinked, looked back again, and a rueful chuckle escaped him. "Oh. Of course—no, I fear I do not, how could anyone? They are rather difficult to make out, after all."

"Quite, quite." Barty nodded, but felt disappointed despite himself. "But you said Doctor Stringer… was he also a resident at this hospital?"

"Consulting, I believe," Gaston said distantly, still frowning. "I admit, this has done more than pique my curiosity, Mister Barty. I wish I knew more about the answers to this mystery."

"What makes you call it such? A mystery, I mean." Barty looked to the picture again. For some reason, he wished he could take it back and put it back in his satchel.

"Two dead men in one picture?" Gaston replied wryly. "Both of them from this hospital? And not to mention, from what I can gather, the year 1883 was a slightly notorious one in this hospital's history." He shook his head. "I believe I am starting to gather why you believe there is a story involved in all of this."

"How so? What happened in 1883?"

The question made Gaston pause, before he pushed himself to his feet and stood at the window, arms folded at his back, a moment of contemplation before he answered.

"You understand that St. Mary Bethlehem has had a less than sterling reputation, in its past. Though it has been rebuilt several times in several different locations, this nevertheless remains true." He looked out of the window as he said it, speaking in a distant tone. "This hospital has been found... *lacking*, shall we say, in the treatment of its patients in the past."

Barty knew the stories of course—practically everyone did. Old Bedlam, the surest prison there was. Old Bedlam where people begged to die, where those being sent there pleaded to be hanged instead before it took hold of them. Men and women, the afflicted and the inconvenient, sent to a place they would never escape, and where in the name of science and *treatment* would be broken, over and over again, until there was nothing left to destroy. Barty was acutely aware that where he now sat was a place of nightmare for many. It made him shiver as he simply nodded, as Gaston continued.

"In the mid 1880's, a scathing report was given of the hospital and its treatment of certain patients. Most of the staff were either immediately removed, or were gradually relieved of their duties and assigned to other tasks," Gaston went on. "I was one of those who came on to replace those who were deposed." He gestured towards the picture while keeping his back to it. "Doctor Heathwood and Stringer were two of those who were made to depart. The rest are likely the same."

"You said *most* of the staff were replaced," Barty pointed out, to which Gaston nodded, his expression still distant.

"Most. There are still those that remain, but some of them are in entirely different positions to that which they once held, I must admit. The only one I can recall at the moment of any sort of prominence no longer holds tenure as a doctor… and yet they are a resident nevertheless."

Barty's expression betrayed his confusion, writ large upon his features before realisation dawned and smacked him fiercely across the face to knock his expression into astonishment. "Are you saying that they are instead a *patient?*"

Gaston nodded, a small, rueful smile upon his face. "Indeed so. Doctor William Markheim was a doctor in this hospital for nearly thirty years. But his repeated experiments, exposure to the addled mind and an inability to properly distance himself from the dangers presented, eventually took his toll, as his mind—a brilliant mind, from all accounts—degraded, as the disease took hold."

"You make it sound like insanity is contagious, Doctor Gaston," Barty said with a shudder in his subdued tone.

Gaston turned to face him then, rotating on one heel, his expression intent in a way that Barty did not quite like. "You instead seem to believe that it is not. Madness *is* contagious, young man. Though it might stem from a seed that takes root in all mortal minds, it is only properly allowed to blossom when it is watered and uncarefully tendered."

"Then that is what happened to Doctor Markheim?" Barty asked carefully.

Gaston nodded, returning to his desk. "His mind is now a thing of fractured delusions. He is haunted by figments and imaginings from his own tortured psyche, screaming at things that are not there and speaking to people long dead. It is a pitiful state, and I fear, despite a healthy regimen of vigorous treatment, he shows little sign of making progress. A most regrettable state of affairs, truly." He sighed and shook his head, his expression pensively thoughtful.

Barty shuddered, imagining all too easily what sort of 'treatment' was being applied, and wondering if figments were truly what was haunting this Markheim. However, he had come this far, and was not going to stop now.

"Do you believe that he would recognise anyone in the picture given? Perhaps the ones who have not been identified? Even the man in the chair?" Barty hazarded, knowing it was a poor chance but trying nevertheless.

Gaston raised a brow at this, and peered down at the photograph, chewing on his bottom lip a moment. He looked from Barty to the picture, then after a moment of thought, a slow smile formed on his lips, flickering away swiftly. "While I cannot promise anything, Mister Barty, I do believe it is worth the attempt. Come, we can go see him together, and see what he can tell us."

This made Barty blink. "Truly?" He had expected a refusal, was even preparing arguments to make, though he had every belief they would be futile. But Gaston had surprised him completely by going along with it. The doctor was nodding, pushing the photograph towards the young man.

"Truth told, I hate an unsolved mystery, Mister Barty. They weigh down my very soul. And you have roused my interest *considerably*. Shall we?" He moved to the door without waiting for an answer.

Barty took the opportunity where it presented itself. He stuffed the photograph back into his satchel and swiftly fell into step behind the doctor, who moved spryly and even eagerly along, his age giving way to his enthusiasm. They crossed the upper balcony to the opposite side—Barty glanced downwards to see the baleful glare of the elderly desk nurse following him every step of the way. While watching him, she reached out and rang a small bell upon her desk.

Leaving her behind, Barty caught up to Gaston. "There is something that yet makes me curious, Doctor." The man made one of those hums, but only glanced back briefly as Barty continued. "Your, interdiction shall we say… what truly prompted it? It cannot have been as simple as what you heard."

The doctor paused. He had reached a large, iron door at this point, and knocked upon it sharply. A metal shutter slid open, a pair of hard eyes looked at the two of them, and then the heavy rattle of chains began to follow, alongside sliding bolts as Gaston answered in a pensive tone.

"I am aware that those who report the news are very good at creating a story if one does not properly present itself, be it with or without supporting facts," he said. "Sometimes striking just enough of the truth to create a problem, bringing things to light. But the whole truth, Mister Barty, is that some things"—the iron door groaned open in front of them—"should never see the light of day again."

The corridor stretched out before them, with iron door after iron door on the left and right sides. The corridor had roof lights, and the floor and walls were painted an innocent white, but despite that the scene was still rendered dark. There was a *weight* to the air suddenly, that had nothing to do with the grim, heavy-set man who stood to one side of the doorway now, gesturing Gaston and Barty enter with a hand that held a baton. Gaston did so easily, but Barty hesitated. The road to the answers he sought was before him, but it was covered in razors. It promised lasting scars and bloody wounds, sleepless nights and memories that would not be shaken free. But he took his first step on it regardless.

"Do not fret, Mister Barty," Doctor Gaston said airily. "The patients are safely locked away at this time of day. They cannot pass their disease to you in their current condition, and most are safely medicated."

A door to the left suddenly rang with a massive, clanging report, the heavy structure shuddering as something struck it with enormous force. Barty imagined a wild beast, driven to frenzy and empowered not so much by muscle and bone but by their tortured imaginings. A moan of despair and fury issued from under the door, before wet sobbing followed. Barty had leapt away from the sound, but Gaston remained entirely unmoved.

"Most, at least," he said sourly, then turned and gestured to the orderly, who was already approaching with a grim look on his face. Gaston turned to Barty and paused, looking past him. "Mister Barty, do take a step towards me. Carefully now."

Instead, Barty followed Gaston's gaze to peer over his shoulder. A wild, staring, bloodshot eye framed in the bars of a small grill set in the iron door of a cell met his, joined by frantic, twisted whispering of what might have been words, but Barty could not tell. Fingers flexed through the small gaps in the bars on either side—reaching for Barty, hungry and needing. The whisper became a growl, desperate and starving, an unspeakable hunger buried within it.

He nearly fell into Gaston, who caught him with one hand, speaking in his pleasant tone. "Please, young man. Keep yourself from drawing too close to the cell doors. The patients that are roused can be quite energetic at most unexpected times." He let Barty go and gave him a pat on the shoulder. "Now then, shall we? Doctor Markheim is at the lower level of the high security wing. It is something of a walk, so we had best be off." The doctor, still smiling that relaxed, untroubled smile, continued on. Barty followed him. Behind them, a door was opened and the guard entered the cell of whoever who made the noise—screaming followed Barty then, interspersed with the sounds of blows and pain.

As they went, he wondered how the man could be so calm. So gathered. Gaston apparently did not feel the slightest bit of fear at their circumstances, of who surrounded them. He was assured of his power here, confident in his abilities. Even going to visit someone who once had been a doctor here themselves and now was apparently quite insane, it was clear that Gaston felt no concern for his own safety, be it of body or of mind.

Barty did not nearly feel so confident. He had encountered monsters, witnessed terrors out of imagining that he still did not fully believe. He now worked for a man who, while he better understood, could not help but recognise that they too were as dangerous as what he hunted. If he spoke of any of this, of any part of what he had seen and done, of the city beneath the feet of this one with the creatures of dream and nightmare dwelling within it, he would be cast into one of these cells in an instant. He would remain there forever also; a subject for experimentation, with no hope of release.

He swallowed and set off after the doctor, who was

humming as he walked, his white coat trailing behind him. They continued on into the depths of the hospital, down long corridors with locked doors. Laughter, screams, sobs, and every sound of hysteria came unexpectedly from corners and rooms, with no clear source. Barty wondered if they were instead the lingering echoes of those that had long died, or perhaps were sounds that simply refused to fade, bouncing through the hospital and haunting the ears of those that heard them before continuing on, perhaps lurking and waiting to strike again. Each cell promised a nightmare, the worst sort of imagining possible, and the faint chemical smell of cleaning could not cover the other smells of the foulest of human expulsions that hovered in the air seemingly everywhere.

Gaston was not troubled. He was still humming as he continued on his merry way, but Barty was sweating cold rivulets down his back. They approached a more secure part of the hospital, with iron bars and a gate separating them from the only slightly less secured cells. Two of the white-clad guards were on this side of it, both sat at a simple wooden table to one side. They sprang to their feet as Gaston approached, but he waved a hand idly, dismissing their attentiveness. "Gentlemen, good day. I was hoping to spend some time with Doctor Markheim. Do be so good as to bring my companion and I to him, would you?"

The guards exchanged looks, before the nearer, a man with a glass eye and a squared off beard, ventured to answer. "Begging your pardon, Doctor. I am afraid Markheim is undergoing treatment with Doctor Hyslop as we speak, in the Water Room." Barty frowned as he listened to the man. He seemed oddly afraid for some reason. Was there something about the 'Water Room' that warranted such a response? Or was it something else that he was missing?

"Ah." Gaston's reply was brief, but his lip curled. "Very

well. Escort us, if you could. You remain here." He gestured to the still silent guard, who nodded gratefully. The glass-eyed man grimaced, but he nodded and set off sharply. Gaston fell into his wake and Barty was dragged along with him.

There were more cells, but these were older; the doors on them were set with bars but it was easier to see into them. Barty could make out twisted figures that might well have been men and women, but it was impossible to truly tell for sure. They did not look entirely *real*, bearing marks of distortion around their features, their faces, their bodies. Jaws that were too large and eyes of different shapes. Twisted teeth and staring eyes that were full of fury, grief, horror, or nothing at all but drooling emptiness. And each of them watched him, followed him, from the depths of their cage. They stared like they all knew his name, all knew what he really was, all knew that he was hiding his true self from the doctor and the guard. The sweat running down his back turned from a trickle to a sheet. Barty did not want to be here.

They reached the end of a corridor, and a door from which the sound of rushing water could be heard. The guard opened the door, leading the pair into the chamber beyond.

It was surprisingly bright within. The room was high and well-lit by skylights, the grey skies above filtering in a bloom brighter than the dark corridors, but the scene within was one of horror. The floor was awash in cold water, with chunks of ice throughout that crunched underfoot. There were five figures in the room—a woman, and three standing men, gathered around the fourth. He was naked, and held aloft by chains at his wrists that kept him standing and with his limbs spread, though he sank to the ground in exhaustion. He was dripping wet, his face covered by a soaked wet cloth wrapped around his head, and Barty could hear the terrified, desperate attempts at breathing. They were painfully thin and ragged, a middle aged man from what little Barty could see, pale and trembling.

The woman wore the outfit of a nurse, carrying a large towel, and two of the men were of the same burly make as the guard, while the last was clearly a doctor—Hyslop, as he had been named a moment prior. Barty halted as realisation dawned as he beheld the scene. While it was not the same precisely, he could not help but see the comparison between it and the photograph he now carried; they were nearly standing in the same positions, all surrounding an equally helpless subject—mad or not, only he was the one who seemed afraid.

Doctor Hyslop was watching a pocketwatch, counting its ticking hands and giving Barty and Gaston an unimpressed look, his lips moving in the count before he finally nodded. One of the burly men picked up a hose, turned a crank, and blasted the shivering, chained man with the high pressure hose as they writhed, choked, and screamed into the wrapped cloth, the freezing water turning their skin red from the pressure of impact. It went on and on, as Gaston stood there waiting, and Barty stared in horror until he could not take it any longer.

"What are you *doing* to him?" He could not keep the sickened note from his voice.

Gaston did not seem troubled however, humming a moment before answering in a lightened tone. "This is shock therapy, in this case, water shock. The subject's mind and body is bombarded to set the conscious and subconscious thought into a desire for survival, to force it towards logical, controlled thought. We seek clarity within these walls, Mister Barty, after all." He peered at Barty, noting his expression, before the man with the pocket watch, Doctor Hyslop, also intervened.

"Were Doctor Markheim fully possessed of a sound mind,

he would recommend this same practice, young man. When we succeed in restoring his wits and returning his once brilliant mind to logic, rest assured, he will be thanking all of us present. This is for his benefit."

"Quite so, quite so," Gaston said softly. Barty was staring at Markheim, who had slumped in his chains with his head downcast. He was breathing raggedly, but otherwise did not move.

Doctor Hyslop stepped forward, snapping his watch shut and putting it in the pocket of his coat. He peered over his glasses severely at the pair, lingering on Barty before focusing properly on Gaston, his peer. A thin-faced man with a narrow, weak chin and wide, slightly-bulging eyes, he made Barty feel more out of place than ever. Unlike Gaston, he did not bother to affect a smile before speaking in a chilly voice. "Now then, gentlemen. What brings you to me?"

"Truth told, dear boy, we are in fact here for *him*." Gaston pointed to Markheim, which brought a puzzled, faint scowl to the face of Hyslop. "There is a puzzle from the past in this young man's possession which he might hold the answers to. I was hoping to be present while some questions were asked."

Hyslop looked unimpressed, giving Barty a short, dismissive looking over before answering brusquely. "He'll be non-communicative for some time yet. Maybe I can be of assistance?"

"I hardly think so," Gaston replied with amusement, which made Hyslop scowl all the harder. "Nurse, get him warmed up and dressed, and you two, bring him to one of the interview rooms on Floor Two."

"You want him chained still, sir?" one of the brawny guards asked and Gaston nodded.

"I certainly do. I am curious, not a fool. If you will excuse us, Hyslop?" The doctor in question was scowling, his features dark, but Gaston was already carrying on with Barty following.

"He does not seem pleased," Barty murmured to Gaston.

The doctor snorted, shrugging. "He never likes to lose his playthings ahead of schedule. But he is no match for the curiosity of my mind. Come along!" His tone was energetic, excited even as he continued on ahead, unphased and untroubled. Barty cast a last glance behind him as they went back into that corridor of the mad, to take in the brightly-lit scene one last time. He knew full well it would follow him long after he left Old Merry Bethlehem.

CHAPTER 13

BY MEANS MEASURED

Doctor William Markheim might have been brilliant once. He might have had a magnificent mind, full of clever anecdotes and witty repartee. He might have been a delight at parties, skillful in steering conversation, a wonderful dinner host, and more besides. Well learned, he was probably handsome at one point as well. He may have been vigorous, engaging, and enlightening. He could have been anything someone could imagine.

The reality of his existence now was such that there was no telling whom he once was. His body was wasted away, scarred and lean, the skin hanging from him incorrectly and loosely. His hair was cut short to his scalp by an unkind hand, leaving him with mismatched clumps and scar tissue. There were scratch marks covering his face and arms, healed, and scabbed gouges into his own skin, and his fingernails were so chewed back as to be non-existent. He huddled now as he was carried under each arm, a tall man on each side of him rendering him small and fragile. Barty had never quite seen anyone so badly beaten down—nor had he ever seen anyone so terrified.

Hyslop had accompanied them. He had not said much, but that was not a problem for Gaston, who spoke enough for the both of them. He had explained how the hospital now treated most cases with a combination of chemistry, electroshock and cold water shock treatments, restraints and, of course, hypnosis. The idea being that the mind could, with sufficient stress, endeavour to right itself again.

"The root of all evil is, in one fashion or another, said to be trauma of some kind," Gaston explained in a pleasant tone that, in the setting, caused Barty's skin to crawl. "It lends to extraordinary expression, it is true, but it also creates our brightest moments as well." He led the group into a small room with a single small window near the high roof, too small for a person to fit through but set with iron bars regardless. "Put him down there." Gaston gestured, indicating a single stool, bolted to the floor with manacles set at its base.

The cringing Markheim, head bowed and his patchwork face shadowed, was led and sat, chained and locked. Both men then eased away—but not too far. They watched with hands folded before them from the corners, but certainly not far enough away as to need more than a single swift step to return. Hyslop lurked at the entrance with his arms folded across his chest and a scowl painted on his lips, fixed into permanence.

Gaston waved idly to his sour-faced compatriot as he stood contemplative in his consideration of Markheim. "The good doctor here believes, as most of those present, that the treatments we offer are our most effective in treating the insane— of keeping the disease at bay, to force our minds to strength by repeated inoculation to trauma; much as might be had in taking a vaccine."

Barty could tell by Gaston's slight frown, and Hyslop's rather irritable stare, that there was a point of contention here, and decided to voice it. "You believe otherwise, Doctor Gaston?"

"He holds a similar stance to others in his field, and those who have come before him," Hyslop interjected with a sneer. "Doctor Gaston believes that words are the most effective tool we have, in that he believes one can talk to the insane, expecting rationale and discourse."

"To a degree in relation to a reasonable time and place, Theo," Gaston replied patiently. "I agree that more firm measures are necessary on occasion, but there *must* be some manner of discourse to suit. Our words are what define us, and they can guide us as well. They are the truest measure of us, surely?"

Barty was about to say something to that, but a hollow, rasping chuckle came from the chained man, as the two doctors and Barty also shot their gaze towards the restrained Markheim.

He was shaking his head, his gaze still lowered as he gave that rusty laugh, a sound full of despair and resignation both. It was an utterly hopeless sound, wrought of enduring misery, as both eyes lifted and fixed the trio with a glittering gaze of hollow malice.

"I always used to think… it was actions, that defined who we are." His voice was a croak, harsh and pained. He swallowed, then coughed, before pressing on. "Actions make us, make us who we are, yes? Make us something, take from us…" The moment of clarity started to fade into confusion, the glitter in that gaze dying as they looked out over nothing. "Take from, yes… take everything…" He fell silent, then started to rock back and forth, letting out a faint crooning sound, barely legible. He was singing. High, reedy, pained, the words illegible—it might have been a hymn, or a children's nursery rhyme. Barty could not tell.

Gaston turned to Barty and, to his surprise, gestured for the younger man to step forward. "Well then, young man, there you go. You have him. I am curious as to how you will manage to ask him, however." There was no cruelty in his tone, just an honest curiosity. Behind him, Hyslop snorted, folding his arms tighter across his chest as he turned his back, shaking his head dismissively.

Barty swallowed, and looked to the now motionless madman, the chains that held him jangling slightly from his shivering. He did not seem dangerous, but the words of Gaston earlier nevertheless made him uncomfortable, insomuch as madness being a thing contagious. After the time he had spent with Jean, with the Undercity, and the encounters he had survived so far, he was ready to believe it more than he liked. But it also strengthened him as he took a brisk step forward. He had made it this far. He could manage this too.

"Good day, Doctor Markheim," he said gently. "How are you feeling today?"

A bitter, rasping croak of laughter, as he shook his head. That appeared to be all the answer on offer, and all that was necessary, so Barty floundered a moment before gathering himself. "I am told you were a doctor here in the year of 1883," he pressed on. "I was wondering if I could talk to you about that."

"Eighty three, eighty three," Markheim hissed. He spasmed, shaking in his chains, rocking back and forth as he continued to hiss. "You were not there. You were not there." He fixed Barty with a single, glaring, unblinking eye, the other squeezed shut as he tried to keep him in focus. "You smell different." The tone was a flat declaration, a statement that brooked no argument, and it left Barty a touch disarmed as he struggled to think of a way to begin—before Markheim shuddered convulsively, and then went still, his head hanging, before he spoke in a voice that was less a rasp and more strained. "…Apologies." He forced it out, not looking at Barty as he tried something approaching a normal response, every syllable clearly an effort. "I am… I am not well, sir."

Barty was inclined to agree with that. But he pressed on, mindful of the stares on his back from the others in the room, none of which were making it easier. "I am… more than understanding, sir," he tried tactfully. "My name is Mister Barty—" he was silenced as Markheim interrupted, loud and explosive.

"Mister Barty, Mister Barty! Seven o'clock, time for a party!" His stare returned, frenzied. "I would adore a brandy, you know."

"Yes. Quite," Barty finally responded. This was not going well. "As I said, I am here asking about events in this hospital in 1883, and I was wondering if you could—"

But again, Markheim lost patience with him. He wrenched at the chains, causing a loud clattering as he snapped his interruption. "No. *Wrong*. Not the what but the who, not the when, but the why." He shuddered again, curling inwards. "Shouldn't have touched it, shouldn't have touched it!" His voice cracked into a sob. "Look what it has done to us." He started to mutter the same words over and over again. "Shouldn't have touched it, shouldn't have touched it…" An endless, stuttering mantra, hunched in on himself.

Barty looked over his shoulder to the two doctors. Both Hyslop and Gaston were watching on—one with a sneer and one with a mysterious look of faint amusement—like a teacher observing a student. Neither doctor looked at all inclined to help, perhaps as mystified as Barty was, but either way he was getting no assistance. So, he reached into the satchel at his side and pulled out the photograph, holding it up in front of Markheim's face, just a few inches away as he continued to rock and mutter.

"Do you recognise this photograph, Doctor Markheim?" Barty said evenly, but with a raised volume—foolish, perhaps, the man seemed entirely capable of hearing him, but maybe he was trying to simply drown out the muttering. "That is Doctor Heathwood, the others are—"

Markheim stared at the picture, his lips moving. Swiftly, opening and closing as he stared without blinking at the photograph. He was speaking, but it was too faint for Barty to hear.

"Doctor Markheim?" He leaned forward, ignoring the fact that the two doctors behind him had paused and come closer as well.

Once closer, Barty could hear that Markheim was murmuring, rapidly and without pause, a long unbroken diatribe that he could make out if he focused. "… *Yes I agree, Doctor Stringer, we can take no chances but as Doctor Heathwood says… now then, good fellows, hold our subject down, down, yes we cannot let him get out of control again, not again—Stringer, we should experiment, yes, we should see what this concoction of the subject can do what it can do, yes…*"

Barty eased back, blinking. "You were there, Doctor Markheim? Are you in this picture?" But Markheim could not hear him. He continued to stare at the picture and his lips continued to move.

"Fascinating," Gaston said quietly, appearing alongside. "Can you understand what he is saying then?"

Barty blinked, and spoke out the corner of his mouth, keeping the photograph held aloft as the madman stared and mumbled endlessly. "A few. I recognise names…"

Heathwood. And Stringer. Stringer was the other doctor that was murdered. Does that mean…? Does he know the others?

Gaston made that hum sound as Barty pushed on. "Who else was there, Doctor Markheim? Do you remember?"

Hyslop snorted, shaking his head. "He won't be much help to you, sir. His mind is broken as surely as any I have ever seen."

"All I need is a name. Just a name I've not yet heard," Barty said firmly. But Markheim was muttering lower now, softer than ever, retreating inwards, curling in on himself. Gaston sighed, shaking his head in seeming frustration, and Barty threw caution to the winds and drew closer, to bring himself within inches of Markheim's muttering form and tried again.

"Doctor Markheim, if you could at all—"

But again, he was cut off. Except in this instance, the circumstances were quite different.

Markheim grabbed him. His hands were as cold as ice, wrought of nothing but bone and nearly entirely fleshless, but nevertheless full of an awful strength that seized him and bore him down. Barty was pinned on the ground, and the chained man was atop him, wheezing desperately. The two doctors were shouting, the guards were shouting as they tried to pull the wizened figure off Barty, who could not even scream as he tried to work himself free. Each figure there was straining as they tried to pry the raving lunatic off of Barty, but all their strength achieved naught; for madness, true, pure madness, is fuelled by a strength that defies all reason. Barty could feel his bones creaking as they drew near to breaking, but the scream in his throat was buried by the crushing weight of chains, his gasp for air drowned by the wheezing muttering from Markheim, who stared at him and through him as he droned on.

"Tell the Professor that we must not, we cannot, the elixir is cursed, *cursed*, must be burned, burned it must, it must be burned and gone, tell Heathwood, tell Stringer, tell Templeton, tell the Professor yes, yes." His eyes focused on Barty, properly, and the twisted wooden expression went first to horror, then to fear, then to pleading. "Please. You have to stop him. You have to stop him! He will never stop!"

Gaston wrenched an arm off of Barty with surprising strength, and Markheim howled in pain and fear as he scrambled away, dragged and forced down with brutal swipes of club and fist from the orderlies, and still he howled. "He knows! He knows, God help me, he *knows! TEMPLETON! I'M SORRY! GOD HELP ME, I'M SORRY!*"

Barty staggered out of the room while Hyslop shouted at the guards, helped by Gaston, who put him up against the wall. "Breathe, Mister Barty. Breathe steady now. It is quite safe."

"That was… what I thought… in *there*," Barty gasped, shuddering. His body ached where the bony man had clutched at him, and he rubbed at his throat where the chains had pressed in. Shivering, shuddering, and for a moment remembering the look in the eyes that had stared at him. Seeing, not him, but a moment lost in time. He felt sick and cold as he remembered the talk of madness being contagious—recalling the feel of strong, clammy hands clutching at him, he felt his skin crawling at the thought.

Something was shoved at him from the side—the photograph, now torn and rumpled. Hyslop clutched it in one hand as he spoke brusquely. "There. And I believe he gave you a name as well." He whipped his hand away the moment Barty shakily took the picture, snapping "*Templeton*. Is it important, do you think?" He cast a dark look to Gaston, then the picture, and frowned deeper. "Where did you get that?"

Barty fumbled for an answer, but it was Gaston who stepped in to save him. "It is unimportant for now. Mister Barty came here looking for a story and we have risked his health and safety." He looked back to Barty and helped him to his feet with an aggrieved expression. "I apologise, Mister Barty. This was completely uncalled for. Truth told, I did not expect any such action from Markheim. He's been quiet and muttering for a decade or so, I've been told."

The closed cell nearby still rang with screaming and pleading, begging and desperate. Over and over again, Markheim would shriek the same words—*"SORRY! I'M SORRY!"* There was a meaty blow that echoed from beneath the closed door, and then silence, save for soft, blubbering sobs. Barty stood quiet and still for a moment.

"I think I have gathered all that I am going to get out of Doctor Markheim," Barty said in a shaky voice. "But I want to thank you gentlemen for your help today."

"Is that all?" Hyslop demanded. "You throw my schedule into disarray, Doctor Markheim's treatment back perhaps permanently, and you just think to depart?" He glowered from Gaston to Barty. "What is this about? Truly, and no nonsense, before I go to the Head of Medicine on this. What are you up to?"

Barty was still shaken, but he interrupted Gaston firmly as the man once again tried to speak for him, having lost patience with it and everything else that had happened that day. "I am part of an investigation into an ongoing case, seeking a lead on the murders of Doctor Heathwood, Doctor Stringer, and two other men, men that I am starting to think if we looked into the record might well have been orderlies here at some point," he said sharply, coldly, looking from one man to the other as they both exchanged suddenly wary looks.

Barty could taste the sudden doubt on the air and pressed onwards.

"Mad or not, that man in there knows something that happened in this hospital, involving those men, and another, one of the ones who might be in this picture—a man named Templeton. What I want to know, gentlemen, is why does only a madman want to tell me about it? And what does he have to be so sorry about?" Silence met him then, both doctors refusing to look at him. Barty's frustration grew, and he stuffed the picture into his pocket. "Very well then. I will be taking this to the correct authorities and we shall see what *they* have to say about it."

"Oh, I very much doubt *that*," a refined, silken voice came out of the gloom behind Barty, causing him to turn. The two doctors with him stiffened up noticeably, as though jerked by a string.

The man approaching moved at a stately pace, a walking stick holding their curved spine upright as much as possible. They were elderly indeed, their skin the colour of old parchment, and greatly wrinkled. They bore a hooked, curved nose and a single monocle on a black cord, and, despite everyone else in the building wearing white coats and some other combination thereof, this man wore an expensive suit of black and grey. He was smiling. But it was a smile that did not fit his face, and certainly did not fit the glitter in his eye.

"I see our good doctors have been giving you a tour, have they?" the elderly man said amicably.

Gaston, standing so rigid as to be at attention, piped up. "He was just in the process of leaving, Professor, and—"

"*Silence,*" the elderly professor hissed, and Gaston went quiet as surely as though his tongue had been nailed to his jaw. The glittering gaze did not shift from Barty, and that not-quite-right smile returned, wrenched back into existence quick as a stroke of lightning. "Professor Ossreich, at your service, young man. And you are?"

"Mister Barty, sir, from the Times." It was worth a shot.

Ossreich smiled broadly before replying, "No, you are not, and no, you are not," he said pleasantly, and Barty froze. "I am quite aware of who represents the Times, and who would be sent to discuss a case such as that which might involve Doctor Markheim. It is not you. And no one by your name works at the Times regardless. I checked, once the desk nurse informed me of what was going on." Barty opened his mouth and closed it as the professor went on, inwardly cursing the hateful desk nurse who clearly had not liked the look of him from the start. "Now, what is going to happen is simple. You shall surrender all effects you have brought with you to these gentlemen immediately, and you will be escorted from the grounds. If you protest in any fashion, then my men here shall turn to force instead."

His tone remained almost benevolent throughout. But Barty was looking at the two men who had come with the professor and there was nothing pleasant about them. They had the heavy, dull look of a hammer that would smash down on the foot of someone, repeatedly, and would keep on smashing without changing expression until every single bone was broken, with as much emotion as a man swatting a fly.

Barty had to caution himself as he slowly removed his satchel to hand it over, knowing full well that he would lose the photograph in so doing—but also knowing he had absolutely no choice. If he tried, these men would beat him, and take it anyway. He turned out his pockets, but there was nothing else on his person. Ossreich nodded at this, satisfied that Barty understood his position quickly enough.

"Very well. I am glad you have decided to be reasonable, Mister Barty," the professor said in that same silken tone.

"Our department Head of Medicine and Dean of this hospital has enough things upon their mind as of late." He gestured with a liver-spotted, claw-like hand, and Barty felt himself being shoved along by a man who clearly wanted him to resist so he could take his time beating him. He did not fight back at all.

Doctor Hyslop dared to raise his voice. "Professor, does that mean Dean Wickham is present at—"

But Ossreich was having none of it. "*Thank you,* that will be all, gentlemen." His tone was cold and flat. Then the smile that was not a smile returned. "Right this way then."

Barty did not resist as he was led along, accompanied by the *click, click, click* of the professor's walking stick, and the haunting, following shrieks of Doctor Markheim, each animal howl a plea for death that refused to come.

CHAPTER 14

THE PRICE OF KNOWLEDGE

Barty expected the first blow, that put him to his knees. He had hoped against the second which had put him on his face, but his hope was ill-served. But its coming betrayed that a third and fourth were soon to follow, and so they soon did. The advantage of multiple blows is that they get progressively less painful at the immediate delivery as sensation gets diffused and senses dull, but each one has the promise of much more pain to be felt later.

These felt like ones that would linger for weeks, if Barty was any judge. Ribs and more beside would leave the lingering touch of pain with every breath to remind him of what had happened.

The two had taken him outside of the hospital to deliver the beating upon him, out of sight of eyes that were not used to seeing such things—something Barty found faintly ridiculous, now having seen what conditions were like inside the hospital. Ossreich had taken great pleasure in observing as Barty was discarded upon the ground outside the servant's entrance, now bereft of the picture, his satchel case, and left with a memory of a great many miseries instead. It had been a poor exchange, he had to admit. The brute that had done the beating was a slab of a man with a face like ground beef, with half his teeth missing and the others all twisted. He had the look of a man who enjoyed the small, cruel pleasures of his work. The other had watched, but Barty wagered a boot to his ribs belonged to him as well. It all sort of blurred together at that point.

But Barty had been beaten before. These strikes had been well given, well aimed, by men who knew how to do them right—but he had endured those before too. He tested his teeth with his tongue and found them all still in place, as he picked himself back up slowly, one arm holding his side as he adjusted to being in an upright position once more.

A slow whistle came from behind him, from the depths of the alleyway. He turned and saw, sliding out of a shadow with his hands in his pockets and head askew, Crook come sidling. He gave Barty a quick looking over.

"Well wish't," he said slow and lowly. "You have not had half a time of it, Mister Barty." He clicked his tongue. "Best we be heading back. The Hunter will be curious about this one."

"I am sure he will," Barty grunted, working his jaw to make sure it was not broken. "Did you see what happened?"

"I had a little bird tell me what came of you," Crook said dryly. "A most talkative sparrow, but then they always are—in a hurry to get all their songs out before they die, like all the rest of them, but they've a shorter life than most." He shrugged and gave a curious whistle—it went low, then high, then low, and lingered on—until the carriage rounded a corner and rolled towards them. With, Barty could not help but notice, absolutely no one driving it, and the coachman standing beside him. This should have surprised him. But he was running out of things to be surprised about; a man had a finite amount of surprise in him, it turned out.

Crook, for once, actually looked a little concerned. He held out one hand as the carriage rolled to a smooth halt beside them, his smile mildly sympathetic. Barty took it, and Crook helped him into the carriage itself. He patted Barty's shoulder as the young man got himself settled.

"Fret not, Singer," Crook said softly. "I quite like the name you gave me, would you know?" Barty, too sore to question, simply nodded his confusion and got one in return. "He who made your bones shriek will come to regret it, and well soon. I shall twist the fates enough to ensure it." He touched the silver hair at his brow then, full of meaning and, despite it all, Barty remembered the terror too, but Crook was already clambering on up to his seat and leaving Barty alone in the carriage— alone, except with a name. *The* name.

"Templeton." He repeated it to himself over and over. He said it again and again so as not to forget it as he lay with his head resting against the window in the carriage. On his lips and in the silent echoes of his thoughts, inside a head that ached and ached, throbbing mightily at every movement and at every sound. And when they reached the Lodge once more, twisting down streets and laneways in that strange and unfurling way until he was able to lurch up steps and back to the study, pushing the door open to the surprised faces of Adam and Jean. He spilled it out, stumbling it from his bruised lips. "*Templeton.*"

There was, of course, a long pause of surprise, before Jean, buried beneath a mountain of papers and books, gestured to Adam. "Get the aid kit, if you could, Adam. Barty, please take a seat, and tell us everything that happened." He kept his tone level. Adam unfolded himself from the floor, but Barty was waving his hand, already pacing back and forth, brushing it off. He launched into a scattered recollection, putting the story together. There was something wet on his neck. Had it been raining?

"And then," Barty railed onwards, furious and strident, "they took my things from me. Took the photograph as well, so that is gone, but I heard him, I heard Markheim say it, heard him say '*Templeton*'. We need to look for him. Need to find him. I am sure that he's the next one, sure of it." He stopped, breathing hard, his body shaking with energy and pain, and looked blearily to the two figures staring at him. Adam held a wooden chest with one hand, looking awkward.

"What is it? Why are you staring at me?"

It was Jean who responded in that same level tone he had used before. "You are aware you are bleeding from the back of your head rather profusely, Barty, and have been since you arrived. Are you not?"

Barty made a snort of disbelief, reaching back—and felt pain, wet pain, immediately. He brought his hand back around, rubbed the fingers covered in thick, glistening red liquid together, said "Oh", and crumbled. The floor rushed up to meet him as he gave a resigned sigh.

A short while later, he was on a couch once more, and jerked awake and upright with a cry of "Templeton!" This proved a minor nuisance to Adam, who was in the midst of seeing to Barty's injuries.

"Yes, yes, we heard you the first time," Jean said with flat irritation to the side. Wincing still, Barty moved gingerly, supported by the careful guidance of Adam, who watched with wordless concern. Barty lay back down on the couch carefully, as Adam's enormous hand once more held a cold compress to the back of Barty's battered skull. It felt wonderful.

Without daring to move his head, Barty shifted his gaze to

his left. Jean was standing amidst the stacks of paperwork on the table, brow furrowed and reading fast. Barty closed his eyes while the world kept spinning and spoke groggily. "So what do we have then? Do you know who he is?"

"We do," Jean said shortly. "Germaine Templeton, a former doctor of Bedlam. Alongside Heathwood, and Stringer, and the other two men who were once orderlies there as well."

Barty could not keep the triumphant smile off his face as he kept his eyes closed. "I guessed right, then." He grimaced. "I am sorry, I lost the photograph."

"It was not for nothing," Jean said dismissively. "We have our next step, and we shall soon take it. I just need to find out where Templeton is located, and I will have Creek bringing the answer to that for me shortly." He mulled something over, giving the recumbent Barty a long look until the young man closed his eyes again.

"It really *was* not for nothing, Barty," Jean said firmly. "Your bruises might have been painful, but take solace in the fact that they may well save a life. There is pride to be had in that. Far more than in other, less noble, means of earning."

"I believe," Adam interjected gently in a rumbling murmur, "that he is trying to tell you, that you did well, Barty. Better than expected perhaps."

"I think I will be more proud in the next morning or so, when this does not hurt so much. It nearly all went wrong, actually." He kept his eyes closed, then blinked and felt his blood turn cold in his veins a moment. "You said this would save a life. You think Templeton is in danger then?"

Jean grunted, turning pages still. "I thought we solidified that already."

Barty winced and shook his head, triggering another exasperation from Adam. "I meant, do you think I put him in danger, by finding out his name?"

Jean paused, turning to give Barty a long, calculating stare. "While I normally would admit that these things coming out tend to start a sequence of events, I wonder what prompted you to make such a rapid conclusion?"

Barty swallowed, staring at the ceiling. "That place is awful, Reynard," he said finally. "And the men who work there are terrible, terrible people." He shuddered. "Not just the professor who had his ruffians see to me... No, the whole place seemed to be screaming. And the doctors do not care. They think of it as an experiment. Something to study." He swallowed. "It must be a terrible thing to be mad, and to be in such a state."

"Some would say that they are unaware of what is happening to them on a fundamental level," Adam said cautiously, but Barty shook his head, grimacing, as he pushed himself up carefully.

"No. They know what is happening to them. Every awful part of it."

Adam was quiet, then nodded and spoke in a soft tone. "I believe you. I truly do." Their tone was gently anguished, before they turned away and started to pack up the box of bandages and tinctures.

Barty fixed Jean with a glower. "I want to come with you when you find out where Templeton is." He expected an argument. Jean opened his mouth, but Adam was the one who answered testily.

"Do not dare. You may have a concussion, as well as possible fractures; bruising at the *very* minimum. You should be resting, having a hot bath. Not going on yet another jaunt into the wild world."

Barty felt his temper flare, though it was an anger that

shamed him after all the kindness that Adam had shown him. "Forgive me, Adam—truly, forgive me, for I am indebted to you a dozen times already since I arrived here—but I earned this. I heal fast. I will be fine afterwards, but I *have* earned this."

Adam drew themselves up to their full, terrible height, but it was Jean who spoke, his voice soft and yet cutting. "He has the scent now, Adam. You may as well be singing to the moon, or entreat the tide to slow." He turned to face Barty fully, his grey eyes hard with intent, but seeing through Barty more than anything else.

"Jean—" Adam said flatly, but Jean shook his head without looking at them as he spoke firmly.

"You could never dissuade me, once I had it. You will not change his mind either."

Adam ground their teeth together, audible throughout the room. "I could not. Not you, nor your son. Gods help me, I wish I knew how."

Jean's expression clouded and his gaze dropped, letting Barty breathe again. "I thought you did not believe in gods," he said absently, to Adam's retreating back.

"The alternative is believing in *you*," Adam snapped over a shoulder, as they trudged down groaning, aching steps.

Barty let them fade away a time before asking the burning question. "What are you speaking of? What is the scent?"

Jean shifted a few pieces of paper in an aimless fashion, before he sighed. "The scent. The trail. The game." He shook his head. "Call it what you want. It is when we can feel that we are getting somewhere, that the pieces are making sense, and the next answer is so close we can taste it—or smell it, in this case." He took a deep breath, closing his eyes before he looked back to Barty. "It pulls us along, drags us if it has to, but it gets us to the next answer." He scrutinised the battered young man for a long moment. "It lets us ignore how much things hurt, it gives us strength when we have none left, because if we do not find out, we might never know, and never knowing will eat us alive."

Barty wavered at that—not least because he felt a wave of dizziness overcome him. "It sounds like a most maddening way to live. Perhaps one of *us* should be inside Bedlam at such a rate." He could not keep the accusation out of his tone. He was tired of this man assessing him.

Another one of those barking laughs, biting the humour out of the air and leaving only bitterness behind. "If that was so, I would not have the pleasure of devouring the mysteries first. They are the only things left to me with any taste, save one other."

Before Barty could ask what he meant by that, the door-knocker boomed from downstairs. A few seconds later it did so again, but there was no sound of heavy footsteps from below —Adam was making no move to tend to it. Having come to this conclusion just before Barty had, Jean was already moving and cursing softly, leaving the scattered notes behind, Barty following.

Creek was there, all but hanging from the door handle, his moustache twitching with irritation, impatience rising off him in a steam. Jean looked him up and down, pausing a moment. "Something biting your toes, Inspector?"

"Montague," he barked back. "The man is on an *exceptional* tear right now. Even for him. He got some upsetting news the other day and it has set him livid ever since." He grimaced. "You have no idea how careful I had to be getting what you wanted. But I would wager you do not have long."

Jean grunted, stepping past him. Barty hobbled to follow, and was nearly knocked off his feet by Creek pursuing Jean, who was whistling sharply. Before the echo had died, the carriage of Crook was rounding a corner—the mysterious and terrifying coachman in question sitting upside down on the driver seat with his feet waving in the air. Barefoot, Barty could not help but notice.

Creek paid him no heed for once. He was growling to Jean, who kept his eyes on Crook. "Montague is in a foul mood, but he has also been putting on *pressure*. Even with his personal problems, he has the *entire* force working on this. Maybe you need to step back, Reynard. Let us handle this one, for once."

"I do that and people die, Creek," Jean said bluntly, opening the door to the carriage, waving the inspector and Barty aboard. "I have enough of that to burden my soul already, thank you very much."

Creek huffed, frustrated, and scrambled in. Barty followed, feeling nauseous from his dizziness, but he forced it down. Jean was last, slamming the coach door and ramming his fist up into the roof, sending the coach leaping off. "Tell Crook where we are going, won't you?" Inspector Creek, in the midst of getting settled, scowled and leaned out the open window, calling against the wind, and apparently immediately getting into an argument with Crook, who started laughing at something.

Jean paid it no heed. He watched Barty carefully instead. "You are all right, are you not?" Barty, surprised at the concern, nodded once. Jean gave the slightest of nods in reply and settled back in his battered coat, as Creek stopped making a scene of swearing at Crook and returned to his seat, slamming the window shut.

"So what has Montague in a state then? Someone salute half a second out of time?" Jean's tone was as dry as dust. Creek scowled as he shook his head.

"Not quite. Someone robbed him. A burglary, and quite the spectacular one."

Jean folded his arms across his chest as he leaned back, slouching in his seat. "Robbed him, you say? I hope nothing of value was taken… they certainly were not after his wit, half of nothing being what it is."

Creek did not laugh, shaking his head. "No. Someone looted his summer home manor in the north. Cleaned it out of anything that was not nailed down… paintings, furniture, everything. He normally enjoys vacations there—I say, is your man all right?"

Barty had taken a moment to figure it out, but once he had, he had choked. The embroidered heraldry on the inside of his pilfered coat suddenly made a horrific sense; Jean had looted the home of the *chief of police*. Barty, right now, was wearing the stolen clothes. Directly opposite him was a police inspector. Any moment now, bells would ring, the jig would be up, and he would be hanged so quickly that his feet would *not* touch the ground.

"He is recovering. Had a bit of a turn," Jean replied dismissively, not looking at Barty as he continued to strangle on his sudden terror. Without elaborating further or even changing tone, the hunter went on. "Tell me what Templeton has to do with Montague then."

Creek gave the near-spasming Barty a wide berth as he went on. "Montague will find his way to Templeton by brute force eventually. When he does, he will come for you next—if for no other reason than the fact he currently wants someone, *anyone* to wear iron right now, rightly or wrongly."

"He's always had a foul temper. It is a shame he remains so unimpressive despite it," Jean replied with a sneer. "He might actually be useful with all that anger."

"Bugger your dislike of the man, Reynard," Creek

snarled. "I just want my name *out* of this. He is still my superior, and I neither need nor require the calamity he would bring to my door if he found out I was helping you."

Barty coughed furiously a few times, his aching ribs exploding each time he did, until pain got him back under control. Creek, halted momentarily by the outburst, glared at him until Jean spoke.

"He will not hear it from me, nor any of mine." He paused. "I do appreciate the risk you take, John. Do not think otherwise."

The use of his first name made the inspector pause. His animated moustache twitched and wobbled, then he spoke brusquely. "Just make sure it was worth it. Put a stop to this, Reynard. Get this under control before the rest of the House of Lords starts noticing."

"And we cannot have that," Jean replied sourly. He banged on the roof of the rolling coach, which came to a halt so abruptly that Barty half-fell out of his seat. Jean leaned forward, opening the door and waved to Creek. "The less you are seen with me, the better. Go on with you."

Creek hesitated then nodded. He was out on the street, a darkened one without light as the city turned towards the pause of twilight, with the depth of night fast approaching.

"Creek," Jean called, as the man was about to turn away. The inspector glared back. "I will repay this trust, inspector. Count on it." The door closed before an answer came. The carriage rolled on, back to full speed in an instant.

"You like that man, don't you?" Barty asked carefully, his voice still a bit scratchy from coughing.

The hunter grunted noncommittally. "He's a better man than he thinks, and unafraid to do the right thing. He is like all police; in over their head at all times, and a hair's breadth from drowning. He just has the good grace to be more aware of it than most, while not allowing it to make him abandon principle." He settled into his seat, frowning and staring at nothing. His tone was absent and non committal.

A more pressing thought intruded upon Barty. "Would you tell him that it was *you* who robbed Lord Montague's house?" His tone was pained, and just a little panicked.

Jean grunted and shrugged, arms folded across his chest. "He did not need to know that, and never shall. Cutter knows better than to drop my name."

"I was *wearing* clothes stolen from his *wardrobe*, Reynard!" Barty snapped, his voice becoming shrill despite himself. Jean flicked his grey gaze to the young man as Barty ranted onwards. "If he noticed, if he remembered what his old clothes looked like, he would have—" He stammered to a halt, making a drawing motion across his throat instead to indicate the slitting thereof. Jean sniffed, and looked back out the window, to the glare at the world rushing by.

"You do not know a great deal about the rich, do you, Barty?" Jean's voice was subdued. "You have seen them, passed them in the street, but you do not know them, do you?"

Barty winced, but shrugged. He could sense a speech coming on, but did not have the strength to make a quip about it.

"Montague did not even see you. He never will, unless something miraculous happens. He will not know your name, what you look like... nothing. Because that is what the wealthy do, what the powerful do. They do not see people, they see the means to an end. If you are not useful, you are invisible." He gave a soft, harsh chuckle, shaking his head. "People die every day in this city. The Ripper was not the first of his kind, just the loudest. The one that made sure everyone was looking." His tone turned darker as he went on. "But the rest? No one sees them. Especially not our chief of police." He snorted, mouth twisting as though planning to spit. "They see what matters. And what matters is what they *choose* to see. They have the privilege of their position to simply ignore that which does not. And they have the power to make what matters to them a very narrow field indeed."

He rubbed his eyes. Barty wondered briefly when he'd last slept. It was, as ever, impossible to tell. "Imagine being so blessed by your birth that you can ignore the lives of those around you. I think part of me would envy it, for how much it meant I would not feel."

He finally looked to Barty and smiled the bleakest smile Barty had ever witnessed. "So, fret not, Mister Barty. The chief of police will not arrest you. He will not see you, notice you, nor save you. Your life or death will not touch him. He would, of course, kill you if he knew—but unless you tell him, he never will. That is the privilege he has. You, on the other hand, have the blessing of being no one. You are a blind hole in the world, faceless alongside all the millions of others who die with no name. You have no idea how lucky that makes you."

The bitterness of his tone sucked all taste from the air. Barty said nothing, and Jean did not elaborate further. The carriage rolled on, the smoothness of its passing in complete contrast to the awkward silence that went on within it.

DOCTOR GERMAINE TEMPLETON'S home was one of the less inviting that Barty had laid eyes upon. It was a town house, quite tall and with a heavy wrought iron fence at its front.

This motif was continued—the windows had bars upon them, secured into the black basalt that made up the exterior. It was also completely and totally dark, hidden in shadows that were at odds with the rest of the street; the place was in a well-to-do neighborhood, and even at this later hour there were individuals strolling the streets in pairs or alone. Crook had nevertheless stopped directly outside of it and, even now, Jean glared up at it, as though the lack of lighting was some manner of personal insult he would not allow to slide—if any such existed at all.

Barty, however, was not enthused. After learning of the rage of Montague, he had no desire to cause a scene in a street where behaviour of an unsavoury or even disruptive nature would bring about police in fairly short order. He did his best to convey his doubts.

"I do not believe the man is home. Perhaps we should try again another time?"

Jean grunted, still glaring at the darkened house. "He is home. I can tell."

Barty looked at the place, then back to Jean, then back to the house. It remained dark and unmoving, with no indication of life. "You will have to elaborate on that," he said, with the tone of a man with little patience.

A flicked gesture towards a barred window. "Curtain shifted. Ah. There he goes," Jean said with satisfaction. Barty followed the gesture and clearly saw it himself—the closed curtain had an echo of motion to it, as though someone had peaked behind it, been seen, and panicked immediately. There was indeed someone home.

Jean was marching to the front door already. The sturdy and high wrought iron gate proved a temporary resistance, however; it had been barred on one side by a slotted pole. Rattling the iron momentarily, he braced himself, then, to the startled looks of passersby, he hauled himself up and over it with seemingly little effort at all.

Barty tried to awkwardly pass this off, giving a little wave and greeting an elderly couple walking past, who were staring in consternation at this display. His strangled "Cheerio!" however, was met with harsh sniffs, suspicious glares, and profound judgement, so he did his best to ignore it and follow Jean over the fence. He had a much more difficult time of it, struggling to get over, and then catching his foot on one of the post spikes before falling in a heap. This short trip back to the ground reminded him thoroughly of the panoply of pain that was already besetting him, and for that reason, he decided briefly to just… sort of remain where he was, getting himself comfortable, pretending his bruised bones were not trying to rip their way out of his body to get away from his mad drive to get himself hurt.

He was not having much luck with this, even as he uncurled himself from the ground to see Jean looking down at him with a completely perplexed expression, before he word-lessly reached above Barty and removed the locking pole keeping the gate barred shut, letting it fall.

"You could have just asked." He sounded bewildered, but had already turned back to the entrance before Barty could answer—while his first thought had been that he did not think the man would have even heard him, he could not help but start to think he was making a mistake in his thinking. But he had no time to debate it, nor the inclination.

Heedless of observers, set on the pursuit, Jean ignored the door knocker and hammered on the sturdy oak with a force that set it to rattling in its hinges, each blow of his fist booming out with a sharp retort. Now *everyone* in ear shot was looking at them and muttering to each other, looking concerned and making the general air of a pack of busybodies with time enough on their hands to interfere in the business of others. Barty, wobbling on his feet, tried the most awkward wave and the most pained smile he had ever given. It worked as well as could be expected, in that it undoubtedly made things worse.

Jean kept slamming his fist on the door. "Doctor Templeton! I know you are there! We need to talk!" His voice was a harsh rasp to echo the thunder of his blows.

Barty winced and, determined to make the best of what was rapidly becoming a completely awful situation, he hobbled up, forcing Jean to step to the side by coming up to the door, speaking in a far more normal tone of voice.

"Doctor Templeton? My name is Barty. I have come from Bethlehem Hospital. I spoke to a Doctor Markheim, and would like to bring you news from him, if you will allow us in?" He kept his tone polite, even hopeful, the wheedling tone of someone coming cap in hand to plead their case. Jean glared, but stopped trying to beat the door to death for the moment. Obstinate silence followed.

But the texture of it was different. A weight of sensation, that there was someone near, and listening, and that the name Barty had said had gotten through to that listener, who was waiting to hear the rest of it. Taking a deep breath, Barty pushed on. "This is about the case of 1883. The one you and Doctor Markheim worked upon... you know which one. Doctor Templeton—we believe your life is in great danger."

Jean went to say something, but before he could, there was a rattling of deadbolts and chains on the other side of the closed door. It opened abruptly by about a hand's width, showing a glittering, glaring single eye in the shadows and yet more chains keeping it shut. A nasal, high voice snarled from that shadow. "Are you with the police?"

Feeling a burst of pride that he had achieved more than

Jean had with his rage, Barty gathered himself up and shook his head. "No, but I—" His words were suddenly cut off.

The revolver had appeared in a flash. Thrust through the gap, held in a scabrous, bone thin hand, Barty had it pointed directly into his face, the barrel quivering in the air but distressingly close to both of his eyes, so much so that it filled his entire world. Everything shrank down to him, that hand, and the gun. He could see the individual bullets in each of the chambers, the fat lead balls set into the brass casings, so small, so simple… and so ready to punch his brains out the back of his head with the single twitch of an unsteady finger.

"If you are not police, you are not welcome here! I am going to count to three. One!" the nasal voice half-screamed, clearly near a state of panic, which was precisely the least desirable emotion to anyone on the wrong end of a firearm. Barty froze. The gun barrel was somehow hypnotic, the shock such that he felt like the entire event was happening far away and to someone else. He wanted to run, to hit the ground, but he had the awful feeling any sort of sudden movement would shock that hand and the bullet would be faster than he was.

"Two!" Came the shriek, the hammer already pulled back, the potency of that pulled trigger and all that stored up force coming closer to its realisation as Barty remained locked in absolute terror.

Jean's hand exploded into his vision, so fast that only in that heightened state of time slowing could Barty perceive it at all. He gripped the gun, jamming his thumb where the hammer was—the trigger was pulled with a jerk, but the hammer slammed down, not on the bullet primer, but on Jean's gloved hand. He grunted, ripped the gun away effortlessly, and, at the same time, kicked outwards at the door.

The chains that held the door shut gave way instantly under the impact, ripping clear out of the frame as the door was torn open. A shadowy figure was thrown backwards with a squeal of terror, scrambling as Jean safely clicked the pistol hammer down, and then turned and thrust the gun into Barty's numb hands. "Three," he growled then, stalking after the crawling figure with menace.

Barty remained where he was, holding the gun in both hands. A simple revolver, black and recently oiled, and one more thing that had nearly killed him in the past week. Dully, he started to wonder if he was, in fact, in the wrong line of work.

Instead of dwelling on it, he stuffed it into his coat, moving without thinking. Ignoring the now obviously watching people in the street, he shuffled inside and closed the door behind him, to track down Jean and his prey.

He did not have to go very far. A crawling, elderly man seldom can get very far. Standing in the gloomy entrance hall, Barty could see a door flung open on his right that he soon made his way to.

Doctor Germaine Templeton was a withered figure. A nova of flame as a lamp was lit illuminated him fully, sitting huddled on a lounge chair. Dressed in stained night clothes, his hair was wild and unkempt, his eyes were set with deep shadows. He looked like a man who had forgotten what it meant to sleep, kept awake by fear.

Jean was shaking out the match that he had used to bring light to the dark room. It was undoubtedly once a finely set place, but in the aftermath of whatever seclusion the inhabitant had undergone, it was now a dishevelled hovel. Rubbish littered into the corners, and open books were scattered here and there. Templeton was shivering in his seat, his wild eyes flitting from one man to the next.

Near as mad as Markheim, Barty thought. He stood awkwardly to one side, feeling the ungainly weight of the gun in his coat as Jean dragged a coffee table in front of Templeton and, after unceremoniously sweeping its refuse from the surface, sat himself down on it, leaning forward bring himself uncomfortably close to the mute doctor.

"Now then," Jean grated. "Now that no one is shooting anyone else, it would behove you to *start talking*."

The wild-eyed man shuddered, his mouth squeezing shut. "I do not know what you mean," he stated flatly, defiantly. Jean seized the arm of the doctor's chair and yanked him closer with little effort, bristling in a bare tooth snarl.

"Do not try that with me, doctor. Not after what you just did. 1883. The reason you're hiding away in here. *Talk.*"

The man shrunk away, trying to dig his way into his chair with his shoulder blades, but there was no escaping from Reynard's terrifying visage and rage-filled glare. "We have all the time we need." Jean was inexorable in his threat. "1883. Your fellows dead. And with us having found you, you are undoubtedly next." He leaned closer, his long nose an inch from the quivering wretch's own. "And you well know it, do you not? Considering how you greeted us."

Templeton's lips tightened, but still he trembled. Barty let the silence drag before he finally found his voice, still feeling light headed. "We can help you, Doctor." He could not believe he was saying it, and even less so that he meant it. "We can get you somewhere safe where whoever it is cannot find you. But we need to know who, or what, they are."

Still silence, as Templeton's eyes rolled in his skull, a trapped rat looking for a way out. His teeth were chattering as he finally managed to speak. "Y-you w-would ne-never believe m-me." He swallowed, frantic and trapped. "Never."

Jean's iron grip settled on a shoulder, but there was nothing reassuring about the gesture. "Try us."

Templeton still shook and trembled, but at those words, he

seemed to slump in final defeat. "This is about *him*. It has to be." He sagged into the chair, covering his face with his hands. "But he is dead. We saw him dead. *We* were the ones who killed him."

Barty and Jean exchanged a look, baffled but refusing to show it, before looking back to the shattered doctor. "Who, Templeton? Who did you kill?"

He refused to look at them, but instead was muttering to himself, under his breath, cursing and pleading in every other word. Jean lost his patience and shook him, forcibly.

"WHO!?" he roared in his face, and it had the sobering effect of a slap as Templeton shrank back in terror.

"18… 1883!" he stammered, stricken numb with his fear. "Patient 1883!"

Jean's expression was completely blank. But Templeton went on, his eyes squeezing shut. "The man with two faces." He opened them again, his expression crumbling, the look of a man already dead. "That is who this is all about."

Barty blinked as revelation gave way to understanding. Not a year. A *number*. A patient number. Jean remained close for a long moment, then leaned back and folded his arm across his chest.

"Then let us start at the beginning."

CHAPTER 15

THE ONE WHO FAILED

When Barty was young, and still trapped in the hell of the orphanage, some of the older children caught a rat. They had used a crude trap, an old wicker basket, and managed to drop it over the rodent as it foraged for scraps, made bold by the fact that, at night, its fellows chewed on the fingers and toes of the sleeping children. When the tables had been turned, it had turned to such desperation that it went mad, ripping at the wicker basket as the children who had caught it—but now did not know what to do with it—screamed in panic. This went on until one of wardens had come, and crushed the shrieking rodent under their boot.

Looking at Templeton, Barty could see nothing but the rat once more. The ragged doctor fidgeted and shifted, gnawing at his bottom lip, looking for that which would save his life.

But the boot was hovering above him; Jean offered no salvation whatsoever. He sat with his jaw jutting forward and his arms crossed, glaring balefully at the wretched doctor. He did not move but he did not have to; there was no escaping that stare, nor him. Templeton realised this too, as he wiped sweat from his brow and sagged, his eyes squeezing shut.

"Patient 1883 was in our care at Bethlehem," he said finally, the words faltering, but he continued on, his eyes still closed. "He was admitted there under most curious circumstances a few years prior."

"Curious how?" Jean asked abruptly. But there was a glimmer in his eyes, a knowing sort of look. Templeton shook his head before answering.

"The man was, to the public, dead. A cover up of the matter of his death was had—he had been involved in some murders, but for whatever reason, whoever had placed him there wanted it kept quiet." He shivered. "No one came looking for him, as a result. And if any had, they would have seen what everyone else saw - a nameless, wordless, bound and gagged lunatic."

"Strange," Barty said, surprising himself as the words slipped out of his mouth, but his curiosity strengthened him to press on. "If he was a murderer, why did they not simply hang him and be done with it?"

Templeton gave a despairing laugh at that, tinged with a hint of madness at its edge. "For the same reason that men do anything that is foolish—curiosity. He had done something extraordinary. He had created… something. Something that should not have existed." He hesitated, then clumsily changed subjects. "Without anyone being aware of his incarceration, we were to use him for our studies, and learn what we could from him. We were… assigned to him, all of us. We knew no one would come for him. So we worked as we wished."

Barty shuddered at that. There was a dread implication to those words, from what little he had seen of the madhouse of Old Bedlam.

But Jean was frowning. "What had he made? You paused there."

The doctor shrugged, caught out easily in the interrogation, but there was no artistry in it and both Jean and Barty recognised it. Templeton plunged on, talking animatedly—as though these words had been chained to him for years, despite all his desperation to be rid of them. "We had originally called it an elixir of youth, but that was wrong. *Emphatically* wrong. To this day, however, I cannot even imagine what I would call it. We simply called it his 'elixir' and left it at that."

Silence followed, and the ruin that was Templeton looked from Barty to Jean before starting to half-laugh, half-sob hysterically, speaking as he did so. "Why am I bothering to tell you any of this anyway? You do not believe a word I am saying. How could you?"

Jean sighed, leant forward—and with a movement faster than a striking snake, slapped the twitching man sharply across the face. Templeton reeled, clutching his cheek, as Jean spoke coldly and emphatically.

"We believe you. Take it as gospel from here on that the more insane this sounds, the more likely both of us are to believe it." Templeton's mouth opened and closed, doubting and pained, until Barty spoke wearily from the side.

"Believe me, I wish he was lying. This will not even be the most outrageous thing we have heard today, and they were all true too." He could not keep the bitterness from his voice, but it appeared to work. Templeton looked doubtful, but there was a glimmer of realisation on his face, and even grotesquely, some hope.

He was rubbing at his cheek. "Y-you have to understand," he stammered. "None of us believed it either. We could *see* it at work, and we did not believe it. Heathwood was the one who accepted it first. He learned more of it than the rest, but then he was focused on how it worked, not how to recreate it."

"I'm sorry, *recreate* it?" Barty could not help but burst out, quite shocked. "After it—whatever it was—was involved in deaths?"

Templeton glared at him, his lip trembling. "You are young. You do not understand what it is like to grow old. And we had it. *We had it*, vivid and bright in our grasp. A means to bring back vigour, and strength!" His tone grew excited, his eyes going wide as he went on. "More! More than we could have ever dreamed." He rubbed his eyes, as that enthusiasm wore him out again. "At least, that is what we wanted it to be. I think that is what patient 1883 wanted it to be. But we all missed the importance of his… changes."

Barty and Jean once again exchanged looks, but the erratic Templeton was now staring at nothing with a look of regret as he continued to explain.

"I do not know how he did it. He would not tell us, not directly. He barely spoke to us at all, but each time he did it was with a different persona." He frowned at that. "I *say* that he spoke with us. But we each of us only met the one… one that was very, uh, *difficult* to speak with. Heathwood managed to speak to another persona who was apparently quite congenial, quite intelligent, and, while happy to converse, confessed to have no knowledge whatsoever of who he even was. He was mostly afraid, according to Heathwood. The other persona was not."

"I was wondering about why you simply called him by a number. You did not know his name?" Barty asked with surprise.

Templeton shook his head vigorously. "He never spoke of it, and we never learned it—I truly believe he had forgotten it. I knew him only as Patient 1883. Something had happened to him to destroy his memory of his previous self, and the entity that had consumed him was something too terrible for words."

"A possession?" Jean frowned, leaning forward. "A wayward spirit, or something more?"

But the doctor, with surprising emphasis, was shaking his head once more. Barty, however, was completely lost. "I do not understand this talk of 'persona'. You had two men in custody? I do not understand this at all." He could not keep the frustration out of his tone. But it was Jean, not Templeton, who answered him, staring intently at the doctor as he spoke.

"He is talking about two people sharing one body, Mister Barty. And that this somehow pertains to the elixir he made." He stated it matter-of-factly, despite how completely insane it sounded. Barty took a moment to try and weigh that statement, and failed.

Templeton however, was shrugging helplessly, his head waggling. "It was even more complex than that. We have had plenty of patients whose personality would shift between one persona and another. 1883 was not like that. He could *change*."

The words hung heavy on the air like spun glass, before Barty shattered them with his ignorance. "I still do not understand. Other personalities? Persona?"

Now Jean did turn to face him, his lack of patience evident from his baleful scowl as he explained in a clipped, irritated tone. "It is a known trait amongst the insane that sometimes they can change into almost entirely different people, as though another soul suddenly takes control, so that they sound, act, and even look completely different. This can be so severe that individuals are only vaguely aware of the other personalities that they might have. They might even have completely separate different memories."

Templeton was now more focused on Jean. "That sounded

like Heathwood." His voice was clearer, more astute, as though he was realising something.

Jean was nodding. "He and I used to discuss this in some detail. I often wondered how he knew so much." He sounded bitter about it, but pressed on. "But you said he could change. How drastically are we talking here?"

Templeton grunted. "Enough that we had to keep him chained at all times. And I say that emphatically… at *all* times. It was not pleasant, and we often questioned it—but it is a measure we have had to take before." He shrugged, his tone dismissive, but something about it touched a cord in Jean. Barty could see his shoulders tighten, his eyes narrow, as his jaw worked, teeth grinding. He forced it down.

"He was a maniac then?" Whatever anger was in him, he kept it out of his voice.

"The gentler persona was incredibly intelligent, clever, and engaging, from what Heathwood told me," Templeton went on, not noticing the flicker of rage in his interrogator as he stared off into the middle distance. "All I knew of him, was not. 'Maniac' barely describes him at all, I have known wild beasts with less ferocity. Even without the most potent efficacy of the elixir, he was strong enough to snap those chains until we both figured out how to strengthen them, and when enough time passed, that the elixir faded." He shuddered, remembering, and reaching up to rub at a shoulder as though it suddenly pained him. "He was… it is difficult to explain."

"*Try.*" Jean's hiss was a thing of venom. Templeton flinched, and again, Barty was reminded how close to violence Jean was at all times.

What manner of chains would they need to keep you caged, Reynard?

"H-he could transform his body," Templeton stammered. "His physical form, his features, would shift depending on what we thought at first was a… a whim…" He stuttered to a halt, before pushing on. "It was not. It was all about what he was feeling at the time, what he was *thinking*. He could mold his own flesh like it was wax, after imbibing the elixir, right down to the bones. And he would heal… I watched his flesh stitch itself back together in front of my very eyes!" A mixture of horror and ecstatic fascination marred his face. "The man had crafted the hand of God himself! He had pulled the divine out of the aether!" He shuddered in a way that made Barty feel even more uncomfortable. "But he was an *animal*. The things he would say… the things he had done. Wh-what he promised to do if he ever got free…

"We called him the Pariah," Templeton said in a hollow tone. "A cursed name for a cursed being. Whatever the elixir had created, it was *terrible*. So terrible it all but devoured the man he had once been, even destroyed his ability to remember who he once was."

"And yet, you tried to get him to tell you, didn't you?" Jean's voice was soft, and distant. "How to recreate it. How to make it for yourselves."

Templeton's eyes were wild as he looked at Jean, pleading. Foam flecked at the corners of his mouth as he nearly gibbered in his desperation. "You don't understand, you don't understand at all! The things we could have done! We could have been *Gods*, all of us, if we just knew how to recreate it, to make it our own! We tried to ask him, to get him to talk. I do not know if the amnesia of the one persona was real or he would not tell us because he knew the danger, and the Pariah would not because he enjoyed the spite of it. We tried *everything*."

"You tortured him." Barty said it flatly. He had seen the hospital. He had heard the screams, smelled the stench under the soap. He knew what they had done. Old Bedlam bore its horrors in its very stones and, having walked amongst them, Barty did not even need to be told to confirm it, after knowing how that place felt; it felt like the orphanage, except twisted even tighter, wrenched even higher.

Templeton flinched, turning inward, as Jean leant towards him, bristling like a growling dog confronting a rat. "A man chained, unable to resist, who had something you desperately wanted, that no one was looking for. All you had to do for *greatness* was beat it out of him." His lip curled, teeth bared.

"He was no angel," Templeton spat, defiant. "No innocent unduly punished. He had blood aplenty on his hands before we tried to get answers out of him. He killed three men while in custody too, as he tried to escape."

"If it had been me trying to escape, I would have killed *all* of you," Jean growled. "So let us be grateful he was less diligent."

Templeton gave a despairing, high-pitched laugh that was nearly a giggle were it not so miserable. "Oh, he is making up for it now. Of that you can be sure."

"But you said he was dead, this… Patient 1883," Barty said slowly. The half-mad doctor shrugged, refusing to look at him.

"I have been keeping abreast of the news," Templeton said sullenly. "I know what has happened, and I know it is him, even if I do not know *how* he survived. Nor do I know how he is finding us."

Jean paused at that. "Why would he not know who you are? How to find you?"

The doctor grunted, but went quiet. Jean reached out, gripped a shoulder, and shook the sulking man until he sobbed and broke. "He was blindfolded! We kept his eyes covered, never gave names!" He shuddered, clutching his head with both hands and nearly wrenching tufts of hair clear. "He should never have known who we were!"

"Added to which, there is the fact he is supposed to be dead. That certainly would make things difficult." Barty could not keep the dry sarcasm out of his tone; the man before him disgusted him. How long had they tortured that man, and for what? Some sort of mad imagined invention? Regardless of his crimes, that did not justify their own.

Templeton shivered. "There was... a collapse. A storm struck, and part of the ward collapsed as the roof filled with water. It crushed three cells, and one of them was that of Patient 1883. We... his presence was kept hidden, and the rescue crew put to work—we could not tell them—but we found a body, strapped with chains, and crushed under rubble. It *had* to have been him. We feared it a trick, that we would hear something on the news but... we never did. For the first year, we were terrified. Then the second. But then time kept ticking by, and we heard... nothing. For ten years."

He was more calm now, as he went on. With a defeated tone in his voice overruling all, Templeton had given his confession. Now, all that were left were the regrets. "And then the killings started. Some of us guessed it early. Heathwood, I think, was first." He made a pained sound, rubbing at his reddened eyes. "He did not deserve what happened to him. He thought he could learn something the rest of us could not, something new in medicine of the mind. He never took part in the... harder questioning. He and the amnesiac were friendly to each other."

The room fell silent, the miserable place feeling all the worse in the aftermath of that questioning. Looking at him now, Barty felt a well of pity; the man was pathetic, wretched, and terrified. He clutched at his head with both hands, sheltering the back of his head, as though warding off a blow, as he rocked back and forth.

But Barty remembered Old Bedlam. He had bruises on his body which were but a taste of the old violence that this man had inflicted upon others without mercy. In the aftermath, it was hard to feel more than disgust, but he tried to hold onto the pity.

But he was not the only one in the room. Jean grunted, and said nothing for a long moment. Then he pushed himself to his feet, and lifted his chin to Barty, gesturing to the exit without a word. There was a moment of confusion, and Barty found himself hesitantly obeying before Templeton seemed to realise what was going on.

"Wh-what? Where are you going?" His voice rose, shrill and high, his features going pale as bafflement gave way to panic.

"Elsewhere. Whether Patient 1883 is your killer or not, he is not here. Good day to you… not that you deserve even *that* much." Jean's tone was scathing, and he was not slowing as he strode to the hallway. Barty was opening his mouth to protest, but it was pushed out of him as Jean shoved him along, forcing him out the door.

But Templeton was in a screaming panic at this point—he dashed across the wrecked room to grasp Jean by the arm, calling out as he came. "No! No! You said you could protect me! Take me somewhere safe, you said—" He gave a yelp as Jean spun and struck him, hard, across the face. The doctor fell on his haunches, a pathetic figure with blood streaming from his broken nose, his eyes wide in fear as Jean turned on him and squatted down, forearms resting on his thighs as he balanced on the heels of his boots, bringing himself low and level with the wretch.

"*He* said it. Not I. And that we 'could', not that we would.

But even if he had, I would not help you. *You* were the one who chose to try and grasp the sun, doctor. You do not get to weep now that your wings have melted away." His words came out in a growl, his eyes blazing. "You know as well as I, you deserve what is coming. And I am not risking myself for one such as you." He tilted his head, cocking it to one side. "Or I could make it simpler. I could it end it right here and now." He reached into his coat and drew out a long, shining dagger, and held it point out against the cowering Templeton's nose. "What do you say?"

He darted the tip forward and Templeton scrambled backwards, sobbing and cursing in a broken tone. Jean straightened, watching as the wretched doctor crawled up the stairs at the back of the corridor and out of sight, before he turned to leave.

Barty felt numb. He followed on leaden legs, his tone subdued with the sick weight of realisation. "You are really going to leave him here, aren't you? To die." He could not believe it as he said it.

"He is dead already. He has been dead for years, his body just needs to catch up to the fact," Jean snarled, stalking along. "The Pariah—if it is indeed him—will be doing him a favour. Sometimes the things you do follow you… and choke the life out of you, in the end."

He wrenched the door open and strode outside. It was properly dark now, the streets only partly-lit, as Barty hurried to follow, his stomach churning with every step. It was not improved when a loud voice shouted Jean's name, full of fire and fury. It was a voice Barty recognised, and he was immediately unhappy about it.

Lord Montague was accompanied by a half dozen officers, bustling out of a police wagon—large, barred boxes drawn by twin teams of horses. They had dark uniforms with silver trim, well-trimmed moustaches, and long batons, and not a one of them looked like they were in a good mood, and were, in fact, in a mood that would put said batons to use. They looked eminently suitable for breaking bones with every swing, and, from the way they were gripped, it seemed that this was exactly the plan in mind.

Jean stood there, his hands in the pockets of his shabby dark coat, his brow raised and looking down his nose at the approaching chief inspector and his cronies. Montague drew right up to Reynard—who, admittedly, stood taller than him, and thrust his jaw out pugnaciously, a vein throbbing on his forehead. "I *knew* it was you, when I heard the description. Breaking and entering! Storming into a man's home! I *have* you now, you unruly swine!"

Jean rolled his eyes, sighing dramatically. "You have nothing, Montague. Just the agonising realisation that I keep doing your job for you." He gave a malicious smile, the glint in his eyes plain. "I could teach you if you like. Pass on some experience of the streets."

Montague nearly blew steam out of his ears at that, but Barty could see the officers behind him shift awkwardly and exchange looks. *He's never been down on the street with the rest of them, has he? What did Jean say? They only see what is convenient. Slumming it on the cobblestones with the rest of the force is not convenient at all, is it?*

"You are interfering in an investigation, Reynard." The chief inspector, despite his rage, was now turning deathly quiet, his words tightly controlled despite his fury. "This should have come to me *first* so we could take appropriate steps." Jean snorted dismissively, but Montague was turning to the men behind him. "Arrest him. He can spend a week in the cells until I figure out what to do to him."

The air changed in an instant. While Barty stiffened up

in sudden shock—and acutely aware of the fact he was in stolen clothes with a gun in his coat—Jean instead visibly *relaxed*. A smile formed on his face, and he brought his hands out of his pockets. For a heartbeat, Barty thought he was going to surrender, but then he realised Jean was reaching to his coat. *He's going to fight them*, the horrified thought bloomed. He was going to fight them all at once—a death sentence, no matter what the outcome might be. And he was *happy* about it.

The six officers paused. They were street men, men that had seen all manner of creature in human skin that would take more than just a stern word, ones that would make a lethal weapon out of a napkin and a handful of sand. Men that would keep fighting for no other reason than the fact that madness, real blood-in-the-teeth insanity, could punch through an oak door and keep coming. They knew what it looked like, and it looked like Jean Reynard, reaching into his coat with a slowly-widening grin.

And then came the scream.

Whatever would have happened to Jean and Barty in that moment became another future, as a scream came from the building that they had just left—above them, from the highest floor, but undoubtedly the same building. Everyone stopped what they were doing and turned towards it, but then a window exploded outwards as something was hurled through it, shrieking in terror as it went.

Templeton came down on the wrought iron gate that fronted his house, face first. His scream of terror was cut off into a gurgling rattle as the black metal of three fence spikes punched clean through his wasted form and out his back, spraying blood into the air, and buckling the fence under his weight as he went as limp as a boned fish. He twitched a moment more, his mind failing to catch on to the fact he was dead, before going still with a sickening wheeze of escaping air.

Everyone froze a moment. Then Montague shrieked something that Barty could not understand in his shocked state, and he and his men raced to the front door, to find whoever had thrown the inhabitant out the window to so dramatically end the argument. But Jean did not follow them. He set off at a dead run down the street instead, towards a blind corner. Barty would have debated for a moment, but with a gun in his pocket and stolen clothes as his outfit—the owner of which was distressingly close at hand—his body made the decision for him and he set off after the hunter while his mind was debating the situation.

He was not far behind Jean, but the distance was widening. The man moved like a deer in full flight, despite the burdensome garb he carried, revealing some of the weapons and more he carried on him. And Barty was tired, and sore. But Jean was not slowing. It took a moment longer for him to realise that Jean was not fleeing from the distracted police, as they turned the corner and plunged down a side street. The realisation was confirmed at the sound of breaking glass, and then, to Barty's astonished eye, a vaguely man-shaped figure *flew* across the street at rooftop level, leaping from one building with arms outstretched, clawing itself up a gutter, and plunging onwards. Bestial and furious, but running away.

Jean was not fleeing; he was pursuing. And as he continued to run, he set his fingers to his lips and blew an ear-skewering shriek of a whistle—one high and long note, and three small, short ones.

They raced on, Barty too out of breath to protest, before there came a familiar clatter of hooves, and the screams of people diving to get out of the way, with a high chuckle. He barely dodged the carriage before Crook came tearing past along the street, standing up on the driving seat and, for the first time since Barty had met him, actually holding the reins of the team of horses he was guiding. And he was grinning. A far too wide grin with far too many teeth, and his eyes cast a strange glow that was no product of torchlight nor the now vanished sun. He thundered past, but Jean clearly expected this; he sidestepped, then leapt bodily to catch the carriage, and hauled himself up on the coachman's rest at the rear. He reached back and, holding the carriage with one hand, he stretched the other towards Barty, hanging by one arm and one foot. Barty did not stop to think. He leapt, reaching out with a stifled, breathless cry on his lips.

When Jean's grip caught his wrist, he thought his arm was about to be torn off. The hunter hauled him through the air like a fish on a hook, yanking him off his feet and nearly crushing his arm. He hurled him at the coachman's rest and Barty got his grip in place—it was either that, or fall.

Jean let him to find his feet, Barty clinging to the carriage as it accelerated. But Jean was not sitting idle. He was pulling himself up onto the roof of the carriage, his expression one of grim determination. Over the roar of the wheels on the cobbles, he called out. "You have eyes?"

Crook laughed like the wind, if the wind was a mad, wild thing of twisting nightmares. "Oh, I do! And they see them true! How bright and *shining* they are to me! I beg for but a dram of their blood, dearest darling! A fingernail! Some hair! Oh, but it would be so *sweet!*"

Jean growled, teeth bared. He was on the roof of the speeding carriage now, standing atop it as his coat whipped around him, as it thundered across cobblestones and down streets. They turned with a bone-juddering skid at one point, as Crook hauled on one lead, turning the speeding mass of surging horses to one side to avoid a full wagon. Barty was nearly flung clear, but held on out of sheer desperation. Jean simply crouched, holding with an iron grip to the roof rack before straightening up again, standing tall and imposing on the roof of the speeding carriage, staring at something.

From his precarious position, Barty followed the line of his stare to see what it was that held the hunter's intent sight. It was not hard to spot—across the rooftops, a figure was racing.

They ran on all fours, pulling themselves by their forearms as they surged with a flowing, propelling motion that rent at the masonry. They were *enormous*—the clothing they wore was strained, as though the figure wearing them had grown twenty sizes and stretched them outwards. Barty could not make out a face at this distance, only the impression of power, and speed. It was human-shaped, but the movement was not—and the carriage, with four horses, could barely keep up. In fact, they were falling behind.

Jean had noticed it too. He spun to Barty, and barked an order. "Get inside! Now!" He pointed furiously at the door.

Barty blinked, and peered around from the back of the carriage that he was clinging to, looking to the spinning wheel just in front of him, just as the carriage wrenched sideways once more, turning far too fast, far too abruptly. Barty was flung lengthways into the air as his feet lost their place and then his grip faded, as the coach shifted again with frantic violence, spinning him in place and all but hurling him through the open window into the carriage interior, leaving his lower half dangling outside, feet frantically kicking in the air as he screamed in sudden terror.

"Stop bellyaching and get moving!" A voice roared above, and a sharp retort was felt on Barty's posterior as he was given a swift kick to the rear that pushed him through. He nearly bit his tongue through as it happened, and landed face first on the floor. He had barely pushed himself up scant inches when

Jean's upside down head appeared through the window above him.

"Enough grovelling down there! Gun! Now!" He reached out with one hand, pointing at something and snapping his fingers twice, as the carriage continued to rage through the streets of London. Barty looked around, dazed, until he saw the case. He knew what was in there. Without thinking, he snapped it open.

Not for the first time he wondered why it was called 'Delilah'. Not just that, but by whom? Jean hardly struck him as the sentimental type. He pulled the twin barrelled gun clear with care, holding it for a moment. There was a strange thrill in doing so, much as there had been the first time he held it, a sensation that it should have been at his shoulder already.

But Jean's shout roused him. He struggled as the coach rolled and raced along, bouncing over the cobblestones with a ferocity that was almost fiendish and threatened to force out his lunch, but he crawled across to hold the gun out to Jean. The man grasped it, nearly yanking Barty back out the window again as he took it, and, for whatever reason, Barty could not quite let go of it quickly enough. The door to the carriage slapped open, and Barty was kneeling there at the opening as the world raced by.

Jean paid him no heed. He set his feet and opened the breech, loading the rifle with two heavy headed shells from his coat, each with a solid brass casing and bright, silvered bullets. The gun went to his shoulder and he aimed, ignoring the shuddering of the wagon as the beastly figure raced from rooftop to rooftop, tearing along through the tight streets of inner London.

The first shot was fired. A boom split the night sky, but it failed to strike. A chimney exploded instead in front of the escaping monster, and it abruptly changed direction and tore away laterally from the racing coach. Jean wasted no time. He flattened himself down on the roof, grabbed the rack once more and roared, "EAST!"

Crook heard him. He sang a cry that ripped through the night with a ferocity that even outdid the blast of the rifle and, at this point, the unfortunate Barty came to learn that many things were possible—even things that absolutely should not be.

Not only was the coach that Crook drove uncommonly, disturbingly fast, but a direct ninety degree turn is something that a coach can normally never quite manage easily. It is a careful thing, to be done on a wide avenue and with plenty of warning to those gathered. What it is *not* suited for is when a wagon is moving so fast its wheels are causing sparks to flash from cobblestones and horses' hooves as it rages along, nor in a rather small, tight street.

Barty felt the world lurch as many things happened at once. The carriage *tilted* to the left and as he was kneeling in the open doorway of that side of the carriage—this all but threw Barty out of the thing onto his face. He barely reached out in time, catching himself on the doorway as he fell partly out of the carriage to find that the road was but inches from his face.

This meant, by extension, that the coach was leaning so hard to one side that it almost horizontal; two of its wheels were in the air. *Well* in the air, in fact. Barty looked down to see the coach's remaining two wheels were barely on the ground at all, and then he looked to his right and wished he had not, because Crook was there, upside down with his silver hair flowing around him in the wind, holding on God only knew how. He was looking right at Barty with eyes that sucked in all light and he was *grinning*.

"Hold on *tight* now, my darling, or the stones will kiss your soul." He winked, still grinning, and then, another shot rang out.

Jean was laying flat on the roof when the coach tilted in the turn, and he had not wasted the opportunity. He had been *ready* for it. And, with his feet braced against one edge of the coach roof rail, he had readied himself, aimed—and fired.

And this time, he did not miss.

Barty did not see it, but he heard the screaming howl of pain that came a heartbeat later and the ear-rending *crash* as something came off the roof and demolished the wall of a house across the street. The coach shifted again, wrenched back into place, and Barty was flung back the way he had come, landing upside down with his legs in the air against the opposite doorway, as the coach shrieked to a halt.

The door opened, and he tumbled out, landing flat on his back. Blinking back stars, he looked up, to see Jean silhouetted against a burning lantern street light. He reached down, yanking Barty up, and thrust something into his hand. "Here. Use this, and come on. Follow!"

Barty was dazed, but soon realised that he held what appeared to be an old flintlock style pistol, the barrel extremely wide. He had no idea what to do with it, but Jean was already running. There were no alleyways here, the houses all tightly packed together. People were already swarming, the explosion of a demolished home loud enough to open every door—not least the still-panicked screams of those that had somehow survived Crook's abrupt turn. Jean kicked in the first door he saw and charged through, cracking the breach of his rifle as he went.

Barty, however, locked in place, until a helpful voice spoke behind him. "Point it skyward, and cast back the night, you poor addled boy. There's a lad."

He jerked his head to see Crook, who against all odds was

staring at him almost bemusedly. "It'll bring folks crawling. I best see to my darlings—they never do well with such things amongst the stone." He ducked away then, and then Barty heard him singing, soft and sweet, the stamp of horses' hooves mixed amongst it. But there was no time to take a proper look of it. He pointed the pistol to the skies and fired, for lack of any idea of what to do next.

There was a *boom* and a *pop* and something that burned bright white shot towards the sky from the barrel, turning all the street stark and blazing. Barty was blinded, closing his eyes in pain before the flare's glow was weak enough for him to look away. There was a ringing of bells now—police bells, fire bells, all manner of bells. And when Barty looked around for the coach as he peered about myopically, it did not take him long to see it was gone, blinked out of existence. There was just a street that was rapidly filling with people, and the screams of residents that had been intruded upon.

This was not a place to remain. He turned and plunged after Jean.

He was still in shock as he plunged through a house with screaming people, aghast and furious at the door being kicked down by an armed man who appeared to be on a safari. Barty ducked someone indistinct trying to grab him, exited out a back door, and tumbled on after a distant figure who had just turned a corner, marked clearly by the long barrel of the gun he carried, leaving the cries behind.

The turn that the coach had made had been *impossible*. No vehicle of that size and weight could possibly make such a turn without turning both itself and everyone on it into match wood. And yet, they had not only made it, they had come out unscathed. Even if it had been all too close.

Jean had only slowed to reload. There was blood on the alley stones and Barty followed it, as surely as Jean had, passing the discarded, still smoking bullet casings. He turned a corner and burst out onto a new street—Jean was there, in the middle of the road. There were people running, carriages fleeing, and Jean had the rifle to his shoulder, aiming at a massive figure already more than a hundred yards away and still running onto a bridge—Southwark, if Barty was any judge. They had come so far as Queen Street? The quarry was blood-spattered, huge, and snarling, sending people and horses fleeing in panic. The crowd parted, just enough. The rifle roared.

Even from that distance Barty could see the burst of blood, sparkling bright and red in torchlight as the bulky brute fell. Jean was already running before it hit the ground, and Barty followed. His heart was pounding in his chest, even as more ringing bells grew closer.

The creature, whatever it was, was getting to its feet. Despite taking two bullets, it was still pushing itself up—with difficulty. The air was full of screams and panicked shouts, and traffic had halted on the bridge, frozen in place by the terror of the scene. Barty and Jean forced passage through the crowd, then emerged through it, to come face to face with what could only be what Templeton had described.

The Pariah was what they had called him, and Barty could see why. And he could see also why the man had such difficulty *explaining* him. The appearance was... contorted. Barty could make out a twisted mess of facial features that seemed to morph even as he watched, the bones and flesh shifting, warping. The hair was dark, hanging lank and dripping with sweat. The clothes were indeed somehow too small, ripping at the seams all over as the body within had simply become too big for them. And on such a note, they were huge. Bulky, brawny, shoulders and chest massively developed, with the skin seeming to strain to contain the freakish power within him. Steam rose off that misshapen body, wisping in the air as though a terrible, potent heat emanated from them. There were great, rent injuries on their body; Jean had hit them in the thigh, and shoulder. There was blood covering the places where the round had ripped through them, but Barty could not clearly make out a wound. He could see blood—but no hole.

But the face... Even as they drew closer, the face was impossible to make out. There was a weird twisting to the muscles and features as they warped and shifted. It never sat still and only vaguely looked human at all. It made Barty stop in his tracks. Jean had raised the rifle again. He still had not said a word, not of challenge nor of anything. He was staring at the Pariah, ignoring all else as an unusually still focus dominated his features. There was a ringing of a bell and rattle of wagons behind. The police, drawn by the flare and the gunshots, were drawing near.

The Pariah knew it too. A growl issued from massive lungs, twisted teeth bared in a snarl, one eye squeezed shut, the other open wide and staring. Jean clicked back the hammer on the rifle. At this range, he would not miss. The moment hung in the air, a sort of murderous intensity settling over all that caused everything to halt as the huntsman and the beast faced off.

Barty opened his mouth to speak—to tell the figure to surrender, to tell Jean that the police were coming, he was not sure yet, but the moment he took in air to speak, both figures moved, as the tightly wound cord of tension snapped. Jean's finger shifted. Delilah roared and spat silver death in an explosion of smoke and brutal force. But the creature—the Pariah —was ready for it, and flung up both their arms.

The bullet fired from the rifle would have stopped an oxen dead in its tracks, and blown a man near in half from the force of it. And so it shattered one arm of the Pariah, and *ripped* through it, rending clean through a forearm bone the thickness of one of Barty's legs, but the trajectory was shifted, and the tumbling round bounced off the Pariah's scalp, ripping a line along the top of the head and knocking him onto his back. Jean swore, and broke the breach open on his rifle, fishing in his coat for more rounds. The Pariah was groaning, a harsh, deep, and terrible sound, but it was already rolling back to its feet, driven by whatever awful potency empowered it. The half forearm hung limp, flopping about grotesquely before abruptly snapping back into place as though yanked with an audible sound of flesh ripping. Jean paused at the reloading of his rifle. Barty felt sick as he watched the thing that was the Pariah start to rebuild itself. More steam rose off it as the wound on the top of its head started to close, the flesh of the ruined arm regrowing with hideous speed—and then his focus shifted.

Behind the horror that was the Pariah, there was a carriage approaching at speed. The driver had not made sense of what had been going on, the dim night bridge hiding too much and warning too little—the sound of horses' hooves and rolling wheels drowning out the noise and the confusion of chaos of fleeing people not enough to warn them. They had, for what it was worth, finally realised something was wrong, but they were too late. Barty could see the coachman, an elderly man, had realised his mistake as he came close enough to take in the awful detail of the monster standing in the midst of the bridge. An unexpected impossibility had frozen them in shock.

"Jean…" he started to say, but then the beast grinned. That single wide eye was mad and staring, *burning* as it made a realisation.

Jean swore, thrust the still unloaded gun at Barty, who

fumbled and dropped it. But Jean was already sprinting forward, wrenching a revolver out of his coat as he went.

Too slow. The Pariah leapt at the carriage, clearing thirty feet in a single, monstrous bound, then sprinted with hideous speed towards it, thundering across the bridge with booming steps. The two horses reared and panicked, and the beast slammed both massive fists down on the ground before them to set them to frantic terror, roaring in their faces to incite them to frenzy. The carriage bucked and turned, and the monster moved amongst it all to lash out with one huge fist, shattering the traces and sending the maddened horses fleeing, dragging part of the tackle with them, as the elderly coachman was flung backwards. But the Pariah was not done; he grasped the wagon with two massive arms—even the one that was still healing—and *heaved*.

If Barty had not been there to bear witness, he would not have believed it for an instant. The carriage was only slightly smaller than the great coach Crook drove, and it was still large enough that it was a laughably impossible notion that any man would be able to lift it. Not just lift it, but *hurl* it. To send it flying into the air, towards the edge of the bridge.

The Southwark Bridge was a mighty thing, all of cast iron, heavy and strong. It was known more as the Iron Bridge, a penny to cross and a fearsome feat of engineering. The iron extended to the sides of the bridge, and so, when the carriage hit it, it ruptured along its frame with an awful cracking of lacquered wood and splinters, caught on the iron and hanging there, rocking back and forth from the force of it. It was a terrible sight, a tremendous show of strength, but that was not what had made Barty freeze. When the carriage had started to move, he had heard high-pitched, terrified screams coming from within. Screams like those he had heard in the orphanage.

There were children in that wreckage.

Jean was still running at full speed, his arms and legs pumping like the pistons of a steam train and equally as relentless. The monstrous form of the Pariah turned and, with a grotesque look of glee, touched its bloodied brow in a strange salute, its misshapen maw twisted into a grin. Jean opened fire without breaking stride, even as the awful figure turned and leapt away, clearing a great bound, and then another, as Jean fired all six shots in pursuit. Barty thought that would be the end of it, but Jean tossed the revolver aside and kept running—not after the departing beast, but at the tilting, shattered carriage.

He seized the doorstep with both hands as the carriage started to shift, the screaming inside growing in pitch. The entire thing was balanced precariously, wedged on the bridge railing, the wheels shattered by the impact, the weight danger-ously overbalanced. Jean held on tight, sliding forward and setting both of his feet on the bridge side rail, hauling himself backwards with all his might. Teeth clenched, his face turning bright red in an instant as veins burst to life on his face, his moustache and beard quivering as his jaw tightened so hard that it looked like his teeth would crack.

He turned his face to the stunned Barty, who stood numb with shock, and, for the first time since Barty had known him, had clear, raw desperation on his face, as he screamed, his voice cracking, "HELP ME, DAMN YOU!"

Barty was shocked out of his frozen state. He ran and leapt at a tilting wheel as it was lifting up, hooking his elbow into the spokes—not bringing it down but slowing its rise just a touch. His feet were hanging off the ground and he franti-cally kicked at the air, as more whistles blew and shouts grew nearer. Turning his head, Barty saw the police wagon rolling over the bridge at a blistering pace, bearing the very officers that had accosted Jean and Barty back at Templeton's. Barty could see Lord Montague, riding on the front alongside the coachman, his expression contorted, and, for a moment, Barty groaned inwardly, thinking that they were about to be accosted once more. And still, the voices inside the tilting wagon screamed.

But Montague surprised him. He pushed the coachman out of the way and hauled upon the brake furiously, shouting orders. The back of the wagon was opening before it had stopped and men were running out, following Montague's shouts and frantic pointing. Hands joined Barty's, pulling him down, and Montague himself took his spot at Jean's side, hauling down the carriage to prevent it tipping. But even with all their added weight to secure it, the entire structure was now cracking apart.

As a couple of officers frantically worked to create some manner of rigging out of manacles and rope to secure the collapsing carriage, Jean let go, letting the rest of the team take the weight. He did not move away, but instead ripped the broken door off its hinges with one hand, hauling himself up into the tilting wreck. "Barty! Help me!" he barked, even as he climbed inside and the screaming intensified.

Barty looked to the man who was holding the wheel down alongside him, a hard-looking man whose jaw was clenched with the fury of effort, a stranger to him before this moment. The man nodded without a question being asked, the vein on his forehead swelling outwards as he increased his weight, even as the sounds of snapping wood and creaks of fracturing structure grew louder. Barty let go and dove to the door.

Jean was already there, passing a very small figure. A child of no more than two, wailing in terror with a red mark across their face, their face awash with tears and mucus. Without thinking, Barty took them in his arms and turned, calling out even over the agonised shouting of the officers having their arms tornout of their sockets from trying to hold on. Someone took the little one; Barty could see nothing but a uniform as he turned back to that open doorway, getting a better look inside.

Through Jean's legs he could see two small children, both boys, clutched in the arms of a woman. She was bloodied, her once fine clothing ruined by her own blood and the debris of the carriage, and yet a lion at bay would have been less fearsome in that moment. She was beautiful despite of all that, even with—or perhaps because of—her ferocity, the same adrenaline that had given Jean the strength to hold on to two tonnes of loaded carriage now giving her the power to protect her children. She was staring with a fixed, blank expression, her face pale and spattered with blood as she sat frozen and unblinking. Jean was, with uncommon gentleness, speaking in a soothing voice to help her unhook her fingers from the second child, who nevertheless clung to her in their panic. The woman had the wide-eyed look of someone not fully aware of what was going on, but singularly focused and incredibly alert. She was staring at Jean with only vague comprehension, but something about the way he spoke, words Barty could not hear, got through to her. She let go at last, and Barty heard her speak in a shaking voice. "Save my children."

The entire carriage creaked. Men shouted for them to hurry, others cried out in pain, as the entire structure shifted again. The carriage had been loaded and the well secured luggage on its roof was now bearing it over as the structure collapsed. But Jean did not jump free, even as the carriage tilted and the horizon sunk lower through the outer window. He took the child and set them into Barty's arms. He turned, passing them along even as they screamed desperately for their mother. But there was no time; Montague was roaring at

Jean to get out, to "Leave it!", but Barty knew that he was not listening. Reynard took the last child, an older boy, and pulled him clear, passing him to Barty, who had to set him down immediately. More men were running closer, shouts and bells and desperation growing into a deafening clamour. Montague was shouting at Barty, shaking him to get Jean out, but his words were frozen on his lips as the carriage began to slide off the edge.

She was reaching. Frightened and shaking, her body was wedged into the wreckage of the shattered carriage, the spine of the bridge railing thrust through the midst of it pinning her in place. She was reaching and Jean had her arms in his, trying to pull her free, even as it all shrieked and groaned around them—and then there was a shout as the officers' grip holding the carriage in place slipped. The carriage began to slide, breaking fully, as Barty screamed Jean's name in warning.

It was Montague, of all people, who did it; he shoved Barty aside, seized Jean by his coat, and pulled, hard. The hunter fought him, refusing to let go. But then Barty and another man grabbed hold of his coat and yanked him back through the doorway, even as the carriage gave way with a scream of terror from within. Too late for the ropes, the desperate attempt to hold it all in place, to buy just a second or two more, too late for her, a frightened mother who had saved her children. The shattered carriage plunged into the dark waters of the Thames with a great splash, and not even a second later it was gone, the scream of the doomed mother lost in the darkened morass, swallowed up along with her.

It took four men to hold Jean back. Before anyone had recovered, he was up and moving, at the edge and about to leap off into the darkness before they grabbed him again. He did not say anything as he struggled against their hold. It wasn't until Montague struck him across the face that he stopped, finally seeming to realise where he was.

"She's gone, Reynard," the chief inspector said, his tone bitter, thick with anger and something more. But vanished was the rage in his eyes when he looked at the hunter. "You go in there and you'll drown with her. You did all you could, man… you did all you could." He ran out of things to say, and just gave an awkward clap to the taller man's shoulder and stepped away, shouting orders to his men, pulling himself, and them, together. In that moment of awful clarity, as Barty watched him in his state of shock, he had a dulled realisation. For the first time since Barty had known the chief inspector, he looked like the leader he was supposed to be.

Jean just stood there. The fire had gone out of him, his expression numb. He stared into the waters of the swirling river and did not move as activity surged around him.

You did not hesitate. Barty stared at him, wondering if at any moment the man might leap forward and go into the waters anyway. *You would have gone over with her, with all of them. Not for a heartbeat, not for a breath, you did not hesitate.*

TIME PASSED. Jean was seated on the back step of the police wagon and no one dared go near him. Barty had retrieved the fallen rifle and revolver that Jean had discarded in his pursuit, and was returning when he paused, finally noticing something.

When the Pariah had been shot, he had bled rapidly. Despite the storming of so many people over the bridge—a bridge now closed as the police took control of the situation and sought the details of the fallen—that blood had been scattered and pooled about. A single flagstone in Barty's path now glistened before his eyes, a flagstone that had a deep divot in its heart, worn there by countless wagon, carriage wheels, and weary feet. It had a shallow puddle of blood now filling that worn groove, and Barty could not help but note that, not only had it not yet congealed, but that it shimmered to even his untrained eye, as though something swirled within it. He paused, then pulled a handkerchief from his pocket, and knelt, the rifle under one arm and the revolver in his coat alongside its pilfered fellow. He soaked the kerchief in the blood, for lack of a better thing to do, though his skin crawled as he did so. Not least because he could have sworn the glinting liquid was still *warm.*

There was a commotion now, from where he had last seen Jean. The bridge was growing crowded, but he moved awkwardly through it. Despite the fact he was armed, someone nevertheless bumped into him, knocking him somewhat off balance. He got a glimpse of a slender, vaguely familiar figure in a hooded coat, but now there was shouting involved, and it had a tone of anger that only one man he knew could summon up in others. He pressed on, still holding the bloodied handkerchief in one hand, the cloth soaked and sticky. Absently, he took some of the sandwich paper that had held the snacks given to him by Adam in the prior days, still shoved in his pocket, and wrapped the bloodied handkerchief in it, stuffing it away as he hurried along.

Jean was standing with his hands thrust in the depths of his coat. A man stood before him, well dressed but greatly upset. He was waving his arms and speaking angrily as Barty pushed through the various officers and others who stood in silence, watching.

"—I was trying to *thank* you, damn you!" the man half-screamed in a strained voice. His face was pale, streaked with tears, and beset by grief. There was no need to be introduced; the soul-blasted look on his face spoke to a loss he could not grasp, a realisation of a world shattered. Behind him, three children were huddled together, united in the aftermath of their rescue. Jean would not look at them. Instead, he looked down his nose at the clearly struggling father, and a sneer so cruel as to spite the devil twisted his lip.

"I would suggest in future you would *best* give thanks to your children by being present when they are in danger. If you had been here, they would still have a mother." He hawked and spat, his hands still in the pockets of his coat. "Was it drink, or another woman that kept you away? Either way I hope it was worth—"

He did not get to finish the sentence. The blow was wild, but it struck true, crashing into Jean's cheek and cutting it, another coming from the other hand that threw his head back. The man was bellowing in rage, but officers intervened and pulled them apart, as Barty hurried forward, putting the rifle down and helping the staggering Jean to sit. The man wavered groggily as various officers dragged the blind-with-rage father, the children following after. One of them cast a look back at Barty as they went. He was surprised to see, in those tear-streaked eyes, there was nothing but helpless hatred.

Montague came alongside, his expression twisted in disgust. "God's blood, Reynard. That was too far, even for you."

Jean, leaning into the hand of Barty's that was holding him up, wordlessly spat blood to the stones. He would not look at Montague, nor Barty, his expression empty. The chief inspector made a sound of disappointed contempt and stepped away, but Jean spoke in a harsh voice without looking at him. "Chief Inspector Montague." It stopped the addressed man dead as, for the first time, Jean referred to him by his correct title, and he turned back.

Without looking up, Jean spoke in a voice that was rusty, his eyes on the ground. "Make sure that man has all he needs. Find family, any that care for him, and get them to him and those children. Get people that love them. They will need them. And above all, make sure they know it was not his fault."

Montague's expression gave way to outright confusion. He stared at Jean, then at Barty, as though the youth would offer an answer, but Barty helplessly shook his head. An awkward moment followed, before Montague simply nodded and stepped away, leaving Barty and Jean alone.

"Why?" It was all Barty could ask, with helpless bewilderment in his voice. Jean did not lift his gaze to him, but looked through the crowd. Barty followed to see the bereaved father holding all of his children in his arms. They were crying together, united in their sorrow, and heedless of whomever might witness it. Officers stood nearby but seemed afraid to touch them, as though grief were a disease, a contagion that would drag any and all it came into contact with down into the same black depths that had claimed a wife and mother.

"They needed to see it," Jean finally said. "They needed to see him strike me down." He grimaced, spitting blood a second time, then wiped his mouth and smeared blood and spittle across his cheek, his gaze still downcast. "When I was taking her children, I swore to her, to them, that I would get them all out. I swore to God that I would. I had to... I would not have broken her grip on her little ones with a crowbar. Ten men would not have shifted her. She looked to me to save her and I did not." His voice fell, and then went silent. Barty could not believe it.

"Reynard, you saved those children. You did everything

that could have been done." He could not keep the shock and bafflement out of his voice. "You were a hero tonight."

Jean snorted, and wiped at his mouth again. "Look at them, Barty. Look at those children. Remember how they looked at me." His other hand withdrew from his coat. It was clenched tightly into a fist. Blood from where he had torn through glove and flesh trying to hold the carriage back welled between his fingers. "They do not see a hero. They only see the one who failed to save their mother. And they are *right* to do so. They have all the right in the world."

Barty wanted to protest. He wanted to argue against it, but he could not. *Sometimes, the truth is not fair. It is not merciful or kind, nor even considerate. It is just the truth.*

Jean pushed himself to his feet. He adjusted his coat, and took the rifle from Barty's nerveless fingers. "Tell Crook not to wait for me. I will be home when I am ready." And with that, he turned and marched away across the bridge, the crowd making way for him. For once, Barty did not follow him. Sometimes, a man needed to be alone.

He reached back into his pockets. With one hand, he felt the wrapped handkerchief and his fingers retreated with a shudder, even as he regretted not mentioning it. With the other, he found a piece of paper.

It took him a moment to realise that, only minutes earlier, it had not been there.

Chapter 16

Time, Passage, and Loss

Lancashire Lane was a deceptive sort of place. With its very name it told lies, as it evoked a cozy sort of air, like might be found in a quaint country village. In that kind of setting, there were apple trees and hazelnut thickets, wildflowers in bloom and comfortable little cottages with a warm fire.

In London, all such convention was nonsense. The reality of Lancashire Lane was a warren, a twisting thing that wound haphazardly through the gloom of towering buildings on each side, occasionally interrupted by a door that clung to hinges with teetering precariousness. It swallowed up sounds from the outside, the passing to-and-fro of London streets not reaching its depths—but that came with the uncomfortable realisation that sound would not escape from its abyss either, promising no safety, and much more danger. There were other things too, lurking shadows that could have held any number of horrors, and from which smells arose that were as awful as they were unidentifiable. It was not a nice lane. It was a lane that waited to murder you if you took too long in it, to leave you in the shadows until you were part of the stones.

Barty made his way along it with care. He moved with the schlepping step of a man who had two revolvers in his coat, while knowing that only one of them was loaded, and he had no confidence in using it anyway. He was tired, and he was nervous… and he was alone. Jean was long gone. But he had not gone back to Crook who, for some reason, had not crossed the bridge. Barty could not understand why, but he had not been inclined to ask. In fact, he had not seen him at all, but then he had not been looking for him either.

Instead, he had been preoccupied with the note he had found in his pocket. It had taken him some moments to realise, upon first seeing it, that it had been placed there by someone else. The figure that had bumped into him on the bridge had seen fit to do so and, upon reading it, his entire plans had been rather forcibly changed.

"Meet where you said. I remember something. Come promptly. B.W."

It had taken him a few moments of absent-minded bafflement before he recalled whom he had spoken to of his previous home address. Though it took him by surprise to recall it, Benji Wrongblood, the wolfcursed adolescent in the Under, was both the mark of the initials and the only person whom Barty had given the location of where he lived. And so, seeing the opportunity in being separated from Reynard, Barty had seized upon it.

He felt anxious despite all that, the notion of returning to his home weighing heavily upon him. He had departed so suddenly and, though he had few possessions, he had still left them unattended at his old domicile. 15b, Lancashire Lane. He hoped that the withered crone of a landlady, the harsh and unfriendly Mrs Hacknee (though he had never heard sight nor mention of a Mr Hacknee and assumed he was either a figment or a man who, when confronted with the reality of his wife, had chosen exile), had not thrown them out. Logic dictated that she probably had.

He found the familiar door. It was unassuming, opening up to the alleyway. Barty knew on the other side of it was a staircase leading up to the left, and a much sturdier door that opened to Mrs Hacknee's own dwelling. She was a harsh matron, with the ears of a bat who would respond with savagery to whomever was situated above her home, making the tiniest sound while she was awake. Barty, being all but destitute, naturally had just that as his home. He had learned to make no movement during the day, and only few at night. It was easier than the screams, the threats, and the assaults by broom on the floorboards below his feet.

He expected it to be locked, but it was not. In fact, it was hanging slightly open, and when he touched it, the door creaked as loud as the rope of a loaded gibbet twisting in the wind. Barty flinched at this, shying back and expecting, even at this late hour, for a screech to be heard of waking fury from a horrible octogenarian of spiteful discernment, but there was nothing. This was somehow even less reassuring. Barty started to doubt and a gnawing, fearful uncertainty that warned him away.

So it was that he nearly jumped clean out of his skin when an exasperated voice spoke from above him. "Are you coming in or not?"

Stumbling backwards, he looked up. An open window was there, a window to his own cramped, tiny apartment that he had never dared to open. A familiar figure leaned out of it, giving him a perplexed look from her expressive eyes, her lower face covered by a mask of cloth.

"Elle?" Barty could not keep the surprise out of his voice

as he stared up at the young woman, whom he had last seen in the depths of the Under.

She rolled her eyes within the depths of her hood, and gestured impatiently. "Get up here, would you? You've dallied enough already." She slid out of sight, back through the window, without waiting for an answer. Barty, still shaken and shivering a little, pushed the door open once more and made his way inside with care.

As he climbed the stairs to his left with a careful step, he slowly came to a realisation that made him feel decidedly uncomfortable. His last memory of the place—hazy, with all the times he had spent coming and going for his investigations—was of something drastically different; while not a bustling sort of place, there had been himself, Mrs Hacknee, and Mr Jenkins, his neighbour down the hall, with three other rooms yet empty. Now, there was an aching silence instead, a sort of listless echo from within that said, *"No one lives here any more."* It was dark, quiet, and dead.

He ascended up the stairs to see the narrowed corridor where the rooms of the boarders lived, the door to his own room open. Elle's head popped around the corner, and then slipped back inside. Her voice echoed out from the opening, light and amused. "From the way you are walking, it is like you are afraid to be waking the dead. You need not worry. They can *always* hear you."

He reached the threshold as she finished speaking, just as a covered candle was properly unveiled, and the room was filled with dim, flittering light. Elle stood at the window, arms folded across her chest, her eyes gleaming from the depths of her hood.

Barty's old lodgings consisted of a single room. Not a very large room. It had a too-small bed, a very insufficient dresser, and enough empty floor to stretch out from head to toe from one side to the next and that was all. There was a window on one wall and a mirror on the other. It was a place where a person survived in, but did not really get to live. His new lodgings were, by contrast, sheer heaven. He gave it a long look, struggling to remember how he lived in it at all.

"You picked a strange place to meet, guv." Benji was sitting cross-legged on the bed. He had covered himself up well, wearing a blazer too big for him that he kept his hands inside, and a large hood that covered his extra hair and ears. But he flung that back now, his expression perplexed, as his nostrils flared. "You got blood on you too." He frowned then. "Except…" He trailed off, then shook his head. "Why'd you say this place was your home?"

Barty was startled at that, looking from one to the other. "Because it *was* my home. I was going to come back here one of these days and get my things, but it appears Mrs Hacknee has already cleared them out." He could not keep the annoyance from his voice as he opened the drawers of the dresser. They were bare as old bones, a stray button rattling around in one, but nothing more. He could not help but swear. "I was only gone a week."

"A week? Are you sure?" Elle asked.

Barty futilely checked another drawer, hoping to see his tools or notebooks, anything at all. He answered with distraction. "Most assuredly. I mean, you can give or take a day or two either way. Since falling into Reynard's employ, everything seems to move a great deal faster."

Silence fell, a heavy sort of silence of shared looks and lingering doubts. Barty turned to see Benji and Elle looking at each other with wary, mystified expressions. "What?" he asked crossly, seeing a question in that gaze as he shoved closed the button-bearing drawer a little more fiercely than was warranted.

Benji gave Elle a querying look, and she shrugged. "Tell him then."

The wolfblooded boy sighed, then, as Barty gave him a questioning stare, he spoke awkwardly. "Ain't been nobody living here for three months, guv. Assured of it."

Barty stared at him. "What in the name of… what are you talking about?" The absurdity of it all made him lose his train of thought. *Something does not feel right though, does it?*

Benji shrugged, and tapped his nose with one errant finger. "Sense of smell. Only thing I'm real good at, truth told. Can smell a penny in your pocket, or a shilling, or the two guns you got in there 'longside the blood." He gave a wink, with a crooked grin that soon faded. "I can tell you, guv, ain't nobody lived here for three months if there was a day." His nostrils flared and his expression went distant as Barty stood there in baffled silence. "Was three people. You, an old lady, and a man down the hall. This was your room."

Barty swung his stare to Elle, who was watching him with surprising caution. She shrugged, but did not break the stare. "You did not ask how we knew which room was yours, did you? He could smell it."

"Well, uh, yes, but…" Barty stammered, but Elle cut him off.

"He is telling the truth, Mister Barty. I would bet my good right hand on Benji's nose. If he says three months, then it was three months, maybe a few seconds either way."

"S'more to it than that." Benji shrugged, rubbing his nose with one clawed hand as he squinted at the roof in thought. "Someone died in the floor below. Someone old. After that, everything faded." He squinted, looking warily at the flabbergasted Barty. "Iff'n I was to be telling, it would have been a day or two before or after you left. You don't remember none of this?"

Barty's mouth opened and closed, and he slumped against the dresser as it became the only thing that was holding him up. He shook his head, trying to make sense of it—but he simply could not. He took a breath, holding it until he let it out explosively, a rush of words coming with it. "That simply does not make any sense. I was looking for Reynard for some time but it was not, it *could* not, have been that long." He shook his head, shuddering, and forcibly dismissed it. "I am sorry. But you must be mistaken."

Benji opened his mouth, his expression doubtful, but Barty did not want to hear it. *No. Not now. It is not important now.* The realisation came down firm, pushing him forward, and he interrupted sharply. "Before you go on, know that I have had a very difficult night already. What happened on the bridge was not pleasant. You did not bring me here to discuss that, or this passing of time, I am sure of it. You said you remembered something—that is what I am here to find out about."

Benji looked annoyed, his nose twitching as his brow furrowed, but it was Elle who gave a sigh of defeat. "Fine, fine. We can bring it up later. Tell him, Benji." She waved a gloved hand impatiently, tugging at her face mask a moment to settle it.

The wolfblood growled a moment, his pointed ears flattening down, before he gave in, continuing to look irritated that he had been disbelieved. "I did not tell the whole truth of what I was talking about with Doctor Heathwood. How I told you of what I did," he said sullenly, eyes on the ground. "Least, I did not tell you all of what happened."

Barty blinked, perking up and pushing up off the dresser. "Go on then. What part did you leave out?" He forced down the disturbing revelation of the missing months as much as he could, encouraged by the realisation that this was more important. He was still struggling to put the echoes of the screaming children out of his mind and this, he hoped, was how he could do that.

Benji scratched the back of his head in nervous irritation before he continued. "I smelled something. Not that you would believe me anyway, seems like," he grunted sourly, turning his face away. Elle sighed in exasperation, giving Barty an annoyed look.

"He is very proud of his sense of smell. He wanted to prove it to you by telling you about… this place," she finished carefully. Barty stared at her, then groaned and looked back to the still sulking Benji, and moved to squat down in front of him at the side of the bed.

"Look, Benji. Today has been a long day. I have nearly died at least three times since I got up this morning. My head hurts, and my ribs too. I was beaten up and nearly shot. So please, try to be understanding."

The wolfblood looked at him warily, and his nose twitched. His brow furrowed down. "You all right?" He sounded doubtful for the first time, his tone hesitant.

Barty gave a ragged laugh, and shook his head; he hurt all over. But he remembered the woman in the river and pushed himself onwards. The scent was on him. There were more pieces of the puzzle to be found—and the Pariah was waiting at the end of it. He nodded, lying through the twinges and aches that would call in their debt later.

Benji looked doubtful, but eventually he shrugged awkwardly. "I said I ran away, but I didn't though. I went up there… or I was going to. Doctor Heathwood, he had a way up the back we used to take so no one would see us, right? But I was getting close, and then I could smell all the blood—a *lot* of it and it… look, it hurts to smell that much blood, see? It being no good for us." He grimaced, his gaze dropping as his jaw went tight.

"Blood has an affect on… on people like Benji," Elle said quietly. "It makes them act strange. Most of them keep to places where smells like that are hard to make out, or teach themselves to tune it out."

"Yeah, which is what I was doing," Benji said sullenly, nodding. "I turned away from the place before I got too close and tried to pick out something else instead. That's when I smelled it, see? Something that didn't make no sense." He shrugged his skinny shoulders, nostrils flaring. "Was soap and ammonia. Real thick stuff, seared right through to my brain." He shuddered.

Barty was nonplussed. "Standard sort of thing for cleaning, really. I am sure any number of housewives use it." But Benji was shaking his head and frowning, looking to him intently.

"Not this stuff. It's the mix, y'see. They grind up the blocks of soap and mix it with the ammonia and mop it out over the floors in the place. Stinks real bad, but covers up all the bad smells. And there's a lot of them there." He gave a spasmodic shiver. "Can't miss that smell. Sticks with you."

"You did not say where it came from, Benji," Elle said gently, but with a bit of wry humour. The elongated ears of Benji flared upwards and then flattened again.

"Oh. Yeah," he said with rueful apology. "They use it up in the madhouse. Twice a day, they mop the piss outta the corridors with it. Old Bedlam." He said it firmly with a nod, his brow furrowed.

Barty rocked on his heels a bit. "But…" His mind raced, and he went to the simplest, stupidest question first. "Heathwood used to work at Old Bedlam, maybe he or someone from there had visited?" he asked in a querying tone, but Benji was already shaking his head.

"Could smell it on the air above me. Lit the sky in a

jagged line, I swear it was so strong I could *see* it. There were other smells mixed into it, but those were the strong ones. It wasn't the doctor. He never smelled like that in all the time that I was knowing him, that's why it stuck out so bad. It was *them* that smelled of it."

"Them?" Barty asked, but he guessed the answer.

Benji's jaw tightened as he nodded. "Yeah. Who done killed him. Whoever killed Doctor Heathwood came from Bedlam."

Barty's mind raced. Bedlam held hundreds of people, hundreds of staff. And they had kept the prisoner—the man with no name, 1883. The man that had created an elixir of transformation? But he was dead. Had someone else figured out the mixture instead? But he had not recognised anyone in the monster he had witnessed on the bridge.

This brought up a thought. He held up a hand. "Benji, you said you saw them enter through the window of Heathwood's home. I saw that window—it was not nearly as large as the... the *beast* I witnessed tonight on the bridge. And something that enormous would be spotted at the asylum."

Benji shrugged, but Elle spoke up. "Perhaps they can change their shape and form as need be. They would not be the only one to do so. And for all you know, the inhabitants of the asylum are in on it. After all, no one who currently works there has been killed yet, have they?"

This brought Barty up short. He had not even considered that, but it was completely accurate. All the murders had been of *former* members of the staff, and a single member of the House of Lords whom they still could not place. But no one within the asylum itself, or even working there, had been touched yet. He nodded, acceding to the point.

"Anyways, I told you what I know... but now you have to do the same," Benji said suddenly, pointing at Barty, who was, for the moment, placed upon the spot. "What you got in your coat there?"

Barty reached into his pocket, but Benji waved him off. "Nay, not the shooters. The right pocket. That blood in there?" With hesitation, Barty pulled out the blood-soaked handkerchief. Benji pushed himself off the bed and snatched it out of his hand, frowning as he held it up to his nose and inhaled deeply, his ears twitching at the sides of his head, before growling deep in the back of his throat.

He took another breath, leaving Barty increasingly mystified. He looked to Elle, opening his mouth to protest, but she was shaking her head in warning, and holding a finger to her lips for silence.

"Backlegs brummer, you got a *mix* in this one," Benji finally said with a mixture of awe and dread, pulling the cloth away from his nose with a grimace. "There's all sorts here. Thought it was just blood at first, but it sure ain't that, not really." He lightly tossed the handkerchief into the air. Still heavy and thick from the gore upon it, it sailed along before Barty snatched it out the air, his skin crawling as it landed with a soft wet splat in his palm.

"You are going to have to explain that one to me, if you could be so kind," he said, trying to keep the depths of the wince out of his voice.

Benji was back on the bed, and shrugged. "There's alchemy in that, some weird stuff. Was it in the laboratory of a wizard or something?"

Barty blinked. "Ah… no. This is the blood of the… that was the blood of our killer. I got it off the bridge."

Benji stared, before his voice returned, weaker than before. "You what? That is how you found it? It wasn't mixed in with anything?"

Barty shook his head, explaining how he had come by the

blood and where it was from. Benji swore weakly, sweat beading on his brow.

Elle stepped forward. "What? What is it?" Her tone was intent, her gaze sharp. "You said it had alchemy?"

"That and more," Benji said fervently. "There's so much swimming in all that it may as well not be blood anymore. I got around a dozen different reagents out of it, and there's more that I just can't recognise. There's blood, sure, at the base. But the rest of it is something else."

"What exactly do you mean by 'alchemy' in this regard?" Barty asked in outright bewilderment. Elle and Benji explained looks, before Benji started speaking.

"It's what you lot call science, but there's magic in it," he said, as though that explained everything. Barty blinked slow and then turned his head to Elle, expression blank.

She rolled her dark eyes and sighed. "He *really* is not telling you all that much, is he? But then again, he never liked it much." She sniffed, and spread her hands. "Magic is taking things from the Other, in different forms or shapes. Some of them are solid. There are compounds, devices, things that can be used for making spells and the like. But some of these can be mixed, or worked with more conventional science. Physics and chemistry, and the like… but it is overwhelmingly danger-ous, and seldom at all stable." She shook her head. "The only way someone would have that mixed with their blood is if—"

"—they were putting it in there themselves," Barty finished, his a mixture of wonder and indeed, a gnawing horror. "I witnessed Adam and Jean working something in the armoury, something they called a foci. It exploded when they tried to combine it with metal." He paused, looking with horror at the handkerchief in his hand. "You are telling me this has *that* in it?"

"Not that one in particular. There are thousands of things

it could be. But yes. Pretty much." She shook her head. "Where would they even *get* something like that?" She sounded baffled, even angry. "That sort of thing is difficult to get a hold of. Only through certain smugglers and means."

"And we can find out those," Benji said with a frown. "Half of them are in the Under after all, and they can get us on the sniff of the other half in a hurry." He nodded, and rubbed his jaw. "We're going to have to keep to the sly with all of them though. You know how that lot are, *especially* Granny."

"We are not talking to Granny Green," Elle said darkly. "She's a headache at the best of times and a nightmare at the worst. No."

Barty was left in silence at this point, as though they had forgotten he was in the room; normally he would be all right with this, but he was tired, he was sore, and he was being haunted thoroughly by the memories of the pursuit. He strode between them, both hands raised.

"Before we go any further, explain what all of this means," he stated flatly. "Starting with the question you have not answered yet." He looked between them both, frowning as each stared at him in surprise. "Why do you both *care* about this? I cannot figure that part out. What is your part in all this?"

Silence fell. Barty rounded on Benji. "You… you I understand, at least a little. You were friends with Heathwood, he was trying to help you. But you?" He spun back to Elle. "You I do not yet understand. You, I do not get. You will talk to me, but not to Jean, and I can think of no reason why you would do that, unless that you know him in some way. And that means you are either his enemy in some fashion, or—" Realisation dawned, and his mouth hung open. Feeling a fool, he shut it again.

Elle had watched the entire tirade with a look of growing resignation. Finally, she sighed, reaching up to remove her concealing mask. Though her nose and lips were twisted in annoyance, she had a rather pretty face, no older than Barty himself. But she bore a jagged, fierce scar that ran down her cheek to the corner of her mouth, giving her a fiercer look, though her expression was resigned. She lowered her gaze.

"My father does not want me involved. Truth be told, he does not want me anywhere near him," she said sourly. "Though he pushes himself, and keeps himself away, he is still my father." She straightened up, lifting her chin proudly. "Elanor Reynard, at your service, Mister Barty."

Barty finally remembered his manners. "It is… it is a pleasure to make your acquaintance at last, Miss Elanor," he said, stuttering. His gaze drifted to the scar, and she, seeing it, lifted the mask to cover her face once more with a grimace, turning away.

"Do not misunderstand me, Mister Barty. I am not doing this for him. I am doing this for James."

"In what way? James is—" Barty tried to ask in a puzzled tone but Elle—no, Elanor—snapped at him firmly.

"Dead, yes, I know. I was there." Her tone was acidic to say the least, hurt in her eyes before she turned away and folded her arms across her chest.

"Because if we don't do something about this, it's the Unders who are going to suffer for it," Benji said quietly, his shoulders hunched. "Her old man nearly blew the pub in two and would have killed everyone in it. Unless we do something about it, he might come back and try again. Best thing we can do is make sure it gets done with quick."

"He does not want nor need our help," Elanor said bitterly, shaking her head. "But we can at least work with you." She gave Barty a doubting look. "I am not sure what he sees in you, at least. Not yet. I don't even know why he has you working with him, to be honest." Her tone turned speculative, arms still folded protectively across her chest. "Why *are* you working with my father?"

Barty needed a moment to answer that one. Finally, he sat himself down on the edge of his bed next to Benji to compose his thoughts. "I cannot tell you his reasoning. Only my own. I needed to know."

"Know what?" she asked with a raised brow.

Barty snapped his response instantly. "All of it. *Everything*. I want to know what is out there. I want to know about what you people know. I want to know my place in it. Because..." He trailed off, looking around the room. He swallowed slowly. "Look at this. This is all I was before. An empty room with nothing in it." He pointed at the floor. "I used to sit there and fix things, make mechanisms by candlelight. And then I would go out and try to find answers to things, to stories. I would find out about the world, about things people didn't know about, because I wanted to find where *I* was supposed to be." He rubbed his brow anxiously with the back of his hand, wiping blood from the handkerchief there in doing so but not caring. "Because look at this. I was gone, and no one knew or cared. I left this place and I cannot... I cannot even *remember* it right. If I look back on my life, it feels like this room. Like I was never even there."

Silence fell for a moment after his impassioned, desperate rant. He felt heat on his cheek from his embarrassment, as both of them stared at him, until Elanor spoke with quiet awkwardness. "Maybe I can see what he sees in you. But what about you? What do you see in him?" She gestured idly with one hand as she clarified. "I know about what you want from him, what you think he can teach you. But what do you *see* in him?"

Barty grimaced, his gaze lowered. "He stares down the dark. I want to know how to do that too. But the more I see of it, the less I think it is something anyone can learn."

"Stares down the dark?" Benji repeated.

Barty shrugged moodily. "Something from the orphanage. On the dark nights, the bad nights, we would look at the lights. Maybe a candle someone filched, or a lamp light out on the street. We would look at the light so we did not have to look at the shadows or what was happening there." He shuddered then. "Sometimes I would look at the dark instead. Not to see what was there; I knew what was there. I stared at it so I knew it was not creeping up on me. Or I tried to, anyway. In the end, I would always find the light to look at instead… just like the rest of us." His hands came together, squeezing the fingers to stop them shaking a moment. "Your father doesn't look away. He looks at the dark. He stares it down. I need to know how to do that."

There was a stretched out silence, and Barty eventually broke it. "You are wrong, you know." His tone was awkward. He was not quite sure how to bring this up. "About your father. He does need your help."

Elanor snorted, chuckling bitterly. "*My* help? He wants nothing to do with me. After James"—she struggled with it a moment before she pushed on, her tone dark and moody—"he turned away all his old friends, he burned all his bridges. He left me, he left my mother, he left *everyone*. Or he forced them away. He blamed everyone. *Everyone*. And he ruined everything." She strode to the doorway.

"He's dying," Barty said, with the sudden finality of dread understanding. Elanor stopped cold mid-step.

"What?" For the first time since their original meeting, her voice was frightened.

"Tonight, I watched him let a man beat him, because he

blamed himself for failing to save that man's wife," Barty went on, the pieces clicking into place with a growing, awful realisation. "He nearly died trying to do it. He *would* have died, if we had not pulled him clear. And he still blames himself, and it was not the first time. He has been reckless from the start, and so, so angry, all the time. When he and I first met, again in the Under, tonight on the bridge." He felt sick, his gorge rising, as it all finally made awful sense. "He did not push you away because he is angry at you, Miss Elanor. He is angry at himself. And he is trying to die. If you hate him, it will make it that much easier."

"For him?" Her voice was ragged, but there was a shining glint of tears in her eyes.

Barty shook his head emphatically. "No. For you. If you hate him, you will not miss him when he is gone."

She trembled, her hand rattling on the door handle before she took it away to still herself. Her voice was hushed when she finally spoke, while Benji seemed to hardly breathe.

"He was not always like this," Elanor said in a strained voice. Without turning towards the pair, she roughly wiped at her eyes. Her voice cracked then as rage swept through her—a rage that by now was quite familiar to Barty—and she rounded on him furiously. "What can you claim to know of this matter? What could you claim to know about my father? Nothing! You have spent but a short while with him! You know *nothing* about him!"

Barty flinched from her wrath and the weight of it. It was more visceral, more powerful coming from her—all the more so because it was unexpected. Her eyes blazed, a volcanic outburst borne of grief. He knew it when he saw it, if only because he had been exposed to so much of it in recent days, to know where it came from. It was one more thing father and daughter shared.

"But I do know myself," he responded, his voice quavering just a touch. "I know why he took me on board now."

"As an apprentice?" Benji asked hesitantly, but Barty was shaking his head.

"Jean has taught me nothing. Consistently, he has given only partial explanations. I have learned more from others than himself much of the time," he said a bit bitterly, as more and more pieces slotted into place. "I am a reporter. An investigator as well, but a reporter." He rubbed his brow. "My work at the Times means I find people of importance, who might otherwise go unnoticed, and tell their stories. Interesting stories, my editor calls them. Little windows into life in London." He looked to each of his audience, who both looked entirely nonplussed, and pushed on in embarrassment. "I try to find people that matter, you see, to record their lives and write about them. The editor tears them to pieces and usually just takes a few lines from it, but that... that is how I get by. And then someone told me that there was a man on the streets who had killed Jack the Ripper, and I..." He trailed to a halt, taking a shuddering breath. "I write the story of people, those who would otherwise be forgotten. I write so that they can be remembered, or learned about, but I thought the story of the man who killed Jack the Ripper would *make* me something, would give me opportunities I never dreamed of!" He smacked his fist down into his hand. "But I never stopped to think why he would *let* me."

He pushed himself off the bed, rubbing his hands together not in triumph, but pure, unfiltered anxiety. "He does not want me there to learn, he does not want me to write about his life. He does not want me to write about how he killed the Ripper—he will not even talk about it. He dismisses it."

"The Ripper was something he and James solved together," Elanor interrupted sharply. "I"ve never seen him work harder on anything in my life. I do not think he even slept until he ran it down and killed it. He was completely consumed in unravelling it." She was shocked, unable to hide it, her eyes wide with surprise. "He will not speak to you about the case, not at all?"

This brought Barty up short. The statement was so at odds with how utterly dismissive Jean had been of the Ripper case, so much so that Barty had all but abandoned it in all the chaos, that it was now brought back into sharp focus. He mutely shook his head. Elanor's strident anger began to waver, her eyes showing shock, doubt, and finally fear.

"I have to go to him," she said numbly.

Benji sat up and pushed himself off the bed, pushing past Barty. "You *can't*," he said sharply. "I can't go near him and I can't go below either. If you leave me alone now—" He cut himself off.

Elanor rounded on him, frowning, before speaking sharply. "Is there something you are not telling me, Benji?"

He looked trapped, the tightness of the small room definitely not helping. "Yarrick told me to clear out for a while," he finally answered miserably, his ears going low and flat. "Some of the others blame me for what happened... and the rest think I'm a teller, because he didn't kill me when he found me."

"Teller of what?" Barty asked in perplexity, but Elanor snorted, answering.

"He means an informant." She swore softly, a range of curses her father used, before easing down and subsiding, the shadow of Jean leaving her gradually as she sighed. "If you are with me, he will not hurt you, Benji. We can go to him and try to... try to get through to him."

Barty was already shaking his head. "You won't," he insisted.

Elanor groaned and turned her head to him, roused into prickly reprisal once more. "Why not?" she snapped, irritated.

"Because he's got the scent now," he said miserably, then gestured around the room. "I know what it is like. I did not come back to this place for three *months* and did not even realise it, I know what it looks like in someone else. If you go to him now, you won't get through to him, and he will push you away, or worse." He grimaced, as Elanor's expression twisted up in frustration. He took a deep breath and pushed on.

"I know why he wants me there now," he went on softly. "It is why he has been harsh to me, why he nearly got me killed more than once; he wants me to write about him, and he wants me to write about him as though he is a monster, a beast... and to do so after he is gone. Then, when you read it, you would be able to do so through my eyes, and hate him." He took another deep breath, not wanting to say more, but knowing he had to. "Because if you hate him," he said in a low, dread tone of dulled realisation, "then you will not miss him."

Elanor's face contorted behind her mask, her jaw trembling as her eyes flooded once more. "I could never hate my father," she said in a ragged voice, lowering her head and pulling her mask up further. "He is my *father*. He is my *Papa*. And I——" She broke down. Benji moved forward while Barty stood frozen, and hugged her tightly. *I should have done that,* Barty thought. *I wish I could have done that.* The realisation made him pause, and he pushed those new strange thoughts down.

"If you want to help, find out about this lead," he said instead, as Elanor gathered herself, patting the wolfblood on the shoulder and slowly, gently prying herself away, even though Benji's grip on her was only loose. "Find out about the alchemy, and bring what you can to us. I will take care of Reynard."

"How?" Benji asked, doubtful. Elanor, too, did not exactly look confident.

But Barty was shrugging his thin shoulders as he spoke with feigned confidence. "By doing my job. What I went looking for him for in the first place… and to get what *I* want as well." He gave a hard smile, and even that false confidence turned more real and solid. "I know what he is playing at now. That means I can stop him doing it."

Elanor stared at him. Abruptly she started to speak. "If you fail—"

"I will not."

She was undeterred. "But if you *do*," she went on emphatically. "You will wish you only had me to worry about. If you fail, then my mother will come after you. And she is *much* worse."

Barty was nonplussed, but then Benji shuddered. "Oh, you *really* better be right then, guv," he said with feeling. "Lady of Ravens is a right nasty witch."

"Benji!" Elanor lightly punched his shoulder in a most unladylike manner, very reminiscent of the Reynard family.

Benji rolled with it, but did not look apologetic. "What? She's mean!"

"Well… yes," Elanor conceded. "But you do not have to go out and just *say* it."

"The point has been made clear, nevertheless," Barty responded awkwardly. Had it ever. The wife of Jean Reynard, if she was a woman of his equal, would be bad enough. The thought that she might well be *worse* was one he dared not contemplate.

Elanor stood there for a while longer, clearly not happy,

but just as clearly finding little she could do about it. She was fierce in her anger, and fiercer still in her frustration. But Barty met her gaze, holding it until she spoke. "You are right about my father," she said with final, flat defeat. "If I went to him at this moment, it would not help either of us. So we will play it your way, for now." She then stuck a finger out towards him, taking a step closer and bringing it towards his face with the aggression of a pistol barrel. "*But* I am telling my mother. So expect to see ravens before long. They are going to keep an eye on you, so don't do anything stupid."

"I saw Adam speaking to four ravens in the library," Barty said, startled into the revelation. "Are you trying to tell me that—"

"They were from my mother, yes." She actually subsided a bit at that, looking relieved. "Good. Maybe she is more aware of this than I thought."

"How the blazes does sending birds help you keep an eye on someone?" Barty asked in absolute confusion, even a little annoyed. It sounded bizarre.

Elanor gave him a pitying look, and Benji sort of grinned anxiously. "I will explain it to you some other time," she said wearily. "Now get out there and find my father." With that, she turned and stormed out of the place, kicking the door open as she went.

Barty wanted to object, but Benji was shaking his head. "Let her go, guv." His tone was gently warning, his ears flattening as he pulled up his hood. "Her dad's a bastard, but he's the only one she's got." He went to follow, but paused. "You'll be right, yeah?" Barty could not find the words, but he nodded. This seemed to satisfy Benji, and he set off out the door after Elanor, leaving Barty alone.

He stood there for a long moment, listening to the pair of them leaving down the stairs. The door opened below, and a second or so passed before he pushed his window open and shouted, "Elanor! Benji!"

There was a pause, as the two shapes below turned to look up at him, and various neighbours who were woken from their slumber cursed the nature of fools, before Barty, feeling incredibly stupid, spoke lamentably.

"I do not know how to get back to the Lodge."

His tone was as helpless as he was, because he did *not* know the way. He had never been able to make proper note of it, and he had never asked for directions. It might as well have been on the surface of the moon.

Elanor stared up at him, clearly seeing how hopeless he was. Finally, she gave a great, defeated sigh. "Yes, of course you do not. How could I have ever hoped different?" She finally beckoned him down. "Come on then. We haven't got all night."

Barty, flushing to the roots of his hair, hurried out to follow them. He paused at the threshold as he went, casting one last look around the darkened single room that had been his life. His little shelter, away from the world, where nothing happened and he did not matter.

He should have felt regret; it was the only home he had ever known outside the orphanage. It was the first place where he had space all of his own. At the time, that had meant something. But now, he could see no trace of himself in it. An empty room, with no memory of the many who had lived in it before him, and would do so long after. He closed the door and hurried downstairs.

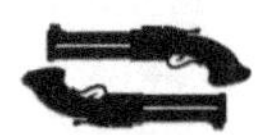

THE JOURNEY back to the Lodge was a complicated affair. Benji and Elanor led Barty through a series of alleyways and back streets, dark places with dark corners that even he had never seen before. Keeping out of sight and out of view, they scurried along and did not speak much. It was not hard to guess why.

"What happens if someone spots you?" Barty could not help asking, as they crawled along a darkened lane beneath a bridge, the trot of horses clattering over flagstones coming from overhead.

Elanor squinted back at him, but it was Benji who answered. "What happens if someone spots the freak, y'mean?" he said sourly without looking back, one clawed hand holding onto the wall to keep him steady.

"I did not mean it like that," Barty tried to explain, but Benji was shrugging moodily.

"Why not? S'true, ain't it?" He sniffed the air, then beckoned them forward. "Mos' times people don't see us. They don't believe what their eyes show 'em to be real and just think it a trick, or some such. It's always dark, and 'sides… who'd believe them?" He chuckled. "We get good at hiding, guv. Have to, if we're going to get far."

"What happens then, for the times that… that you don't?" Barty asked warily. It couldn't be that easy, could it? There had to be more to it than that.

Benji shrugged. "That's when her Dad, or those like him, come for us, isn't it?" He jabbed a thumb at Elanor, who scowled angrily.

"My father never did anything like that, Benji. That's not what he does and you know it." Her tone was sharp, and Benji flinched as though struck. He finally shrugged and kept moving, head lowered.

"There are others out there," Elanor said finally, speaking

to Barty without looking at him. "They have many names, but we call them the Black Coats." She grimaced, her eyes dark with distaste. "They're there to hide the evidence of the existence of the unnatural. No matter what." She looked ready to say more, but then pushed onwards.

"How is that different from your father?" Barty asked, following in her wake. She tensed at the question, and he followed up hurriedly. "I am asking from a place of ignorance. Please. I just want to know——"

"Everything, yes, you already told me," she interrupted in a clipped tone. "My father investigates killers and mysteries of the hidden world amongst us. He saves people in doing so. The Black Coats do not do that. If someone, or something, is revealed, they are the ones who make sure the evidence is lost and people involved disappear. They do not save innocents. They just get rid of the ones who are too loud."

"They sound powerful," Barty ventured. "And dangerous."

"They are," Elanor said shortly. "I hope you never meet one. They are more likely to kill you than anything else. They are few in number, and mysterious, but utterly merciless."

Barty was silent for a long moment, following after her, before the question came to his lips that he had to ask. "Like your father, in France?"

She stopped. Benji was a little ahead, ducking into a side alleyway. For a long moment, from the way that Elanor tensed up and straightened, Barty felt she was about to turn and strike him. The moment hung like that before she strode onwards, saying nothing. Barty hesitated, then followed, chiding himself for not biting his tongue earlier. It made little difference. The rest of the journey went by in frosty, hard silence.

The twisting journey continued, but soon Barty got

glimpses of corners and structures that seemed vaguely familiar, though twisted by the pall of darkness. It was nevertheless
sudden when they emerged from an alley barely wide enough
to walk down single file, to find himself in the street of the
Lodge, the building looming dark and dire amidst all of its
fellows in the nominally unremarkable street.

"And here we are," Elanor said quietly, the subdued words
the first she had spoken since their talk. She stared at the
place, her eyes haunted in the dim light of the street lamps,
torn, even in her stillness, by what conflicting emotions her
mask could not hide. Barty could read the intent if not the
specifics, and he was reminded suddenly of how he wished he
was the one to reassure her, not Benji, and it prompted him to
speak.

"I have learned a great deal tonight, let alone those previous," he said quietly, without looking at her, as Benji remained
huddled in the depths of the alleyway, afraid to see or be seen
by the place where he expected Jean to be lurking. Barty
pressed on, even though Elanor continued to avert her gaze.
"A great deal of names and more besides. This world is far, far
greater than I imagined. I am not sure if I am ready for it…
but, I will do my best to remember it all."

She gave a noncommittal sound and turned away, but
Barty was not done. "Your father is teaching me not simply of
the world you all seem to inhabit, but how to survive in it,
even if he does not quite know it yet. But I *will* use this—all of
it—to keep him alive." He nodded to her as she turned to face
him. "I owe you that much, at the least." His tone was firm,
and he held her eyes with his, perhaps for the first time since
he had met her.

She stared at him for a long moment, then shook her
head. "You had better, Mister Barty. Now, go on. The clock
yet ticks, and ever faster." With that, she turned into the alley,

vanishing into the murk of the shadow. Barty saw the glimmer of Benji's eyes shine for a moment in those depths before they, too, winked out, both of them swallowed up by the night. Barty watched them go, then sighed and turned straight into a grin that robbed him of the ability to scream, and left him making a very small sound like that a startled mouse might make.

Crook had not made a sound, and had not announced his presence at all. He was simply *there*, grinning like a skull with too many teeth, knowing the joke and already howling with silent laughter. Barty would wonder later—when he was not wondering how he did not wet his trousers—how he ever thought Crook was somehow *human*. The smile was too wide, the eyes too bright, the silver hair and the face that looked a thousand years old and yet younger than him, too smooth and ageless and, altogether, too perfect. The lamplight reflected silver in the iris, and the pupils were a black void of the darkest abyss.

"You, young man, are late," he purred triumphantly. "Late to the dream and later *still* to the waking, where have you been?" He inhaled as Barty stood in frightened silence, eyes closing as though inhaling something to savor. "You've blood on you, and a blood so cursed it is *crawling*. A touch of magic in a place it does not belong?" He skipped then in place, dancing to stand beside Barty and, taking his elbow, dragged the stiff-legged young man onwards.

"I have been singing your song for *hours*, Mister Barty," he went on mournfully, his face pulled into a comic expression of sorrow. "High and low in every cranny and hole, whispering in the ear of the dead to see what they might tell me. Nothing! Not a word or reason." He sighed, touching his brow and flicking his finger away dramatically. "I am, for lack of finer words and better melancholy, exhausted. But now I have found you." He frogmarched the still frightened Barty to the door of the Lodge, and patted his shoulder, sending him on his way to stagger up the steps. Barty had just reached the door knocker, when Crook spoke again, "Oh, and Mister Barty?"

Barty turned and felt his blood turn to ice, locked solid in his veins.

Where Crook had stood, there was now a shadow. A formless shape, etched in darkness and silver. It flowed in place, sucking all the light into itself. There was a grin there, in the midst of that darkness, but the eyes of dark light within what might have been a face were terrible in their malice.

"Never run from me again, Mister Barty. Never go where I cannot find you. I'll make your song a scream to drown Heaven in your wailings." The voice spoke with a sound like cracking ice and splinters driven under fingernails. It reached down Barty's spine and spoke of dark times in dark places, back when man was but a brute in the skins of beasts, and outside the edge of the firelight, that voice *waited*.

He blinked, nearly falling over, but in that blink the nightmare *thing* that had been Crook was back to that smiling figure, but there was an edge to that smile now that spoke of many different things.

Barty fell onto his rear, trembling, shivering with the cold racing through him. "There… there was a n-note, I had… I had…" he stammered through chattering teeth. Crook stared at him, and the smile faltered, fading, and his head tilted in a birdlike fashion, a lark spotting something wriggling amidst the soil. His expression turned quizzical.

"Oh," Crook said slowly then, his nostrils flaring. "You had *reason*. Mayhap valid reason." His nostrils flared again as he inhaled deeply. "Hm… Now this does leave me at a loss, and perhaps one well deserved." Barty barely heard him, but

Crook straightened—and gave a small, but flamboyantly, courtly bow. "An apology, Mister Barty. I thought you had chosen to neglect me, not seek other duties." He straightened, shaking his head and chuckling, his tone rueful but light. "What a most mortal assumption I made." He jauntily strolled off down the street at that point, leaving Barty quivering alone in his terror, until he passed a corner and was out of sight. The moment he could not see him, Barty scrambled through the door behind him, and slammed it shut.

The Lodge was silent for a moment, then there was an ominous creak from the landing above, and Barty looked up to see Adam's twisted visage, warped yet further with a look of concern, peering down at him. There was a moment of pause, then the giant brought a hand into view. "Welcome back, Mister Barty." Their voice was troubled, no doubt picking up the state of Barty's mood fairly easily. "Is everything quite all right?"

No, the coachman is a demon made out of shadows and teeth, nothing is all right or ever will be again, was what Barty wanted to say, but he immediately wondered what the point would be; of course they would already be aware of this. And of course, they probably would find it hilarious to see his reaction. So he brushed himself down firmly, and forced himself to stand steady. "Everything is fine, Adam. Thank you for asking." There had been a slight pause between each of his spoken sentences, as he made sure to take a breath to keep his voice steady. Nevertheless, he guessed quite rightly that his tone carried the strain.

Adam, because they were Adam, was far too polite to make a note of it, but their face did have a gentle frown of concern, a kind expression marred by the patchwork of their features. They simply nodded instead, and then gestured.

"Best you tidy yourself up. Reynard got back quite some time ago."

That brought Barty up short. Like a jolt up his spine, as that terrible memory of what waited for him outside faded in to the immediacy of what he was *also* facing. He sprinted up the stairs, startling Adam still further, but Barty drew up to him waving a hand in a frantic gesture to indicate quiet. "Is he all right? Jean. I mean, is he——"

Adam raised a craggy brow, nonplussed, but lowered their voice regardless—as much as could be done. "Reynard continues to be Reynard, with all that it entails. He marched up here without a word and went to his room. Why?"

Barty took a deep breath, and quickly, carefully, explained the events of the evening—while leaving out Elanor and Benji as well. If Adam decided to tell Jean about them, then things could become unnecessarily difficult, and Barty felt that to keep things orderly, he would need Adam's help more than his interference. The giant listened, impassive, their expression giving away nothing and not least because Barty struggled not to stare when he looked at them. Adam deserved better than his rudeness, and he regretted the omission—but needs must.

"Show it to me," Adam said quietly, holding out a hand, as Barty came to a close. Barty was confused, before Adam gave a hurricane-like sigh. "The handkerchief, Mister Barty. Please." A hurried movement later, Barty yanked the much drier handkerchief out and placed it in Adam's hand. It looked tiny in that vast, dinner plate-sized palm, as Adam rubbed their jaw thoughtfully.

"You said that the blood is infused with alchemical mixtures," they said slowly, and then flicked a glance towards Barty, the dead eyes nevertheless sharp. "How exactly did you come to such an erstwhile conclusion, pray tell?"

Barty gaped, then grasped desperately. "I thought... I

mean, I think I recognised some of the smells down there in the armoury, from when you were working," he stammered. "It seemed obvious, so I just… well." He made a shrugging gesture, a futile movement that was supposed to stand in the way of an explanation, and failed to do so. Adam just made a soft *hrmm* sound and looked back to the handkerchief.

"You also took quite a while to find your way back here. Jean took the long way and yet you were the one to come after."

"Yes, well, I stopped by my apartment, as I said," Barty fumbled along. "To make sure I did not leave anything behind. I felt that I might as well, with the time that I had."

Adam made another noncommittal *hrmm* sound, and then nodded. "Very well. I will take this below and see what I can learn from it, though I doubt that I will get much in the condition that it is in. However, this is my speciality. I should have something shortly." He nodded to Barty ponderously, who felt the tension at his lying flow out of him like water poured from a well handled jug. "Get some rest, Mister Barty. I am sure Jean will need you in the morning."

Relieved, Barty turned to his room. In truth, he was exhausted, and sore, and the day had taken more from him than he cared to admit. Hearing those words brought a powerful sense of relief, and he gave a ragged chuckle before nodding, heading to the door of his room.

As he stepped within, Adam spoke from behind him. "Mister Barty, I must commend you however."

Barty paused, even as he was closing the door. "Commend me, Adam? For what?"

The giant was turning the handkerchief over, frowning. "The Lodge is not the simplest place to find, unless one knows the way. Surprising, how fast you picked up the knack really.

Well done." The dead-eyed gaze flicked towards him, as Barty held his breath. "Perhaps there is more to you, as Jean thinks."

Barty stood stock still, until Adam's lips turned up in a semblance of a smile. "Good night, Mister Barty."

"Good night, Adam," Barty mumbled, and closed the door. He stood in the darkness for some time, listening to the retreating steps of the giant outside. They merged with the thud of his own heartbeat, pounding in his ears. He was back in the dark again, and this time he did not try to stare it down.

CHAPTER 17

THE PIECE THAT DIDN'T FIT

Barty did not remember falling asleep. He did not remember his dreams either, save vague insanities that were uncomfortable things with hard edges and dark lines, and smoke that tried to eat him while apologising.

He would have either ruminated on this further, or plunged deeper into the twisting void that kept his aching sleep uneasy, but the waking world was approaching, coming for him, and it would not wait. Especially not when its chosen avatar was Jean Reynard who, upon finding that knocking and calling did not work, rapidly lost the last shreds of his patience and threw a water jug over Barty's head.

At least Barty desperately hoped it was water, and not the contents of a chamber pot, as he sat up shrieking and spluttering. An unwilling tasting proved to his minor relief it was not the latter, and indeed the more inoffensive of liquids, but this was little comfort. Jean stood there with a stony expression, jug still in hand, his face marred by the bruise where he had been struck the night previous.

"We have work to do, Mister Barty," he said flatly. "Sleep

can come afterwards." He turned and marched out of the room, leaving the door open as Barty stared after him, choking on his frustrated rage. He left the room, and then reappeared in the doorway, holding two steaming kettles. "Tea and coffee." His voice dry. "They shall warm you up. Now move." He set each of them down on the dresser beside the door, and then pulled a battered tin cup out of his coat pocket, and set it down deliberately beside them. And then once more he was gone, and did not return a second time.

The shock of the cold water from a London autumn, hardly the quaintest of weather at the best of times, did not, unfortunately, hide the fact that Barty hurt all over. The previous day had beaten him down, then up, and then all about, and it had mocked the idea of mercy. He was feeling it today, in the very core of himself as his bruises upon bruises all called out to him in protest. They were not pleased, and determined to spread it around.

But Jean proved correct. The coffee was hot without being scalding, the tea soothing. He had one of each before he pulled off his cold, wet clothes and dressed himself once more from the closet; Adam had found him some more trousers, some shirts, of the same sort of make as that which he had been wearing, but there was but the one coat, and the one hat. As he pulled on the stolen coat, Barty was once more reminded of the brace of revolvers he had in the inner pockets. He felt he should probably do something about that, particularly since only one of them was loaded.

But time waited for no man, and neither did Jean Reynard. "Mister Barty, if you please!" Came the shout from below and the aching, battered Barty stumbled dejectedly down the stairs soon after. Jean stood there, his hands in the pockets of his heavy coat.

"Where is Adam?" Barty queried, even as he half-stepped,

half-hopped downstairs, his position precarious. He only had one boot on and the other was not getting on easily while traipsing downwards.

Jean, staring at him, merely shrugged. "I have not seen them. I do believe they are in the armoury." Vaguely, Barty figured they were probably still working on the blood-soaked handkerchief. But how much more could they manage? He wanted to say something, but Jean was already opening the door and marching outside. Barty hopped along on one foot, yanking a boot on the other, half-falling outside of the door.

The coach was there once more with its four silent horses, all of them turning their heads to look at Barty and Jean, though their eyes were covered with blinders. Their driver was there as well; Crook sat at a jaunty angle, with an odd lean that looked like he was about to fall out of his seat, but he was crooning a song in words that Barty did not recognise. Jean paid him no heed but Barty froze in terror at the sight of him, remembering the thing that he had been for just a heartbeat on this very same darkened street.

"Lady Amberley will not wait, Barty. Get in the coach," Jean said sharply, his tone harsh and his eye narrowed. He was on edge, Barty could clearly see by this point, as though coiled through with razors and spikes, ready to burst. There was menace enough in that impatient rage, and Barty did not have the strength to try and fight against it. He nodded, and pulled his bedraggled frame into the coach, even as Crook's song took a high note and then lowered, in a queer sort of greeting.

"Bedlam," was all Jean said, a short, sharp bark of a word as he got into the carriage and sat down, his arms folded across his chest, staring straight ahead with the enraged intensity of a man chewing down fury. Barty, however, was at a loss.

"I thought you said we were going to see a Lady Amberley?" he queried.

Jean's gaze narrowed but he did not turn his head. "That would be quite difficult to arrange, Mister Barty. She is dead."

"Then how—" Barty began, but Jean went on in that same acidic, hardened tone.

"She died last night, because a fool failed her twice and got her killed. Even now, the police are trying, and failing, to find her body in the river depths. They may never do so." His jaw worked, the beard and moustache bristling as he turned his gaze to the window, as Barty fell deathly silent. "Lady Rebecca Amberley. Wife of Lord Grayson Amberley, mother of three boys. Edward. Timothy. And Richard." He paused a moment, perhaps remembering all four of them, and how they had looked at him the night before. Barty did not know. He did not dare to ask.

"I am told she was a caring woman, who spent her time managing public charities. Her family was not one of the wealthier ones, but she was well respected for her work, and was noted for being a fine mother to her sons." He bared his teeth then, angry in a way that Barty had not yet seen him. "She deserved better than to become a footnote in a case about foolish men fumbling with things that they do not understand."

"Then what are we off to do?" Barty asked hesitantly, his tone neutral despite his dread. There was violence in Jean's voice. The sort with blood, and broken bones, and terror.

"We are going to Bethlehem Hospital once more, Mister Barty," Jean replied, eyes burning out the window as though he could already see the object of his ire and, by sheer dint of his fury, might cause it to explode into flames sent by the Almighty. "And I am going to get the answers I want, any way that I must." He closed his eyes with an effort, and settled back into his seat. "Now do be quiet, Mister Barty. I need to think." His tone was still that flat, empty note. It had been that way ever since their last talk on the bridge.

Barty was quiet from that moment. There are moments in one's life when it is apparent that another word spoken is not worth the punishment that it would bring, and this was one of them. Barty instead sat silent, and stared at the man he had promised to keep alive, promised to his own daughter that he would do so, but now, once more in the presence of that implacable fury, that caged down rage that seemed to burn black in every fibre of his being, Barty was inexorably driven to the realisation that he could not stop Jean from doing anything.

He could follow in his wake. Observe him, hear him maybe, and learn something of him, but it was now he realised how hard it was to *reach* him. There had been moments, cracks in the broken armour where Jean had spoken to him. Shown that beneath that fierce exterior was something else, something more. It was in pain and it was dying but it was there, struggling to endure amongst all the blood. It had been there on the bridge, when he had to be pulled from his death rather than give up. It had been there, when he had let himself be struck down by a grieving father in the hope it would give them some closure, and to punish himself for failing at something he could not possibly have given more towards doing. And it was there, when he had told him about James, the son he had gunned down to save a daughter. Buried beneath the fearsome brutality, the searing aggression, and relentless drive, the face he presented to every-one, the ferocious killer that everyone feared or hated, and often both. Probably none more so than Jean himself.

Elanor was right; Barty did not know him. He wished to, to unravel the mystery of the man who killed demons, and took away nightmares while allowing himself no peace of his own. It made Barty's hackles rise to think he sat across from a man determined to die, driven to do the only thing he knew how and hoping to perish in the process. Between him and Crook, the terrible *thing* that happened to steer a carriage at impossible angles and speeds with but a thought, Barty was caught in a waking dream, and was drowning in it.

"You are staring at me as though I have something stuck to my face, Mister Barty." Jean spoke in a testy voice, with both of his eyes still closed. "And I know there is not. What is on your mind, since your silence has become more deafening than your voice?"

Barty swallowed, nearly choking on his tongue a moment. He floundered for a second, to think of a question that was not simply asking the man if he was planning to shoot himself. "I was, ah, meaning to give you back your revolver." It was not at all the truth, but it was something that was weighing nevertheless. He fumbled in his coat, and pulled the hand gun out to offer it to the man.

Jean opened one eye, gauging something. "I forgot I gave that to you. You still have that other one, do you not? The one that man waved in your face before he went sailing out the window."

Barty swallowed and nodded, reaching in to pluck it forth. Of the two, the revolver of Doctor Templeton was in significantly poorer condition. It was worn and scuffed, the barrel short and the sight poorly marked, with a weak latch near the hammer to hold it closed. Jean's revolver, on the other hand, was longer and, despite being cast to the stones during the pursuit of the horrible Pariah, it looked in better condition. Jean reached out and took both of them, before giving each a cursory inspection. He sniffed at Templeton's gun, and then cracked it open to tap each of the bullets out of it into his hand before tossing it aside.

"Same calibre, fortunately," he grunted. "The bullets are new enough, but that gun is better off melted down to scrap." He held his revolver back to Barty, the bullets soon after. "Take this, and these. I want to see if you can figure out how to load it on your own." Barty blinked, holding them in his outstretched hands, unsure of what to say.

"First. You want to open the lock, then pull the holding pin beneath the barrel." A single finger pointed out a catch to one side of the cylinder that held the rounds. Barty flicked it, eased the pin to break the catch, and the heavy cylinder swung to one side. "Empty out the casings, then practice firing it while it is unloaded a few times." Jean's voice was no longer angry. It was patient, steady—a teaching voice. Barty shortly realised that he was not only being taught, but that Jean was using the time to take his mind off of other things. He set to work, but not too swiftly. His mind was already figuring things out, finding the mechanism remarkably simple, far simpler than others he had fixed and mended, which made him quite uncomfortable; a thing with so much power being so overwhelmingly simple was just concerning. He soon had the hammer back and the trigger ready on the emptied revolver, but paused a moment, looking back to Jean, who watched him steadily with an unreadable expression.

"Are you expecting violence at Bedlam, Reynard?" he asked the hunter with a worried tone, thinking he had already had enough of such things. Jean gave a grim smile, and closed his eyes again, settling back into his seat as they rattled and bounced along.

"I sincerely hope so, Mister Barty. Now, keep practicing, and load it once you are done. We shall be there soon."

Barty swallowed, clicking the trigger by accident. There was a snap of the hammer closing that startled him, but Jean paid it no heed as his student fumbled through putting the revolver back together, this time with the bullets loaded, a notion that now made his skin crawl as he put it back inside his coat. His mouth felt dry. He was returning to Bedlam with bruises still fresh, and in the company of the most dangerous man he had ever met. Something told him this was not going to go well.

THOSE WHO SEEK to create their future generally have the most control over it. That was the notion that occurred most sharply to Barty, as Jean marched up to the gate of Bethlehem Hospital, his pace rapid enough to set his coat to billowing in his wake. He reached the gate and lifted one boot to kick at it once and fiercely, seemingly disappointed it did not fly open at that ferocious gesture. But a shouted voice of shocked anger instead made him cheerful, as the guard that Barty had once convinced to be let inside came storming out, baton in one huge hand being thumped into the other. "What's all this then?"

He saw Barty and stopped short, scowling at him. "You! Didn't you get enough the last time?" He smacked the iron gate with the baton, making Barty flinch. "I got given a talking to because I let you in. You must be daft if you think—"

Jean cut into his line of vision. He was smiling—that is to say, his lips were turned upwards and his teeth were showing. In no measure whatsoever did it approach his eyes which, instead, glittered with an altogether different sort of glee, spiked through with waiting malice. "Hello there, good sir. I am a madman and I am here to speak to one of your doctors. Do be so good as to let me into your care."

The sound of Crook's coach rolling away became very loud in that moment. Barty blinked several times, and the dull witted guard's jaw worked a few times in his perplexity before he reached out to reason the only way he knew how. "You what?" he asked in a note of disbelief.

"People do admit themselves into professional care, do they not? This is a hospital, correct?" Jean asked in that same cheerful, utterly out of place tone. "I am as I say I am, sir. A madman, and in need of care." He held up both hands, wrists turned inwards. "Come now. I promise you will not regret it."

A lie never laid thicker upon the air, Barty thought with sick horror as the guard frowned, then, still holding his baton in a threatening manner, he moved to open the gate.

"Don't go doing nothing funny there. Either of you." The gate slid open, and he pointed towards the hospital entrance along the road within. "Both of you, hop it in front of me. And no nonsense," he growled, but Jean was already striding through the gate with that same horrible, cheerful air.

Barty followed, his steps altogether more leaden and dragging. The guard fell in behind them both, still smacking that baton into his palm, Barty flinching with each hit. Which baffled him, because he also knew he had a gun and the other man did not. But he *also* knew that while he was terribly, deathly afraid to fire the revolver, the man behind him was not at all hesitant to wield the baton that he carried.

They marched up to the great front door of the place, and Jean pushed the doors open with grandeur, striding within with his hands raised up beside his head in an almost comical fashion. "Good day! I would like to speak to the Dean of the hospital immediately," he ordered pleasantly and loudly, as Barty and their escort drew in behind him.

Much as before when he announced himself a lunatic, Jean's proclamation could have made the drop of a pin unto velvet audible. There were several in attendance in the lobby, and Barty recognised all of them. There was the attendance nurse at the front desk, who still looked as though she dined regularly upon a lemon to maintain her expression, and to one side was Doctor Hyslop, who was a problem, and the cadaverous Professor Ossreich, along with his two thuggish attendants, who was a nightmare.

The two physicians were looking towards the dramatic entrance, and the elderly Ossreich formed a thin, needle-pointed smile at the sight. "Mister Barty, I see you have returned… and with company." He turned his glassy gaze to the guard. "Care to explain why you let these two in, orderly?"

The squirming gate guard grimaced. "Begging your pardon, sir, but he said he wanted to have himself committed on account of being a madman. He seemed a bit… y'know." He waggled a finger at his temple, the universal sign language of a disturbed mind.

Jean continued grinning even as he spoke. "Ah, but you see, that was down at the gate. I am already feeling quite well by now, and I would like to speak to the Dean instead."

Ossreich's smile widened. "Well then, that should make things simpler, especially with an eyewitness." His silken voice of dusty malice rose slightly. "Gentlemen? Take that man into custody." He sounded pleased, in his ancient way of taking pleasure in spite. "And give his assistant a thorough reminder of his previous visit again, if you would."

The two thugs were chuckling, reaching to their belts for their own batons. The guard with Barty pushed forward, lifting his baton to place the point of it at the back of Jean's head in a warning. "All right then, you heard the professor. Now hold still, there's a good chap."

They were ignoring Barty, paying no heed to him whatsoever. He was not a threat and they knew it, which made him wonder for a brief and terrible moment if this was all a test, if he was supposed to pull out the revolver, if he was supposed to be the one to step in.

But Jean spoke idly. "I take it from the sound of things, I am not being taken to see the Dean."

One of the approaching orderlies chuckled in a phlegm-filled voice. "You'd be right, mister. Right this way then."

The huntsman sighed, and shrugged. "Shame." And then, violence happened.

It was terrifying in its sheer ferocity, Barty could not help but think while he stood frozen into place. Jean somehow got the baton out of the hands of the guard behind him and, in the same movement, broke it across the face of one of the approaching men. He caught that one's falling weapon as they tumbled to the ground, with a jaw shattered so completely that it would never work again, as teeth spilled across the floor like dice at a gambling table. Barty had seen men fight before, had seen fist fights and other drunken brawls, but as Jean beat three men into being crippled and unconscious, none of that previous violence in its *entirety* came close to matching it.

Bones cracked and splintered with horrendous speed, as a coiled spring came undone all at once with explosive force. It was over so fast that there was hardly a sound made apart from the crunches and the blows, no screams or shouts, whatever sound might have been made shocked thoroughly out of the systems of the observers.

But when the nurse dove for a bell, Barty drew out the revolver and pointed it and she froze in bug-eyed terror while Barty wondered what the hell he was doing, but then Jean was tossing down a baton—there were shards of teeth embedded in that wood—with a clatter, stalking towards Ossreich. None of the men were smiling any more; Hyslop was cowering and Ossreich looked stunned, as though he could not understand that, suddenly, he had no power at all.

"First man that screams will eat his own tongue after I rip it out," Jean growled as the withered form of Ossreich stumbled backwards, seeking safety and finding none, as Jean continued. "Patient 1883, otherwise known as the Pariah. That is who I am here for." Ossreich did fall over then, onto his behind as Jean stood over him, crouching down to the terrified elderly man with all the mercy of a vulture. "Your Dean, what was his name again? I never remember what you vicious old bastards are called."

"Wickham," Hyslop croaked. "Dean Edwin Wickham." He was huddled in a corner, staring at Jean as though he was a living nightmare. "That is his name. B-but he is not here. He has not been here for weeks."

Jean tilted his head, still looking down at Ossreich. "With a killer hunting him and every other who had anything to do with the Pariah—how terribly coincidental." He lowered his head once more, sneering as though to spit. "I wonder, do you still think it worth it? All that blood, was it worth it?"

Ossreich, pale and caught between rage and terror, was unable to answer, clutching at his chest as his breathing became a wheeze. Jean snorted and spat a glob of something foul to the side of the old professor's head, and stood. "What am I saying? I would wager you never even hesitated." The scathing tone unbridled in its contempt, he turned to the still cowering Hyslop, his head tilting once again. "You seem at least helpful."

Barty was shaking, with the gun still pointed, the nurse staring at him in horror, frozen in place. Barty was at the very *least* as terrified as she was. *Why did he give me this why do I have this what am I doing* ran through his mind over and over, the only variation of his thoughts being that he would sometimes change the order of his internalised ranting, while occasionally adding curse words he would seldom, if ever, dare utter in public. And all the while, he refused to look at the three twisted forms laying with splayed limbs in the centre of the entrance hall. They twitched at the corner of his vision. Occasionally, they made bubbling sounds and red was leaking from them in a slow spreading pool, mixing together on the well-scrubbed floors.

"Th-the Dean is not present. He is… he is…" Hyslop faltered as Jean approached, pressed up against a wall, and the hunter sighed in frustration.

"Speak, man. You are only useful to me while you can make words."

Doctor Hyslop swallowed, but it was clear he had no spine for this. Men and women in restraints, broken and drugged by a regimen designed to leave them shattered, *that* was something he knew to deal with. This was something well out his realm of determination. But Jean was not going away. Barty almost felt sorry for him. Far more so than he felt for the recumbent Ossreich, who was, even now, trying to crawl away from the scene with not a scrap of his dignity left to him.

"There… he has been in seclusion for weeks now. W-we have not seen him at the hospital for all that time. Professor Ossreich has been running things." The haggard Ossreich glared back as Hyslop sang his sins, but he did not stop crawling towards a distant doorway. Jean ignored him. Barty did not dare pull the gun he held from the nurse in case she moved. He barely dared to breathe.

"Then where is he?" Jean barked. Hyslop hesitated, but Jean smacked his hands together sharply with a crack before he barked. "Where, damn you! His life is in danger as we speak!"

Hyslop gaped like a fish on a dock, ripped from its watery home and aghast at the shock even as it suffocated in open air, but he stammered on. "He is… he is at a funeral!"

"Someone died?" Jean growled, his head still tilted, as Hyslop nodded in panic.

"His brother in law," The doctor replied. "Lord George Foxgrove. His service is being held at St Paul's Cathedral."

Jean went completely, entirely rigid. The room went silent, as the bottom of the world dropped away and everything started falling. Barty could see Jean's face, could see the realisation he himself did not understand, but before he could ask anything, the door that Ossreich had been crawling towards opened abruptly and struck him in the face with a loud retort.

The nurse that walked in was quite young, rather pretty in a busy, harried sort of way in her pristine uniform, and she had a few seconds to take in the sight in front of her. She saw three broken bodies on the floor, a rolling, cursing Ossreich who was clutching at his face, a frozen solid desk nurse and, of course, Barty with a gun. At this point she did the entirely reasonable thing and started screaming at the top of her lungs, a long unbroken note of sheer panic as loud as a foghorn.

It got Jean moving. Shaking him out of his stunned stupor, he bolted across the room, picked Barty up bodily with one arm, and ran to the door, the scream following him out as the sound of a ringing alarm bell soon joined in as the two fled from the doors. And Jean was swearing. The sort of cursing that would turn an innocent child to the life of a hardened criminal, that would set a nun to smoking cigars and tarnish the crown jewels with their very blasphemies. It was difficult in all of his panic, but Barty was nevertheless able to deduce his companion was rather upset.

They were sprinting down the gravel road, as shouting, bellowing, alarms, and more went off behind them. Whistles were being blown and people were in uproar, but Barty did not dare stop to look. Jean pushed him up the gate and started climbing up after him as the orderlies charged after them, clearing the iron spikes with difficulty and falling in a sprawl on the other side. Crook was already racing along the cobble-stones—*laughing uproariously, damn his hide*, Barty thought—to collect his two bruised and battered charges before whisking them away from the furious attendants behind them.

"Where to, my playful wonders?"

"St Paul's!" Jean roared. They were both clinging to the back of the carriage, riding in the footman's rests instead of inside. Crook did not look pleased to hear this, his mouth twisting as though tasting something particularly unpleasant, but he did not argue. Jean was already opening the rear coach compartment without caring a jot about the police running on foot towards the hospital, and pulled out his double barrelled rifle, crooking it under his arm.

Barty clung on tight, but finally had his air again to speak. "Why? Why are we going to the funeral? Can it not wait?"

Jean shot him a murderous look, grinding his teeth. "The only one that did not fit, Barty! Lord Foxgrove, the man who learned to fly and fall!"

At first, Barty had no idea what he meant, but then it slid into place with freezing clarity, and he nearly slipped.

"The man on the roof?" Flattened out and crushed, thrown clear across a street to land on a rooftop—their first crime scene. The Pariah had killed him, having hurled him as clearly as he threw the carriage on the bridge. The piece that did not fit. Barty had tried to forget the sight, but some things remained no matter what.

Jean nodded, holding on with one arm, glaring as the carriage raced along, kicking up sparks. Barty felt the realisation widen. "He was never the target, was he?"

"No," Jean snarled. "He was just to get the real one in the open." He thumped the stock of the rifle against the roof. "Whatever you have in those things, now's the time to use it Crook! Faster!"

"I assure you, beloved," Crook called back over one shoulder, his voice somewhat peeved, "nothing shall get you there faster!" The reins were not flicked, and no whip was cracked, but nevertheless, the four strange steeds found extra strength somewhere, as the carriage barrelled over the stones towards the distant looming spectre that awaited. Barty held on with both hands, praying and hoping he did not lose his grip. He had come too far to be a smear upon the stones now.

CHAPTER 18

TWO DEAD MEN AND ONE COFFIN

The Cathedral of St Paul was a structure as magnificent as it was imposing. Standing more than three hundred and fifty feet tall at its tallest peak, the white stone of its massive structure shone at the highest point of old London. It was a place of great importance, where important people went when they were made more important, when religious observations of great importance needed important people to attend and be seen to reflect their importance, and of course, it was where important people went when they were dead, to be seen by as many people as possible one last time. Because they were important, but also dead.

Barty had never dared to set foot inside it. The notion that he would be doing so in his present circumstances was something that made his spine quiver, as though it sought a way to leave the rest of him. The revolver was back in his coat, heavier than ever this time—the weight of having pointed it at another living being made it darker, denser. Would he have shot her, if she rang that bell? Of course not. The very notion seemed impossible.

Ah, but you would have said the same to the very idea of pointing a gun at someone, wouldn't you? Until you did.

Cursing the treachery of his thoughts was futile for the time being. They had roared across bridge and down streets, that looming titan of structure drawing ever closer as they went. It was impossible to miss the cathedral, but never before had it featured so prominently in awareness; for all its incredible design and sheer, vast size, the cathedral was a thing that was simply always *there* for the observers. Occasionally visible, depending on where you were in London itself, sometimes reflecting the light of the sun off its dirtied white stones, when that fitful glow was able to pierce the miasma that cloaked the city in its thickened soup of filth.

It was so noticeable that, eventually, the eye learned to ignore it. A thing of wonder that with familiarity became nothing more than a feature of the geography, drifted over and ignored. It did not help that the place was very much for *other* people. London was full of such places. Places that an orphan from St Mary's did not get to see. Places that they did not look at if they could help it, keeping their eyes down as they toiled along and told themselves it could be worse, so much worse. The world, Barty knew, was separated into two groups of people. Those that kept their eyes lowered, looking to the ground. And those that looked out on the world, and wondered how much of it was theirs, and how to get more of it. St Paul's Cathedral was for the latter.

Except now, things were a shockingly different situation. And as the carriage rolled into the square in front of the cathedral, the sky above bloated with thick, rolling clouds, with Barty's arms numb from clinging so tightly to the carriage rear, it was all the more apparent as to why.

There were many other carriages arrayed about the place, all of exceptional fine make and work, and a six horse hearse carriage with everything a-gleaming black. As Crook brought his own carriage closer, the horses of each and every one of the gathered carriages began to dance and shift in their traces, whinnying nervously and pawing at the ground, getting more agitated as the newcomer drew closer. The horses of Crook's carriage were steaming—all over, in fact, but when they slid to a halt without a touch upon the brake, they went still and rigid once again, steam rising off them, but otherwise showing no signs of exertion. Nothing like horses at all, and every other horse in the place seemed to know it as they went into a bucking frenzy, the air full of their whinnying cries, before that, too, was drowned out in a rising tumult.

The doors of the cathedral had been closed out of respect for the dead. They were violently thrown open now by people much too preoccupied with other matters to continue to respect such convention, and were mostly screaming. A flood of stumbling, screaming mourners flowed out of the massive structure, wearing various styles of very expensive black, as Barty stumbled off the back of the carriage and righted himself. Jean was snapping shut the breach of the rifle as he growled, low and bestial in his throat, "Damn it all. Too late."

Barty did not have to argue. There was no point; the screams were proof enough, along with the rushing, falling crowd. But Jean was moving now, keeping the rifle raised and shouting *"Move! Move!"* as he went. The harshness of his voice, paired with the inevitable authority of *having a gun* created an effective parting of the waters, and the crowd melted around him, with Barty doing his best to carry on in the eddy of his wake. People were scrambling, some being helped and many being forgotten and near trampled as the horde fled, all pretence to society, all dignity of station, completely forgotten.

They moved with the hurried, terrified panic of animals fleeing a predator, that instinctive rush of movement and adrenaline to *get away* no matter what and without thought to guide it; all save for the one man pushing through it, striving to get to where everyone was running from, and the poor, driven fool in his wake, bound to this fate as though chained.

A man in a bishop's garb tumbled past, and Barty was nearly knocked off his feet more than once, but they reached the threshold as the last of the crowd fled out of the way, and at last both Barty and Jean could make out something new. Shouting from within; a terrified voice, gibbering in panic, and another, monstrous and terrible, echoing from the depths of the vast hall, bouncing off the walls and growing ever more fearsome. The voice of an affronted deity, come to the house of another God, and demanding it in turn be heard.

"Mercy!" the horrible voice was roaring. "Where was mercy when I begged for it? Where was mercy, when I wept for it?" The voice was thunderous, pulled from vast lungs on heated breath, wrought hot from rage. Jean stalked forwards as Barty took in the scene.

The interior of St Paul's Cathedral was a magnificent sight. High, vaulted ceilings, glowing with the light of candle and the soft, muted light from the grey skies outside shining through the windows. It was a vast hollow, the exterior of the mighty dome and the cross shape of the building itself reminiscent of the crucifixion, reflected entirely on the interior. There was a long central nave, leading up to a circular space under the dome, with two arms making up the transepts to each side holding yet more space for observers, with the rear quire behind. Amongst that space for the clergy and choir was the vast shape of the grand organ, thousands of pipes, five keyboards and other vast complications making up, not so much an instrument, as an entire process of them.

The space closer to the dome and the altar was in a state of disarray. Pews were scattered and fallen here and there, along with various discarded belongings and fallen, snuffed out candles. The floors were a mixture of black and white marble squares, and the high, high ceiling a mixture of frescoes and other artwork. All told, it was a grand piece of both architecture and art and, if Barty could have managed it, he would have enjoyed his time to look around it.

That was not possible in that moment. Quite far from the entrance that he and Jean had walked in through, just past the circle reflecting the dome directly above, was where the altar stood. In the middle of the circle itself was a fallen table, a white cloth crumpled in a heap—and to one side of it, cracked and broken, the coffin of the unfortunately twice fallen Lord Foxgrove. One stiff arm stuck out at an awkward angle from the shattered wood. Time had not improved his death, nor his circumstances.

But it was the sight at the altar itself which was the most immediately arresting. The vast bulk of the Pariah was there, seemingly even larger than the last time, and his twisted, misshapen form was bellowing at a smaller, wriggling figure that they held with one huge hand upon the altar, roaring their rage and wrath in accusations that shook the firmament.

"*COWARD!* You sent others to torture me, to maim me! My secrets are not for YOU! THEY NEVER WERE!"

A shrill, terrified shriek met those words as the Pariah straightened. It was lit by the light of candles, the dimmed cathedral giving the entire scene a strange, otherworldly edge to it. The vast rumble of that enraged voice, mixing its echoes with that panicked screaming, made that sensation nightmarish as Jean continued to move forward, pulling back the two rifle hammers with a *click* that the Pariah heard, their great head coming up, still lost in shadow in that gloomy place. They wrenched the screaming man—the Dean Wickham, presumably, a man of advancing years and a terrified countenance—and thrust them between their own body and the approaching hunter, holding them by the throat with their feet kicking a whole two feet from the floor.

"Houndsman!" the bestial being snarled, but there was a wretched sort of chuckle in their voice. "I was wondering when you would arrive!" The voice was as twisted as their body. It echoed strangely, harmonising with itself but in a bizarre sort of discordance. It was like hearing several people talking at the same time except in pain, or louder, or with a vile sort of leer in their words as might come from a lecherous drunkard.

Jean was stepping sideways with the rifle raised. He never looked away from down the sights, even as the Pariah shifted, moving with him and keeping the squirming Wickham held in one hand easily between them. "You know me then, Pariah? How fortunate."

The vile, twisted voice chuckled in a menacing rumble, sneering. "I was told to watch for you from those in the Under," they growled. "They *hate* you down there. And I thought I knew what it was to be loathed, but you… you make it an *art*."

"Strange. Never seen you down there," Jean replied flatly, as he continued the side stepping, the two circling each other as Wickham whimpered, begging and pleading, before Jean snapped, "Do shut up, Wickham. We are talking." He flicked his gaze from the dumbstruck, gibbering doctor, to focus back on the obscured Pariah instead, before realising the huge figure had stopped a moment.

"You do not know who I am yet, do you?" the Pariah rumbled, slowly, its tone one of dawning understanding. "Hah. Hah hah. HAH HAH! You don't *know?*" The tone in their voice was one of astonished glee. "Hah! I though you would have figured it out days ago. Locke would have known. He'd have gunned me down in a heartbeat." There was cruelty in that mixed voice, and joy also. It had the purring malice of a voice that knew where to put the knife and grind it in, and would enjoy every moment of it.

Now it was Jean's turn to go still. "You knew Locke?" The beast was laughing still, a rolling and bubbling sound.

"Oh I *knew* him. He was the bastard to track me down the first time. Think he thought me dead, but no, not me. Not me. I am not the one who dies. Never I!" The glee was growing, burning brighter and almost drunk with happiness.

"If I put one of these in your skull I wager we'll test that theory good and quick," Jean snarled, as Barty huddled back, terrified, afraid to get in the way. The Pariah was circling towards him, the very notion of which made him panic. He did not want that nightmare anywhere near him. The monster continued his slow walk, carrying his human shield with him as he went, still giving that twisted, mangled chuckle.

"Oh, you might be right, houndsman." The indescribable face warped further as a rotted grin appeared like a knife wound in the midst of it. "Locke would have shot me by now. He raised you *soft*. Your master made a mistake when he chose you, from the sounds of things." The hellish grin only widened further. "From what I hear anyway."

Jean went still, and Barty knew what he was going to do before he did it. The barrel of the rifle dipped and fired with a boom that bounced off every wall and holy image louder than Barty could have thought possible, and the Pariah howled and went down on one knee as the leg they were standing on was blown out from under them. But they did not drop the wriggling Dean Wickham as they did so, and instead the howl turned into a rasping laughter instead, as that massive hand closed.

The sound of bones collapsing under a crushing pressure is an awful thing to hear at the best of times, and this was not one of those times. Wickham went limp as a sackcloth doll amidst a final gurgle of air leaving lungs dead so quickly that muscle contractions were cut off in the midst, before the body was flung at Jean in the same instant. In retaliation Jean fired the second shot in reply, but he was forced to dodge the hurled corpse.

The shot went wide as Jean weaved and rolled, letting go of the rifle and wrenching the heavy twin barrelled pistol out instead, even as he came back to his feet in a fluid movement. The body of the unfortunate Dean flew past Jean and crashed into the fallen coffin and table, sending both skidding across the dome floor, the two corpses tangled together in a way that could only be called unseemly.

The Pariah scrambled away. Their leg was untwisting as they went, the blast that had ripped a hole six inches wide in their lower leg already healing, leaving a trail of their tainted, cursed blood as they went. Jean fired, once, twice, each gouging a massive hole in the vast back and ragged clothes of the Pariah, but it did not go down, until, with a howling shriek, it dashed into the southern transept and leapt through a window, which exploded outwards amidst a chorus of screams from outside. Jean and Barty both scrambled in pursuit, but a cursory glance showed it was hopeless—the tremendous speed and power of the Pariah had it leaping amongst rooftops in moments as the bullet holes in its twisted body already had healed.

Jean's teeth were bared, but Barty could not help but stare in horrified wonder. Jean glared at him from the edge of the shattered window. "I was hoping you would remember your gun and shoot him, not hide," he snapped.

Barty shook his head, too stunned to apologise. "How does alchemy *make* something like that?" He could not keep it inside, even if he thought it a stupid question as he asked it.

"*Alchemy?*" Jean said then, his voice sharply curious. "How do you know that this is because of *alchemy*, Barty?" His tone turned rapidly accusing instead, and he pointed the barrel of the pistol he carried at him; even though it was not loaded any longer, Barty could not help but flinch.

"Because of... of the handkerchief, and there were... there were reagents in the blood, Adam said, they said they were going to investigate it—" He stammered to a halt as ice flowed down his spine. "But I thought we went to Bedlam because... because you knew about... " He trailed off in horror. "You did not speak to Adam?"

I didn't tell him, he suddenly realised. Despite learning about the fact that the killer had been residing in the Asylum, despite knowing alchemy was present in the blood of the Pariah, despite knowing the importance of it all, he had not said a word of it to Jean. So caught up in the pursuit and everything that had happened, he had simply assumed that Adam had told Jean about it. But then, he also remembered, that Jean told him he had not seen Adam that morning at all.

"I did not speak to Adam, no," Jean said scathingly, furious, as he swore loudly and explosively then, a further desecration to go along with the bullet holes and other violence in the cathedral. He glared balefully at Barty, his fists clenching, then exhaled with volcanic anger as he turned away, quivering with fury, leaving Barty standing in huddled shame.

There was shouting coming from the nave then. A bustling crowd of running police charging up the aisle, with a familiar duo at their head. Jean marched towards them, pausing only to pick up his fallen rifle with a brief crouch.

"Reynard!" Montague was furious, shaking a fist, as Barty came up hesitantly in the wake, feeling awkward and stupid. As the chief inspector berated the wordless Reynard with Creek huffing for breath, bent double at his side, Barty took every angry word and put it to himself.

He should have spoken earlier. He should have said something. He should never have assumed, least of all because he was afraid of looking foolish. Though he had asked many a foolhardy question, and given many a pitying look for his lack of understanding over the past few days as the world pulled surprise after surprise and rattled his wits in his skull, he had no real excuse. If he truly wanted to help Jean, if he truly wanted to be part of the investigation themselves, he had no business not sharing things that he knew with him, even the simplest of revelations. But what he had learned from Benji and Elanor was far from that, and he had sat upon it like an idiot.

"I know who they are," Jean said flatly, the words cutting through the furious shouting just as Montague was getting warmed up and gesturing furiously at the shattered window, and in the aftermath of that statement, echoes merged into silence, save for the sounds of harsh breathing as from many men that had run too far, too quickly.

Montague, one hand still raised with furious finger pointed, blinked rapidly several times. "Who?" he demanded then, shocked.

But Jean shook his head before speaking harshly. "A dead man. Twice dead already in fact. The next time for good." He ground his teeth as he spoke, coldly furious.

"That is not an answer, Reynard," Creek wheezed, for once looking as annoyed as Montague.

But the hunter shrugged, dismissive. "It is the best you are going to get for now. The point is, I am going to run them down now. Anyone else is just going to get in my way." He pointedly looked to all of the police gathered before him, before focusing on Montague. The chief inspector looked conflicted, furious still, but he set his jaw pugnaciously, his moustache quivering.

"You swear to me, Reynard. That you will kill this wretch before anyone else gets hurt," he stated flatly. Creek and Barty both looked at him in astonishment.

But Jean was nodding. "Before dawn. If I do not, feel free to lock me up yourself. I will even give you the chains." He said it without a trace of humour, radiating truth with every word.

What has he figured out? Barty wondered.

Montague glared at him. A shared look passed between them then, echoes of the two of them upon the bridge lingering around them still, in the aftermath of the disaster they had both been part of. He shook his head, muttering, before stepping aside and gesturing down towards the main doors. "Go then. Do not make me regret this, Reynard."

"You probably will, some day," Jean said dryly, as he marched forward through the rows of parting police. As Montague started to bark orders and organise them, Barty was left standing alone, withered by his shame, and wondering quite sincerely what he was going to do now, before Jean turned and looked at him with annoyance.

"Stop standing there like some lost pup, Mister Barty, and hurry up. We do not have much time." He took off again without looking back. Barty remained frozen for a moment, then, as the volume of Montague rose, he set off after Jean, scurrying awkwardly along and trying to push through as yet more police thronged onto the scene.

Crook and the carriage waited at the end of the steps, with every other carriage keeping a wide berth from the scene. There were crowds, and people shouting conflicting orders, and many others watching in wide-eyed fascination and confusion. Voices were shouting louder from the direction that the Pariah had fled off towards, but Jean paid them no heed. He stalked towards his carriage, with police stepping out of his way as he went, even if he got some strange looks in doing so. But Barty, racing awkwardly behind him, felt himself stopped abruptly and dragged back—a young officer, his eyes suspicious, bustled him about and gave him a looking over, but before he could ask a question, Jean's voice barked from behind him. "Hands off him, if you do not mind." He'd halted on the step, his rifle under one arm. "He is with me."

The officer looked conflicted, until an older man with the look of a sergeant about him took him by the shoulder and shook his head in warning. Barty felt himself released with reluctance, and scurried into the carriage after Jean as, with a whistle, Crook set off into the milling crowds surrounding the cathedral. More were coming to view the street theatre, the inevitable curiosity of those seeing opportunity and wonder both bringing those of all stripe and colour to see what was going on. It would likely be all over the newspapers for the evening edition. Barty could not help but regret he was going to miss out on the scoop, but no one would have ever believed him anyway.

The scorching glare of Jean finally could be ignored no longer, as Barty turned reluctantly to face the man sat opposite him, his arms folded and his jaw set pugnaciously. One eye was partly screwed shut in that echo of rage, until Barty finally spoke.

"I am sure you are quite angry at me, sir, but—" was as far

as he got before Jean bit back at him with a tone that evoked a headsman's axe.

"A correction, Mister Barty, I am, in fact, *furious* with you. I would even go so far as to say I am utterly bloody livid in my state of distress at this venture, and Lord help me, if I was less restrained I would be in the midst of giving you a thrashing." He ground his teeth as Barty quavered, then finally exhaled his annoyance, reaching into his coat to pluck out a cigarette and match from its depths. "However, we do not have time for that. We need to go figure out what Adam has learned from this handkerchief you are talking about—but first, and I mean this quite sincerely, do tell me absolutely everything that you know."

Barty took a deep, shuddering breath, and rubbed his face, shivering as a second realisation sank in; this time, he would not be able to keep much of what he had learned secret. He did what he could to twist it, to protect Elanor, even if he was unable to fully understand why it was so important her name be kept out of things.

"I met with Benji, after the bridge," Barty said, his voice faltering. "He told me he smelled the Pariah, after Heathwood died. He told me that he recognised the smell of cleaning liquids used in Bedlam, swore it could be nothing else. And then... then he smelled the handkerchief of blood I got from the bridge. Said it was full of alchemy." He fell silent, as Jean continued to glare at him balefully from his seat as the carriage rolled along. Barty could not help but think of how much time he had spent bustling about in London in this carriage with this very angry man over the past few weeks. It was a distraction to alleviate himself from the weight of that angry stare.

"I will tell you this one time, and one time only, Barty," Jean said with a terrible finality. "Once, because I suppose you are afforded that leniency. You *have* been important to this investigation until now, which I will not deny. But next time you learn something about a case, you are to come to me *immediately* and tell me. Do not rely on another to do it for you. Do not expect anyone to do the work because you will not. Do it yourself, or do not bother further. The next time I have to wait to get answers from you I will *beat* them out of you." His tone was hard, cold. There was no mercy in that expression nor in his eyes, which were frostier than the northern seas. "Are we clear upon this matter?"

Barty sat huddled upon his seat as though it would swallow him up. Finally, without looking up, he spoke in a small, hesitant voice. All his aches and pains, all his bruises and strained bones came through in his words in that moment. "I should have said something. I thought Adam would tell you, I thought you somehow already knew, I thought—" He cut himself short, then took a deep breath, without looking up. "I should have said something," he went on quietly. "It will not happen again."

Jean grunted, sourly, but the worst of his rage seemed to subside into quiet frustration. He gave a dismissive snort and looked away, as Barty glanced up hesitantly, before the youth struggled on.

"You said you know who he is, to Lord Montague," he stammered, rubbing his hands together. Jean grunted again. "Who, then? Who is the Pariah?"

Jean looked irritable, but he shook his head and struck a match, lighting the cigarette held between his teeth. "Well." He took a deep breath as the carriage rolled on, the crowd thinned now as they rattled down the street. "It would be hypocritical in the utmost now for me to keep that to myself, after the tongue lashing you just had to endure from me." His tone was sour, and he was shook his head, before he turned his steely gaze back to Barty.

"The mistake I made was a simple one, born out of both arrogance and missing information." He exhaled smoke as he went on, speaking swiftly. "I failed to find anything because I was looking in the wrong places. I presumed to find what I needed in either studies of various creatures, *or* in open cases." He took another inhalation and then blew more of the somewhat acrid smoke around the carriage. "The machinations of the hidden world are beyond numerous, Mister Barty, but there are usually common aspects to them that have been explored before. However, on occasion there have been unique cases, that defy normal expectations." Barty waved a hand in front of his face, coughed, and pushed open a hinged window—noting that the mechanism to do so was strangely organic, as though grown instead of shaped. Jean frowned at the momentary distraction before he pressed on. "Many years ago, my mentor, Theodore Locke, tracked down a relentless killer. It was a difficult one, because it was trying to find a man who had uncovered something that had never been seen before." He grimaced, shaking his head. "It was before my time with him started, and I remember him mentioning it, and I think I read about it once, but only now does it all make sense—only after speaking to him, do I finally understand who the Pariah *is*." He took another drag from the cigarette, then leaned over to cast the stub through the opened window.

"Through alchemy and science, two things which normally do not mesh well at all, this man—a doctor and a genius—managed to create something completely unheard of. A means to change his form, to rejuvenate himself to a younger, more powerful state." He shook his head. "It was unheard of, and for good reason. Alchemy is *incredibly* unstable, and used with extreme care and generally trusted materials." He rubbed his cheek as he went on. "Materials which are extremely difficult to come by, and seldom by those who do not know what they are looking for. But somehow, this man figured out something that had never been done before, and more than that, he was so sure of his work that he *injected* himself with it, refining it as he went to make it more potent." He snorted. "I admire his bravery, but only until such a point that the cracks began to appear... the side effects."

"I think I can safely say I know what those look like now," Barty said meekly, remembering the twisted form of the Pariah, a twisted hulk of a being with that awful, unnatural strength.

But Jean was shaking his head. "No, you do not. Not fully. The Pariah is just the end result. What the alchemy was actually doing was warping him, body and soul. It was *wrenching* his mind into a new state as well, and turning him not just into a different person physically, but also mentally—so much so that the new shape, the younger, stronger form, was not a different aspect, but a different person altogether." He clenched a fist, striking it into his open palm as he growled in realisation. "Heathwood, the studies, all of it... it all started with this man. The split in personality, the different personas in the same body, all of it began with *this* case. It all came from this... but he died. Locke wrote that himself. The man poisoned himself, just before he was brought down for good. Guilty and ashamed of what his other half had done—and it was bloody and wretched indeed—he took his own life as Locke and the others broke down the door to his laboratory. That was supposed to be the end of it. The case was closed. A cautionary tale warning of the dangers of the unknown, lost to myths and legends."

He sighed, leaning back then, and closed his eyes. "But now, I am to understand that not only is he still alive, despite being declared dead more than once, he is at large in the city, and has been operating out of the very asylum that he was locked into as a prisoner, somehow, without anyone even realising." He shook his head, and gave a chuckle that rang of disbelief as he fell silent.

Barty swallowed. "Who was he? Who *is* he?"

Jean opened his eyes, staring balefully at the carriage roof, as though to pierce the rolling clouds above that hovered heavy and laden with rain. "His name is Jekyll. Doctor Henry Jekyll."

"Jekyll," Barty said slowly, before he nodded. "And what are we doing now?"

Jean grunted, and closed his eyes once again. "We are going home to the Lodge. And there we are going to find a way to kill him, once and for all, and have it done before the moon slips from the sky." He gave another soft, snorted chuckle. "No pressure, of course."

Barty stared at him as the carriage rolled on, a hollow sensation in his gut. "Indeed. No pressure at all," he murmured. It did not matter if he wanted to believe it, even as the rain began to fall at last, heavy and full, turning the world outside the window into a drenched haze. In that moment, that very pressure, ignorant of being denied, felt singularly inescapable. It crushed down upon them as they rolled along the road, trailed by the voices and cries of streets turned to panic on a rainy London afternoon.

CHAPTER 19

THE STRANGE CASE OF DOCTOR JEKYLL...

"What do you *mean* you have no idea what he looked like?"

The door to the Lodge opened with Jean at stride, Barty following him in with an expression wrought of frustration and disbelief.

Jean stopped abruptly and rounded on Barty. "I am stating the facts, Mister Barty. The elixir he created allowed him to change his appearance whenever he took it." He turned again, striding towards the lower stair that would lead to the elevator. "Locke theorised that it had a relative morphic charm involved; it is possible that he looked different to every person who observed him. Everyone who tried to describe his alternate shapes could not find the words to do so, which is indicative of such an enchantment."

Barty was locked in place for a moment out of sheer bewilderment. He shook himself both mentally and physically, shut the door, and hurried off after the inexorable pace of Reynard, who was clearly in no mood to wait. "That makes no sense at all, damn you!" he called after him in anger.

"Magic, Mister Barty!" Jean snapped back, already moving to the next staircase as Barty half-jumped down the descending staircase to catch up. "Alchemy is the science of magic, the distillation of the impossible into physical form—and changing form is the core of it! But if you want it to make sense, I am afraid we do not have the time to explain it here."

"But if that is true, you have no way of figuring out who they are!" Barty said in despair. "Let alone how we are going to get into the hospital, which the police are probably still present at, after what happened there!"

Jean paused once again, halting at the door to the elevator. His expression twisted a moment, before he turned that shadowed gaze back to his charge for a moment. Barty halted, thinking he had gone too far for a moment.

"Part of me wishes to blame you for that, Mister Barty. If I had known that our quarry was there, things would have gone differently—however, since at that moment he would have been murdering the Dean halfway across the city, it was perhaps fortunate happenstance." He considered a moment, running his fingers through his hair and sweeping it back behind his ears as he thought. *He looks tired*, Barty realised. The man always looked tired, but today especially so, and he realised he had taken it for granted that he had fallen asleep the previous night after the incident at the bridge. Jean probably had not slept at all, and if he had, Barty could not imagine what his sleep had been like, as he remembered Lady Amberley and the bridge.

His face had been the last she saw, he thought. Barty felt a chill dance its frost-coated fingertips up the length of his spine. He would not have been able to sleep either.

"However," Jean was saying, "You have been but briefly been exposed to my methods in this case. I will get us into that hospital, and I will track Jekyll down. It is a certainty."

Barty felt a question rising in his throat, but the look on Jean's face said it plainly; he was not interested in hearing more on the subject. Not now.

"Very well, fine then," he said stiffly instead. "But how are we going to get into the place? I doubt the same front door trick will work twice, even on a different guard."

"Well, it is most interesting that you should ask, you see—"

Whatever answer it was, however, would have to wait, because at that moment there was a very loud noise.

The entire foundation *shifted* as, from the elevator shaft, came a rush of displaced air. A massive, subterranean boom as well, that could have only have come from one thing above all else—an explosion. Dust rained from the ceiling as both Jean and Barty looked at each in shock, then dove for the elevator, heedless of the risk as they shut the door and wrenched the crank to bring about the descent. Barty shifted in place anxiously as Jean stared with a squint through the dust at the number, before violently yanking it back into place and halting the descent abruptly, shoving the gate open and charging out, shouting for Adam.

The doors were hanging open, broken off their hinges in the process. There was a great cloud of dust and other materials on the air, and a singularly horrendous smell like that of several kinds of burning metals, and other materials beside that which Barty could not identify. Jean kicked one of the heavy doors out of his path and charged in, reckless and desperate. "ADAM!"

"If you could be so kind, Jean," a voice said faintly from within the murk. "I would appreciate your assistance immediately."

The air and Barty's watering vision cleared. The armoury was a wreck, with a great cleared area apparent in the centre of the chamber. The ground was blackened, charred and still smoking, and it did not take Barty long to realise that, not only had there been an explosion, but it had originated here, blasting outwards in every direction and hurling away everything from that point.

Adam's voice had come from *somewhere* and it was Jean who figured it out first. He started shifting a shattered cabinet and shelves, a great pile of rubble that Barty was starting to recognise as a familiar shape. *Most* of one anyway.

"I rather regret to report I am somewhat at odds right now," Adam continued in a tone that was mildly vexed. "My curiosity somewhat got the better of me." With a heroic effort, Jean finally lifted a heavy wooden counter and hurled it aside with a cry, to reveal both Adam, and the cause of their vexation.

Whatever had gone off, Adam had been a little too close to it. Directly in front of it, it would turn out. They had managed to get their hand in front of their face—there was an outline of a hand on the face, the parts not covered now blackened and obscured. The bloodshot, yellowed corpse eyes blinked a few times up at Barty as he came alongside, and the battered, twisted face nevertheless twisted further into an attempt at a polite, reassuring smile. "How do you do, Mister Barty?"

Barty gaped in horror. Both of Adam's arms were severed, one at the shoulder and the other at the elbow. The heavy coat that they wore was rent apart and there was exposed muscle, metal, wires, and bone and more things that Barty could not explain that apparently made up the giant and their body. And yet Adam themselves did not look too upset about this entire development, instead nodding to Jean, who was crouched alongside the fallen figure, and carefully, gently removing the last bits of debris covering them. "Do help me out a moment, won't you?" Adam asked politely, and Jean sighed, but nodded.

"I do not suppose you will explain how this happened?"

Adam shrugged, as Jean began searching. It was difficult; most of the lights in the place had gone out, but a few still cast a fitful glow that allowed Jean to search even as Barty stood in horror, a scream lodged in his throat. But eventually Jean found what he was looking for, and reached down to pick up Adam's forearm, grunting with the effort of doing so.

"You've ruined your coat, you know," Jean said accusingly, as Barty wobbled in place.

"Is that all you've got to say?" he half-shrieked in horror.

Both Adam and Jean looked at him in confusion, before realisation dawned, as both man and giant said "Oh," at the same time.

"Oh? *OH?* Adam, what *happened?*" Barty said in a shrill tone of horror.

The giant shrugged from their recumbent position. "Unfortunately, an experimentation into alchemical compound neutralisation yielded a resultant thermic force of outpouring energy, that was both uncontrolled and terribly unexpected." They paused, and gave a grin, lifting the stump of their arm as Jean arrived at one side. "In short, Mister Barty, I made something explode." Jean pressed the neatly severed joints of the limb together, shifting them about. Barty was aghast, about to make a complaint, before Adam rumbled, and nodded. "Almost... there, that should do it."

Barty was about to say something, when the fingers of the severed arm twitched. As his jaw dropped and his thoughts fell out of his ears entirely, he watched Jean let go and, instead of the limb tumbling to the ground, it remained in place, the hand opening and closing slowly before it started to move and shift. It had been reattached. Adam had *put their arm back on.*

"She really knew how to make you work, didn't she?" Jean said with uncharacteristic subdual, as Adam nodded, twisting their arm about slowly as they grimaced. Jean watched, attentive, and oddly gentle.

"That she did. Regrettably so, in fact." The arm came up, and pointed past Barty. "The other one is over there. Could you drag it over? I can do the rest. The legs are still putting themselves back together." They sounded incredibly apologetic, even embarrassed, but Barty just nodded numbly, and found the arm laying amidst the rubble. He reached down to grasp the arm by the coat it was still wearing, and started to awkwardly drag it over.

"So, I take it you figured something out," Jean said dryly, looking around the room as Barty grunted and dragged an arm almost as large as himself and indeed somewhat heavier across the ground.

Adam nodded gravely. "The blood Mister Barty managed to collect had a variety of compounds I could identify, but plenty more I could not. It was most fortunate that"—they paused, glancing to Barty, who looked over to catch that glance in the midst of his trek—"that someone was able to get in contact with me about *someone* in the Under managing to get a hold of some very rare alchemical components."

Elanor. Benji, Barty thought, swallowing. Had Adam just nodded slightly, as he stared at them? The giant continued as Barty drew near, dragging the arm along and breathing hard as he did so—the limb was heavy, and had it just *twitched?*

"Aegisium, trimatrius of Thereus," Adam said shortly. "Essence of the sixth aether, and oldsblood. To name but a few." None of these made any sense to Barty whatsoever as the giant reached over to grasp their severed limb—with a hand that had been severed itself but a few moments ago—and picked up the still detached arm, shifting it about to place it back where it belong. There was a grunt and a strange *twang* sound, before the air smelled briefly of ozone, mixed amongst the strange chemical smells of the place, before Adam twisted their now somehow reattached limb.

"That will take weeks to work properly," Adam said mournfully, then started to pat themselves down, grasping various parts of their form and *wrenching* them back into place with awful sounds and terrific force. "Now where was I? Ah! Yes. The explosion."

"Yes, we were wondering about that part," Jean said in a deadpan tone, his expression flat as Barty cringed in on himself at the sight of Adam putting their broken body back together, even as they continued to speak.

"Our killer has a slew of things running around in their blood. A significant amount of materials of transformation, and the seven gates of changing." They carefully pushed themselves up, wobbling. "So I started looking for counteragents." They pushed themselves up, rolled their shoulders, and straightened. There was a horrible noise of bones snapping and popping back into place—at least, Barty thought they were bones—and then Adam made a sound of relief. "Much better. Fabulous," they said cheerfully, then looked around the wrecked room. "Nominally so, at least, considering the present circumstances." They sighed, and spread giant hands wide. "So regardless, I managed to isolate at least some of the regenerative components and the transformative, and I have to say whoever it is, they have an absolute *genius* mind for this sort of thing, and I would sincerely love—"

"It is Jekyll, Adam," Jean said bluntly. The armoury fell

silent. Adam's hands dropped, then they sighed, the twisted face showing regret.

"I thought them dead. And I have tried to forget them for some time." They grimaced, looking back to Jean then with a frown. "You are sure?"

Jean nodded grimly, before going on. "He was dead. At least one more time after that also. Whatever the elixir does, it does not allow him to die, either. So I need to know what you know… and I need to know it right now, Adam."

The giant rubbed their eyes a moment, then took a deep, slow breath, before letting it out in a rushing sigh. They looked to Barty, who had stood still to one side. "Thanks to the contacts that brought me word of what… Jekyll… has been securing for himself." They paused a moment before pressing on, "I was able to isolate that two primary compounds were activated in the blood, both binding together with two others being used as a bonding agent—the ones I mentioned, in fact. Now." They limped across the rubble, their body cracking and snapping back together as they went. "All separate, but most of them did not really *do* anything. They cannot influence the material world *normally*, but a variety of reactions allow them to, in this case. My idea was to introduce a new variation to the primary components of the mixture, to cause a dissolution of their bindings." They hesitated. "I added two primarium metals, one in distilled form to the mixture. And then things became quite noisy almost immediately afterwards, before you happened upon me." They gave an apologetic smile. "Thanks awfully for that, by the way. Being trapped down here for a day or two would have been horrendous."

Barty nodded, but Jean was losing patience. "Adam, what—"

But the huge figure placated them with a waving hand.

"Yes, yes. Silver nitrate and mercury." Jean gave them a perplexed look, but Adam continued. "Silver nitrate on its own is explosive, I know, when it is dry. I took its liquid form instead. Mixed with mercury it normally does not create much of a reaction, but when mixed with the components in the blood, they cause an enormous release of energy. If distributed right."

"What exactly does that mean?" Jean stated wearily, rubbing his face in annoyance.

Adam gave a guilty shrug and continued. "The two materials must be mixed in the bloodstream. Thoroughly. Which means you would need to apply them separately, one after another, to create the highest level of distribution." Adam looked regretful. "I doubt that the reaction will be comprehensive enough without that. From what I can gather, Jekyll's formula is frankly peerless."

Jean glared up at them, and for a long moment, the air was tense in the wrecked armoury, before Jean turned and marched away, heading down towards some cabinets that had escaped the destruction, opening them one at a time with a violent flourish.

"What are you looking for, Jean?" Barty asked hesitantly.

"Mercury!" came the answer, angrily as Jean held out a glass bottle filled with silver glinting liquid, which he shook around angrily. "Silver nitrate!" He growled then, holding out another bottle which was very firmly stoppered and this one he did not shake much, but swore in such frustration to show he very much wished to. "There is hardly any left of either. Enough for a round each, no more." He swore again, but his jaw set in determination. "Now show me, where is the bullet press?"

There was a *thump* from nearby as Adam righted a bit of ruined debris, to unveil a series of clamps and a strange device that looked like a machine press. "There is not much, Reynard," the massive figure said apologetically. "Much of what you need went up when I used, uh, the Reynard method of combining the components together to create, well… this mess." They gestured guiltily, but Jean paid no attention.

He dug out two brass bullet casings—quite large, Barty could not help but note—and two strange bullets to set into them. They looked more like cases themselves, made of solid material and lined in lead. As Barty watched, Jean opened each and started the process of filling one with the shining silver liquid mercury, and the other with a glittering dark liquid before snapping each shut and then proceeding to set them into the brass casings. It was rapid, efficient, and furiously done. Jean looked quite put out, muttering to himself. "Two. All these supplies and I get *two bloody shots*." He gave Adam a glare. "What have I told you about using the Reynard method of science, Adam?"

"Quite succinctly, 'do not'," Adam said glumly. They looked to Barty, who was very perplexed, before they shrugged guiltily. "Basically, I put everything together and then hit it with something. The response was as immediate as it was upsetting. I fear I rushed things a little."

"Yes, I can see why you call it the 'Reynard' method," Barty said weakly, recalling a week of rushing from one thing to the next and what it had done to him for that time, and in whose wake he had been doing so.

Jean was placing each round into the press, one at a time as he continued to swear, before he straightened up, and held up pair of heavy, enormous shells, glaring at them. "One of each. It is a good thing I do not miss." He pulled the heavy twin barrelled pistol from his side holster, cracked open the breach and loaded one after the other with a grimace.

"Careful with the silver nitrate," Adam cautioned. "You know how it stains skin terribly, Jean."

"Turns it black, I know," Jean said flatly. "But it is fine. Two shots. One chance with each." He shook his head in irritation.

"That does not feel like much of a chance, Jean," Barty said nervously.

But Jean was not listening as he firmly snapped shut the breach and closed down the two hammers to set it safe. "It is the only one I need, Mister Barty." He moved further down the long hall of the armoury, pausing as he went, picking this and that off the racks, tossing something away, taking something else.

"Two bullets?" Barty said weakly, as Jean strapped on a sword belt, before seizing up an antique longsword, testing the edge and then slamming it home emphatically and continuing on. "He is going to fight that thing with just two bullets to do the job?"

"And they both have to hit, as well," Adam replied, their tone subdued and brow furrowed. "If it was anyone else, I would have my doubts, but…" They trailed off, rubbing their massive jaw with a trembling hand. Barty looked up at them, frowning.

"If it was anyone else, perhaps, but is he still enough of himself to do it?"

Adam said nothing, but that twisted visage furrowed into a further frown.

Jean, however, was done. He adjusted his coat, his person now altogether more bristling with armament, and straightened. "No time to waste, Mister Barty, now come along. We've an appointment to keep with a dead man, to make sure that this time, he *stays that way.*" He turned, marching off with purpose towards the exit, striding through the broken doorway.

"Go with him," Adam said quietly. They gestured about the ruined armoury with a rueful expression, the limb twitching as they did so. "I've a great deal of work ahead of me to make this right, and my body will be useless for quite some time except at this. And from what I understand, having spoken to a mutual acquaintance… he needs you now."

Barty swallowed, understanding who it was Adam meant; Elanor had gotten word to him. He was about to say something before the barked shout of his name came from the distant elevator—he sufficed himself by simply nodding, and hurrying out. Jean slammed shut the elevator door and hit the lift crank before Barty had come to a halt.

"I trust you still have your revolver," Jean growled as they started to ascend. He had his eyes fixed on the roof of the elevator as it rose, his glare as intense as a scenting hound fixed upon prey it could not see, but knew was there.

Barty swallowed, patting his coat and nodding. "It is, but I will be sore pressed before I ever use it again. I would rather I just threw it away, to be honest."

"Do not dare. It is a fine weapon, and you will need it at some point, whether you like it or not. Such is the way of things. Those who bear arms are those who will eventually have cause to use them." His tone was flat, sour.

"That is not the most comforting of statements, sir," Barty said with a bit of hesitancy in his voice. Jean snorted as the ascent continued, flickering a brief glance.

"What about a weapon is supposed to be *comforting?*" he asked in a tone of disbelief. "It is a statement of intention, not an offer of comfort. I thought you would understand that after today."

Barty fell silent, trying to puzzle his way through that,

while quietly noting that Jean fairly *bristled* with various forms of weaponry at this point. *A statement of intent, indeed—to fight a monster, or all the world?*

He decided it was time to change the subject, finding this one too uncomfortable. "All right then, but returning to an earlier question, how exactly are we getting into the hospital? You failed to answer that."

The elevator clanked into place as Jean wrenched the crank into position with an emphatic movement, but now he was grinning, a sharp grin that had a spite which outweighed any trace of humour. "Well, Mister Barty, that shall be the interesting part. But I can assure you of one thing." He sounded cheerful, which filled Barty with dread.

"And what is that?" he asked, prompted to do so and hating that he did.

Jean strode on out, chuckling darkly. "You are *absolutely* going to loathe it."

He was right. Barty hated it.

The world was still a wet, grey haze as they approached Old Bedlam. It was a proper London late afternoon in autumn, as the bloated, sooty clouds above, that rolled low and threatening, vented their grumbling displeasure on the stones, washing away some of the accumulated sins... some, but never enough. Never all of them.

It was a proper time to be indoors. Perhaps satisfying oneself with tea, and a little toast. Enjoying a warm fire and possibly a spot of reading, a most excellent way to pass the time in practically any situation. So, as Barty found himself clinging to the roof of the wagon as they sped along all too close to the fence of the hospital grounds, soaking wet and freezing cold, hungry and tired, he wondered not for the first, second, third or even the last time what in the *Hell* he was doing.

Crook was speeding the coach along with his silver hair plastered to his head and grinning the sort of grin that reminded one of a snarling wolf, the eyes alight with joy and hunger both in the spirit of the hunt. He had glanced back once at Barty as they went, fixing him with that hungry stare, and so it was that he felt a genuine gratitude towards Jean, who grabbed him by his collar to drag him upright. The hunter had that double barrelled rifle, as well as the rest of his paraphernalia, and they were kneeling on the coach roof, obscured by the rain, but not nearly enough that they could do this for long. Not that Barty wanted to remain near to Crook for longer than was necessary.

The fenceline was rushing past, almost close enough to touch. It would still take an effort to clear it, the high iron fence threatening with its spikes, high and tall enough to keep people from getting in, but more importantly, from getting out. However, as mad as such people might be, they didn't have a speeding coach to leap from. A barked command came then, and Jean wrenched Barty forward even as he leapt himself, and the world turned all manner of topsy-turvy before it then proceeded to hurt instead.

They had landed in some thick bush, but it only absorbed so much of the fall. The many bruises that Barty had thus far acquired proceeded to sing their upset even louder than before, each and every one of them calling for attention and payment due. He bit his tongue and forced back tears as he hung suspended in a tangle of branches, until a hand took his shoulder and wrenched him clear.

Jean was wheezing, and after he righted Barty to his knees, he collapsed a moment, breathing hard. "Damned… going… too… fast," he wheezed, angry, as he took a deep, forced breath and then slammed his rifle down by the stock to push himself to his feet with a grunt, swinging it around to his shoulder, as he glared up at the building before him.

Under the darkened, raining sky, the hospital had a far more menacing air than it already did. The thick granite walls were dark and cold, the white dome over the main entrance a grandiose gesture at odds with the barred windows. Jean was glaring at it as if it had personally offended him.

"Should we not… take cover?" Barty grunted and gasped as he spoke. He still could not get his feet under him. It was too much to even think about in that moment. His ribs were trying very hard to convince his stomach to throw up, but he had not eaten nearly enough over the past few days to give up such hard won morsels so easily. Jean grunted, and then Barty heard him pull back the hammer on the rifle, the sound menacing and loud even amongst the rain.

"There is something wrong," Jean hissed. "Listen."

Barty struggled to hear anything over the ringing in his ears for a moment, but eventually he did hear it, underneath the rain, coming from the great dark structure before him. Hysterical sounds, shouting, laughter and screaming. Uncontrolled, uncontained, distant and echoing, but present nevertheless. And the building itself was dark—completely dark, with no trace of any lighting whatsoever in any part of it, which was a warning sign in of itself.

While the asylum was a dark place in every sense of the word, something was off. It was on the air and the tune it was playing was high pitched, the strings out of tune and broken. Barty felt his stomach churn further, and now it had nothing to do with pain.

But Jean was already moving. That inevitable stalk across the grounds, his movement bold and heedless. It cared not if anyone saw him, even if the weather was keeping most eyes from being cast towards him. Barty scrambled, then followed off into his wake, grimacing as he went at the flickers of agony, but each step became easier than the last as he got himself moving.

Reaching the wall of the building, Jean proceeded to hug it and follow it around. He kept away from the front entrance —with good reason, Barty figured—and the pair of them skulked along, temporarily sheltered from the rain. The complex of the hospital was huge in of itself, promising multiple exits, and it was one of these that Jean found. A large iron door, locked and barred from the outside. A most peculiar notion until one realised it was very firmly designed around keeping people *in*, and that no one in their right mind would want to get in themselves. Even more so, those that were out of their mind wanted nothing to do with the dreadful structure. Some places exuded nightmares. Bedlam was one of them.

Removing the bar was no effort, but the lock took more. Barty expected to see lockpicks, or some other manner of roguish chicanery, but instead Jean fished a crowbar out of his coat and started wrenching the door off its hinges with practiced barbarism. He waved off Barty's efforts as he the door groaned, then cracked off its frame as Jean demolished it, falling to the ground with a loud *clang* and with it, the sounds from within became all the more apparent.

The door opened led into a corridor, the depths of the hospital stretching out before them. Jean entered slowly, rifle at his shoulder, stalking into the gloom. And from within came cries, and shouts, pleas, and screams. And laughter. It sounded like what the place was, a madhouse, and for whatever reason all the silences that had come from the place before had been drowned out, now buried under the mixed nightmare sounds coming from many tortured throats.

Jean walked the corridor carefully, opening the door at the end with one hand before sliding through it and rapidly turning left and right to check each direction. He then paused, and beckoned Barty forward in silence, his expression even more grim even in the gloom of the darkened interior. Barty nevertheless obeyed, and drew in close, holding his breath.

They were in one of the wing corridors. In each direction, the corridor stretched on, lined with doors to one side, the other set with high, barred windows that looked to the interior square that the hospital itself surrounded in a great rectangle. Normally those doors would be firmly closed, each of them containing the poor, wretched individual within who would lay there in wait for whatever terror disguised as treatment would come to cure them, but instead this time, those doors were open. Each and every one of them.

"God help us," Barty whispered in horror.

Jean grunted, his own voice a murmur. "I do not think God can see this wretched place, Mister Barty. If he did, he would not approve." There was however a grunt as he surveyed the corridor. "Bastard. They've gone and opened every one."

Barty could make out movement now, amongst the gloom. Lumpy figures in crude sack cloth clothes, barely distinguished as more than shadows as they moved in erratic, disjointed fashions down the length of the corridor, shuffling away in an awkward manner from the pair of them. Even in whatever haze they existed in, the sight of Jean bristling with anger and firearms addressed a primal instinct to recognise danger, and to get away from it.

"They knew we were coming," Barty said softly, in realisation. He swallowed, as more understanding flowed in after to add different, uncomfortable layers to the revelation.

"Indeed. An effort towards misdirection, and concealment, but without taking the time to simply flee," Jean said sourly, his voice dark and growling. "They seek to finish this here. This has become a trap for us."

"What do we do then? Do we leave? Find the police?" Barty whispered hurriedly, turning on the spot as the hackles on the back of his neck stood up.

But Jean was closing the door that led to the corridor they had passed through. "No. We do the exact thing that they are planning us to do. We spring the trap."

"We do *what?*" Barty hissed in horror. But Jean's expression was implacable, hard.

"We put them in a place to strike, Mister Barty. I cannot kill him unless he is close enough to die."

He said it as though it was the simplest thing in the world, and, seemingly choosing a direction at random, started to move along the corridor. Barty was frozen for a moment before he hissed a frustrated response. "That does not make any bloody sense!"

But he was following, and Jean was leading, as they delved deeper into the belly of the beast.

AT FIRST, Barty was terrified of the madfolk who were wandering the place. He shied away from them, unwilling to even let them touch him. He remembered the demented screaming and frenzied, staring eyes of the mad doctor Markheim the last time he had come to the place, seized and shaken by arms that should not have held the strength that they did. But as they went, it was hard to keep the same feeling.

Most of them scurried away as they drew close. They wept and gibbered, seeing things that were not there but nevertheless filled them with dread. They were, in short, almost entirely afraid of the hunter and his assistant, wanting nothing more than to remain invisible to their gaze. Many were still in their cells, that prison which held them that they were unwilling to leave.He paused at one cell, the door hanging open. A middle-aged woman sat on a crude, broken bed, huddled in a corner, staring at the barred window and crying, sobbing, from bloodshot eyes. She was wasted away, a shell of a person, and would not even look at the door, instead sitting with eyes fixed on the heavens above that seemed to weep with her.

Jean appeared at his elbow and gently nudged him along, refusing to look at the inhabitant. "You cannot help them, Barty. Come on."

"I do not understand," Barty whispered, as he hesitantly fell into step once more. "She could leave... she could escape. Any of them could. If I could have left the orphanage before I did..." He trailed off, shaking his head in confusion.

Jean did not slow, moving with careful steps and checking each corner and open door as he responded, speaking quiet and firm. "To where, Barty? Where could she go?" They reached an open arch, leading to a larger hall that appeared to house a surgery and observatory. "They are imprisoned more surely than any mere cell. Those are simply to keep them in place, to stop them wandering." He said it with clear distaste, even disgust for such weakness. "They are far from the only people trapped in the terrors of their own thoughts.

But they will never be free of them, no matter how much one tries to show them the way."

Barty frowned, looking back over his shoulder, as they hesitated at the archway. "That is not right. I thought this place was supposed to help them." He felt weak saying it himself; he had seen so much of this place already. Jean snorted, giving him a look that said a lot before wordlessly shaking his head and taking a step forward.

A figure leapt screaming from the shadows. Barty dove for the floor, as a loud *crack* echoed out. Jean had, without hesitation, swung the stock of his rifle around and smashed it into the jaw of the pouncing attacker—a ragged man of elderly years with wild hair and wilder eyes. Barty did not recognise them. After being force-fed a mouthful of fine walnut rifle stock, they lay in a sprawl, twitching, and very clearly no longer a threat.

Barty lay with his hands over his head, blinking. Jean had his rifle back to his shoulder, squinting down the sights to the still figure, before finally dismissing them and looking around the room. He grimaced at something, seeming to understand.

Barty brushed himself off as he got shakily back to his feet, noting the look of distaste on Jean's face as he did so. "What? What is it?" He looked about nervously.

There was a table with straps, heavily reinforced, and smaller tables for surgical instruments nearby. Overlooking the scene were tiered rows of benches, so that whatever was done on the table could be witnessed by those looking down. There was a strong smell of alcohol on the air, sterile, and drying the tongue. Something about the theatre made his skin crawl.

"This is where they teach lobotomies. Amongst other things," Jean growled, with the look on his face like he would very much like to set the place on fire. "A whole new generation of doctors, learning how to burn out a soul." He spat, disgusted. "I do truly hate this place." He was moving as he said it, past Barty, and something about his expression shifted, the eyes narrowing. Before Barty could ask what he was doing, Jean lashed out with a boot and kicked over a chest of drawers, spilling medical instruments all over the place, and bringing a panicked scream from the figure hiding behind it, who whimpered in terror, covering their head with their arms as though warding off a blow. In so doing, it was immediately clear whoever they were, they were wearing a suit. Not a patient, but a doctor. Both men had seen this one before.

"Doctor Hyslop?" Barty said in surprise. He had been reaching for his coat and the revolver within before realisation set in. The notion made him feel quite ill for a moment.

Jean made no such surprised inquiry. He simply reached out, grabbed Hyslop by the collar, and dragged him from his hiding place as he screamed and whimpered, before Jean slapped him sharply across the face. "Be quiet. You will have them all down on us if you do not shut up." His tone was harsh, but the slap had worked. Barty had a curious twist in his stomach at the thought of a doctor who treated insanity being struck out of his hysteria, but the humour was, at that moment, wasted.

Hyslop stared up in terror at Jean, hardly recognising him in his dazed state. "Where is he? Do not tell me you do not know who I mean," Jean growled in a venomous hiss, but Hyslop looked too frightened to respond, his jaw hanging open slack. Barty finally took pity and slid forward, pushing himself past Jean to intercede.

"What my colleague is trying to ask, is… what happened here?" The doctor stared at Barty, then squeezed his eyes shut. Jean stepped forward impatiently, no doubt to strike another blow, but Barty stopped him with an upraised hand, even as Hyslop spoke.

"I-I do not know. Someone opened all the patient doors about an hour ago. I-I have been in hiding, ever since."

"No guards? No alarms sounded?" Jean asked in disbelief, but Hyslop was shaking his head, his whole body trembling in his terror.

"None. I do not know what happened, or how." He looked around frantically, then grabbed Barty with both hands. "You have to get me out of here. They are *hunting me!*" His voice rose several octaves, but Barty took him by the wrists, his voice steady.

"Doctor. Calm yourself, and we will deal with this." He surprised himself at how calmly he said it. He even believed it. Hyslop, too, seemed to believe it by how he shuddered and nodded.

Jean did not. He snorted, turning away to scan the dimly lit gloom. "We let everyone out, and *he* will escape in the mob. This place is a prison first and foremost. Let us take advantage of that fact." He looked around, scowling. "A lack of light is definitely a problem. He could be nearly anywhere, and a slap across the face will not do much to him." He contemplated a moment, then swore softly, turning to Hyslop. "We need to narrow this down. Do you have keys to the rest of the hospital?" Hyslop shook his head, and Jean grimaced. "Very well. Where would we find them?"

Hyslop hesitated a moment, then spoke slowly. "The front desk would be the only place guaranteed. It is the most secure part of the building, and where I would..." He quavered, giving Jean a glance as he doubtless remembered the sheer brutality the man had unleashed there but a few hours previous. Shying away, he pressed on regardless, hurriedly. "We can get out that way as well. It would not be far from—" but Jean cut him off with a growl.

"No one leaves. Not until our killer is dead. And they are

still here." Jean turned, his eyes on the roof as he frowned. "They are close, in fact. I am sure of it." Both Barty and Hyslop followed his gaze—for the first time Barty suddenly felt a thrill of fear and realisation. Until now, he had not truly appreciated the depth of it, feeling removed from the danger somehow. But Jean's expression was intent, dimly lit and cast in shadows, and there was a wariness to him that only grew more and more palpable with each passing moment, all but infecting those around him with that deadly paranoia.

Barty tried to shake it off, angry at himself. "We cannot do this alone, Jean. Not the two of us." He said it sharply but softly. "Not with everything else and all these patients wandering about. We need the police at the very least!"

Hyslop nodded furiously, and Jean glared at them both, furious for a moment before, surprisingly, he relented, exhaling sharply. "Fine. Front desk first. Is there a means to contact the police from there? I would wager there is with how quickly things progressed this morning," he said dryly, making the doctor flinch in terror once again even as he nodded frantically.

"A telephone. Yes." He swallowed, and then got to his feet, his legs shaking. "You will keep the patients away from me, yes?" He sounded pathetic in his terror, Barty thought, even as he helped the man stand. He was not sure why he was not as frightened himself. Perhaps after all that had happened that week, he just did not have the strength to do so.

How surprising then, that he had the energy for this instead. To help Hyslop along as they turned back, heading towards the entrance. Hyslop went first, with Barty beside him. Jean stalked in the rear with the rifle held low, and moved with such silence that, several times, Barty had to make sure that he was still with them. Rather than reassure him, this only made him more nervous.

As they moved, it became increasingly apparent that the hospital was going to need more than a little work to be up and running again. Twice they had to stop as they drew nearer to the front entrance as they came across large groups of patients. Most of them seemed docile, quietly wandering about and acting in disquieting, but harmless ways—they avoided them with ease, but did not try to interact with them. But there was a definite undercurrent of danger, that was assuredly heightened when they found the dead. Two guards and what must have been a doctor at some point, all crumpled and still, hidden in dark corners and twisted into uncomfortable shapes. There was no sign of life or the *possibility* of life in those still figures, sprawled amongst the debris of the riot that had claimed their life. Barty paused, Hyslop also, but Jean did not and pushed them forward.

They drew closer on the centre of the hospital, and the entrance hall, Barty starting to recognise features, from when he had been brought through the hospital himself. Then there was a sound, of a door being opened in front of them in the darkness, and the three of them rounded the corner.

In truth, it mostly consisted of Hyslop and Barty diving to one side, and Jean turning the corner with his rifle raised, but then the tableau became better illuminated.

Doctor Gaston stood there. His clothes were ragged, torn, and there was blood on his face. He was breathing hard, and looked frantic for a moment before he blinked and gave a great relieved breath. "Thank goodness you are here." He sounded genuinely happy, and, despite his clear distress, he gave a great, broad smile.

Barty hesitated. He was not the only one—Jean did not lower his rifle, frowning down at the man. But Hyslop pried himself free and rushed over to Gaston, seizing him by the shoulders and hugging him tightly. "Gaston! You are alive!

God's own, it is a miracle." He nearly sobbed in relief and clung to the first friendly, familiar face he had seen in all the mess. But Gaston gently disengaged himself from the doctor, holding him at arm's length with a smile.

"It was a near thing, Theo," he said wryly, almost cheerfully. "More than a few close calls! But everything is all right now." He turned his gaze to Barty and Jean, and nodded with a smile. "Thank you for looking after him."

"You look like you have had a time of it, doctor," Jean said slowly, lowering his rifle only slightly. Barty, however, pushed himself up to stand between the two, shaking his head.

"Gaston was the one who helped me into the hospital the first time I was here, Jean," Barty said firmly. "He got me to speak with Markheim, and that led us to Templeton. He is a friend." Jean said nothing, giving Barty an emotionless stare that said much to the notion of friends and their making. But Barty was already ignoring it, having grown far too used to such judgements from the hunter already.

"Are you hurt?" he asked the ragged doctor, who shook his head.

"Oh, the blood is not mine," he said apologetically. "I am quite fine." His gaze shifted from one to the next, looking nervously at Jean, who remained at the back with his rifle still at his shoulder.

"Well, we need to get into the main hall," Barty urged. "There is a telephone there, apparently?"

Gaston hesitated, then nodded slowly. "A little battered, but yes, at the main counter, I believe. But surely it would not be working at this point—"

Hyslop was pushing past him. "We've got to try! And if not, we can flag down some police in the street. Come on!" He was excited, desperate now as freedom seemed so close.

Gaston froze up a moment, then awkwardly fell into step

himself to follow. Barty did the same, but Jean, for whatever reason, hesitated. Barty started to feel uncomfortable, but could not put his finger entirely onto why.

They passed into the entrance hall. There were still faint smears on the ground from where Jean had confronted the guards earlier in the day. There were other signs of violence however—overturned tables, and broken windows. Several desks and sets of shelves had been cast over the front entrance, effectively creating a barrier to prevent anyone getting in, or out. The upper gallery of offices were also partly ransacked, with doors hanging off their hinges, but not a soul was to be seen.

Hyslop broke the inspection with a wail of despair from the wrecked counter and desk that, last Barty had seen it, had been the home of the nurse who had welcomed guests, amongst other things. She was nowhere to be seen now. *Probably took the day off after a maniac pointed a gun at her, who could blame her?* Barty's treacherous thoughts crept up on him once again to lather him with shame.

Hyslop was holding a length of snapped cable in one hand, with one end going into a box that was now a collection of splinters and shattered mechanical components—the fabled phone, a marvellous invention when it functioned and nothing but false hopes when it was in pieces. Hyslop stared at it with the lip-wobbling despair of a man who had seen a glimmer at the tunnel's end and found it to be naught but an incoming train.

"Well, that settles that then," Gaston said wryly. He turned to the group and shrugged helplessly. "I have an idea. Why don't you three wait here, and I will see if I can perhaps signal from a high window?" He pointed vaguely upwards. "I am sure there is a way up to the roof from here or something. But here is safe. Why don't you wait here until help comes?"

Barty blinked, surprised at this. "That is… that is very helpful of you, Doctor Gaston, but surely we can handle something like that. Maybe the two of you could remain here instead—"

"You were coming out of here. Why did you not do that already?"

Jean's voice was quiet, soft, but had an undeniable edge to it. There was a *click* as the hammer on the rifle was pulled back. Everything went very, very still.

"I am sorry?" Gaston said in a puzzled tone, but there was an edge to his words as well. He was close to Hyslop and Barty. Barty felt a sudden, skin crawling realisation, as he looked between the two men now facing off against each other, as Jean gave the doctor a hard, cold stare.

"You were coming out of here when we found you. If you had a plan to signal for help from the roof, you would have already done so. Why did you not?" He remained where he was, but the twin barrels of the rifle raised up as he set the gun to his shoulder, his gaze fixed on his target throughout. He was asking questions, but from the way he was speaking, he already had the answers. "What did you say your name was again?"

Gaston held up one hand in apology—*only one*, Barty noticed, the other inside the torn and ragged coat that Gaston was wearing. *Torn, but how?* Barty at first thought the doctor had been in a fight with patients, much like the fallen that they had seen. But that blood on his face, splattered there, it was not his? How had his clothes taken that much damage but he had not? Realisation started to sink in, the little whispers of something being wrong becoming all the more apparent, becoming louder and louder with each passing moment until the scream of alarm bells was all Barty could hear inside his head.

"I assure you, I do not know what you are talking about, Mister Reynard. I was, as your esteemed companion said, the one who helped you through this whole endeavour, and I do believe that you owe me—" But Jean's voice cut him off, soft but nevertheless laden with venom.

"Strange. I do not believe I ever gave you my name."

Gaston froze, the words dying on his lips, but instead of looking frightened, his eyes narrowed down instead, turning dangerous.

"How good is your French, Barty?" Jean said quietly. "Because last I checked, Gaston also means—"

But he did not get to finish what the word otherwise meant, because in that moment, several things happened.

Gaston ripped his hand out of his pocket, a glint of glass and metal flashing as he brought forth a syringe full of dark liquid and stabbed it into his own neck, quick as lightning and without hesitation. Jean stopped mid-sentence, raised his rifle and fired. All in a heartbeat. And still, he was too slow.

The rifle blasted the syringe clear, taking with it two fingers as the round ripped through flesh and bone. The syringe itself, only partly injected, flew away and was lost in the gloom as the boom of the shot and the howl of the target combined together, as Hyslop screamed and Barty ducked away. But that partial injection of whatever had been in the syringe was enough.

The change was not slow—it was immediate, violent, and horrifying. One of Gaston's arms shot out even as Jean was pulling back the hammer, and kept going, growing longer by far than it had been and long enough to grasp the paired barrels of the rifle and wrench it out of Jean's hands, hurling it away.

The huntsman was not done, however. In the same movement, he whipped the twin barrelled pistol at his side—the one that held the two paired bullets of the mixture that he had crafted back in the armoury—and fired, slick, fast, and from the hip.

Gaston was *warping*, his flesh shifting and changing with horrifying speed and intensity, as that second shot caught him high in the chest. It made him howl, but the sound was horrendous, monstrous, and *twisting* in the air as it was ripped out of his shifting lungs. Jean was already preparing to fire the second shot—*too early!*, Barty thought, *it has to mix in the blood!*—but there was no time. Gaston was on him already, and he was not stopping.

The bloodied hand with missing fingers was useless, but the other was untouched, and it grabbed at the heavy pistol, squeezing down with the same force it had used to turn bones to powder, to rip a man's head off before he could so much as scream. There was a hideous *crack* of wood and mechanisms breaking apart as Jean snarled and tried to fire the second barrel, but could not. The mutated hand of Gaston broke the gun apart and then, still holding it, yanked Jean off his feet towards him, caught him by his coat, and with a roar hurled him away.

Barty watched in horror as Jean was flung through the air like a ragdoll. He sailed up to the upper gallery, tumbling helplessly through the air before crashing into Gaston's own office and through the window with a hideous smashing of glass, and vanished from sight.

"*JEAN!*" Barty screamed. There was no answer, and Barty's heart stammered in his chest. *No. I failed her. She wanted one thing from me and I could not give her that.*

Elanor. He had promised Elanor, had he not? And Charlotte too, before she vanished from the world. He had promised both of them, different promises each, and failed both times. But Jean understood that, did he not? He had promised the Lady Amberley, before she had fallen to her death. *How strange,* Barty thought, *just how much the pair of us suddenly have in common.*

These were the thoughts that were moving almost sedately through his mind in that moment. In stark contrast, his body was moving all on its own, directly in defiance of his own thoughts. Barty abandoned Hyslop, and slid across the stone floor on his knees to scoop up the fallen rifle. He ignored the fallen, shattered pistol, spun around in the middle of his slide and scrambled after Gaston. The doctor was a twisted figure, shifting and changing as he went, his body warping and distorting in a way that made the stomach churn as he lumbered madly for a distant door at the back of the hall. As Barty sprinted in pursuit, the twisted figure smashed through a closed door—a service passage, or so it seemed, and plunged off into darkness. And Barty chased after him.

It was only when he passed through the splintered remnants of the doorway that his senses caught up to him at last, even as he stared about wildly. *What in God's name am I doing?* he asked himself in horror, even as he heard a thump and clang from above, and his head shot up to see a figure racing up a flight of stairs towards the distant roof.

This was a disused part of the hospital, leading up to a place that seemed seldom used and never really tended to, from all the dust, cobwebs and grime that lay everywhere. *Just beneath the surface,* Barty thought. With all the clean and tidy corridors, all the careful presentation of sanitation, the rot was still there, hidden away but yet plain to see when it was uncovered.

He followed taking the stairs two at a time, as they creaked and groaned underneath him, half-rotted in places and brittle in others. But he had the wind in him now and the thrill of fury and the hunt drove his pain far, far away. He was moving without thinking as *something* else took over his body and pushed him on. Maybe it was the promise to Elanor. Maybe it was what he had told himself after Charlotte was not there. Or maybe, just maybe… it was that same thing that had driven him to lose track of days, weeks, as he set off in pursuit of Reynard, the same man who he, even now, did not know if he was dead or alive.

Whatever the feeling was, it had picked him up by the scruff of his neck and dragged him along with a gun in his hand, as he found himself once more wanting, no, *needing* to know. He raced up a flight of rickety stairs, then another, barely able to see in the gloom, the faint light from mostly shuttered windows and the setting sun giving him just enough light to see, just enough for a boy who had learned to stare into the shadows to see what he already knew was there, so that it could not hurt him.

The stairs ended, but now there was a gantry that raced along into murkiness, at the end of which was another, much shorter set of stairs. A trapdoor burst open ahead, a ragged figure tumbling up into the room above, but Barty was right behind them and a few moments later, staggered into place, rifle at his shoulder, to take in a most peculiar sight.

It took him but a moment to finally understand where he was standing. They were in an odd, circular structure, a dome covering them, raised upon close set pillars which a man could squeeze through. The entire place was somewhat exposed to the elements but nevertheless had a plenty of cover from the outside—more so, with the crude timber walls someone had set up around the interior to conceal any movement within. The space was large, and wide, plenty of room for someone to work within. And someone most assuredly had been.

There was a collection of glasses in odd shapes, desks, and small, contained braziers full of ashes and charcoal. Ceramic plates, and scattered syringes with heavy bore needles. Several glass beakers with thermometers and more besides, all of it reminding Barty of the laboratory within the armoury—at least, how it had appeared before Adam had blown it up in their efforts to try and solve the riddle of Jekyll's elixir, the crux of which was standing in front of Barty right at that moment.

Gone was Gaston's friendly, easy smile. His expression was wild, untamed, a bestial savagery in his very expression that defied civilisation. Closer to madness than any face worn by any in that place, this home to insanity that secretly had been the refuge of a sort of animal insanity that was beyond any other. They were frantically searching the syringes scattered on the desk, and even as Barty brought up the rifle—how easy it was, to sling it to his shoulder, even if it horrified him, he could not deny the ease—their hand closed on something small and gleaming even as Barty pulled back the hammer and shouted hoarsely in a voice that barely had any air, "JEKYLL! STOP!"

Everything went very still. Gaston—or Jekyll, or whoever he really was—turned slowly towards Barty, holding the syringe still in his bloody hand, missing most of the fingers. His eyes were narrowed and hard, his upper lip curling into a snarl. They were far bloodier at this point, and small wonder; Jean had not missed his shot. The hole the round had ripped through Jekyll's chest however was already closing—much slower than it had in his more monstrous form, but neverthe-less the blood flow had already stopped.

Barty stumbled up the last few steps, the barrel of the rifle waving before he steadied it, keeping it levelled at his target, who twitched… but did not move. Barty kept himself together with difficulty, and though he had not nearly enough experience with this sort of thing, he stood his ground, even as he kept the gun in place.

The twisted visage of the doctor shifted then, slowly, sliding around as though it were liquid, and morphed into a smile. And suddenly the creature was Doctor Gaston again, smiling, cheerful, and friendly. "Well, Mister Barty. It would appear neither of us were who we pretended to be, in the end. What a thing, eh?"

"You used me," Barty said dully, the barrel still weaving slightly. It was both so easy and yet so difficult to keep it pointed at the smiling doctor. "You needed that picture, didn't you?"

The doctor shrugged ruefully, almost apologetically. "Not so much the picture, as what the picture could tell me. I knew some of the names in it, but not all of them. I needed Templeton. He was the last piece I was not sure of." He made a face, sighing. "Shame you got there first. I think that was where you got too close." He sounded regretful, but dismissive about it.

"But *why?*" Barty spat, his teeth grinding. "Why kill them, why kill any of them?"

The smiling face vanished, wiped into a snarl so quickly that the warping seemed almost unreal. "Because of what they *took* from me, what they *wanted* from me. My work, Mister Barty! *Mine.* They *tortured* me for something that was never theirs to have!" The voice changed too, twisting into something fearsome and mangled, an animalistic howl at its edges.

"You killed all those people, you caused all this death, just for some research? Because of… of science? But—" He shook his head. "Doctor Jekyll, I—"

He was cut off by a furious roar, and as he nearly pulled the trigger in sheer fright, the face of the doctor distorting in his rage as he snarled.

"You know *nothing*. Not even my name—do NOT call me that! My name is *Hyde*," he raged, teeth bared. For all that Barty had the gun, he was the far more fearsome entity.

Barty steadied himself, swallowed down his fear, and took a deep breath. And at last, called upon the very thing that had gotten him into all this trouble in the first place; curiosity.

"All right then. Mister Hyde," he began slowly, his voice steadier than his racing heart. "Then explain it to me. I am listening."

CHAPTER 20

... AND MISTER HYDE

When Barty had begun this venture properly, bound and gagged on the floor of a coach, surrounded by men, wondering how he would soon die, he pondered how many of them would have guessed that his current situation was, in fact, the most likely one. Not in a ditch or in the depths of a peat bog, but instead staring down a shapeshifting maniac while holding a gun, knowing that if he missed he would be torn to pieces.

If one had guessed, he would be upset at them for not sharing their clairvoyance. The fellow could make a fortune at festivals.

The figure before him growled, the lips pulled back in a snarl as he stared with eyes full of blazing rage, teeth bared in animalistic hatred. *Curious*, Barty could not help but think. *He appears more a monster now than he did even when his body was warped and twisted.*

"Presumptive to think I will tell you anything," the murderer spat.

Barty shrugged, keeping the rifle levered. "We have time

enough. And I am willing to listen." He said it with more confidence than he felt. "And if I shoot you right now, I do not think you are going to shrug it off easily enough to run."

The malformed face warped further in the depths of that hateful scowl. "True enough… unless you happen to miss." There was a purring threat in those words, and Hyde tensed like a wolf about to leap.

Barty steadied the grip on the rifle and squared it more into his shoulder, aiming down the sight like he saw Jean do. When you have nothing else, you bluff. "Think that I will?" His voice was high in his panic, but the rest of the bluff worked. Hyde eased down, and then spat a glob of black phlegm to one side, snarling.

"Very well, pup. What exactly did you want to know?" There was caution in his voice, caution and anger. The syringe remained held aloft, but the fingers holding it shifted, making sure the grip was secured. Barty noticed but was careful to keep the rifle pointed straight.

"I wanted to know why you killed all those people," Barty said slowly. "Why you did any of this… why even come here at all? To this hospital?"

Hyde sneered, but his eyes narrowed somewhat. For a moment he said nothing, then spoke in a hard, grudging voice. "Curious. I half-expected you to be as simple as them, and ask about this instead." He waggled the syringe, then, as Barty glanced at it, slipped to one side. But the glance was just that, and Barty tracked the movement with the rifle. "My life's work, and God's own curse," Hyde spat in disgust. "My key and my chain both merged together. Those dead fools would *never* shut up about it." He growled, shaking his head. "Millions of questions, and never once understanding the answers. Fools, children grasping at the knee of a God, hoping for a glimpse of a secret forbidden to them." He sneered once more, shifting another step as Barty followed his every movement.

"You killed them because of your research? Was it as simple as just that then?" Barty asked again the question, but this time Hyde did not disappoint and growled his response.

"That was but the part, not the whole. It was not theirs, it was *never* theirs, and they would never have understood the process to begin with. How does one split a soul? How does one unchain one's own heart?" He scowled, shaking his head with a pained grimace. "No, their greed disgusted me, true… and for that alone, I would have gladly ripped them limb from limb, chewed on their twitching tongues and made them grovel in their own blood, but that was not *why*."

Barty swallowed, that stomach churning description of possible fates making him feel sick, but Hyde was animated now, speaking faster. "They clawed and clawed and wanted and *wanted* and they would do anything for it, oh yes, *anything* to get what was not theirs, and they did not care what it cost, not when it meant *nothing*." Foam flecked the corner of his mouth and his eyes were wide and glassy, staring into nothing. "They broke me again and again to see me heal, to watch me stitch myself together even though the elixir was fading, and they would make sounds and write little notes and leave me there to *bleed* in the *dark*, Mister Barty, day after day after *DAY!*" he roared, snapping back to focus and making Barty flinch. "Has your dull, plodding mind figured it out yet, Mister Barty? Have you grasped the depth of what you dare to ask?"

Barty felt sweat dripping down his brow, but did not dare to brush it and his hair out of his eyes, blinking rapidly as he felt his breath catch. "You… you wanted revenge?"

"Ah! Brilliant, you've a mind in that fragile skull of yours after all—of course I wanted revenge! Do you have *any idea* what it was like? Blindfolded, chained at all times, with no awareness of my surroundings but for pain, and what pain it was… they would cut, they would break, they would test again, and again, and again, chatting amongst themselves while I screamed, laughing at little jokes while I begged, discussing dinner plans while I wept." The fist that did not hold the syringe closed inwards, the voice turning hoarse in a mixture of frenzied rage and old, unforgettable agonies. "*Look at me*, Mister Barty," he snarled, and his free, bloodied hand ripped his ruined coat and shirt away to expose his torso. "Look at what not even I could heal."

Barty recoiled; it was impossible not to. Hyde's body was a wretched, vile nightmare of scar tissue, signs of surgery that became increasingly sloppy. "Can you imagine it? Once they knew what they could do, they carved away piece after piece just to watch it grow back. Once they made me *eat* pieces of myself to see what it would do!" he went on in a rage. "And then the regeneration… it got slower, and more difficult, and they stopped and used *other* methods. Water, electrocution, intoxicants. Whatever they had not tried, all to get the answer of how I did it." He bristled still, glaring at Barty with eyes bloodshot in their fury. "You have no idea, boy. They deserved to die. Every last one of them. I only wish I could have made it *slower*." He glared at Barty. Staring at the fearsome figure, Barty could not help but feel a horrified sort of understanding, and an entirely too uncomfortable realisation—in this moment, Hyde reminded him of Jean, all too much.

"Then, I was afforded a chance…" Hyde continued. He seemed to be relieved to finally telling everything, like a pressure had been unstoppered and now all the words, all the truth was flowing out with it. "I was given the one thing that they never expected. I *died*. My body gave up and there was nothing but blessed darkness once more, just as it had been before—when I was first caught, I flooded my body with poison, and that is how I found myself in custody at all; my death was over too swiftly, as my body regenerated even from that. This time? I made sure of it."

"You could not have known you would come back a second time," Barty said in a shaking voice.

Hyde snorted, giving a rasping, hysterical chuckle. "Listen to what I am telling you, Mister Barty. Do you think I even *cared?* I wanted any existence but what I had, even if it was but the void. Hell itself could not be worse than what I was wallowing in."

He shuddered then, his entire form contorting, spasming so fiercely it looked like his bones were trying to jump out of his flesh, hissing and spraying spittle. He half-turned away as Barty shifted, drawing closer.

"Why take so long? You… whatever happened to you, why the waiting? So many years? What made it happen now?"

Hyde growled, low in his chest. Still holding the syringe in his mangled, bloody hand, he turned back on Barty so quickly that Barty could not figure out *how* he stopped himself pulling the trigger on the rifle. Hyde glared at him, gauging the distance, the question of how easy it would be to leap across the room and attack him, the wondering if the shot would or would not hit. All question asked and answered in a moment, but then overridden by the overwhelming urge as Hyde twitched once more, speaking in a growl.

"Because I forgot. I forgot how to make it," he snarled, turning back to Barty and speaking quickly. "I forgot how to make the formula, because *pieces* of me had been burned away. Dying, and coming back, the body repairing itself, putting itself back together but after so long, and after so much damage, there were *parts* of me that stayed buried. I forgot even my own name, and I crawled in the dark. For years. A beggar on the streets." He snorted, then started to make an ugly, demented chuckling sound. "And then, lo and behold—a miracle! A voice. That was all it took. A *voice*." He grinned, wide and sharp, the gleam of madness in his eye. "A voice that I knew. Heathwood." The grin splitting his face warped, as though something inside wrenched it away, and Hyde's voice changed, becoming sorrowful, and subdued. "He did not have to die. He was the only one that did not hurt us, you see—" and then the voice snapped back to harshness between one syllable and the next. "He was *part* of it, how many times do I have to tell you of this?"

"Who are you talking to?" Barty asked in a quavering voice.

Hyde snarled at him, turning back, and this time he was not grinning. "Shut your trap, boy. I was not talking to you." He grimaced, then turned away, as Barty dared to steal a glance around the room. Who was this madman even speaking to? He was starting to feel queasy just being near him.

"You have no idea what it cost. How *difficult* it was," he growled, and there was a pleading edge to his voice that jarred with what he was saying. "We heard his voice while we were begging, and it all came back to us. He gave us a shilling and told us it would be all right, just as he used to do when we were in the cells and he tried to help, tried to cure us, tried to *fix me* but I do NOT. NEED. FIXING!" His voice rose in a howl, as the rain and wind spilled in from the open embrasures around them.

He's arguing with himself, Barty realised. A second voice was fighting with the first. *Two personas,* the doctors had said, and Jean also. Two people in one body, but only one of them used 'I'. Barty was trapped between fascination and simply pulling the trigger and ending the diseased ranting, but Hyde was continuing on.

"I remembered how to craft the formula. I remembered where I had hidden things, things I could use, that were still there. I remembered my learnings, I remembered my intellect, and I learned, I *learned* how to control it. To make my body do things unlike *ever* before. My emotions! Hah! All I had to do was control how I felt!" He was giggling, then plastered a broad, familiar smile on his face, and in that moment he was friendly, cheerful Gaston again, his features warping into that same expression that Barty had been greeted by the first time he met the man. It took a moment to sink in, for it to become clear what he was looking at. *No one could describe what he looked like*, that was what Jean said; because Hyde's face was a chaotic cavalcade of warped expressions and features, twisting endlessly from one moment to the next.

But Gaston's face was warm, and friendly, and steady… and entirely a lie. It was horrific, to realise that the reason for that amicable smile was so that Hyde's shape remained fixed, instead of the shifting, warping horror it otherwise became. Hyde was able to disguise themselves as a different person *entirely* by changing how they were feeling—the notion of which was nearly impossible to grasp, especially in a person so utterly driven to madness. It was a sign of a terrible, inhuman determination, a driven desire for vengeance so awful that it overrode even the most basic human emotions. The smile was wrenched away, turning into the hideous nightmare as Hyde growled like an animal.

"I had to walk into this place with that smile after all they *did*. Shake hands with them without faltering, attend their meetings without flinching, be their friend and colleague without breaking—so you can rest assured, I was going to kill them. That was the thought that kept me smiling, that I was going to kill them all, and they had no clue it was coming. Every last one of them. And now I have."

"All of them?" Barty said in a shaky voice. "Was Wickham the last?"

Hyde shook his head, chuckling. "No, no, but he was the one who oversaw all of it, the doddering old fool. No, the one who managed it, who worked for it the most was Ossreich." He gave that high, rasping giggle again. "I opened all the cells just so they could chase him down, do you know? All the people here, I was not the only one he hurt. They all *hated* him, wretched thing that he was… and oh, how his tender mercies were repaid. They tore him apart. I listened to him screaming as they ripped him to pieces, and then found my way back here, to get the last of what I needed before I left." His expression twisted into disgust, sneering. "And to deal with the last of the loose ends."

He narrowed his eyes at Barty, who had a sudden sinking sensation, deep and terrible, as that look spoke volumes. He had seen the look of promised violence, of threatened death many times over the past week. This look did not promise that. It announced, with surety, that death was approaching. It was both soullessly calculating and utterly malicious, and his feet wavered.

"I do have to thank you, Mister Barty, for two things," Hyde said slowly, his voice turning dangerously even, as that unblinking stare continued. "The first and the most obvious, for helping me find the last names. I had to make sure those that were here were the last, to prevent suspicion, to make them feel like this place was *safe*. But I could not find the others. You did that for me… and I thank you for it." He smiled, but there was nothing friendly in it this time. It was knowing, and smug, and spiteful.

Barty swallowed, and with his voice shaking, his finger

aching painfully from trying not to pull on the trigger, he responded, "And the second thing?"

Hyde's smile widened, turning reptilian. "For giving me enough time to grow my fingers back, of course," he said in a horribly cheerful voice, as he waggled the fingers of his hand that held the syringe—fingers that Jean had blown clear off, regrown and covered in oddly pinkish skin. Barty blinked in astonishment, aghast, and unlike Jean when he saw the moment, he simply did not react in time, as Hyde spun the needle around, slammed it into his throat and, with the regrown fingers, pressed the plunger.

The dark liquid shot into his vein and Hyde screamed. The wind and rain of the storm suddenly intensified, the air turning dense, and a strange smell thickened on the breeze—a smell of metal and something else at the edge of senses that drifted up the nose and into the depths of the brain.

Barty pulled the trigger. There was nothing but a click.

He gaped, half-turning the gun to see, to his horror, that there were *two* triggers. Because of course there were. One to fire each barrel, with their own round and their own hammer. He had just pulled the wrong one, but then the howl of Hyde changed, turning into something deeper, more terrible, as the wind whipped up yet more. There was a flickering of light, the setting sun turning the scene to a terrible mixture of shadows, and briefly Barty wondered if he was in fact going mad entirely, as he watched the absolute horror of Hyde's transformation.

He did not simply get larger, though the mass and weight definitely increased at a shockingly fast rate, the clothes bursting from the inside as the figure grew larger and more distorted. The entire form seemed instead to *blur* in weird, horrific ways. A dozen arms forming, coexisting in the same space for a moment before blending together in size and mass into a hideous mixture of all of them. A dozen, no, *dozens* of different faces, all screaming out of their many mouths, forming on the shoulders as the face warped and twisted like clay.

Not one persona. Many of them. However it had happened, Jekyll, Hyde, whoever this monster now was, they were a fractured nightmare of pieces of different people, each mood a different person. The voice that he screamed with had rage, ecstasy, terror, and grief. Every aspect of human emotion all at once, to create one terrible voice that was, above all else, frenzied in its insanity.

Barty stared in horror, unable to think or breathe. So long in tension with the rifle and holding the trigger had him feeling like he was suddenly made of stone, but as the beast turned towards him once more and raised a giant, warped arm to smash him to the ground into a bloody paste, his body moved without thinking. The rifle was back at his shoulder. He did not bother to aim, his finger shifted and finally, the gun fired.

He had expected it to kick harder than it did, but it *did* still kick, and hard. His arm was knocked back, the rifle lifted high into the air—and he did not miss. Hyde stumbled as the massive bullet ripped into his torso, staggering him in the midst of his murderous charge, but it did not hit him in the head, and so it might as well have been nothing but a wad of spit and paper for all it managed to do to him. A fist lashed out even as Barty dove away, bashing the rifle out of his hands. It smashed into the stone embrasures surrounding the dome and the beautiful wooden stock broke under the force. Jean was going to be unhappy, he felt in an absent fashion as he rolled over the ground. If he was even alive.

Barty, however, did not have time to think about that. He did not have time to think about anything in that moment, rather than staying alive. He dove for the makeshift laboratory with his heart racing. It was the only thing in the dome that provided even a shred of cover, and he had to hope that it would give Hyde at least a second of pause, that the many beakers and the array of strange compounds and alchemical mysteries would give him reason to slow down. This hope was sorely disappointed as the beast that was Hyde smashed into the laboratory table and hurled it aside with a tremendous crash of broken glass and wood. Something caught fire immediately, flaring into light with a rush, and Barty scrambled to get clear, leaping backwards and scrambling away. And Hyde kept coming, destroying everything in his path as he lashed out in mindless fury.

Barty was cornered in a heartbeat. The monster reached for him as his back touched to stone, but the feel of wind and rain reminded him—he ducked left and then slipped out one of the gaps of the embrasures of the dome without even thinking about it.

He immediately regretted his decision. At more than a hundred feet in the air, he was now outside of the building, off solid ground, and holding on to wet, slick stone. The rooftop sloped down and away beneath him, rain slewing off dark rooftop slate. This was not a great place to be in.

And it was only made worse when a huge, clutching hand reached after him through the gap he had just slipped through, like a cat grasping after a mouse hiding in its hole. He scrambled away, half-slipping as, with no real alternative, he started climbing away from the grabbing hand, that whipped back through the gap and out of sight. Barty moved a couple more unsteady paces, his breathing not yet under control as he got a moment of respite, before realisation sunk in. As much difficulty as he was having in moving, Hyde was having no such problem. He turned his eyes front just as a hideous wash of stinking air burst over him, as he came face to face with the insane, twisted grin of his pursuer, Hyde's bulging, warped eyes glinting with malicious glee. And then, with shocking ease, he smashed apart the white stone between him and Barty, sending chunks of rubble flying outwards. His grip gone, Barty let go and began to fall, before a hand closed around his midsection, blasting the air out of him, as he was yanked bodily back into the dome interior, his feet dangling and kicking uselessly, trying to pry open the hand that held him.

"Now now, little mouse," Hyde growled, and his grip tightened. "Cannot have you taking a fall and a tumble first. Not *yet*, anyway." He grinned in a knowing fashion, and Barty nearly swallowed his tongue in realisation before he was slammed bodily against a pillar that held up the dome roof, leaving him breathless and seeing stars.

"Who else knows of me?" Hyde snarled. "Who else did your little lying tongue tell? If you do not answer, little Mister Barty, I will break each and every bone you have to make you sing." The grip tightened, and Barty, unable to get any air into his lungs, writhed in agony. His chest was burning. The bones were about to collapse. Any moment now his ribs would cave in on themselves and crush his lungs, his heart, and he could not *breathe* let alone speak as everything went darker, red appearing at the corners of his vision, before—

"If you could let my assistant go, I would be very grateful for it." Flat, cold, and in that moment, it was the best sound Barty had ever heard. The pressure relaxed as he was whipped about, held aloft between Hyde and his returned foe.

Jean had shed his coat, something Barty could hardly imagine as he was so used to seeing it. He had one eye shut and there was blood streaming from his hairline over one side of his face, and more staining his shirt. The antique longsword he had brought with him was in his hand, and he looked tired, battered, and very, very annoyed.

"What a fine mess you have gotten yourself into, Mister Barty," Jean drawled, his tone sardonic, even exasperated. He took a step forward. Without the coat, Barty could now see the harness that Jean wore, with a large knife at his back, smaller ones perhaps for throwing set into the vest, and an empty holster where a revolver might sit. Something about this nagged at Barty's thoughts. "Are you all right?" Jean asked, taking another step, his feet crunching on glass.

"Oh, he will be vomiting out his *guts* in a moment if you take another step, houndsman," Hyde spat over Barty's shoulder, his enormous grip tightening before Barty could answer.

Gamely, he tried anyway. "Never better, sir," he croaked. Something about the holster tickled his memory again. And then realisation clicked, just as he felt it inside his coat.

Hyde's huge hand held Barty on his left side, the arm wrapping around his front and holding him up in front of Hyde's body as a shield. As it so happened, the grip that Hyde had, with his thumb pressing at Barty's chest and his fingers curled around him, meant that he entirely failed to notice that on Barty's upper right side of his coat, the revolver that Jean had given him, that he had taught him to load and fire, was sitting safely in place. Barty's heart, already racing, started to pound fire alongside the ice into his blood as a mad plan began to take shape.

Behind him, Hyde was talking, snarling his words right into Barty's ear as he kept his grip tight. "You could have stopped me well before this, Reynard. This is *your* fault, as much as it is mine."

Jean simply snorted and took a step to the right, the sword still held low, with both hands now as he kept his feet well set and balanced. "Yes, I have heard that one before."

"You could have just let me go and carried on, and *none* of this needed to happen," Hyde growled, with growing frustration.

"I have, in fact, heard that one too." He took another step. The gleaming sword remained low.

Hyde, for whatever reason, was getting desperate at this point. There was something about the way Jean moved; unhurried, untroubled. Easily shifting his weight, with his gaze clear from his one open eye. He did not sound tense, or frightened, or even thrilled. He seemed not simply calm, but even, and flat. Disinterested. Unlike everyone else who, when confronted with Hyde, backed away, who ran screaming or froze in fear, Jean appeared as excited about the conversation as about one about the weather. Bored even. But his eye was fixed not on Hyde; it was fixed on Barty.

"You have played a good game, houndsman, but this is where it ends. You put down the sword, and let me leave. I will let the boy go when I am clear. No one else needs to die," Hyde grated. He stopped moving. "I will count to three."

Jean sniffed, and shifted his stance. The sword, gleaming red in the firelight from the growing blaze in the wrecked laboratory, lifted overhead as Jean set himself, the sword pointed towards Hyde from his own shoulder. "I do believe I have heard that one as well." His mouth twisted. "Rather think that was a lie all those other times, also." He moved forward a step.

Hyde made a grunt, shocked. Then growled. "I see the boy means as little as your son did to you, maybe even less." Jean went very still. "Still. I will count anyway… and after I am done, I will kill you too. You cannot kill me, Reynard. Nothing can."

"Maybe not," Jean said amicably. "But I can hurt you." His grip tightened, his gloved hands shifting on the sword hilt.

"I can hurt you very, *very* much indeed." His tone changed, to become a low, snarling menace, and Barty felt the hand on him tense as Jean and Hyde locked eyes—and then Jean looked at Barty and nodded.

While the conversation had gone on, Barty had not been idle; his hand had stolen up and into his coat with slow, deliberate care, gently sliding the revolver out of his coat where Hyde, using his body as cover, could not see it. And as Jean nodded, Barty remembered his lessons, pulled back the hammer with his thumb, set the barrel against Hyde's wrist pointing down, and fired, even as the hand started to tighten around him to crush him like an egg, he was—barely—faster.

The bullet ripped through flesh and stuck into bone, and the huge hand opened reflexively, but the explosive reaction of force, rage and the ear-splitting howl at his own sent Barty tumbling to the ground as he was half-flung away, the gun tumbling from his grip. He rolled to see the massive form of Hyde raising both of his enormous arms to smash him into the stone and reduce him to a messy red paste, but then Jean was there, with a flash of steel and a spray of blood, as Hyde shrieked in his murderous hatred, and turned on the hunter who stood with his teeth bared, hurling himself at the mountainous foe before him.

It was an incredible sight as Barty lay there, sprawled amongst broken glass and splintered wood, as man and monster strove while lit by the light of flames, as wind and rain howled around them in the growing storm. Jean moved like a striking snake, the sword he carried losing all of its archaic nature in his hands as he wielded it with grace, poise, and murderous lethality. But Hyde was in a frenzy now and, even as Barty watched, his ruined wrist and hand knitted itself together. He swung huge arms around with such killing force that a single blow would have smashed Jean to pieces, but to his credit, the huntsman danced out of step, countering with sharp, compact sweeps that ripped flesh and sent blood spraying until the stones were slick with it—but each time the wounds soon closed.

Hyde was snarling with laughter as he attacked, Jean sliding on his knees beneath a blow and turning as he rose to slash across Hyde's back, rending his clothes further apart as the beast snarled. "You trying to make me bleed to death, houndsman?"

"If I have to kill you an inch at a time, I will," Jean spat back, before he leapt into the fray. But he was tiring, his breathing hard, and he was already weary. Soon he was attacking less and defending more, avoiding rather than striking, as Barty stared in horror, trying to find an opening, crawling to his knees as he struggled to think to find something to do, to figure out how to help…

He saw it in the light of the flame. The clothes Hyde wore were now destroyed almost entirely, his upper clothing ripped away further by Jean's sword. And the bullet that had struck him in the chest before, fired by the pistol, the spot that it struck was clearly visible—but in a different way, that made it stand out.

Barty could clearly see the black lines emanating from the spot where the bullet had struck, and stopped. Under the skin was a network of blackened blood vessels, stained by the chemical within the round that had punched through that flesh, and then proceeded to flow into the bloodstream. What had Adam and Jean said? Back at the armoury, they had talked about how Jean needed to be careful with the silver nitrate, for how it could stain skin black.

Until this moment, Barty, and probably Jean, had no idea which round had hit the monstrous Hyde, of the two that had needed to hit. But suddenly, right there, as Jean stumbled back from a strike that unsteadied him, Barty knew which shot had landed. And that meant…

His head turned around to the wreckage. He scrambled over to the pile of broken glass and ruined instruments. There had to be one there, right? There *had* to be. He felt jagged shards bite into his knees and hands, and they hurt like acid digging into his flesh, but he did not care as his hand closed on what he needed and lifted it up. His other hand scooped up the revolver, and he turned back to the fray.

This was insanity. He knew it as he started charging towards that massive figure. Hyde finally bore Jean down and forced him to the ground, the sword caught between flesh and bone as he pinned his opponent, ready to finish it. And still Barty came on, his mind clicking everything together. Everything hurt, every part of him hurt so badly he would have been screaming in pain otherwise, but he charged anyway. The mad thought of his promise, the driving urge to know more, and the simple, primal urge to survive gave him a clarity he never knew he had before. So, as he drew closer, he raised the pistol and fired, even as Hyde went to beat Jean into the stone, sending a bullet ripping through the beastly Hyde's back.

The monster howled and spun, lashing out with a massive backhand. But Barty had seen it coming. Every strike from the beast had been given in anger, with wild and reckless force and without finesse. Fatal if they struck, certainly, but it was how Jean had survived. For all his power and brute force, Hyde was an animal more than he was a fighter. And Barty only needed one opening. He ducked underneath that wild backhand—he heard it roar as it ripped overhead, tearing the air apart in its passing with horrifying power—and brought his right hand up, stabbing it towards Hyde's chest. There was a crunch of glass as it slammed home, jammed into the dark spot like a target on that broad, brawny chest, and then Hyde brushed him with a glancing blow that sent Barty flying across the room. He dropped the revolver as he went, as Jean was also sent tumbling away, flung with ease, his sword lodged in the forearm of Hyde. But it was not the only thing trapped in his flesh.

Hyde looked down, to see a long, thin rod of glass sticking out of his chest, buried about six inches into the cavity. A rumbling, rasping chuckle escaped him as he started to laugh in surprise. "A thermometer? You stabbed me with a *thermometer?*" He was laughing, in complete surprise at the sight, ignoring any pain it might have caused—if any at all.

Barty clutched his left arm. It was undoubtedly broken, the limb hanging useless and the pain screaming in his head so loud that all he could do was sob in agonised despair. He had broken the end off the long, laboratory thermometer before he had stabbed it home.

"Indeed, I have. A thermometer." He looked then to Jean, who had gotten groggily to his knees, and by happenstance, his hand landed on the revolver Barty had dropped even as the young man locked eyes with him and finished speaking. "Full of mercury."

The realisation flared bright in Jean's eyes. A simple laboratory object, used undoubtedly to measure temperature and more besides in this hidden workstation, and filled with the metal needed to correctly mark the temperature. Without even meaning to, Hyde had led them straight to it—the second part of the antidote. Jean snatched up the revolver, pulling back the hammer. Hyde reacted by instinct, and raised both arms to cover his face like he had on the bridge.

But Jean was not aiming at that. And as he himself liked to say, he did not miss.

The bullet tore through the thermometer itself and into

the flesh beyond, but all it had truly needed to do was the breaking. For the slender, fragile glass tube, stuck directly into the black mark of the silver nitrate where Barty had stabbed it, burst open and poured the silver liquid mercury into the wound. There was a decent amount in the quite large thermometer, as long as a Barty's forearm, but there did not need to be.

Hyde clutched at the wound, making a grunt of confusion, then his eyes widened, as from between his fingers there came a glow, brighter and brighter, before he started to howl—no, to scream. His entire form seemed to warp then, much as it had when it was transforming, as though every aspect of the monster was trying to escape the prison of its flesh all at once, as that searing, eye-watering glow began to spread through his entire figure, getting brighter, and brighter, as Hyde flung out his arms—dozens forming all over his form, a dozen screaming faces and heads pushing out all over his body, braying in all the different voices in different kinds of terror—and then Jean grabbed Barty, dragging him out of one of the embrasures, leaping down to the sloping roof below as the dome exploded outwards.

As Barty flew backwards through the air, he was afforded the sight in detail. His mind focused on the spectacle rather than confronting the reality that he was plunging backwards into open air, a not-insignificant distance from the ground. There was no fire in the explosion that ripped the dome outwards and sent chunks of white stone flying through the air, pebbles flung by the kick of an angry god as the structure burst. The dome collapsed inwards in the aftermath of the blast, the structure ripped apart by a blast far more powerful than that which had ripped through the armoury, as Hyde was transformed into an altogether different warped state; that of a living bomb. The sound was a shockwave, setting ears to ringing, but Barty could not think about that anymore as he landed on the rooftop and started to tumble down it. His shattered left arm flopped underneath him and the world turned into darkness and red stars as pain shrieked louder than any explosion. He was rolling, tumbling along, unable to stop himself, and the edge of the roof drew ever closer until—

Until Jean was there. An arm like an iron bar seized Barty and held on tight, a foot slamming through a roof tile to force a halt as they were jolted around awkwardly, left sprawled on the rooftop amidst the debris of the blast, with the rain from the wretched London sky falling upon them both. Barty held to Jean, and the man held to him, and for a moment all was still at last.

Barty felt an urge to say something. This was an important moment, and he should speak something to mark the occasion. They had survived, they had tracked down their foe, and they had unravelled the mystery. This was a moment to say something witty, something clever, something that truly underpinned the gravity of the moment.

So it was to his great disappointment that he merely said "Argh", and the world went dark, as he blacked out into blessed nothingness, his battered body finally deciding that was quite enough for the day, and turned itself off.

CHAPTER 21

───────

THOSE THAT HOLD ON TO FEAR

When he awoke, he immediately wished he had not. Though his circumstances were now far better—he was no longer on the roof, though he did not know how—he was, instead, in the ruin of the entrance hall of Bethlehem Hospital, though it now truly lived up to its name of Bedlam. There were shouts of police outside, the ringing of bells and hand wound sirens. There was a great deal going on and all of it was terribly noisy, and Barty was in a horrible amount of pain.

Jean was pulling his coat back on as he stood amidst the rubble. Barty found himself on a somewhat uncrushed bench —only somewhat—that was to one side, having clearly been placed there while unconscious. How Jean had got him there, battered, bleeding and exhausted, he would never, ever know. It barely seemed possible. With care and gritted teeth, he pushed himself to sit upright, to better take in the scene.

Jean was walking through the ruin. The dome and much of the roof had collapsed in on the interior beneath, and now the ceiling was open to the night sky. Rain still drizzled in from the clouds above. As Jean approached something that lay small, shattered and utterly broken in the debris, Barty pushed himself to his feet, drawn to the sight even though he was horrified.

Hyde was gone. But there was a figure that yet remained. They were a wrecked remnant of a person—indeed, there was only half of what was needed to be classed as a whole person at all. Bones were exposed, flesh ripped away… half of the face was simply gone. One arm was torn off, and no legs could be seen at all. And yet, in some truly ghastly fashion, it yet lived, clinging desperately to life that it should not have had.. The little of the body not blown apart was old and withered, and the eye that remained stared at Jean, blinking slowly. Barty felt his gorge rise. There was no way that the thing that remained should still be alive, let alone conscious. What terrible will drove that mangled corpse? What desperation to live?

Jean stood over him, looking down for a long moment before looking to the sky. "I wish I could say it was good to finally meet you, Jekyll. But circumstances do not allow for such novelties."

A rasping breath, a gurgling sound. The broken jaw opened and closed, and a liquid voice finally forced out one word. "*Why?*"

Jean's head tilted at that. A look akin to bewilderment coming to his features, his mouth twisting into bitter disbelief. "Come now, Doctor. You know why.'

His tone was oddly conversational. There was no one else in the room but the three of them, but voices were getting closer. Given time, half the police of London would descend on them, but it would take time. Jean continued on, unhurried.

"I do understand why you did some of it. Why you wanted revenge. Anyone would want it, for what they took from you." He gave a bitter chuckle. "That I understand all too well."

The single remaining arm lashed out with surprising strength, grasping Jean by the ankle. But there was nothing else that could be done except hold to him as that maddened eye stared, filling with tears. "...*Th'n why?*" The wretched voice gurgled it out in a sob. The will that drove it to speak such words left Barty in horrified awe. This, he understood now, was a man who had twice defied death outright to claw his way back to life. Even now, he still clung to existence.

Jean stared back at the wretched, living corpse with a grimace. "You know why, Henry." His tone turned colder. "You were not going to stop. Lady Amberley, the woman on the bridge. How many others? How many more? You would not stop, until you were made to." He reached into his coat and pulled out the revolver. Three shots yet unfired, as he pulled back the hammer. "I saw you then, and see you now. I know you like I know myself, be you Jekyll or be you Hyde... I know you are never going to stop. We have that as our kinship —too much of each other to turn away."

The hand let go of his leg, and lifted. A shaking, bloodied hand, the flesh withered like that of an ancient corpse, pointed up at Jean, and still gurgling, Jekyll, or Hyde, or whatever this terrible creature was, spoke clearer with a desperate, accusing effort, as though anger drove his body to function beyond what it could possibly manage. "*Hypocrite,*" he spat, that trembling finger pointing at Jean in his rage.

The huntsman tilted his head as Barty held his breath. "A valid accusation, in truth. I have taken many lives for the same cause as you." He nevertheless raised the revolver to aim down the barrel at the helpless figure. "But I am not here to grant you excuses, Doctor. Just as I have earned none myself. My sins are not an absolution for yours. Nor are they a penance. You killed the woman and you do not get to excuse that. I should know."

He looked down the length of the gun, though there was no missing at this range as he kept on, cold as the inevitable grave. "I remember every face. Every name. Every pleading beg and desperate prayer, every angry curse and sobbing entreaty. I remember them all. The day I forget so much as a single one, the day even one fades in my sight… well. That is the day I will join you in Hell, Doctor. By my own hand, if not by that of another. But until then, as long as men like you exist, I will take comfort in knowing that if I did not stop them, they never would—and that too, would be my sin to bear, if only it were mere guilt—but it is so much more than that. Something you forgot. But I have not." His finger tightened on the trigger, but he paused and tilted his head once again, staring down.

"Tell me something, Jekyll," Jean said quietly, though it looked like he would pull the trigger before he finished speaking. "When you died the last times, what happened?" Silence, a sort of heavy pause. Jean tried again. "What did you see?"

The staring eye turned to the sky, a sort of deepening horror in that gaze as the destroyed Jekyll stared into the boiling void above. His voice spoke in a ghastly, agonised rattle, made all the more terrible for the fear that filled it.

"*Everything.*"

The first shot came a heartbeat later. Then the second, the third, and then the dry click, once, twice. Each one was sent into the skull and shattered it into an ever more horrible display, as Barty closed his eyes and looked away. Jean reached into his coat and pulled out a flask, pouring the contents over the corpse. The flick and flare of a match soon followed, before the broken body flared into light and began to burn, much as the ghoul in the cemetery had all that time ago. *Not that long*, Barty realised with a lurch. It felt like a lifetime ago.

He wanted to say something, as running steps drawn by gunfire thundered closer. Jean, however, was wandering away, and the words stuck in his throat regardless. In that moment they felt, not just cheap, but unnecessary. Regardless, by the light of the blazing corpse, Barty watched as Jean bent down, and picked up something from the ground that gleamed in the firelight. A syringe, set with brass, with two fingers still in place from where they had been shot off the hand. There was still liquid in the cylinder. As Barty watched, Jean casually tossed the two fingers into the corpse fire, and put the syringe into his coat.

He was about to speak when the door leading to the broken chamber ripped open and lantern-bearing police thundered in. Inspector Creek was at their head, and he stopped and swore at the sight before him, looking at the fire, then Jean, then Barty, then back to Jean.

"It is done, Inspector," Jean said wearily, in the vast silence. He then moved again, and to Barty's surprise, picked up the shattered rifle that Hyde had broken in the dome during the battle, before continuing on. "A little past nightfall, but I am sure that I can be forgiven for that." He shrugged, while standing amidst the absolute devastation that he had caused of the destroyed hospital. "Now, if you do not mind, I would like to take my charge and go home."

Creek looked torn, particularly after giving the battered, bloodied Barty another look. He looked about to say something, to make some complaint, to protest. Instead, he turned sharply and barked an order. "Clear the way! Injured men coming through!" The uniformed officers responded with a shuffling of feet and confused consternation, but they obeyed. Barty felt Jean come alongside, and then a supporting hold at his back.

"Hold the left arm up with the right," Jean said quietly. "Take the pressure off it for now. It will help."

Barty swallowed and did so, nearly falling over as he took the weight of his broken arm. He barely heard the conversation between Jean and Creek, but it was there nevertheless as his senses swam.

"Montague will want a report of all this," Creek growled. Jean snorted at the notion, but nevertheless nodded at the corner of Barty's blurry vision.

"He will have it, with the parts that are relevant."

"Damnable mess here, Reynard," Creek's tone was exasperated. He raised his voice then. "Someone put out that fire—"

But Jean stopped and raised a hand, speaking sharply. "No. Let it burn."

As Barty's vision cleared, the huntsman turned to the inspector and the officer that had paused midstep towards the burning corpse on the ground.

Creek looked baffled, looking to the fire then back to Jean. "What would have us do with it?"

Jean shook his head, grimacing as he glared at the flames a moment. "Put more fuel on it. Anything you can. And keep it burning until even the bones are ashes." He turned his gaze back to Creek. "And when it is done, scatter them to the wind. Can I trust you to do that?"

The inspector paused, his jaw twisting. Then he nodded, and irritably jabbed a thumb over a shoulder. "Go on then. And mind your step as you go."

Jean nodded, and, still propping Barty up, the pair of

them passed out the door, into the corridor beyond. The front doors were sealed by all the rubble collapsed in upon them, so they were to go back the way they came. There were plenty of police around now, rounding up the patients, dragging them back to their cells. Some seemed barely aware of what was going on. Others screamed. Others wept. It was haunting to say the least, the desperation of those that were once again being confined away palpable in their every gesture. In the light of it, as Barty limped along with Jean at his side, it hardly seemed a victory. These people would remain here, unnamed, forgotten, and now made to suffer more than ever.

It reminded him of something, his tongue thick in his mouth as they continued on slowly. "He tried to help, you know."

Jean was roused out of whatever silence buried his thoughts, grunting and looking down to one side. "What? Who did?"

"Heathwood," Barty said slowly, blinking once or twice. "Hyde… or Jekyll, one or both of them, said that he tried to help them, instead of just torturing him like the others. He actually tried to help him."

Jean was silent at that, before he nodded. "Thank you. It troubled me to think Ulysses could be part of something so terrible." He exhaled, then his lips twisted as though soured, his bloodied moustache bristling. "He was a friend of my mentor, you know… Jekyll. It was how he learned so much of the esoterica." He sounded bitter about the matter, for any number of reasons. "Locke did not speak of the case much. He simply regretted it deeply. If he had, I might have solved this sooner." He snorted. "Did you wonder why I asked you of your French, when you told me of Gaston's name? Gaston is a name that is derived from *guest*, or *stranger*." He paused, then shrugged. "Quite literally, 'the hidden man'. A fitting name for them, I suppose. I wager he thought himself terribly clever when he thought that up."

Barty swallowed, and went quiet again as they continued to stumble along. He was tired at this point, more tired than he could ever remember being. They passed through the corridors and through the milling bodies and then out into the night beyond. There were horse drawn carriages and lock up wagons, men running and milling everywhere, and a general atmosphere of great irritation, as well as the bellowing of many voices asking questions and wanting answers. Reporters and more, and idly Barty wondered what answers were forthcoming. Fewer than anyone hoped, that he was sure.

"Why did they do it?" he said as though to himself, but Jean stiffened at his side, and it prompted him to think the question through more fully. "Why did any of them... do it?" Absently, he felt a trickle of worry at the memory of the syringe Jean now carried, hidden in the coat. Jean shrugged, his broken rifle still under his arm as he considered a moment, looking skyward to the uncaring clouds.

"This world we live in is a dangerous one, Mister Barty. Not because of what is in it—though that is indeed very dangerous—but because what we, as humans, bring to it. We are confronted with the unknown, the unknowable, wonders and powers beyond reckoning. But what we mere mortals bring to that... is our fear." He turned his dark gaze to Barty then, those tired eyes still hard as stone, the will behind them as terrible as it was indomitable. "Those men feared death, and each of them died regardless, stained by that fear and all they did to avoid it. Human ego, human fear, human self-righteousness and above all... human greed. They will kill more of us than monsters ever could."

He started off again, and Barty moved with him with difficulty, limping and stumbling as they made their way to the gates and the exit. No one tried to stop them. Barty was relieved by this; he was too tired to do much about it at this point except fall over, but they pressed on. "You said this world we live in, Jean," he said then, his tone curious. "Does that mean I am now properly part of it?"

Jean snorted. "You were the moment you gave up everything to find me, Mister Barty. Though I am sure you regret it at present."

But Barty shook his head, surprising even himself. He gave a crooked grin, squinting at the man holding him up. "Honestly, sir… no. Not really."

Jean blinked, then, for the first time since they had met, he gave a chuckle that was without bitterness. A genuine, quiet laugh at fearsome odds with their surroundings, but honestly amused. "You are a strange bird, Mister Barty."

They drew closer to the gate and the thronging crowd beyond. Barty quailed a little at the sight, but Jean drew himself up firmly, squaring his shoulders as he frowned, then looked down to Barty and helped him straighten.

"Before we head on, let me give you one more lesson, Barty." His voice was firm. "Though those before this one have been poor, this lesson is important. Hold on to your fear. Hold it close in your heart and remember it. Hold it and cage it, that it might grant you humility in your choices. But never let it guide those choices. A choice made in fear is a choice towards death, in a myriad of ways. Those men that died over these past few days, and tonight… they listened to their fear. They were ruled by it. So I say this—know fear. But never let others see it in you—and never let it choose for you." Barty blinked, suddenly realising that Jean was no longer supporting his weight. He wavered, wondering if he might fall.

"You are stronger than you know, Mister Barty. And you already know how to think without fear. Tonight you proved that to me and, I hope, to yourself. Now stand. Show the world who you are." Jean said it quietly, but Barty heard every word. It stiffened his spine and straightened it. Everything hurt. But he had enough left of him for this.

Jean watched, then nodded, and turned to the street. He whistled , one high and long note, and three short and sharp, and began to stride forward, with Barty forcing one foot in front of the other so that he might walk at his side.

The crowd laid eyes on them and started to shout questions, seeing someone without a uniform and expecting answers, but seconds later there were more high pitched shrieks from those amongst the street as the inexorable advance of Crook and his four disturbing horses moved through the throng, forcing them out of the way. Amongst the confusion, Jean yet still strode forward, and Barty followed.

The spectre of Crook grinned down at the pair as he sat, perched comfortably, holding reins that Barty knew he did not need. He licked his lips at the sight of the battered duo, ignoring the protests of the crowd who had been obliged to make way, clearing the way to the front gates, which now opened as Jean yanked one of them back and made space for Barty afterwards. Despite all that Crook terrified him, he was grateful to see him; that short walk had taken everything. And yet it had meant something.

Jean helped him into the dark of the carriage and closed the door before thumping the roof once. The coach lurched forward, to the screams of those getting out of its way, but no bones were crunched beneath inexorable wheels. The coach rolled on. After a moment, audible even over the sound of the rolling over cobblestones, Crook started to sing. A wordless tune that slipped effortlessly into mourning lows and cheerful highs, a discordant mixture that nevertheless was somehow comforting. Barty leaned his head against the window frame and looked out over the dark, misty haze that was night time London after rain, blinking slowly, seeing nothing, feeling his thoughts gently fall apart. Jean started to say something, but it was too far away. He closed his eyes and eased back into the quiet dark.

CHAPTER 22

A FORTUNATE REALITY

Time crawled, leapt, slithered, and otherwise progressed in its normal method, ticking with the heartbeat of the universe towards each, ever climbing moment.

Barty had slept, and then slept, and for the sake of variety, slept some more beyond that. It had been helped with various wonderful tinctures that Adam had prepared, that not only took away much, if not all, of the pain from his many injuries, but seemed to speed along their healing as well. Barty soon felt well enough to get around the Lodge again, and even spent a little time exploring. He had wandered the stacks of the library, peered through volumes with difficulty—his broken arm remained in plaster and splint—and helped Adam fix the armoury, though the heavy lifting he had left to the giant.

Montague had been by, but Barty had not seen him. Others had as well, all to speak to Jean. And himself it turned out, but for some reason Jean had shielded him from that, and answered what questions they might have had himself. Barty had been grateful. He needed the rest.

Now he was back in the library. He kept returning to it, over and over again. And each time he found himself drawn to the same place. It was here that Jean found him, striding into the study with something heavy in his arms that Barty, spinning from his spot, immediately recognised.

The phonograph was carefully tidied up, and much as Barty had last seen it… with a few minor scuff marks. Jean placed the heavy thing easily upon the sturdy central table, then stood there for a moment, frowning at it and rubbing his jaw. His bruises had already faded. Whatever it was that Adam had concocted as a restorative clearly had worked its wonders upon him as well, but for some reason, he now seemed ill at ease. He finally glanced at Barty and then focused past him, and frowned deeper.

"You keep coming back to her, don't you?" He gestured vaguely to the painting that was at Barty's back, which made the young man flinch for reasons he did not quite understand, but he turned to look.

"Well, it is a curious case, I have to admit," Barty confessed. "The Woman in Red… Carmilla. If she really has been the enemy of the Society for all this time, then she must be very powerful."

"She is," Jean said shortly. "But not nearly as powerful as she is clever. She is a manipulator, a careful planner, and easily the most dangerous opponent any member of the Society could hope for. Quite inscrutable in many ways, really."

"You sound like you know her personally," Barty could not help but point out, staring up at the painting. It remained compelling, but not simply because of the beauty of the woman captured within it. There was something else about it that tugged at his mind. Something that remained on the tip of his thoughts, but he could not give voice to.

"We have met," Jean said abruptly, frowning at the artwork, before turning his gaze away. That startled Barty, and he looked back to Jean in surprise before staring up at the painting again, that knowing smile and darkened gaze, but Jean went on without looking at him. "But that is not what I wished to speak to you about today."

Barty dragged his eyes away, to see Jean tapping one finger on the phonographs frame thoughtfully. "I thought of a way that you could use this, that I would accept, Mister Barty. You could not use it elsewhere, but it could be useful to the Society itself. A means to record the lives of those that have lived within it."

Barty blinked, and then felt a sense of unease. He opened his mouth, then closed it. He remembered all at once his revelation to Elanor and Benji. After the brawl with Hyde he had forgotten it, but his realisation that the man before him sought out his own death—or so he felt—returned with full force. Jean noted his silence, and taking it for confusion, continued on.

"I would like to record details of... of a life. There are several I can think of, but there are some more than others. This could help do that. I have tried to write it down, but it has been difficult. More than I would care to admit." He exhaled slowly, still tapping the phonograph, as Barty remained rigid, his thoughts racing. "Perhaps you could use it too, Mister Barty."

The rolling, plunging thoughts bounced into a brick wall and stopped abruptly. "Pardon?"

Jean shrugged. "I want to speak to you about James," he said slowly, without looking up. "I want to talk to you about my son, to tell you about him, what he was like, what he did."

He straightened, setting his shoulders and taking that sturdy, unyielding posture that Barty knew so well, even if the world was weighing down upon it. "And perhaps you can tell me about people you remember afterwards. The names that you remember. The people… and what they meant to you."

Barty felt things tilt a moment. This was not what he expected, and it brought with it buried memories. Suddenly, to his shame, he realised that he had never even considered telling the story of his fellow orphans, of those that had been left behind. Of Charlotte, the girl he had never seen again save in his nightmares alongside all the others. Starkly, he was made aware that he and Jean both had difficulty talking about such things. He kept his eyes downcast.

"I am sure you do not care to hear of such trivialities," he mumbled, trying to avoid that sore spot. "We never really mattered, you see. I do not think anyone would care about our existence."

"I do," Jean said simply, and Barty raised his eyes. Jean's expression was inscrutable, but his gaze was hard as he watched Barty wordlessly for a long moment to study his expression. "No life is ever meaningless, especially not an innocent one. You saved my life, Mister Barty. I saved yours in kind, perhaps… but that should have been my task alone. You should not have been necessary to my protection, and yet you were. And when the moment came, despite all that had come before, you rose to the occasion." He subsided, sighed, and shook his head. "We would not have defeated Hyde without your abilities, and your cool-headed reasoning. And I wish to recognise that."

Barty needed a moment, to process all that he had heard. Jean looked awkward. This was not a speech he had enjoyed giving, but nevertheless felt like he had to. And since he was being honest, Barty could not help but be so in kind.

"I…" he stammered, and tried again. "I thought you wished to die, truth told." He had, in fact, wondered more than once if he had done the right thing in saving the man, despite his promise to Elanor. But suddenly confronted with that most alien thing from the hunter—the simple nature of *gratitude*—he could not help but confess.

It had an effect on Jean. The man blinked, his mouth twisting, before it set again in a hard line, and he gave a contemplative grunt, his eyes lowering back to the phonograph thoughtfully.

"I would admonish you for such a statement, and thoroughly, but I suppose in retrospect, it is hardly so wildly erroneous a conclusion," he confessed in a stiff tone. "I have not been performing at my utmost."

"A little reckless, yes," Barty muttered meaningfully, a bit embarrassed. The fact that Jean had not exploded at the statement was surprising even to him. But something seemed to soften in the air at that moment, even as a realisation made Barty's hackles rise.

"So," Jean went on, moving past the moment with a gruff tone. "I thought that this would be the better middle ground. I have little interest in speaking of myself; I find such a notion nauseatingly egocentric, such that it makes my skin crawl." He took a deep breath. "Talking about James will, in many ways, be more difficult."

"Then why him, over yourself?" Barty asked as he shifted closer to the table. Jean shrugged, as though it were the simplest thing in all the world.

"Because unlike myself, Mister Barty, the message my son wished to impart, the lesson he tried to teach, and the world he tried to create… it was all something worth saving."

It was delivered so easily, so simply, as Jean once more showed the depth of love for his son, while showing just how far his own self-loathing ran. And in that moment, Barty knew what he needed to do.

He pushed himself forward, moving easily now despite the aches. "Before we begin that, I would like to do something first," he said firmly.

It took Jean off guard, his head tilting and his expression perplexed. Then he shrugged, sighing. "If you so wish."

Barty nodded and headed with purpose to the exit. As his hand closed on the door handle, however, Jean spoke thoughtfully.

"Before you go, Mister Barty, allow me an answer to something."

Barty froze, turning first his head, then letting go of the door to face the man properly, his determination giving way to trepidation. Had he already guessed what he was heading off to do?

"When this venture all began for you… do you remember it?" Jean was staring off at nothing, his brow furrowed.

Barty blinked, off guard once more, and then he shrugged his good arm. "I was… well, I was in the pub, if you must know. Going over old newspaper readings about the Ripper." He coughed. "And then someone told me about you. They talked about the great hunter and tracker, an investigator without peer." He chuckled, rubbing the back of his head. "The way she spoke about you, she sounded like she was a very great admirer of yours, truth told."

Jean did not laugh. His gaze instead narrowed as he looked off into that middle distance. "Strange that you listened to them, then. This stranger. A woman, you say?"

Barty blinked, confused. There was an edge to Jean now that he did not quite understand. "Well, she was very compelling." He made a rueful face. "Compelling enough to make me forget myself for weeks in the effort to find you." He shook his head again, laughing despite himself at the strangeness of it all. "Do you know I cannot even remember how she looked? I mean, not really. She had very bright eyes though." He rubbed his jaw. Thinking back on it now, it really was quite odd. "Still…" He could not help but go on, trying to reassure Jean. "It was fortunate that she found me, was it not? Seeing how everything turned out."

Jean was still for a long moment, then nodded slowly and thoughtfully. "I think you might well be right, Mister Barty. Now run along to whatever errand you have planned. I am in no hurry to go anywhere right now." He waved a hand dismissively. Barty cracked a wry smile and turned back to the door, shaking the thoughts away once more.

He hobbled down the stairs, passing Adam on the bottom of the steps. They were cradling the broken rifle in one enormous hand, pausing as Barty stepped clear and nodding to him politely. Their movements were still slow, deliberate and careful, and much of Barty's help in the armoury had been with detail work and putting small things away with delicate care—which made the broken rifle a curiosity.

"Good morning, Adam," Barty started cheerfully. "Going to try and fix that as well?" He nodded to the broken gun, but the giant shook their head.

"I fear I have never sought to master the creation and management of firearms. That was Cosgrove's doing." They hefted the rifle a moment, looking thoughtful. "He shall be quite upset. He was quite proud of Delilah."

Barty could not keep his surprise and curiosity from his features as he looked down at the weapon. The major mechanisms of the rifle seemed intact, but the barrel was bent and the stock cracked and shattered.

"I never asked why it was called that, to be honest," Barty said, looking curiously up at Adam, who gave a rumbling sigh.

"An affectation of his. Cosgrove names each of his murderous little devices, to try and impart a sense of uniqueness, perhaps a personality to them." They snorted softly. "Personally, I have ideas towards that peculiarity, but the fact remains implicit—he will not be pleased. Delilah was an exceptional bit of his work. When he finds out you were the last to use it, he will probably be very upset at you." Barty quailed at that, remembering the vicious butler all too well. The fact he made weapons did not surprise him. The fact he *needed* them to kill a man, however, did. Adam clearly saw the upset, and a slow, sly smile formed on their face. "*If* he finds out, of course."

Barty swallowed. "I sincerely hope he does not, truth told." Adam's smile grew wider still, and their free hand came around to pat two fingers on the top of Barty's head. It was a strangely comforting gesture, even if the realisation was that if Adam actually put some effort into it, they could have driven Barty feet first into the floor like a nail struck by a hammer.

"Fret not, Mister Barty. He shall not hear it from me. My lips are sealed." They lifted that huge hand to tap at said twisted lips, and winked. The smile faded after a moment, eyes flickering to the arm still in a sling. "How are you feeling? Forgive me for not asking earlier." They were mournfully apologetic in that moment, so much so that Barty waved his right arm about frantically in an effort to placate them.

"No, no! I am fine, Adam. Better by far because of all the help you gave."

The giant beamed at that, clearly relieved. They nodded shyly as they went on. "A mutual friend brought instruction via some feathered assistants in regards to what I should do. She is very skilled at such work. I will make sure to pass on your gratitude."

The mysterious witch wife of Jean. Barty was surprised to

learn of her involvement, but he was honest in his next words. "I hope to meet her soon then, and tell her so in person."

Adam nodded, their smile turning mysterious. "I think that shall shortly be the occasion, yes." They straightened then, nearly touching the distant ceiling, and nodded. "For now, however, I must bid farewell. We have a great deal more work to be done below." They touched their brow in a salute.

Barty did the same, and carried on. One day he would learn the name of the woman who had helped him heal, he decided, idly wondering why no one gave her name. A flicker of worry passed through his mind, in that perhaps it was simply because everyone was too afraid to.

This worry continued on into outright fear as he nevertheless opened the front door of the Lodge and trudged down the steps. It was a surprisingly fresh and bright day, the sun high and the clouds blessedly broken for at least the moment, a most unusual thing in the autumn months, and to be well savoured because of it.

However, Barty was having trouble enjoying it. He knew what he needed to do in this moment, but he was far from happy to do it. The last time he had encountered Crook on this footpath, he had seen a glimpse of something terrible, something fearsome, and it still shook him. The fact that Crook was not a human at all was something that weighed on him each night as he slept, and each time he stared into shadows he imagined the thing he had momentarily become was there, waiting for him. Despite that, he remembered what Jean had said to him at Bedlam. The conversation about fear, and it being a thing that people brought with them.

If he was going to do this, he had to do it correctly.

He was terrible at it, but he gave his best. A single long high whistle, and three sharp ones. He paused, waiting and listening, but heard no rattle of coach wheels. He took a few steps and started again, but was startled into a coughing fit as a familiar voice spoke from behind him. "Please, *do* stop that. I heard you the first time and it was quite enough."

Crook was where he had just stood, though there was no way he could have approached without being seen. A clear and empty street was suddenly filled by the dapper, twisted stance figure, his long white hair tied back and his smile askance, those silver eyes that did not reflect the sky fixed on Barty and wary. Barty needed a moment to compose himself. *Fear. Remember that fear is what you bring with you.*

"I was starting to think you did not like me any more, Mister Barty," Crook said mournfully, but there was a wicked smile tugging at their lips. "And I had hoped so to see more of you. I am sure you are a most interesting thing in your dreams."

Barty coughed at that, a bit off guard. "Actually, I was hoping to ask a favour of you, Crook," he said slowly, but with formality. "A boon, if you could call it that."

The delicate eyebrows shot up and the smile turned into a wide grin as the eyes brightened. "Oh, a phrase I *do* love to hear." The grin was closer to a leer then. "Ask what dance you wish to play, and I will see about the song."

Barty grimaced, not liking *that* phrase either. "Well… could you find Elanor? And Benji too, but they are likely together." He paused. "I do not know what you are, Crook, but if you could do that, I would be most welcome."

Crook's smile turned faintly glassy, and his head tilted what looked an awkward angle, with that smile still there but now without the same glitter to it. "Say I can, say I cannot… the greater question here is, what purpose would that serve?"

Barty swallowed, then shrugged. "I think it would do Jean good to see his daughter again. And I think Benji deserves some protection after all that has happened. I think this is the right moment. The right time, as it were, to try and work towards that."

Crook was quiet at that for a while, head still tilted and still standing in that odd, scary stillness before he finally spoke, his voice turning distant. "You have grown since the last I saw you, Mister Barty," he said slowly. "You have stretched and strained your spirit in directions it was not used to going, and proved thoroughly entertaining because of it." He sighed, straightened, then threw up both hands in a gesture of exasperation and surrender. "Fine! Fie upon it! You have me at a moment of weakness myself. You pressure me too greatly!" Barty was about to give a puzzled thanks, before the silver-haired trickster bowed low. "You have grown into your naming, Mister Bartholomew Bartleby. And thus, I grant your name back to you."

Barty's tongue stuck to his teeth. Or rather, *Bartholomew Bartleby's* tongue stuck to his teeth. A rushing stillness crashed into him as he realised that, ever since he had given Crook his name, he had been without it. He had forgotten his name. But now it was back, burned into his thoughts, as though a screaming that had been silenced finally rose back to the surface. He was Bartholomew Bartleby.

Crook was still bowed deep and low, and glanced up, a look of annoyed expectation upon his face. This, Barty—no, Bartholomew— realised raggedly, was an important moment. There was expectation of something in kind. His first thought was to kick this name-thieving deceiver and flee. His second was to run screaming. But the third was the stronger. *Remember that fear is brought with you.*

So he returned the bow, as low as he could, his arm aching and all. He bowed low, despite the fear, defying it, and matching the gesture, and spoke as evenly as he could.

"Th-thank you. For giving that back to me."

Crook nodded and straightened with a smile, and Bartholomew followed suit. Still smiling, Crook lifted one hand and turned the wrist, and the coach with its four silent horses approached from behind Bartholomew, who ignored it, as his mind was racing. Something was important here, something he had the edge of. Crook slid up into the coach seat as though drawn to it.

"Farewell, Bartholomew Bartleby. I will return with your master's daughter and her friend." But he was stilled then, as a hand was raised by the young man on the street before him.

"If I may be so bold," Bartholomew said with a rueful smile. "Perhaps you were right about the name. I rather think I might have grown… but I do believe I have grown into the name that was given. Please. Do keep calling me Mister Barty, Crook." He cast himself at whimsy, without knowing why, but wanting to find out.

A lizard blink, and then high and clear laughter, and for once, there was no glee, nor malice, nor hidden wickedness. This was something else, a genuine and honest laugh of sheer joy, the laugh of seeing something new and wonderful. A long-fingered hand touched their brow in a playfully mocking salute. "Please, darling Mister Barty, call me by name, for it was granted by the first starlight, and I fear that you have earned it." He winked. "Though I have grown fond of your title, it is time to cast it aside. Call me Puck."

A strange weight seemed to lift off Barty's sore shoulders at that. And he was Mister Barty again, his name taken, remade, and now granted again. He was still Bartholomew Bartleby as well, but for the time being—Mister Barty felt a kinder name. A simpler one. It was, as he had said, a name he had grown into. He nodded to Crook—no, Puck.

"A time of names and truths indeed, Puck." He inclined his head, and felt the fear lift. Perhaps there was still cause for it, underneath it all, but there was reason enough to be without it.

Puck laughed, still overjoyed, and the coach rolled away smooth, as smooth as oil over stone, and that laughter rolled with him as the coach picked up speed, and Barty was left to contemplate alone but unafraid. This was a new day, and the sun yet shone. A future unknown reached out for him, but for the first time, Barty was sure of the fact that he would be part of it.

The fact that the future was full of monsters, magic, and the unknown was not lost on him, of course. But after all he had seen—how much worse could it possibly be? In the face of the brisk autumn breeze, those things felt far away. He could worry about them tomorrow. Today, he would talk about a man he wished he could have met, and see a father reunited with his daughter. And it would be enough. He turned back to the door and went back inside.

B arty did not see it. But Jean stood where he had left
him, staring not at the phonograph, nor at the empty
air, but at the painting of the mysterious dark-eyed
woman. He stared at it with a clenched jaw and a narrow
gaze, stared at it as though it held answers. It probably did.

Adam was there, their expression even more unreadable
than usual. "You think he knows?"

Jean shook his head with a grimace. "No. That is not how
she works. He has no idea what his purpose is, and nor do we.
We can only guess."

Adam nodded slowly, and for a moment it seemed that
they would say no more, before they gave a genteel but significant cough before speaking. "For what it is worth, Jean, I do
not think that he means any harm, knowing or otherwise."

Jean scowled. "Things would be simpler if that were the
case. But no. That is far too prosaic for her. I know her well
enough for that. I know her better than anyone alive—or
otherwise."

Adam gave a small hum before speaking delicately. "I

would presume as much. After all, she *was* the one who raised you."

A frosty silence was Jean's reply, his expression stony. He stared at the giant Adam, before finally looking away. "*Locke* raised me, Adam."

"So you say," Adam replied in a mollifying tone that indicated none of their disbelief. "Regardless, put it aside for now. Barty is innocent in all of this."

Jean subsided. He nodded, falling quiet, and Adam let the matter drop. Nodding to the hunter, they made their way out of the library, leaving Jean Reynard in silence, staring up at the picture of the woman in red.

His gaze did not waver, but the lines of his face hardened into resolve. "If you sent him this way, it was for a reason, Carmilla," he grated, quietly. "If you set him on this path, I will find out the reason why." His eyes narrowed further, and his voice turned dark. "Should I find it not to my liking, I will end him for it. And then come for you."

Silence. Stillness. Jean held his breath, but only for so long before he exhaled. There was an answer to the question some-where—but Barty was not the only one with a talent for finding answers. For now he would wait, until the moment came.

And it would be enough.

ACKNOWLEDGMENTS

When I was very small, I was handed a book far too large for me. My grandmother gave me a copy of Lord of the Rings, and having cajoled me with promises of there being violence within (a very important caveat to a young boy) I was set loose. It took me months to get through it.

I learned something very important. Getting through a story takes work, and time. Too much time perhaps – I cannot give her this tale, as much as I think she would enjoy it. I shall read it to her grave, hoping she can hear it. I wrote this for her.

However, it was not written *because* of her. Nor my father, who left this life before I could even share dreams with him. This book was written because of the staggering kindness, the gentle guidance and unyielding patience of those who simply told me again and again that I could, that I should, that I must, until I did. I apologise for making it so difficult. My doubts were the mountain you carried me up, until we reached the peak.

To my wonderful, brilliant, and (justifiably) inexorable editor and publisher, Renee April. This simply could not be, without you. The time, effort and patience to bring us to this conclusion is staggering. Your friendship is beyond any price imaginable. This is not mine. It is ours.

To my best friend, Christopher Watt. Not only the single reason I got this opportunity at all, but the unyielding rock in the face of all my nonsense. He's a better friend than I deserve. To Gareth Keenan, a brilliant artist with an unrivalled knowledge of old lore passed down over generations of old legends and myths. Jean was born and built in his head as much as he was in mine. I truly hope we collaborate some more—the creativity he wields is unique, brilliant, and immense.

Beyond that—there is a *staggering* amount of people to thank for their belief that I could make this happen. My friends Glenn Penridge, Daniel Timbrell, Ron Fenton, Andrew Locke, Emily Judson, Torrey Donner, Sean Stephens, Andrew Agnew, Lachlan Boughton, Jason Huynh, Dale Sweigart and the *dozens* of online community members who not only demanded the story, but encouraged every step of the way. To Lydia Fuller, the assistant editor and the first true blind reader of the story. To the advance readers who were both beyond generous in their time and praise, to giving me my first reviews of effusive praise. And to Dayna Watson, the long suffering cover artist, who did *too* good a job if you can believe it—I am sorry, we simply couldn't choose which one we loved most, we loved all of them. And lastly Reordan J. Carey the concept artist who gave not only flourishes and touches, but also brought the world within to life in image—a feeling that truly is hard to describe in how wonderful it is.

In the end, there are too many to thank. I would thank each and every one of you for being there and reading this. It is more than I could ever deserve, and ever repay. Thank you.

But I must make a special mention of my family. On my father's side, of men and women who embody the best there is of people that can be ever found. I learned more from you than you might think. All of it is what is best in me. My flaws are my fault alone.

On my mother's side, I have the reasons I am alive at all. My grandfather, the strongest and kindest man who I could ever know, who taught me wisdoms and lessons no one else could. His son and my uncle, who has kept this family standing near alone with an effort that defies imagination and *cannot* be repaid. And my mother, who has only ever wished the best of me and for me. I am sorry I have made it so very difficult. I know you tried. Let this prove then, that it was enough.

If I missed you, know I have not truly. If you think I left you out, I did not—I just ran out of space on the page. You *are* in here, in some small way. You all are.

Thank you, all of you. We did it.

Jonathan Maloney

About the Author

Cursed from a young age for picking up a copy of Lord of the Rings without proper authorisation, Jonathan has long pursued a career in writing. To his great surprise, he actually found one.

He lives nominally in rural Australia but prefers to dwell in either his own head or the internet, neither of which is any better.

He has a cat named Biscuits who is far more interesting than he is.